LOCK 'N' LOAD

FEDERAL K-9 SERIES

LOCK 'N' LOAD

FEDERAL K-9 SERIES

TEE O'FALLON

Entangled Publishing, LLC
2614 South Timberline Road
Suite 105, PMB 159
Fort Collins, CO 80525
rights@entangledpublishing.com

Amara is an imprint of Entangled Publishing, LLC.

Edited by Brenda Chin and Karen Grove
Cover design by Erin Dameron-Hill
Cover photography from Getty Images and Deposit Photos

Manufactured in the United States of America

First Edition May 2018

To all the wonderful dogs I've loved in my life: Chief, Frosty, Kobie, Kiska, Taz, and Jet. And to the beautiful puppies I hope to have again one day.

To all the working dogs: K-9s, military dogs, guide dogs, therapy dogs, companion dogs… For all that you do to keep us safe and make our lives better.

Last but hardly least, to all the dogs currently living in shelters worldwide. May you one day soon find the loving human you deserve.

Prologue

Forty years ago

She squeezed her eyes shut, willing the unbearable pain to stop. It didn't.

With every breath, her ribs screamed in agony, to the point where she nearly blacked out. The muscles in her abdomen spasmed from the fresh blows, never having completely healed from the last beating. Her left eye throbbed and was so swollen, she could barely see out of it.

Gritting her teeth, she pressed her palms on the cheap linoleum kitchen floor, trying to push up on her hands, but there was no traction and she fell back down with a painful *thud*. It was impossible, she now realized. In her weakened state—and with the floor so covered in blood—her hands kept slipping.

"Mama!" her little boy cried.

"Stay there!" She held up her hand, gasping as another shaft of pain speared her entire upper body.

Her son's pale cheeks were streaked with tears, as were

hers. Although she didn't know whether his were from seeing her like this or the terror of what was before them.

Lying in the ever-widening pool of blood surrounding her was her husband's deer-gutting butcher knife. And her dead husband.

The flow of thick, sticky blood that had poured from the gaping wound in his belly and the deep slice in his neck had gradually slowed to a trickle. From the amount of blood, she'd guess the knife had sliced into an artery somewhere.

"We have to get out of here, Billy," she whispered on a strained exhale. She took another agonizing breath, this one shallower, so it didn't hurt so much. "Walk around the blood and help me. Careful not to step in it." She didn't want to leave any sign that her son had been there, including any bloody sneaker prints.

Billy stared at her, his watery blue eyes wide, his hands trembling. Still, he didn't move, and the realization had her worrying that he'd be mentally scarred for life.

First things first.

"Billy, sweetie. I need your help. Can you come over here and help Mama?" Painful though she knew it would be, she raised her arm, wincing as her ribs screamed in protest. Surely several of them were cracked. "Come quickly. *Please*," she added when he didn't budge.

"O-okay." His chest rose and fell, and to her relief, he began skirting around the blood, keeping his back to the kitchen counter.

She grabbed the bloody knife from the floor and began wiping it clean on her shirt. Even though her husband had a lengthy record, the police would still process this as a crime scene and look for the killer.

Another spasm ripped through her, and she dropped the knife, squeezing her eyes shut as she stifled a scream. When she opened them, her heart thudded. The knife had slithered well beyond her reach into the center of the bloody pool. Looking up at the ceiling, she sent out a silent prayer that she'd managed to clean off all the fingerprints.

"That's good," she said to Billy as he approached her from behind. "Now hold out your hand and keep it steady while you help me up. No matter what I say or do, just keep helping me to stand. Okay?"

Billy nodded, and after placing her hand in his, she took several deep breaths. What happened next would be excruciating, but it had to be done. Will's brother, Avery, was due over shortly, and if her brother-in-law caught them there, she and her son would both surely die. Most likely, Avery would hack them to ribbons and enjoy every second of it. *The son of a bitch.*

She and Billy locked gazes. "Pull me up, and remember what I told you. No matter what I say, don't stop."

Without hesitating, he pulled. The scream she let out was high-pitched, like that of a wounded animal. Which was exactly what she was.

"Mama!" Billy cried when she was halfway to her feet.

"Don't stop," she hissed. White stars exploded in her vision, and she wavered, reaching frantically for the nearby counter. Billy was small for his age and might not be able to fully support her. If she fell to the floor, she doubted she'd be able to rise again.

Fumbling through the haze of agony, she grabbed for the edge of the laminate, gripping it so tightly several of her nails cracked. She sucked in shallow breaths, exhaling through her mouth until the spasms passed. Vaguely, she recognized Billy's cries of concern, although his voice was muted, as if he were far, far away.

"I'm okay. Just give me a minute." *You don't have a minute.* Avery was coming, and his rage would be ten levels beyond Will's worst. That was the way of the West Virginia Sands clan. Violence was their family legacy.

Gradually, she could begin to make out shapes from her one good eye. She blinked and shook her head to clear it, but that only intensified the throbbing.

Behind her, Billy threw his arms around her waist, plastering his body against hers. Covering her mouth with her hand, she muffled the scream rising in her throat from the tight contact around her battered midsection.

Grimacing, she eased away from him and snagged Will's pickup truck keys from the hook by the kitchen door. "Let's go." She turned and tugged Billy's hands from her waist, leading him to the door. With every step, her chest ached. Her eye throbbed. More than once, her knees nearly gave way out from under her.

"Mama, can I get my mitt?" His hopeful voice made her heart ache as they made their way slowly to the truck.

"No, sweetie." Her steps were slow, mincing, but eventually they got to where Will's pickup was parked in front of the old shed. "I'll buy you a new one. I promise."

As Billy helped her up into the driver's seat, she wondered how or where she would get the money to pay for a new mitt. She cranked over the motor, grateful for the engine's loud, reliable rumble.

Billy climbed into the passenger seat, and she waited while he buckled up. An ironic snort of laughter bubbled in her throat. An evil, violent man would soon be coming for them, and all she could think of was that her son needed to fasten his seat belt before they drove off.

Taking one last look at the dilapidated house that used to be their home, she suddenly saw that her path moving forward was the clearest it had been since she'd made the horrible mistake of marrying Will. Once again, she prayed that this time she'd be able to find the resources and courage to do what needed to be done next.

Then she and her son would disappear. Forever.

Chapter One

Present day

Trista dug into her bag for her ID and pushed through the heavy glass door of the George Bush Center for Intelligence, aka CIA headquarters.

Though it was early September, summer was still in full swing, and the building's cool interior was a welcoming, icy whisper over her face. Of course, on a day like today, she probably shouldn't have worn her long gray pencil skirt with its matching long-sleeved knit blouse. But the outfit was comfy and covered nearly every square inch of her, which was precisely why she'd chosen it. Baring a lot of skin had never been her thing.

Voices echoed in the cavernous lobby as she walked briskly across the sixteen-foot-wide circular floor seal bearing the well-known eagle-and-shield symbol of the CIA. Trista groaned inwardly. She hated Mondays. Not because she hated work. Hardly. She absolutely *loved* her job and had ever since she'd interned with the CIA during college.

With majors in math and computer engineering, she'd been recruited by the agency only days after graduating from Columbia University. Having interned for several summers in St. Petersburg, she was also fluent in Russian and naturally gravitated to the agency's Directorate of Analysis, focusing on Russian politics. But her true love was computer cryptography, part of the Directorate of Science and Technology. There, she'd quickly discovered she possessed that ultra-rare talent for seeing things in codes and ciphers that no one else could see, and finding patterns and associations hidden beneath layers of jumbled data. At thirty-three, she was one of the youngest—and the *only* CIA employee—to work on projects simultaneously for both directorates. Including her current assignment: surveil the cultural attaché to the Embassy of the Russian Federation in Washington, D.C. On the internet, that was. And she was eager to log in and get back on his digital trail.

I really, really do hate Mondays.

Mondays were reserved for tours, and sure enough, an early morning student tour of the building was already clogging the lobby, partially blocking the two employee lines to the security checkpoints. Even those lines were unusually long this morning. The magnetometer occasionally beeped from someone who failed to remove keys from their pocket, and the X-ray machine's conveyor belt rattled and thumped as visitors placed their bags and briefcases down for inspection. Until recently, Langley didn't allow public tours, but now that they did, they weren't taking any chances with shoddy security.

She got into one of the two employee lines and began tapping her ID card against her thigh. Her latest assignment was the first one in months that had really gotten her juices flowing, and she was eager to dig in. With her analytical aptitude for anything requiring a computer and all things coded, she was a whiz at her job. Hence, the additional security clearances that came with the embedded circuitry in her ID card.

"C'mon, c'mon." She tapped the card harder against her thigh. It was just before seven a.m., an atypically early time for a student tour. Due to the seven-hour time difference between Virginia and Russia, she'd altered her shift to start an hour earlier, and the delay at getting upstairs to her computer was irritating. Eavesdropping on someone eight time zones away was a royal pain in the *zadnitsa*.

To keep herself occupied, she turned her attention to several boys who were part of the tour. She'd learned early on as a child that she was a people watcher, and she was good at it. Ironic, since she considered herself socially inept. Her three gifts in life were her analytical mind, her ability to read people, and, of course, her fluency in Russian. *Beyond that, I got nothin'.* With her, social skills and good looks must have skipped a generation.

The boys had caught her attention partly because they were big, seventeen she'd guess, and partly because they were standing close to each other, leaning in and whispering. *A clandestine huddle.* She wasn't an operative—a CIA agent— but she loved the lingo.

In unison, the boys craned their necks, eyeing the employee checkpoints. One of them grinned slyly, nodding his head. She'd bet he was the leader of the pack and was trying to act cool in front of his friends by doing something totally brainless.

She snorted. *Don't do it.* He wouldn't be the first idiot to try to blow past the visitors' screening checkpoint, and he probably wouldn't be the last.

"Hey, Tris!" a bubbly voice called from somewhere behind her.

She looked over her shoulder to see her friends, Bonnie

and Kevin, at the back of the employee line. She waved back, grinning at Bonnie's attire. Her friend was everything Trista was not—gorgeous and a social butterfly extraordinaire.

Bonnie Mistrano was tall, about five foot eight, voluptuous, and wore skintight clothes. She had that whole Italian beauty queen thing going, and it worked for her. Men loved Bonnie, and she loved men. Ironically, Bonnie had it bad for Trista's teammate, Kevin Lowell. But Kevin was so blockheaded and job-obsessed that he appreciated RAM, memory space, and a super high-speed internet connection more than a beautiful woman's attention.

Kevin was a classic, pocket protector–wearing computer geek who had eyes only for his computer screen. The man was totally oblivious to how much Bonnie lusted after him, and Trista had been sworn via pinkie oath never to reveal how much Bonnie loved the guy.

The familiar *whooshing* from the glass shield entry panels opening and closing meant she was closer to the checkpoint scanner, with only a half dozen people in front of her. That's when she noticed the new cop standing in front of the scanner visually checking IDs before people swiped in. *Holy moly.* It would have been impossible *not* to notice him.

He was tall. *Really* tall. By her estimation, several inches over six feet. In her sensible, boring, flat shoes, he would easily tower over her measly five foot one. Perhaps he was new to the CIA's Security Protective Service, because she didn't think she recognized him. Then again, she probably needed new glasses.

Pushing her thick trifocals up higher on the bridge of her nose, she peered around the man in front of her to get a better look.

Wide shoulders and an impossibly broad chest filled out the cop's navy-blue uniform shirt. His short sleeves were filled with thick, bunching biceps. Her gaze traveled down his torso to his trim hips and from there to a pair of long, muscled legs flexing beneath his uniform pants, then back up to his duty belt loaded with, among other things, a large holstered gun.

With the line shortening, there were only three people ahead of her now, giving her an even better view. Pathetic though it was, she couldn't stop herself from cataloging more of the cop's assets.

Short, dark-brown hair curled boyishly around his ears, as if his cop haircut was on the verge of needing a trim. Deep, chocolate-brown eyes. *Like Ghirardelli. No, Lindt. My favorite.* With his straight, patrician nose, high cheekbones, and chiseled square jaw, he was *GQ*-handsome, in a rugged kind of way.

The vigilant way he scanned the visitor line reminded her of a panther surveying the forest from the treetops, ready to strike its prey at any time. But what he did next was totally juxtaposed from the wild image she'd just created in her mind.

Alvin Sykes was the CIA's oldest living employee, and Alvin refused to use a walker, instead preferring to lean heavily on his cane. As he hooked the cane over his forearm to swipe in, he tottered, and the officer shot out a hand, steadying Alvin and allowing him to use his arm for added balance.

Unable to tear her gaze away, she continued watching the cop, alternately fascinated by both the infinite gentleness he showed to Alvin and the rippling play of thick muscles in his forearms. She'd definitely never seen him before. His was a face she could *never* have forgotten. He was unbelievably gorgeous. The man was like a living, breathing Greek statue cut from marble by the most gifted stonecutter in history.

Her perusal momentarily paused at the gold, rectangular name tag on that incredible chest. *Sgt. M. Connors.* When she looked up at his face, he was staring at her intently, almost…

thoughtfully. She froze, her throat clogging. *Oh, pooh.* Her face heated with embarrassment.

Why can't I be as fluent around men as I am with computers?

Yet another major flaw in her social abilities, or lack thereof. Getting outcast as a brainiac early on in school had led to social awkwardness—the source of her hot-guy anxiety. The minute she found a man even remotely attractive, she got flustered, and her ability to converse like a normal Homo sapien went totally out the window, as if someone had switched off the power button to her brain. Sadly, that had only worsened over the years.

She quickly averted her eyes from his and moved up in line until there was only one person standing between her and the scanner. She couldn't wait to get upstairs and escape to the comfort of her office—the one place in her world where she felt truly competent.

Dark brows drew together as Sgt. Connors stepped aside for her to access the scanner. That's when she noticed it. A tan-and-black dog sitting obediently at his side. She'd seen the other CIA K-9s before but never so close that she'd have to pass within inches of the animal in order to move through the checkpoint.

Unable to move, she froze. Dogs were definitely not her thing. Ever since a horrifying encounter with a dog when she was a little girl, she went out of her way to avoid them entirely. The fact that this one was a badge-carrying K-9 didn't alter her perspective on the animal in the slightest, and she intended to give it a wide berth.

"Good morning, Miss Gold."

Sgt. Connor's smooth, rich voice was so in sync with her whole melty chocolate analogy it wasn't funny, and Trista could swear she felt the reverberation of his words like a warm caress on her skin. Sure enough, goose bumps zinged up her back to her neck, and *wow* did it feel good.

How does he know my name? Duh. Cops know everything.

"M-morning," she mumbled, averting her gaze as she sidestepped both man and dog. In reality, she was more flustered by the man than the dog. She swallowed hard, gripping the ID card tighter in her hand. Her nervousness around Sgt. Connors was ten times worse than it had been around any other man.

No, make that a hundred times. A thousand. For crying out loud, what is it about this *guy?*

Trying not to appear flustered—*yeah, good luck with that*—she raised her now-trembling arm to insert her ID card into the scanner when she was shoved roughly aside and found herself falling ass-first to the floor.

When she landed on her butt, the abrupt jarring knocked her glasses off and sent her tight hair bun flying apart in disarray. Everything went blurry. Something big and dark blue dove past her, followed by something tan and black.

A dog barked, followed by a loud grunt as something—or *someone*—hit the floor. People shouted, and heavy boots pounded past her.

Trista got to her knees, skimming her hands along the floor's cool surface, searching for her glasses. Her hair had come undone, and her blurry vision was that much more obscured by her own hair, making efforts at finding her glasses completely futile.

"Tris! You okay?" Bonnie shouted from beside her. "Here." She shoved Trista's glasses into her hand.

Her fingers closed around the plastic frames, and with shaky fingers, she pushed them on. Despite the audible chaos seconds earlier, the scene she focused on now was unexpectedly controlled.

Face down on the floor, not five feet in front of where

she kneeled, was the same kid she'd rightly surmised would stupidly try to bolt through the employee entrance.

Bonnie sighed. "Will they ever learn?"

"No," they both said in unison, then laughed.

It had become trendy to try to blow through Langley's security, then post the video on social media.

The doofus was lying on his belly, his face plastered to the floor. The K-9 had its jaws clamped around the kid's forearm while Sgt. Connors had his knee planted solidly in the boy's back.

"Ouch. That's gotta hurt," Bonnie said, grimacing. "Although I don't see any blood."

"Sheba, *pust*," Sgt. Connors ordered.

The dog immediately released its jaws from the boy's arm, backing off and lying down, but still uttering an occasional growl. Even lying down, the dog's body quivered with obvious readiness to re-engage if necessary. The thought of all those sharp teeth clamped around her own soft flesh made Trista shudder.

In a matter of seconds, Sgt. Connors expertly and efficiently handcuffed the kid and hauled him to his feet. She noted that the boy's sleeve didn't appear to be torn by the dog's teeth. *Amazing.*

"Did you see that?" One of the other boys in line laughed and pointed to his friend.

"That was *so* cool," another said, laughing with his buddy.

"Young man"—one of the building's assigned tour guides shook her finger—"needless to say, your participation in this tour is over. Permanently."

Trista gave a snort as Sgt. Connors handed the kid over to two other uniformed officers. That must have been the pounding of booted feet she'd heard—the cavalry had arrived. Granted, she'd been almost blind at the time, but she'd been impressed by the speed and efficiency with which

Sgt. Connors and his dog had taken down the punk.

With a satisfied smirk, she watched the other officers walk the kid away. To where, she wasn't sure, since he looked to be under eighteen and, as such, a minor. Still, he *had* tried to breach a federal facility.

"Are you all right?"

Trista jerked her head around to find Sgt. Connors crouching on the floor beside her, his face only inches from hers, his incredibly broad shoulders blocking out all else. Big brown eyes pinned her, and she couldn't tear her gaze away. No, his eyes were more like cocoa, coffee, and caramel all rolled into one. *Yummy.*

The look he continued to give her was intense. His dark brows drew together as he searched her face, as if looking for injuries.

"Are you all right?" he repeated, frowning. Actually, it was more of a scowl.

Yes, she wanted to say. But her throat was clogged again, and no matter how much she tried, her lips wouldn't move.

She took a deep breath, praying it would kick her brain into gear. It didn't. The only thing it did was send his sexy, way-too-appealing aftershave directly to her lungs and her brain.

Say something, stupid.

"I—" She swallowed. Lord, she'd thought he was good looking before, but this close…*OMG*. She might not be able to speak to certain men, but that didn't mean her libido was dead. For a man, he was utterly stunning.

"Tris?" Kevin asked. "You okay?" Only then did she realize he'd come to her aid as well and was now crouching next to Bonnie.

"Do you think you can get up?" Sgt. Connors held out an enormously large, incredibly strong-looking hand. "Let me help you."

Now staring stupidly into his eyes, she placed her hand in his, noting several thick scars on his hands and forearms. As he began pulling her to her feet, an inhuman snort ruffled her hair.

A large brown-and-black muzzle thrust its way into her peripheral vision. Trista gasped and scrambled in the opposite direction—straight into Sgt. Connors's hard chest.

Her pulse pounded. Her body trembled as she took in quick breaths. The dog stared at her steadily from amber-gold eyes, a shade lighter than Sgt. Connors's.

She tried pushing herself farther from the dog, but not only weren't her sensible shoes gaining traction on the shiny granite floor, Sgt. Connors's body was an immovable mountain of muscle.

Still holding her hand, he hugged her tighter against his body, wrapping his other arm around her waist. "It's okay…" His deep voice rumbled in her ear. "*Sedni.*" In response to his command, the dog sat. "Sheba won't hurt you. She's here to protect you."

"I d-doubt that." Cynophobia—fear of dogs—was something she'd lived with since she was six years old.

He gave a slight tug and pulled her to her feet. Blood rushed to her head, and she wavered, instinctively putting out a hand for balance. Her fingers contacted the center of his chest. His shirt felt odd, and it occurred to her that he was wearing a protective vest under his uniform. That, and he smelled really, really good. Like cedar, leather, and dark rum all rolled into one intoxicating scent.

Concern etched his chiseled features. "Do you need to lie down?" He released her hand, clasping her shoulders gently.

One of her hands still remained on his chest. Worse, her other hand was now gripping his forearm.

When did that happen?

She looked up. And up, until she could meet his gaze. As

predicted, he did indeed tower over her by more than twelve inches.

The arm beneath her fingers was warm and thickly muscled, with a light scattering of coarse hair covering rough, slightly raised skin. Scars aside, strength and confidence emanated from the man like a halo of raw power.

She shook her head, snatching her hand back. "I'm f-fine. Thank you."

Jeez Louise, I'm babbling like an infant.

Avoiding Sgt. Connors's intense gaze, she stepped to the ID scanner, feeling his—and everyone else's—eyes boring into her back. Her hands went clammy as she shoved in her ID card. Somehow she managed to punch in her code and make it through the checkpoint. When the glass panels *whooshed* open, she bolted through and speed-walked to the elevator bank. After wiping the sweat from her brow, she pounded on the *up* arrow, willing an elevator to arrive before anyone else could join her. A bell sounded and the doors opened.

"Hold the doors!" Bonnie shouted as she and Kevin bounded in next to her.

Trista pounded again, this time on the button that would close the doors before anyone else could intrude on her ultimate embarrassment. When the elevator began to rise, she let out a groan.

"That was an exciting way to start the morning, huh, Tris?" Bonnie giggled. "And holy shit, that new K-9 guy is h-o-t *hot!*"

Trista opened her eyes in time to see Kevin roll his.

"Do you ever think about anything else besides hot guys and sex?" He arched a brow.

"Well…" Bonnie stuck her finger in her mouth, momentarily looking up at the ceiling while she pretended to think. "No. I don't."

Trista laughed. Bonnie did think about sex constantly,

but only with Kevin. He just didn't know it. Yet.

The doors opened, and they made their way into their office.

"And he was awesome," Bonnie continued as she settled behind her desk. "The way he took that kid to the ground, he was like a giant panther." She placed her hand over her heart and let out an exaggerated breath. "Be still my heart. I think I'm in serious lust."

Trista dropped her bag onto the floor, amused that Bonnie had also likened Sgt. Connors to a panther. As she powered up her computer, she noted Kevin was frowning. *Could it be he's a tad jealous? 'Bout time.*

"You're pathetic." He shook his head in obvious disgust, turning on his own computer. "All it takes is a few muscles and you go weak at the knees. Trista doesn't need muscles on a guy. A guy's gotta have a brain. Isn't that right, Tris?"

"Huh?" She looked up from the log-in screen, already focused on her new assignment. "Right," she answered and caught the wistful look of longing on Bonnie's face as she watched Kevin from across the room.

As she logged in, she couldn't stop shuddering at how close that dog—Sheba—had been to her. True, the animal had seemed well behaved and responsive to commands, but she hadn't been that close to a canine since she was six, and she'd hoped to keep it that way. Besides, she had Poofy.

She glanced at the glossy photo on her desk of her beautiful, pure-white male Angora cat with enormous blue eyes. She and Poofy could do without dogs, thank you very much. And they could do just as well without gorgeous, muscle-bound cops with melty chocolate-brown eyes. She and Poofy had each other, and that's all that mattered. Most of the time, anyway.

After inserting her ID card, she tapped her fingers on her desk, waiting for the password prompt.

Sgt. Connors certainly did have a lot of muscles. She'd felt them beneath her fingers as she'd leaned on his forearm for balance. While he'd been wearing a vest, it didn't take a genius to figure out that, had he not been wearing one, her other hand would most certainly have come in contact with two of the hardest pectorals on the planet.

Get real.

Not that she was thinking about him or anything. Guys like him didn't notice women like her. She knew what everyone thought of her. Mousy. Dowdy. Plain. Blending into the woodwork, so much so that at some point in her life, she'd actually begun *trying* to disappear. Hence the gray clothes. People didn't notice gray so much, and she liked it better that way.

She typed in her password and clicked the enter button. While she waited for the various search programs to boot up, she realized her social clumsiness and humiliation weren't the only things bugging her about what had happened in the lobby. She realized she was envious of Sgt. Connors. He was so confident and self-assured. Unlike her.

When the boot-up finished, she clicked on the Dark Curtain icon on her screen, then opened an internet search engine. A slew of news stories populated the screen, all concerning the U.S. presidential election in just over two months. Typing in the address for one of the many secret chat rooms on her list for the morning, Trista dug in.

Her short nails clicked on the keypad's buttons so quickly it sounded like the *pitter-patter* of rain on a metal roof. The target—Alexy Nikolaevich Lukashin—was out there somewhere in cyberspace, and it was Trista's new assignment to track his diplomatically protected butt down and uncover what he was up to. Unofficially, of course.

Alexy Nikolaevich Lukashin's official cover was as cultural attaché to the Embassy of the Russian Federation in Washington, D.C. The CIA, however, knew him to be the *rezidentura*—a legal resident spy. Lukashin was an older man in his sixties, a product of the Cold War. Surprisingly, he was techno-savvy with a preference for utilizing social media. His favorite method to hold long-distance meetings with colleagues was hidden in black net chat rooms.

Glancing at the task bar, she verified Dark Curtain was running then proceeded to enter one chat room after the next, searching but not finding whom she was looking for. "Where are you, Lukashin?"

As her fingers flew across the keyboard, the clicking grew louder. Faster. Her heart rate kicked up, and her breathing went shallow. Darting her eyes from one quadrant of the screen to the next, she scanned the many pop-up windows for signs of the elusive *rezidentura*. This was her forte, an incomparable technical expertise few in the world possessed besides her. She might be a total dork where men were concerned, but there wasn't a code she couldn't decipher or a computer network anywhere in the world she couldn't hack into.

During the next twenty minutes, she lost count of how many chat rooms she entered and exited using the Dark Curtain program she'd developed several years ago. Dark Curtain ran in the background, allowing her to penetrate any chat room, bypassing the standard username and password requirement. Once inside, it was like hiding behind a thick, dark curtain and listening to everything being said in a room without other participants ever knowing she was there.

The program was incredibly powerful, allowing her to get around military-class encryption and secret, complex passwords. She'd even added an enhanced feature that allowed her to capture plain-text conversation in a folder on her computer before a secret chat room's auto-delete function kicked in, permanently deleting plain text after a preset amount of time had elapsed.

"There you are." She smiled as Lukashin's code name—Karakurt—popped up in a Russian-language chat room.

Months ago, she'd discovered that code name, musing over the symbolism. The Russian Karakurt spider was one of the ten most dangerous spiders on Earth. Poison from a single bite caused intense pain that would quickly spread throughout every muscle in the body.

Focusing on the conversation already in progress, she again verified Dark Curtain was still running on the task bar. The chat was in Russian, but with her fluency, it was no obstacle.

Karakurt: *He is not who he says he is.*

White: *If this comes out, it will ruin everything. Who made the discovery?*

Banks: *A reporter. Thomas George.*

White: *Does anyone else know?*

Karakurt: *Aside from our own people, none.*

White: *He must be stopped before this information is released to the public.*

Banks: *Understood. Although, other matters are moving forward. I leave for Iqaluit in an hour.*

Karakurt: *I'll take care of it.*

Iqaluit? Trista strummed her fingers on the desk. *Where have I heard that name before?*

The images on her screen flickered, and she froze, staring at the now-black screen. "What the—" Her screen came back online and she relaxed.

White: *Good. Report in when—*

Trista waited impatiently for White to finish his sentence, but he didn't. "When what?" she said out loud.

A red pop-up window—a warning window—appeared in the upper portion of her screen, and she darted her gaze to the task bar.

Dark Curtain was no longer running.

Bolting upright, she grabbed the mouse and clicked the Dark Curtain icon, but it refused to engage. "No, no, no!"

Wide-eyed, she clicked the icon again and again, already knowing the program—and everything else on her computer—was frozen. Worse…if Dark Curtain wasn't engaged, that meant…they could *see* her. Well, not literally see her, or her actual identity. But when the program froze, it was the equivalent of someone ripping the curtain off the wall, revealing her standing there in the room, listening.

She didn't understand what had just happened or, more importantly, *how* it had happened. She'd designed Dark Curtain with three times the number of safeguards that CIA protocol required. *This should never have happened.*

The chat screen went dark. Conversation was over. Resting her elbows on the desk, she dragged her hands down her face, considering the likely cause of the program's failure. The flicker of her monitor could have been a power surge, but all classified systems at Langley were on a backup generator.

"Tris?" Kevin looked at her, brows raised.

Bonnie also eyed her from across the room.

"Did your monitors just flicker?" Trista asked.

"Yup," Bonnie said.

Kevin nodded. "For a second, yeah. It happened to me yesterday after you'd left for the day. I reported it to facilities, and they said they'd look into it."

"Apparently, they didn't fix it." Leaning back, she

crossed her arms. One would think the CIA, of all agencies, would have quicker network repair response. Now she'd have to start over with Karakurt. He might even change his code name, but she'd find him, wherever he was. She just wished she'd heard the entire conversation before the system had glitched out on her.

She had no idea what Karakurt and the others were discussing, and she'd been excited to hear more. For that matter, she didn't have a clue who Banks and White were, although White seemed higher in the food chain than Karakurt, and Karakurt was pretty high as it was.

Opening up her chat folder, she clicked *print*. Whatever they'd been discussing, at least she had a transcript. Maybe the spooks could make something out of this. She grabbed the single sheet from the printer and slipped it into a large envelope with the appropriate security restrictions stamped on the outside, then headed for her boss's office to drop it off.

Trista's stomach let out a growl as she parked in the side lot of the Mellow Moose Tavern. The Moose was just about every Langley employee's favorite place to eat. Unexpectedly, there were quite a few cars in the main lot. Then again, the Moose was one of the only restaurants around that served decent food this late at night. Or morning, really.

It had been nearly midnight when she'd turned off her computer and headed home. Despite missing lunch *and* dinner, all her successive efforts to find Karakurt again had proved fruitless. She yawned, looking forward to grabbing some takeout, then falling into bed. She'd been at it for nearly seventeen hours, and she was exhausted.

Tomorrow, or rather later today, she'd get back on her board and surf the chat rooms. Sooner or later, Karakurt would show himself again.

Another gurgling growl low in her belly had her reaching for the door handle, but it was jerked from her grasp as the door opened. A hand gripped her wrist, twisting her arm as she was yanked up and out of the car.

A hand clamped over her mouth. She tried to scream, but the sound came out in a muted squeal. Her attacker spun her around and shoved her against the side of the car. Rearing back with her elbow, she tried jabbing him in the ribs, but all she connected with was air.

Something sharp bit into her neck. *A knife.* And with every quick inhale, the knife pressed deeper into her flesh.

Her heart pounded, terror twisting in her belly as her attacker dragged her across the pavement toward the tree line. She twisted in his grip, swinging her arms out, trying to hit him.

But she was no match for his size and strength.

A moment of horrific clarity hit her. *I'm going to die.*

Chapter Two

"Let's get out of here, girl. I'm beat."

Matt waited for Sheba to jump in the SUV—a CIA-issued Explorer, specially equipped for K-9s—before closing the door behind her. He wiped the sweat from his brow, relieved to be heading home. These double shifts were killing him, and he couldn't wait to grab some food and kick back.

As he got into the driver's seat and buckled up, his thoughts rewound to events of that morning. More specifically, to Trista Gold.

Having been newly assigned to Langley, he hadn't gotten to know many of the employees, but he knew who *she* was. The CIA's crack analyst.

"She's a little thing with a lot of power at her fingertips." The remembrance of her petite form in his arms had him realizing just how tiny she really was. And how unexpectedly curvy her body was beneath that head-to-toe gray outfit.

Hearing his words, Sheba thrust her snout through the cage opening between the headrests and gave a soft snort.

Cranking over the engine, he pulled out of the lot and

headed to the main gate. Only one place would be open this time of night and still serving. Luckily, the Moose was on his way home.

He wondered where Trista lived. Actually, he wondered a lot about the woman, something that shocked the shit out of him. She was nothing like his type. Trista was shy, unassuming, and wore minimal, if any, makeup. Rather than trying to hit on him as most women did, she couldn't seem to get away from him fast enough. Still, there was something about her that intrigued him. He just couldn't put his finger on what it was.

As Matt drove past the security gate, he waved to Mac, the officer on duty, then turned toward Dolley Madison Boulevard and the Langley Shopping Center.

"You know, girl," he said, reaching out to stroke Sheba's velvety-soft muzzle, "I'd bet my ass that beneath those librarian glasses and those god-awful schoolmarm clothes she wears, there's a stunning beauty itching to cut loose."

Woof.

Sheba's warm breath blew against his ear. She knew he was talking to her, and he loved their late-night chats. Unlike most women he dated, Sheba was a great listener. Some nights after a double shift, their conversations were the only thing keeping him from falling asleep at the wheel. It also helped him unwind.

He and his Belgian Malinois had been together for two years now, and he couldn't imagine being teamed up with anyone else. They'd become tight, anticipating each other's next moves and thoughts, the same as any human partner ever could. Maybe more.

Sheba was the only female constant in his life, and he preferred it that way. It was the way things had to be. Years ago, he'd figured out that as soon as he began to feel anything resembling true happiness with a woman, guilt would smash the relationship into smithereens. As a result, he had a long list of pissed-off ex-girlfriends who'd been unceremoniously dumped. Ten in the past twelve months, if his count was accurate. It wasn't that they'd done anything wrong, or even gotten too clingy.

The old saying *It's not you, it's me* was far too accurate. They never believed him, but it was true. What he didn't tell them was that he didn't deserve any happiness. Not after what he'd done.

He dragged a hand down his face. Twenty years later, and the guilt was still as raw and fresh as if it had happened only yesterday. The only good thing was that he hadn't had a drop of alcohol since that day.

Slowing the Explorer through town, he passed the supermarket. He hated shopping but had next to no food in the house. With his buddies and their K-9s coming into town to stay with him during the upcoming pre-election events, he'd have to pick up a ton of groceries. Pretty much the only thing he had plenty of was kibble. Turkey and salmon flavor. Sheba's favorites.

When he lowered the window for some fresh air, the smells of greasy fast food wafted into the truck, and he scowled. Trista Gold smelled a whole lot better.

When she'd fallen into his arms, he'd breathed in pretty-smelling woman. It must have been her shampoo or perfume. Vanilla and sweet spice. He'd guess she was in her early thirties, and had no ring on her finger. Come to think of it, she hadn't been wearing a single piece of jewelry. Odd, but the woman had something about her that really got to him.

Her heart-shaped face included a cute nose and lips so rosy pink they didn't even need lipstick. He hated the stuff. Most of the women he dated usually wore red or deep pink that inevitably wound up all over his face or on his shirt collar. He didn't know what they made that shit out of, but it never seemed to completely wash out of his clothes.

Without those gargantuan, dark-rimmed glasses hiding half of Trista's face, he'd finally gotten a good look at those sparkling green eyes of hers. They were the same color as his mother's ferns just before they unwound from their spiral bud. With those thick waves of honey-blond hair all messed up and escaping from that prim bun, she'd looked less like a schoolmarm and more like a woodland nymph on a bad hair day.

Now it was his turn to snort at the imagery he'd concocted. It wasn't like him to wax all poetic-like. What he ought to do was tell her to ditch the bun.

"She sure doesn't like *you*, though." He gave Sheba a quick scratch under her chin, and she leaned farther through the opening, resting her head on his shoulder. "She took one look at you and almost had a heart attack."

Sheba gave his ear a quick lick.

"Hey!" He gently swatted her muzzle away.

Woof. Sheba snorted and lay down in the back of the truck.

Not that he could ever see himself in a relationship, but if by some miracle he ever got his head out of his ass, any woman of his had to like dogs. No cringing in fear the way Trista had. It was obvious from the all-consuming panic in her eyes that the woman had been severely traumatized by a canine somewhere in her past.

Too bad. She didn't know what she was missing. In his opinion, dogs had better character, honesty, and loyalty than most humans. The only exceptions he'd encountered lately were the guys he'd gone through K-9 school with.

At the traffic light opposite the Moose, he flicked on the turn signal and braked to a stop behind another vehicle. He'd take the guys here next Saturday. They'd get a kick out of the place. Especially Mo, the bartender. Glancing at the Moose's main parking lot, he was gratified to see plenty of cars. That meant he could still get some food.

Motion near the adjacent tree line caught his eye. "What the fu—"

A woman was flailing her arms and being dragged across the parking lot toward the woods. There was barely enough light to make out details, but was that—*Trista Gold?*

Matt slammed his foot on the accelerator and cranked the wheel, zigzagging around the vehicle in front of him and blasting through the red light.

The Explorer's engine roared as he sped into the lot. At the edge of the curb next to the tree line, he slammed on the brakes, tires screeching.

He flung open the door, simultaneously pushing the remote button on his vest that would automatically pop open Sheba's door. *"Zadrrz!"*

Instantly responding to the Czech command, Sheba leaped from the vehicle and bolted ahead of him.

He took off at a dead run, blood pounding in his ears as he charged into the woods, catching a glimpse of something shiny—a blade—at Trista's throat.

Ahead of him, Sheba growled, leaping and latching her jaws on the attacker's arm. Then he heard another growl, this one human, as her teeth sank into flesh. At the same time, Matt barreled into the guy, tackling him to the ground.

The son of a bitch immediately resisted, giving Matt an excuse for pounding his fist into his jaw again and again. Several gratifying pained grunts later, the guy went limp. Matt was about to flip him onto his belly and cuff him, when an eerie screech broke the silence.

He jerked his head around to see Trista's hand at her throat, her eyes bulging wide. Her mouth was open as she gasped repeatedly for air.

Holy fuck!

Terror gripped him. *I'm too late.* Her throat had been sliced open.

He went to her side. "Trista. Trista!" he repeated when she didn't respond. The only sound coming from her throat was that same horrible wheezing.

Which meant she was still breathing but not well.

Grabbing the mic on his lapel, he called for an ambulance and local PD assistance. As the dispatcher relayed his requests, he tried examining the wound on her neck, but Trista refused to move her hand.

"*Pozor*!" he shouted to Sheba, giving her the command to guard the unconscious man's limp body.

Trista gripped his arm, her nails biting into his skin. "In-inha—"

"*What?*"

To his left, leaves rustled, and Sheba growled. Matt's heart pounded as he whipped his gun from its hol-ster, pointing it at the noise. Trista's attacker was up and hauling ass through the darkened woods. But Matt couldn't leave her. Not like this. Not until the paramedics arrived. "*Shit.*" He hated letting the fucker escape, but she needed him.

Sheba's body quivered as she repeatedly lifted her front paws off the ground, eager to give chase yet obediently awaiting his command.

"*Revier!*" Sheba spun and charged into the woods to search for the guy. Seconds later, Matt heard sharp barks slice the air, then a human *yelp* from somewhere deep within the tree line.

Clenching his teeth, Matt cursed and reholstered his weapon. He didn't like the idea of his dog out there alone with a murderous, knife-wielding asshole.

He grabbed a flashlight from his belt, shining the beam on Trista's face. "Stay with me. Don't you dare die on me."

Her eyes were still wide and panicked, one of her

hands still clutching at her throat. He expected to see blood streaming through her fingers, but all he saw was a thin trickle from a narrow, superficial cut.

She pointed over his shoulder. "Inhale—" More high-pitched wheezing.

"Inhaler?" *Fuck*. He was an idiot.

She's having an asthma attack.

Pushing to his feet, he ran to the only car in the lot with its door wide open and grabbed her purse from the passenger seat. He dumped out the contents, easily finding the inhaler. As he ran back to her and knelt, he shook the inhaler, then put it to her mouth.

She wrapped her hands around the canister, pushed the button, and took a fast, deep breath, holding it.

Fear twisted his gut as he watched her face, waiting for the meds to take effect. Fuck, he felt helpless.

More rustling from the tree line had him whipping out his gun again, resting his flashlight on top of the barrel. Sheba's eyes glowed red in the high-powered beam. Panting, she sat at his side, sniffing Trista's arm.

Sirens wailed in distance. Trista's eyes were closed, and he noticed her glasses were gone. Her chest rose and fell rapidly. She was getting more air now but might need another hit from the inhaler.

He holstered his gun, then cupped her cheek, which was cold and clammy. "Hang in there. An ambulance is on the way."

When she began to shiver, he worried she was going into shock. Shifting on his knees, he encircled her in his arms, trying to transfer his warmth to her slim body. Resting his chin on the top of her head, he inhaled that same sweet flowery scent he'd detected that morning.

Sensing distress, Sheba lay down on the ground beside them.

The sirens grew louder, then red and blue lights lit up the parking lot and the trees. Police cars and an ambulance rolled in, grinding to a stop.

"Over here!" he shouted.

For a second, he had a vision of the other cops blasting him to kingdom come. He'd reported a woman being attacked, and here he was holding her tightly on the ground.

"Police, don't shoot!" Matt called out as he maneuvered Trista so the badge on his shirt would be clearly visible.

Then she went limp in his arms. Matt placed his hand on her sternum, and his blood ran cold. She was barely breathing.

Correction: he didn't think she was breathing at all.

Chapter Three

People yelling at her. Radios squawking. Trista took a shaky breath, and when she opened her eyes, she was nearly blinded by all the flashing red-and-blue strobes.

Emergency vehicles.

Something covered her mouth and nose. A mask. Make that an inhaler. Not hers, but a big one, the kind hospitals had used on her when she was a kid. A nebulizer. She struggled to remember what had happened, then it hit her. She'd had an asthma attack. A bad one, this time.

People standing and kneeling over her were blurry. *My glasses.* Where were they? When she tried raising her arm to find them, someone squeezed her hand.

"Hey, Trista," a deep voice rumbled softly near her ear. "Welcome back. You scared the hell out of me."

I know that voice.

"Sheba, *lehni*," the same voice commanded.

Sgt. Connors. Beside him, his K-9 lay on the ground, panting, water dribbling from her muzzle.

What are they doing here? For that matter, where is *here?*

The Moose. Attacker. Knife.

She tensed, and her heart began beating faster. Her attacker was nowhere in sight, but Sgt. Connors was there. He'd come to her rescue. Relief flooded her, and her pulse slowed. No longer did her chest feel tight. No wheezing or coughing. The inhaler had done its job opening her airways. Struggling to rise to a sitting position, she realized she already *was* sitting. Had they propped her up against a tree?

As a child, when she'd had bad asthma attacks, the doctors would put her in a sitting position, making it easier to breathe. But this tree was moving, breathing, and she knew what it was.

Sgt. Connors's broad chest.

The night air had chilled, but his breath against the top of her head was even warmer. Feeling self-conscious about his proximity, she struggled to rise, but his arms prevented her.

"Easy there. Let the paramedics do their thing."

Having no other choice, she relaxed against his chest and it felt good. Warm. Solid. Protective.

"Respiration and pulse are back to normal." A paramedic peeled off the Velcro blood pressure cuff on her arm. "Does your chest still feel tight?"

She pulled the mask from her face. "No."

A second paramedic reached out a hand, stopping her. "Leave it on for a few more minutes, then we'll take you to the hospital to get checked out."

"No." She swatted the medic's hand away, dragging the mask from her face. "I'm not going to the hospital. I'm fine now. I've been through this before." Not in ages, though. She only carried an inhaler in her purse out of habit.

"Trista," Sgt. Connors said. "Let them check you out at the hospital."

She twisted in his arms and found his face *sooo* close to hers that for a moment words fled. Even in the shadows of the trees and all the flashing red-and-blue lights, he was still the most handsome man she'd ever seen. "Th-this was triggered by stress. N-now that the trigger is gone, I'll be fine." Aside from stuttering, that was.

Dark brows slashed together in a scowl as he looked from one paramedic to the other. "What do you think?"

One medic shook his head. "I don't like it, but she's conscious and seems lucid. We can't force her to go if she refuses."

"I put a bandage on her throat," the other one said. "Luckily, it was only a shallow nick."

"I'm right here." She fisted her hands. "So don't talk around me. I've made my decision and that's final. I have plenty of inhalers at home if I need them. If I have another attack—which I won't—I'll call 911."

"I think you should take their advice and go to the hospital." Sgt. Connors was shaking his head at her.

Shoving his arms away, she pushed to a kneeling position and faced him. "I d-don't care what you think." It irked the snot out of her that she could tell off both paramedics without stumbling over her words, but the second she looked at Sgt. Connors, her brain waves shorted out.

Her knees wobbled as she struggled to stand. Sgt. Connors reached out to steady her, helping her rise to her feet. She twisted her neck in every direction, although her vision was still blurry from not wearing her glasses.

"Where is he?" Common sense told her she was safe in the circle of emergency responders, yet her chest tightened a bit just the same. "The g-guy who grabbed me, where is he?"

"He got away." A uniformed cop came forward.

"I think my dog got a piece of him," Sgt. Connors said. "I'll swab her mouth in case he left any DNA to run through CODIS."

"Uh-oh," someone new said, a voice she recognized as

one of the Moose's waiters. "Sorry, man. I, uh, gave your dog some water. She was panting so much, and I just thought... Fuck, I'm sorry."

"Forget it," Sgt. Connors said, although from his tone, he sounded annoyed. "We probably couldn't get a decent swab anyway."

"Matt." A tall blond man in slacks and a dress shirt rolled up his sleeves and pushed his way through the small crowd of people encircling Trista. On his belt was a gold badge and a gun. "Thought I recognized your voice on the radio." The detective held out his hand to Sgt. Connors, and they shook. "What've we got here?"

"This is Trista Gold." Sgt. Connors dipped his head in her direction. "She works at Langley. She was attacked in the parking lot." He paused, pressing his full lips together in a hard line. "Her attacker got away."

"Ms. Gold, I'm Detective Sorensen. I'd like to ask you a few questions." Detective Sorensen tugged a small pad and pen from his shirt pocket.

"Jake, let's go to my truck so she can get more comfortable."

Without waiting for a response, Sgt. Connors placed a hand at the small of her back, urging her in the direction of the parking lot. As they walked, she felt his touch clear to her toes. She knew he was only keeping his hand there in case she passed out or something, but she had to admit, it felt kind of good.

"*Kemne*," he said, and the dog trotted along beside them.

Moments later, she was seated in the front passenger seat of his truck with the door open, Detective Sorensen facing her. "Can you tell me what happened?"

She opened her mouth to speak, pausing to watch Sgt. Connors wordlessly point. The truck swayed slightly as the dog leaped inside the open door behind her. Turning, she bolted upright, preparing to jump from the truck.

"Relax, Tris. She won't hurt you." He leaned in front of her and slid the metal grating between her and the dog shut. As it had earlier that morning, his sexy scent came to her, and she couldn't help but breathe him in.

She cast a wary eye toward the dog that sat only inches from her, staring back with big, golden, satanic eyes.

And when did he start calling me Tris?

That was a nickname only her parents and close friends used. His use of it should have annoyed her, but it didn't. Oddly, it sounded…natural.

"Ms. Gold?" Detective Sorensen was staring at her with raised brows.

"I drove into the lot just after midnight," she recounted, pausing to watch the ambulance roll out of the lot.

It took only a few minutes for her to relate what she knew, and it took all her resolve not to look at Sgt. Connors, who'd come to stand next to Detective Sorensen. Even the dim light cast from the passenger compartment's overhead light was enough to make the thick muscles of his forearms stand out in vivid detail.

"When I got here," he said, pointing behind them to the woods, "some assho—" He paused and cleared his throat. "Some guy had his arm around her, a knife to her throat, and was dragging her into the woods."

Detective Sorensen scribbled on his pad. "Can either of you describe him?"

"No." She shook her head. "I never saw him. He was always behind me." She put a hand to her throat, running her fingers over the bandage covering the knife wound.

"Matt?" The detective turned to Sgt. Connors.

"About five-eleven, one-eighty, dark hair, wearing gloves, and he reeked of cigarette smoke."

"You saw all that?" She widened her eyes at the specificity

of his description. And she couldn't even remember the cigarette smell.

Probably because he had a knife to my throat, and I couldn't breathe.

"I got a look at him. You didn't." Sgt. Connors then proceeded to recount his observations, including him tackling her attacker to the ground.

"You saved m-my life." Her words came out a harsh whisper.

He shrugged. "Just doing my job."

"N-no, really." She locked gazes with him, only now fully realizing how close she'd come to dying. Or worse. "Thank you."

The sides of his mouth lifted briefly in a reluctant smile, and again, she was struck by how incredibly gorgeous he was. Especially when he smiled.

"Does Sgt. Connors's description sound like anyone you know?" Detective Sorensen asked. "An old boyfriend, current boyfriend, enemies?"

"No. I don't have any of those." Definitely not a boyfriend, not even an old one. At least, no one who'd lasted very long.

"Did he try to grab your purse?" Detective Sorensen asked.

"No." She shook her head.

"Did he say anything to you?"

"No."

Detective Sorensen looked up from writing. "He didn't say anything about what he was going to do to you?"

"No. He never said a word. Like I told you, he pulled me from my car, grabbed me from behind, then dragged me to the woods. The next thing I knew, I was on the ground." Helpless and unable to do anything, including breathe.

"Did he say anything to *you*?" Detective Sorensen turned to Sgt. Connors, who shook his head, then frowned.

The detective tapped the pen on his pad, pursing his lips. Whatever both men were thinking, it wasn't good.

"What aren't you telling me?" Neither man responded, just exchanged suspicious looks. "I may work for the CIA, but I don't like secrets. If there's something I should know, say it."

Detective Sorensen shoved the pad and pen into his pocket. "On the surface, this seems like either a robbery or a sexual assault. However, he didn't go for your purse, and granted, he may not have had the chance to assault you sexually, but he didn't say anything to you."

"I hadn't realized rapists carry on lengthy discourse with their intended victims."

The detective nodded. "Normally, they say something."

"Some use words designed to lull you into a sense of safety," Sgt. Connors said, his jaw hardening. "Some ask if you need assistance. Others use outright profanity. Some like to tell you exactly what they plan to do to you."

Wrapping her arms around herself, she shuddered at what an easy victim she'd made. Parking in a darkened section of the lot probably hadn't been the brightest thing to do. She might have a kick-ass analytical mind, but when it came to practicality, she was as dumb as a stump.

"Hey." Sgt. Connors briefly rested his hand on her shoulder. "You're gonna be okay. I won't let anything happen to you."

Seeing the sincerity in his eyes, she believed him. Or, at least, she wanted to. She'd been alone for so long now, she hadn't fully understood how nice it was to have a man care about her well-being. But this wasn't him caring for her. This was simply a police officer exercising his duty to protect.

Detective Sorensen then proceeded to ask her a slew of other questions, which she answered to the best of her ability.

"If it wasn't robbery or rape, then what was it?" she asked

him.

"Don't know. At this point, my guess is it was a random attack." He waved his pen in the air. "We'll review the Moose's video cams, but last week they were offline. We found that out after a hit-and-run in the parking lot." He made another note on his pad. "Since he wore gloves, dusting your car for prints is a waste of time."

Detective Sorensen pulled a wallet from his back pocket and handed her his business card. "If you think of anything else I should be aware of, give me a call. If you see or hear anything suspicious, don't hesitate to call 911. In the meantime, we'll run every tag in the lot and both adjacent lots in case he left a car here. If anyone red-flags with a criminal history, we'll pay him a visit."

"Can you have a car run by her place for the next few nights?" Sgt. Connors asked.

"Sure thing, Matt."

"Thanks, Jake." Sgt. Connors extended his hand, which the detective shook.

After Detective Sorensen walked over to the few remaining officers still processing the scene, Sgt. Connors faced her. "Do you have someone to stay with you tonight?"

She shook her head, wishing there was someone. "I just w-want to go home. I have to feed my cat."

"I'll drive you home."

"What? No! I have my c-car." She began getting out of the truck.

"Stay here." He pushed gently on her shoulder, forcing her back into the seat. "I'll have one of the uniforms follow us in your car."

She opened her mouth to object again, but he ignored her and carefully closed the passenger door in her face.

A minute later, he got in and handed over her purse. "Where do you live?"

"Uh, I uh—" *Oh great, here we go again.*

His brows rose in question, his gaze locking with hers. Bonnie was right. Even blurry, Sgt. Connors was h-o-t hot.

She gasped. "Wait, my g-glasses!"

"I put them in your purse." He guided the truck through the lot toward the road. "I hope you have a spare set, 'cuz they don't look so good."

Digging into her purse, she found her glasses and tried shoving them on. Both lenses were still intact, but the frames were twisted and mangled beyond repair. She'd have to hunt deep in her bathroom closet for some contacts to tide her over until she could order new glasses.

"Th-thank you." She rolled her eyes. *I sound like such a dork.*

"Where do you live?" he asked, checking his side mirror, probably to see if the deputy driving her car was behind them.

"Arlington. 442 Roseb-bud Lane."

For the first few minutes of the drive, neither of them said a word. Trista couldn't. Tonight, her social ineptness was at an embarrassingly all-time high, although not with the paramedics and not with Detective Sorensen. *Only* with Sgt. Connors.

"You shouldn't be parking in lots that aren't well-lit at night," he said, gunning the truck onto the ramp for I-66.

"Thanks for the t-tip."

"What are you doing out at this hour?"

"I was working late and needed f-food."

"Great minds think alike." He chuckled, and she liked the way his laugh came out all rumbly and rich. "I was waiting at the light to turn in and grab some grub myself. Best burgers in town."

She laughed. "Definitely." At least she'd managed four syllables without tripping over her words.

"What were you working on so late?" he asked, then held

up his hand. "Never mind. Top secret, right?"

She gave him a brief smile. "New assignment. I was stuck on something and didn't want to leave until I broke through it."

"That's job dedication." He nodded. "How often do you have asthma attacks?"

"Not often anymore." She shook her head. "Stress can trigger one, b-but it's not usually this bad."

His hands tightened around the wheel. "Getting attacked at knifepoint definitely qualifies as stress."

"My doctor always told me to avoid mental pressure, and to exercise d-daily to keep any stress under control."

"Do you?" He glanced at her. "Exercise every day?"

"The only parts of my b-body that get any exercise are m-my fingers." She let out a heavy sigh.

"You okay?" he asked, giving her a quick glance.

"Fine. I was thinking that if I'd b-been stronger, or had taken some self-defense cl-classes, this m-might not have happened." At least, she might not have been so totally helpless.

"Don't kick yourself." He slowed as he took the exit. "Even if you worked out every day with weights, you probably wouldn't have been strong enough to fight him off. But the self-defense classes are a good idea. I can get you a list of courses in the local area."

"Okay."

The rest of the ride passed in silence until they braked to a stop in front of her modest ranch house. She watched her car pull into the driveway, then a marked unit parked in front of them at the curb.

A snort and a puff of hot air at the back of her head made her jump, twisting in the seat to find Sheba standing directly behind her, the dog's golden gaze holding her transfixed. Her heart beat faster, and she forced herself to breathe slowly, praying she wouldn't have another asthma attack.

"Sheba, *lehni*." Sgt. Connors turned to her as the dog lay down obediently. "One day you'll realize she'll never hurt you. I promise."

She swallowed, only somewhat comforted by the cage between her and the dog, then cast him a disagreeing glare. "Sure I will."

This time, his mouth lifted into a full-fledged smile, and her heart rate kicked up even more but not from stress this time. *Hardly.* The sight of all that manly deliciousness bestowed upon her mousy, dowdy little self did all kinds of unexpectedly appealing things to her body. Like making her belly tingle.

Even though there was no chance a man like him would ever be hers, she was gratified to know her body was at least functioning on a normal level around this guy. Even if her brain wasn't.

Taking a deep breath, she held out her hand to him. "Thank you, Sgt. Connors. For the ride home, and for saving m-my life."

Smiling, he took her hand in his. "So formal. Call me Matt."

Before she could process how his large hand completely engulfed hers, he was out of the truck and walking up to the officer who'd gotten out of her car. Matt took the keys, then shook the other cop's hand.

When the marked unit drove off, she reached for the car door handle when the door opened.

"C'mon. I'll walk you in."

She slipped off the seat and nearly plowed into his chest. Standing so close to him made her realize just how big he was. "How t-tall are you?" she blurted out, then felt silly about the childlike bluntness of her question.

With his hand at the small of her back, he closed her

door, chuckling. "Six-four. Six-five or more in these shit-kicker boots."

"Wow. I'm f-five-one."

"Don't shortchange yourself. You're at least five-two in your shoes."

A squeaky laugh bubbled from her throat. When they got to her door, he handed her keys to her and waited while she opened it and turned on the porch and living room lights. She turned to see him standing just outside the door. "Th-thank you again, Sgt.—"

He held up his hand, interrupting her. "It's Matt. And from now on, maybe you'll stop to say hello on your way into Langley. Although I expect you to call in sick later."

"Why?" She frowned.

He gave her a *duh* look. "Really?"

"I feel fine, and I need to g-get back to my assignment."

Dark brows bunched as he watched her thoughtfully. "You know you have to file an incident report."

"What?" Her stomach knotted. She'd totally forgotten about that. Or maybe it was selective memory.

"Agency policy requires any employee involved in a police matter to report it to the security office within twenty-fours after the incident."

"I kn-know." She quickly averted her gaze, hoping he wouldn't detect her hesitancy.

"I can help you fill it out," he offered.

"No! I'll take care of it." *Not.*

There was a rumor in the analysis branch that an analyst who'd once had a seemingly inconsequential interaction with the police had his security clearance revoked. If her clearance was yanked, she couldn't do her job. And if she couldn't work, she might as well not exist. Her work was *everything* to her.

Matt continued staring at her, saying nothing. Blood pounded in her ears as her heart began beating faster, something it did whenever she told a lie.

Uh-oh. She gripped the doorknob tightly. He was a cop and could probably see right through her.

"Is there someone you can call and talk to about what happened tonight?" he asked. "Your friends from this morning, Bonnie and Kevin?"

How did he know everyone's names? *Cops know everything, remember?* Worry boiled in the pit of her stomach. Bonnie and Kevin were the last people she would ever tell. If she did, word would get out. She couldn't put her clearance at risk.

"Why would I d-do that?" She heard the telltale quiver in her voice, and sure enough, he scowled down at her.

"Because they're your friends, and after a traumatic experience, it helps to talk about what happened."

"Maybe." *Maybe not.* "I'll think about it," she lied again, hating herself for doing it. He'd saved her life, after all.

"Where's your cell phone?" he asked.

"Here." She indicated her purse.

"Get it out."

She crossed her arms. "Why?"

"I'm going to put my cell number in your phone. That way, if you need anything tonight, you call me."

"Why would I c-call *you*? Shouldn't I call 911 if I need help?"

"Humor me." Mimicking her, he crossed his arms, too. Then he surprised her by leaning in so close that their noses almost touched. "Now get out your damned phone."

"Okay, okay." She dug the phone out of her purse, and unlocked it. "What's your n-number?"

Sighing, he grabbed the phone, entered his number, then handed it back to her. "Call me if you need anything. *Anything*," he reiterated but remained standing at her open door.

"What?" she asked.

"Close the door and lock it. I'm not leaving until you do."

"Fine," she said with a huff, then slammed the door in his face, cranking the dead bolt with more force than necessary, so he'd be sure to hear it. Muffled chuckling sounded on the other side, followed by receding footfalls. Hurrying to her living room window, she watched his taillights as he drove off.

Meow.

A soft, furry head nuzzled her leg, and she reached down to scoop the Angora into her arms. Big blue eyes stared back at her from a pure-white face. "Poofy, you must be starving."

Despite her own stomach being empty, she had no appetite. She fed Poofy, then washed up and slipped into her favorite cotton nightshirt.

Exhaustion pervaded her entire body. Her limbs were suddenly boneless, and she all but fell into bed. When Poofy jumped on the mattress and snuggled next to her, she could barely lift her arm to give him his usual good-night scratch behind the ears. When she did, her hand trembled.

Why me?

Why had she been singled out?

She could have died tonight. Alone. In the woods. If Matt and Sheba hadn't come along...

The trembling in her hand spread to her arm, and suddenly her whole body shook as everything came back to her with vivid clarity.

One of the man's arms had banded her chest, the other tight around her neck, holding the knife to her throat. When he'd been dragging her across the pavement, he'd laughed. She hadn't remembered that before. The bastard hadn't said anything, but he'd laughed. Then they were in the woods, and the knife bit into her skin. The next thing she knew, she was on the ground, and—

"Breathe," she whispered. "Just breathe." She took in slow, even breaths, trying to stave off another asthma attack.

Poofy's soft fur beneath her fingers soothed her, and she focused on his steady purr until the trembling lessened and the growing tightness in her chest dissipated.

The numbers on her bedside clock were blurry, but she could still make them out in the dark. It was nearly three a.m. In a few hours, the alarm would go off, and she'd be back at work. Assuming Matt would be there as well, she'd have to find a way to avoid him when she went through security. The last thing she wanted was to have a discussion with him again about filing that report with the agency.

Tucking Poofy closer against her offered some measure of comfort.

She thought again about Matt. Funny, but he'd had his arms around her twice in the past twenty-four hours, and both times, she'd felt completely protected and safe.

Trista grinned sleepily, but her last thought before drifting off wiped the grin from her face.

What if the attack wasn't random?

What if he tries to kill me again?

Chapter Four

"What is she doing at work only five hours after getting attacked?" Matt said to Sheba as he watched Trista deliberately get into the longer of the two employee lines—the one he *wasn't* stationed at. "And she's avoiding us."

Sheba's ears flicked, and she dipped her head, as if in agreement.

"Why would she do that, girl?"

Sheba let out a soft snort followed by a series of low whines. She did that whenever he talked to her, as if they were carrying on an actual conversation. Which, they were.

Narrowing his gaze, he tracked Trista's progress in the other line, realizing she wasn't wearing her glasses. Not that he was surprised. The frames had been pretty mangled. She must have contact lenses in, and he wondered why she didn't wear them more often. She was beautiful wearing glasses. Without them...she was a knockout.

When she finally got to the checkpoint, she shoved her ID into the reader and punched in her code. No sooner had the plexiglass doors *whooshed* open than she cast him a furtive look and took off like a shot to the elevator bank.

What the hell is that about?

People's voices echoed in the lobby as he yawned and dragged a hand down his face. "Women," he muttered, shaking his head. It could be he'd never dated one long enough to figure out the way their minds worked.

"You look like shit, Connors," Buxton McIntyre, aka Buck, his boss and head of Langley's security division, said as he came to stand beside him. Though the man was a full six inches shorter, he had the presence of a Great Dane in a room full of Chihuahuas.

Matt nodded a greeting to several employees passing through the checkpoint. "Feel like it." He'd only managed a few hours' sleep before reporting in for duty.

"From what I read in your report," Buck said, "sounds like you had a late night."

Stifling another yawn, he nodded. "And then some." He'd written up a quick report for Buck before coming on duty, and he'd also left a message for Jake Sorensen to email over the police report.

"We'll discuss it at the meeting after lunch. That should give Ms. Gold time to file her own incident report. Make sure to attach the PD's report to hers."

"Will do."

Buck turned to leave, pausing. "You really do look like shit. Take off as soon as the meeting's over. I'll get someone else to cover the rest of your double."

"Thanks, boss." He gave Buck a grateful look. With several of the other security officers on vacation, he'd been working plenty of double shifts. Normally, that didn't bother him, but it wasn't even eight thirty, and he was already dead on his feet.

Not only did he like working for Buck, but the hours at the CIA were a boatload better than they'd been at his former employer. Usually, that was. Last night had been an exception.

After six years as a military K-9 officer overseas, the Alexandria PD had picked him right up after he'd left the Marines. But after five years, a spot on the PD's K-9 squad had never materialized. And his heart was always with the K-9s. And so he'd moved on.

The other good thing about working for the CIA was his commute, which was now a fraction of what it used to be. Less time on the road meant more time working before and after-hours at his place. *Jerry's Place*. His charity organization for kids and canines was a work in progress, and he still had a shitload more to do before it was up and running.

A quick glance at his watch told him it was only five minutes since the last time he'd checked it. As soon as the weekly security meeting was over, he'd get in a quick workout at the gym, then take Buck up on his offer and head home early.

After downing the last of his coffee, Matt headed to the printer to get the police report Jake had emailed over. On the way back to his desk, he poured himself another cup and sat at his desk to give the report a quick scan.

Beside him, Sheba lounged in her bed, her muzzle between her legs, her eyes half closed and wearing an expression of utter contentment. It always amazed him how happy she was just to be near him.

Jake's report was thorough, although there hadn't been much to report on. Jake had even sent uniforms back into the woods behind the Moose early this morning to look for evidence, but there'd been none. The ground was so dry, they hadn't even found any shoe prints.

What he read still bugged him, more than it had last night. Sure, some crimes lacked motive, but his cop instincts were buzzing. Something about last night seemed off.

Is it because Trista is so petite and helpless?

He doubted she had the strength to hurt a fly. When she'd lain there in his arms, unconscious, she'd seemed so fragile. That fucker had meant to hurt her, if not kill her. He didn't want to think about what would have happened if he and Sheba hadn't been there. When he'd witnessed her being dragged into the woods, he'd been out for blood. And when he'd pounded his fist into the guy's face, it had felt good. Damn good, because he'd wanted to kill him.

Matt looked at the crumpled report in his fisted hand. Just thinking about what a close call she'd had and how her attacker had escaped got him pissed off all over again. He hated seeing innocent people get hurt, and he'd do everything in his power to help someone in need.

Trista had needed him, and he'd been there for her. That was what being a cop was all about. Helping people. It was something he needed to do. *Had* to do. He had a lot to make up for in his life. He couldn't change what he'd done all those years ago, but he intended to spend the rest of his life trying to be a better person.

"Hey, Matt. Heard you had some fun last night."

Olga Miller, one of the other K-9 officers in his unit, leaned down to pet Sheba, who rolled onto her side, exposing her belly for Olga to scratch.

"I wouldn't call it fun, exactly." Grabbing a paper clip from his drawer, he attached the reports together, intending to staple them to Trista's incident report.

"Rescuing a damsel in distress?" She placed her hand over her heart and let out an exaggerated sigh. "If I wasn't married to the love of my life, you'd be at the top of my list of the most manly men to get rescued by."

"Lucky me." He narrowed his eyes, sending her a warning look.

After giving Sheba another scratch, she snickered and stood. "See you in the meeting, Stud."

"Wiseass," he muttered, then grinned. Secretly, Olga was one of his favorite people. She was like the sister he never had. Well, the sister he hadn't talked to in years.

Grabbing a pad, he rose and went to the main office to check again for Trista's incident report. The office's in-box was empty, so he began searching all the other boxes on the counter, in case it got misfiled.

"Can I help you find something, Matt?"

Matt turned to find Ava, the security division's administrative assistant, who was watching him from the doorway.

"Yeah." He turned back to flip through some of the other loose documents on the counter. "I'm looking for Trista Gold's incident report."

"No one's dropped off any incident reports today." Ava began tidying up the mess Matt had just made. "Except for you, that is. I read your report. What you did last night was so heroic. Like something out of a movie. A knight in shining armor rescuing a damsel in distress."

Matt froze as he reached for the top in-box, then turned to glare down at Ava. "You've been talking to Olga."

"Yesss." She batted her eyelashes and sighed.

"Christ," he mumbled. "Just let me know if you find it."

"I'll do that, Matthew. Now scoot." She made a *shooing* gesture with her hands. "You'll be late for the meeting."

"In a second." He picked up the phone, then dialed Trista's extension. His call went directly to voicemail, and he hung up. He'd already left her a message an hour ago about the report. At this point, she'd been in the office nearly six hours. She'd had plenty of time to get the damned report in.

But, he suddenly realized, she never intended to file it.

When he'd talked to her about it last night, she'd assured him she would get it done, but her response had been bullshit. He'd seen it in her eyes. She might be a whiz at digging up analytical secrets, but she wasn't a very good liar.

Not your problem, Connors, so stop thinking about her.

Rubbing his forehead, which had begun to ache from lack of sleep, he headed to the conference room and found everyone else, including Olga, already there, standing.

"Grab a chair, Connors." Buck gestured to the empty chair at his left. "Everyone, let's give a big round of applause to our resident white knight."

Ah, shit. Matt ground his teeth as his colleagues clapped heartily.

"All right, all right." Buck sat, as did everyone else. "Let's get down to business."

Matt handed Buck the crumpled police report. "Here's the PD report from last night."

Buck took the report, quickly flipping through it. "And Ms. Gold's incident report?"

"It's not here." Matt met Buck's questioning look.

"Meaning what?" his boss asked. "That it's not here? Or that she didn't write one up?"

"Can't say."

A series of *oohs* and *uh-ohs* resounded around the table.

Buck sat back in his chair. "Did you call her?"

"Yes." Matt hesitated to mention that he'd called her twice. She'd nearly been killed last night. Throwing her under the bus for a missing report didn't sit right with him. There must be a damned good reason she hadn't filed it.

"How many times?" Buck prodded.

Shit. "Twice. Got voicemail both times."

The *oohs* and *uh-ohs* got louder.

"All right, all right." Buck held up his hand for silence,

then made a note on his pad. "Give us a quick rundown of what happened."

Matt summarized everything from the moment he'd seen Trista being dragged into the woods to the time he'd dropped her off at her house.

"Wow!" Olga laughed. "First, the kid yesterday at the checkpoint, and now the guy last night. You've been doing a lot of tackling lately."

"Reliving your old college football glory days?" Mark Waters added with a smirk.

With his head pounding full force now, Matt sent them each a silencing glare. A good workout before heading home and sacking out would definitely hit the mark to ease the tension creeping up his neck.

"So, no obvious motive, nothing to show the guy knew Ms. Gold. You really think the attack was random?"

Matt rubbed his jaw. "I don't know. Could be it really was just a crime of opportunity."

"But you don't think so."

He met his boss's gaze. Buck not only had thirty years of federal law enforcement under his belt, but he could also read his people and knew what they were thinking.

"I can't put my finger on it. But the locals have no leads to follow up on."

"Anything connecting the attack to agency business?" Buck asked.

Matt shook his head. "Nothing I know of."

Buck made another notation. "As long as there's no connection to agency business, there shouldn't be any fallout from this. After the meeting, I'll notify Ms. Gold's supervisor about the report."

Matt winced inwardly, hoping Trista didn't catch too much heat.

As the meeting went on, they discussed other security

matters, including that stupid kid who'd tried to barrel through the checkpoint to impress his friends. The idiot would probably get off with a warning.

As Buck passed out the coming week's schedule, Matt's thoughts drifted back to last night. There were too many unanswered questions. Including why he'd insisted on her having his personal cell phone number. It made him feel better knowing she had it. Until this thing with her attacker was figured out, he couldn't shake the protective urges welling up inside him. Not that he had any delusions of heroism. But he and Sheba *had* saved her life, and now he felt somewhat responsible for her.

As they filed out of the conference room, Mark Waters and the other K-9 handlers clapped Matt on the shoulder.

"Your damsel's not gonna like you much after today," Waters said.

Yeah, no shit.

Matt put Sheba up in her office kennel, then headed for the locker room. The idea of Trista being angry with him—or anyone else, for that matter—was unlikely. She was so shy and demure, he doubted she had an angry bone in her body.

Chapter Five

"You're *what?*" Trista stared at Wayne Gurgas, her boss and the deputy chief of the Strategic Programs Section.

"Revoking your security clearance." Wayne leaned over and flipped off the switch on her computer.

The room went deathly silent as Bonnie and Kevin stopped whatever they were doing to listen. The sound of her computer shutting down was like a gunshot to Trista's heart. Biting back a scream, she widened her eyes, gripping the armrests of her chair. She stared at the blank screen, then shifted her eyes back to Wayne. "You can't do that," she whispered, paralyzed by shock, barely able to speak.

"I can, and I did." Wayne crossed his arms, hiking up the sleeves of his suit jacket. "I'm sorry, Trista. The head of security just notified Genevieve and I"—he nodded to his assistant section chief, Genevieve Grujot, who stood beside him—"and the decision is final. Until we can verify the attack on you last night has no connection to agency business, your clearance is revoked."

Regaining her wits, Trista stood, fisting her hands. *This*

can't be happening. Her entire world was imploding before her eyes. "If my clearance is revoked, I can't do anything on the computer or online. I can't run Dark Curtain or find Karakurt again." Though she'd been searching for him since the moment she'd arrived that morning. "I might as well not come to work at all."

"Exactly." Wayne gave a curt nod. "Until this is figured out, consider yourself on paid vacation. You've got half an hour to gather your things and go home. Langley security will stay in touch with police regarding the attack."

"Is this because I didn't file an incident report? I'm sorry, I'll do it right now if it will help." She knew it wouldn't. It was too late for that.

"At this point," Wayne said, "that's not necessary. We read about what happened in the police report and Sgt. Connors's report."

"*Sgt. Connors's* report?" Last night she'd told him she would take care of it. Looks like he'd gone behind her back and filed one of his own.

Wearing a sympathetic expression, Genevieve walked around Trista's desk and laid a hand on her shoulder. "I'm sure this will all be resolved soon, and then you can return to your assignments. For now, go home. Enjoy the free time. None of this is a reflection on you."

The hell it isn't.

Something was wrong. *Very* wrong. True, she had concerns about filing the report, but she never really believed this could happen. Not to *her.* It wasn't like Wayne and Genevieve to take such drastic action without consulting her first.

Wayne uncrossed his arms and pointed at her. "I expect to see you checking out of here within the next thirty minutes."

"But—" Her body began to tremble as the enormity of what had just happened sank in.

"No buts, Trista." Wayne turned and headed to the door.

"I don't want to hear anymore. Just leave. I mean it. Thirty minutes, and I want you gone."

With a sudden spurt of desperation, Trista rounded her desk, pushing past Genevieve, stopping Wayne before he could leave. "Please, don't do this. I *have* to work. If I can't work, I'll—" She couldn't say the words. *I'll be nothing.*

Wayne opened his mouth, then closed it. A glimmer of something she couldn't identify came to his eyes, but then he yanked open the door and left without another word.

Again, Genevieve's hand came to rest on her shoulder. "This will all be over soon. You'll be back at work in no time." Then she turned and followed Wayne.

As Trista watched the door close behind Genevieve, tears pricked her eyes, irritating the contact lenses she'd been forced to wear.

"Aw, honey." Bonnie guided Trista back to her desk, forcing her into her chair.

Kevin came over and sat on the corner of her desk. "Sorry, Tris. I've never seen Wayne act like that. Guy's got a bug up his ass about something."

"Yeah, but what?" Bonnie frowned. "And what *incident* are they talking about? What happened?"

Letting her head fall forward, Trista moaned, then told Bonnie and Kevin everything.

"Oh my God." Bonnie's mouth gaped open. "That's why there's a Band-Aid on your neck? You could have been killed. You should have told us about this when you came in this morning, and taken at least a day or two off after an experience like that."

"We're your friends, Trista." Kevin crossed his arms over his chest, tapping his fingers on his pocket protector. "You should have called us last night."

"I'm sorry." Trista shut her eyes, wishing she could erase everything that had happened in the past twenty-four hours.

She knew her friends were only expressing their concern, but her head was seriously starting to pound. "After it was all over, it was late and I was so tired, I practically passed out the second my head hit the pillow."

Kevin narrowed his eyes. "And you have no idea why this guy attacked you?"

"Well, I can guess." Trista shuddered at the truth. He was either going to rape her, kill her, or both. She supposed there was a remote—albeit *very* remote—possibility that the attack had something to do with her job, but she hadn't been working on anything dangerous, not even earlier in the chat room. Certainly it hadn't been anything to *kill* her over.

Bonnie gave her a sympathetic smile, then pressed her hand over her heart. "Sgt. Connors saved your life. That is so heroic."

"Give me a break." Kevin glared at Bonnie, and she glared back.

Watching the wordless exchange between her friends made Trista smile. Kevin was jealous, and he didn't even realize it.

Returning his gaze to Trista, Kevin resumed his tapping his pocket protector. "Sounds like whatever's in that report triggered something in-house."

"The police report, or Sgt. Connors's incident report?" Bonnie asked.

Trista's head pounded even worse now. She hadn't thought of that. "Good question. It's one I intend to find the answer to."

Pushing up from the chair, she stormed out the door into the hallway, ignoring the curious looks from others she passed on the way to the elevator. During the entire ride to the ground floor, she clenched and unclenched her fists.

When the doors opened, she charged across the lobby to the security office. Ava, the administrative assistant Trista had met on occasion during agency Christmas parties, smiled as she looked up.

"Ms. Gold, glad to see you're okay after last night."

"Thank you," she managed politely. Stemming her rising temper, she took a deep breath. "I'd like to see the police report and Ma—Sgt. Connors's report on my, uh, *incident.*"

"I just made you and your supervisor a copy." Ava handed her a manila envelope. "Here you go."

"Thank you." She pulled out the contents and read Detective Sorensen's report first. At the bottom of the form, she noted the detective's assessment. *Assailant unknown. Random attack presumed.* Then she read Matt's report.

At first glance, she was impressed by the detail and his manner of writing. Clear, concise, and to the point. But when she got to his assessment of the incident, she understood why her clearance had been revoked.

At the bottom of the agency form was a question requiring the reporting officer to indicate whether the incident had any connection with agency business. There were three possible answers: *Yes, No,* and *Unknown.* Matt had checked off the *Unknown* box.

Bastard. She wanted to call him worse, but cursing had been drilled out of her by her mother at a very young age.

He'd had no justifiable reason to say that, and because of that one checkmark, her rock—her lifeline—had been snatched away. She resisted the urge to scream at the top of her lungs and, with shaking hands, carefully placed the reports back into the envelope.

"Where is he?" she asked Ava, proud of herself for keeping the rising anger from her voice.

"Who, dear?" Ava looked up at her with raised brows.

She clenched her teeth. "Sgt. Connors."

"He's in the gym." Ava pointed through the security office opening to the doors across the lobby.

"Thank you." She plastered on a smile she didn't feel in the slightest, then spun and charged across the lobby.

With every click of her short heels on the granite floor, her temper flared hotter. By the time she reached the double doors outside the fitness center, her heart thumped faster, keeping rhythm with her rising anger. She paused before holding her ID card to the reader on the wall, uncertain whether her clearance revocation included access to certain locations as well. Even if it meant kicking the door in, she'd gain entry if it was the last thing she did.

Time was ticking down on her thirty minutes. But before she vacated the building, she fully intended to give Sgt. Connors a piece of her mind.

When she held her ID to the reader, the light blinked green and the door clicked. She pushed the door open and was assailed by the smell of the black rubber mats and blaring music.

The gym was empty, save for one person: Matt. At the far end, he lay with his back on a weight bench, pressing a barbell loaded with huge circular weights at each end. With quick, angry strides, she charged forward.

The barbell clattered as he set it on the rack, then he stood and grabbed a bottle of water from another bench. As he lifted the bottle and drank, she froze, her gaze traveling down then up his body.

Black sweats covered his long legs. A sleeveless, sweat-soaked gray T-shirt with the words *Alexandria PD* on the front clung to his chest, outlining finely honed, incredibly cut pecs and abs. Sweat glistened on bulging biceps as he held the bottle to his mouth.

She watched, fascinated at the way his throat worked as he swallowed half the bottle. When he lowered it and caught sight of her standing there, the corners of his mouth lifted into a slow, easy grin.

Pressing her lips together, Trista gripped the manila envelope even tighter in her hand and stormed over to the radio, cranking the volume off. When she turned back to

Matt, he was no longer smiling. As she stalked toward him, he set the bottle back on the bench, canting his head, eyeing her suspiciously.

Her chest rose and fell rapidly. Her pulse beat wildly in her ears. She threw the envelope at his chest. "How *could* you?" She gritted her teeth. "How could you put down *Unknown*? Do you have any idea what you've done?"

He stepped closer, towering over her. "What the hell are you talking about?"

Pointing her finger at him, she poked at his chest, somehow noting through the depths of her rage how hard it was. "Because of *your* report, *my* clearance was revoked. I'm banned from work. Banned from the whole frigging building because of you."

Narrowing his eyes, he scowled at her. "Because of *me*? I doubt that. *I* wasn't the asshole that attacked you."

Her voice rose, and it took everything she had not to pick up a weight and throw it at him. "You took everything from me. If I can't work, I have nothing. *Nothing!* Do you hear me?" Again, she jabbed at his chest.

His jaw went hard, anger flashing in his eyes. When he spoke, his voice was low and even. "I had a duty to report the incident as I saw it. Maybe," he added, leaning in until she could feel the heat from his body, "if you'd returned one of the messages I left for you, you would have seen this coming."

"Seen this coming?" Widening her eyes, she took a step back, so angry now she was quivering. "Why did you have to file a report at all? *I* would have filed one." *Eventually. Maybe. Probably.*

"Doesn't matter. I have a duty to file my own report. You didn't know that, did you?" He took another step toward her, forcing her to crane her neck to look up at him. "You had no intention of reporting what happened last night, and you damned well know it."

Lowering her gaze, she focused on his chest. His broad, heavily muscled chest. He was right, but that wasn't the point.

"Look, Tris." His tone softened. "You were attacked. You could have been killed, and we don't know for certain if it was a random attack, or something else. I'm sure as hell not gonna lie on a report just because it pisses you off. I checked *Unknown* because that's what I believe to be true."

She parked her fists on her hips, refusing to back down. "You had to know it could impact my clearance. It's happened before, to another analyst."

"I don't give a shit if it happened to a hundred analysts before you. If I think there's even a remote chance of a threat to the agency, or to you, it's my duty to report it. I won't lie just because you don't like the truth."

She shut her eyes, squeezing them tightly, willing the flood of fury shooting through her to calm. Somehow, she knew he was right, but he'd just sent her entire world tilting on its axis, and she couldn't handle it.

Letting out a soft breath, she covered her mouth with her hand. The rage and fury seething within her fled like air from a popped balloon. Then, to her horror, tears pricked her eyes. Before she could stop it, she was gulping down air, but it didn't help.

"Are you—" Matt halted in midsentence. "Oh, no." He began shaking his head. "Hell no. Don't you *dare* cry on me."

She couldn't help it. The tears began to fall, and she couldn't stop them. The next thing she knew, Matt uttered a groan and his arms were around her, pulling her against his chest.

Intending to shove him away from her, she clenched her fists, but then his hands were on her back, making gentle, soothing motions, and it felt too good to move. She clutched at his damp shirt, digging her fingers into his flesh through the soft fabric.

"Shh," he whispered, his lips grazing the top of her head,

then her temples. "Everything will work out okay. I'm sure of it."

Still holding fast to his shirt, she took a series of short breaths, trying to rein in her meltdown. She hoped he was right, but at the moment, it didn't matter. Until further notice, the one thing that meant more in the world to her than anything else had been cruelly taken from her.

"I'm sorry, Tris. I didn't mean for this to happen."

He pulled away enough that she could look up at his face. It was only then that she noticed the tiny gold flecks floating in the midst of his deep brown eyes.

When her mouth opened, his gaze dipped, and he bent his head. His lips brushed hers, softly at first, then with more pressure. Without realizing she was doing it at first, she kissed him back.

With a groan, he sifted his fingers through her hair, covering her mouth with his. His lips were warm and soft, his touch gentle. Using light pressure, he urged her lips open with his tongue.

Biting back a soft cry, she opened her mouth. The instant his tongue tangled with hers, her body trembled with need, and she clutched at him tighter. Cupping her nape, he deepened the kiss, angling her head, massaging her neck with long, strong fingers. His taste on her tongue was so new, she couldn't find the words to describe it. It was hot and wonderful, stirring up a fiery, passion-fueled craving she'd never experienced before.

His hand skated across her back, leaving a trail of delicious tingles on her skin, and still his tongue sought hers again and again. An unfamiliar ache started low in her belly, uncurling, blooming into something she *did* understand. *Desire.*

The hunger in her belly spread lower, hotter, until something inside her snapped, unleashed like a wild animal sensing freedom for the first time.

She molded herself against Matt, when he abruptly pulled away, thrusting her from him. His mouth was open, and his nostrils flared as he drew in heavy breaths. As he watched her, she glimpsed the heat in his gaze morph into something else. Regret.

"Fuck." He tightened his jaw. "I'm sorry. I shouldn't have done that. It was a mistake."

His words were like a slap to the face. Here she was, her body quivering with the absurd and inexplicable need to kiss him again, and he'd told her unceremoniously that she was a *mistake.*

Backing away, she glared at him. "I'm *no one's* mistake."

"C'mon," he said as he reached for her. "I didn't mean it like that."

Evading his grasp, she glanced at the clock on the wall and gasped. The half hour Wayne had given her was nearly up. If she didn't get back upstairs and collect her things quickly, she might be tossed from the building like a common criminal.

"Whatever," she lied then brushed past him and walked calmly to the doors, resisting the urge to run. Once outside in the lobby, she leaned back and closed her eyes. Placing her fingers on her lips, she couldn't help remembering how his lips had felt on hers. How he'd tasted on her tongue.

But kissing her had been a *mistake*?

He'd actually said that. Curling her fists, she pushed from the door and headed to the elevators, where she punched the *up* button with far more force than necessary.

Matt might regret kissing her, but he'd made her body experience things she'd never imagined. New things. Exciting things.

Every square inch of her rational brain told her she shouldn't, but she wanted those things again.

With *him.*

Chapter Six

Why the hell did I kiss her?

Matt stomped on the gas pedal. Behind him, Sheba let out a gruff sound of annoyance as she struggled for balance on the bench.

"Sorry, girl." He held his hand to the cage opening until she leaned her head into his palm. Stroking her velvety ears normally soothed him during the drive home after a rough day. Not today.

He'd been an ass and a shithead to kiss Trista, and he still couldn't come up with an acceptable reason for doing it.

To stop her from crying?

Initially, yes. The sight of her tears twisted his guts like nothing else.

Or to take her mind off getting her clearance revoked?

Maybe. No, that was bullshit.

He cranked the wheel, turning onto the road that ran in front of the Moose. He knew damned well why he'd kissed her. He just hated admitting it to himself.

I kissed her because I fucking wanted to. Needed *to.*

The plan had been to hold her, comfort her, knowing he was partly to blame for her losing her clearance, but when she'd looked up at him with those watery green eyes, his brain had detached from his body and the next thing he knew, he was tasting her beautiful, rosy lips. Just a quick taste, and then he'd stop. Or so he'd told himself. But when she'd kissed him back, he lost control and his inner-asshole had asserted itself. And he'd liked kissing her. A lot. It had felt too good, and that was the real reason he'd stopped. He didn't deserve to feel anything that good in his life. Not since the night his drunken stupidity had gotten his best friend killed.

This was his self-imposed penance. Jerry wouldn't get to feel anything good ever again, so neither should he. Including kissing Trista Gold. Because kissing her had by far been the best thing he'd experienced in years.

"Goddammit." *Goddammit to hell and back.*

Braking for a red light, he slapped his other hand back on the wheel. If only she hadn't kissed him back. Didn't matter. Taking advantage of a woman who was upset, and who'd just been attacked the night before and was undoubtedly vulnerable, made him the biggest shithead on the planet. Worse, with her soft, full breasts pressed against his chest, it had been impossible not to ogle her assets. Again making him a royal shithead.

As the light turned green, he stepped on the gas. He'd noticed she stammered when talking to him but not other guys. *What the hell is that about?* But when she'd been chewing his ass out in the fitness center, she hadn't stammered once. She'd given him a piece of her mind and then some. Never again would he be taken in by her shy, demure exterior, not when he'd had a run-in with the fiery hellcat hiding within.

He shot past the Moose, hazarding a glance at the wooded area behind the restaurant's parking lot. Jake had assured him uniforms had scoured the area for evidence both that night and in the morning when it was light out. But they didn't have Sheba.

Yawning, he noticed a few heavy raindrops hitting the windshield. The forecast was for a heavy downpour within the hour. He took his foot off the gas pedal.

Was it worth a second look?

It was a long shot, but after tonight's rain, there'd be no chance at all of picking up a scent.

Checking ahead and behind for traffic, he hung a 180 and pulled into the restaurant's lot, parking adjacent to the curb edging the woods where Trista had been attacked. He wanted Sheba to try to find a scent in the same location. Shutting off the engine, he got out and popped the side door button. Normally, he'd keep Sheba on the leash, but rain was coming down harder by the second.

"Hledej oznac." Her ears twitched, then she leaped out and bounded onto the pavement. Without him needing to point, the dog immediately put her nose to the area where Matt had tackled the POS to the ground. He pointed into the woods, and they both took off running, Sheba leading the way.

Breathing hard, Matt could barely keep Sheba in sight. The dog was a highly trained, highly motivated animal, and when she got on a hot track, there was no holding her back.

About a hundred yards ahead, he caught sight of her tan-and-black tail bounding in and out of the trees. Overhead, rain on the tree canopies got louder, and even beneath all that leaf cover, large droplets spattered onto his forehead.

Finally, Sheba lay down, panting, alerting him to something she'd found.

Slowing to a jog so he wouldn't mash any evidence into the ground, he eased up next to Sheba, placing his hand gently on her wet back. Beneath his fingers, the dog's muscles quivered with excitement. "Whatdya got there, girl?"

Between Sheba's paws, and half obscured by leaves and pine needles, was a jagged piece of cloth stained with something dark. Possibly blood from Trista's attacker.

Working quickly, Matt pulled a small plastic evidence bag from his thigh pocket and carefully scooped up the cloth without touching it. After sealing it, he stuffed the bag back in his pocket. Lightning lit the sky through the tree cover, followed by a crack of thunder.

"Let's get outta here."

Back at the truck, Sheba shook, sending droplets of water flying everywhere. Rain pounded on their heads, but Matt took the time to give his dog her reward for a job well done: an orange ball secured to the end of a rope. She clamped her jaws around the ball, and he held the rope taught for a few minutes while she tugged and pulled, twisting her head from side to side, growling in delight. By the time they were back in the truck, they were both soaked to the skin.

Matt wiped dripping water from his forehead and guided the Explorer out of the lot toward the police station.

Twenty minutes later, he was handing over the bagged evidence to Jake. "This was in the woods near where Trista Gold was attacked. Sheba found it, and I know she got a piece of that guy last night. Can you do me a favor and have your lab run it through CODIS?"

"Could be blood." Jake held the bag up to the light, examining the cloth. "All right. I'll send it in, but it could take a while. Weeks, maybe."

Matt handed Jake the CIA chain of custody form he'd already filled out. "Could you do me another favor and put a rush on it?"

Jake barked out a laugh. "Dream on. The lab's booked up solid. I've been waiting on a simple fingerprint ID for over a month now."

"I've got a bad feeling about this guy. Maybe this *was*

nothing more than a random attack, but if it wasn't…Trista's attacker is still out there. And the kind of guy who would do this probably isn't exactly a stellar citizen."

"Tell me about it." Jake nodded. "I'll do my best, but I can't promise anything."

"Thanks, buddy." Matt stood to leave, turning. "Find anything on the video cams?"

"Negative." Jake shook his head. "Still offline. And before you ask, our boys talked to everyone inside the restaurant after you left. There were no witnesses."

Shit. He'd really hoped Jake would have turned up something else by now. "You've got my cell," he said on the way out the door. "Call me as soon as you get the results. I owe you a beer."

"That you do." Jake nodded.

When Matt opened the door to the truck, Sheba stuck her head through the opening. Again, her body quivered at the prospect of getting out there and doing her thing. That was just one of many outstanding aspects of being paired with a K-9. Most of his human partners over the years hadn't exhibited half that excitement about their jobs. Sheba, on the other hand, was eager to go on patrol every day, rain or shine. Unlike a human, the dog almost never had a bad day. Speaking of bad days, Trista's past twenty-four hours definitely qualified as shitty.

Shaking his head in disbelief that he was doing it, Matt turned the Explorer in the direction of her house.

Chapter Seven

"You *yelled* at him?" Bonnie set the glass of Dalwhinnie on the kitchen table, her eyes wide. "You actually *yelled* at Sgt. Connors?"

Trista gave a reluctant nod, then took a sip from her own glass, savoring the spicy caramel and vanilla tones of her favorite Scotch. Her parents had given it to her as a gift after one of their walkabouts in Scotland, and she'd been hooked on it ever since. Not that she was much of a drinker, but it helped her to unwind after a stressful day. A light buzz was already working its way through her system, and she welcomed it.

Kevin abruptly stopped swirling the ice cubes in his glass. "What'd he do?"

Poofy readjusted himself in her lap and purred louder when Trista sifted her fingers through his thick scruff. "He told me he had a duty to report the incident, and that he'd done it for the safety of the agency, and for me."

She still couldn't believe she'd given Matt a serious tongue-lashing. A side of her personality she hadn't known existed—an outspoken, confrontational side—had taken that moment to make itself known. Equally shocking was that during her entire tirade she hadn't stammered once. A first around Matt.

"Did he get angry?" The corners of Bonnie's lips curved up at the corners, and she leaned on the table. "Did he whip out the handcuffs? Get all manly on you?"

"No." Trista rolled her eyes. "He was in the fitness center working out." Looking all sweaty, and muscular, and gorgeous.

"Did he yell back at you?" Kevin asked.

Trista shook her head. "Not exactly, although he was definitely mad at me. Matt is so big and intimidating, he doesn't have to raise his voice to get his point across. All he had to do was stand over me, scowling with those cop eyes— he's good at that, by the way—and I felt about yea big." She held her thumb and forefinger a quarter inch apart. Compared to him, she *was* yea big.

"Whoa, stop." Bonnie held up her hand, scrunching her brows. "You just called him *Matt*, not *Sgt. Connors*. When did you start calling him *Matt*?"

"I—" *Don't know.* She stared back, knowing she had a deer-in-the-headlights look on her face. Even though he'd told her to call him by his first name, she'd never really intended to.

"Did something else happen that you're not telling us about?" The beginnings of a sly grin began forming on Bonnie's lips.

"No," she said a bit too quickly, feeling her cheeks heat at the memory of having Matt's arms around her, his lips on hers, his tongue deep in her mouth. *Oh God.*

Bonnie reached across the table to grip Trista's arm. "Something *did* happen. I knew it. Give it up, GF."

"Leave her alone," Kevin said with a note of annoyance.

"She's been through enough."

"No way, José." Bonnie shook her head, then leaned back in her chair, crossing her arms. "This is serious girl stuff. If you don't want to hear it, go to the bathroom or something. Stick your fingers in your ears. But I," she said, pointing to her chest, "need to hear it."

"Okay, okay." She might as well get this over with. Bonnie would eventually pry it out of her anyway. "It wasn't that big a deal. One minute I was yelling at him like a crazy person, then I realized he was probably right, and I started to cry. I think he took pity on me because the next thing I knew, his arms were around me, then he was kissing me. I started kissing him back, then he said it was a mistake, and I left because Wayne and Genevieve told me I had thirty minutes to leave the building, and—"

"Wait." Bonnie smacked her hands on the table. "Dial that back. He was *kissing* you?"

Now her cheeks really started to grow hot. "Well, yeah. But he said it was a mistake, and he apologized."

"Oh, no." Kevin waggled his finger at her. "Men don't kiss women by mistake. Trust me."

"I agree." Bonnie nodded. "Why did he say it was a mistake?"

"I don't know." Trista groaned. "Maybe it was a pity kiss, or an I'm-sorry-for-getting-your-high-level-security-clearance-revoked kiss."

Either way, he'd made it painstakingly clear he regretted it, and the realization still twisted her insides. She hadn't been able to stop thinking about his kiss since she'd stormed out of the fitness center.

It had felt good kissing him. Crazy *good.*

His body had been warm and damp with perspiration, his muscles hard as steel beneath her fingers, flexing and bunching. And his hot mouth had been demanding one minute, soft and gentle the next. God help her, when his tongue touched hers, her body sizzled to the ignition stage in record time. She'd melted in his arms, boneless, like a limp noodle. Never in her life had a man's kiss scrambled her brains to such a degree. *Then again, it's not as if I've been kissed by many men.* But Matt had been responsible for her security clearance being revoked, and no way could she forgive him. Not entirely, anyway.

"Again, no." Kevin waved his finger. "Guys don't give pity kisses. Guys kiss when they want to kiss because it feels good. Trust me."

"I agree." Bonnie nodded. "Something triggered this. A spark, a connection, a—"

The doorbell rang, and Poofy swiveled his head to the door with a loud, inquiring *mew.*

"Excuse me," she said to her friends, picking Poofy up and depositing him gently on the floor, where he made another protest, louder this time. A sure sign of discontentment at having been ousted from his regal perch on her lap.

At the door, Trista peered through the peephole. At first, all she saw was navy blue. Then she recognized the gold badge and name tag, and her heart rate zoomed into the stratosphere.

Matt stood on her front porch, looking all big and commanding and able to leap tall buildings in a single bound.

Why is he here? If he'd come to apologize again for his *mistake*, she'd die of embarrassment.

Suddenly self-conscious, she tugged at the hem of her white lounging shorts, wishing she was wearing something that covered more of her backside and upper thighs. For that matter, her snug green knit tank top didn't do much to conceal anything, either. She'd only worn them because she was stuck at home for who knew how long and hadn't expected any visitors, not even Bonnie and Kevin. But they were close friends of hers, and Matt was not. And he was far too male for her narrow little comfort zone.

The doorbell peeled again, and she took a deep breath and opened the door. Their gazes met, then his lowered to her legs, then slowly slid back to her face, but not before lingering on her breasts.

To her horror, her nipples had begun to pucker and were now hardening beneath his gaze. She quickly crossed her arms. *Talk about embarrassment.*

In the ensuing and painfully awkward silence, he cleared his throat. "Can I come in?"

"Wh-why?" *Shoot. Not again.*

"Because I don't want to have this conversation out here on your porch." His gaze flickered again to her breasts, and his jaw went rigid.

"Fine." Sighing, she stepped aside for him to enter, although she couldn't stop the zinging in her belly as he brushed past her.

Through the kitchen doorway, Bonnie and Kevin craned their necks to see who was at the door. Bonnie elbowed Kevin, whispered something in his ear, and they both rose and joined them in the hallway.

"Sgt. Connors." Bonnie offered Matt a megawatt smile. "How nice to see you. Are you checking up on Trista after last night's, uh, incident?"

"I am."

"Sgt. Connors." Kevin held out his hand, which Matt shook.

"We were just leaving." Bonnie threw Kevin a meaningful look, then hooked her hand around his elbow, practically dragging him out the door.

"Apparently so." Kevin gave Trista a pointed look that spoke volumes. "Call if you need anything. I mean it. You can stay with either of us if you want to."

Matt's brows drew together as he narrowed his eyes on Kevin.

What's that about?

"Thank you, but I'll be fine here. Goodbye, you guys. And thanks for stopping by."

Before she'd closed the door, Bonnie turned at the bottom porch step, putting her thumb to her ear and her pinkie to her mouth, mouthing the words "Call me later."

When the door closed, Trista turned, and her mind went blank. Matt's dark brows were still knitted, and a distinct air of disapproval swirled around him. He sure had that scowling cop thing down.

"Can we talk?" he asked, his deep voice sending another delicious shiver through her body.

"Sure." She indicated the kitchen, and he stepped aside for her to pass. As he did, she breathed him in, catching an all-too-disconcerting whiff of his leathery, rummy aftershave, although now it was mingled with the clean scents of soap and shampoo.

He'd undoubtedly showered after his workout, and the image of Matt naked, water cascading down all those corded muscles, popped into her brain, sending goose bumps parading up her neck and making her nipples even harder.

Grabbing a sweater draped over the back of a chair, she quickly slipped it on and sat, automatically reaching for her glass of Dalwhinnie. He pulled out the chair next to hers and when he sat, she nearly laughed. He was so big, he seemed to take up half the kitchen. Or maybe it was his enormous, brooding presence that only made it seem as if the square footage of her kitchen had instantly decreased by a factor of ten.

"Can I get you a drink? Scotch?" She nodded to the bottle in the center of the table. *Wow. Two entire sentences without a stammer.* It didn't matter that they were two very short sentences. It was a win nonetheless.

"No, thanks."

"No d-drinking in uniform?" She groaned inwardly. *So much for my winning streak.*

He shrugged. "Something like that."

Hmm. He'd declined with an air of casualness, but she detected something else, a hidden meaning behind his words.

"You don't drink at all. D-do you?" she asked, suddenly curious about what made him tick.

His gaze hardened. "No."

She shouldn't ask but couldn't stop herself. Must be the alcohol lowering her inhibitions. "Are you an alcoholic?"

"No." A hint of a smile tugged at his lips, softening the hard, rugged planes of his face.

"Then why d-don't you drink?"

That got her a full-fledged smile, and her heart skipped a beat. "What's with all the personal questions?" he asked.

Honestly, she didn't know. Especially given her long-standing proclivity to social awkwardness.

"Tell you what," he said, leaning back, stretching his long legs out under the table until one of his boots touched her bare foot. "I'll answer your question if you answer one of mine. Deal?"

Uh-oh. What had she gotten herself into? But she still wanted the answer to her question. "Deal. You first, though."

"Okay." He nodded. "Not drinking is a personal preference."

"Have you ever had a drink?" she asked.

"Yes."

"When was the last time you had a drink?"

His eyes darkened, and she sensed a subtle shift in his demeanor. "Twenty years ago. When I was sixteen." Then he grinned, and again her heart did some weird, skittering thing. "That was three questions, by the way. My turn. Why do you only stammer when you talk to *me*? You don't do that with anyone else."

"That's not t-true," she said with a huff.

He nodded. "It is, from what *I've* seen."

Poofy stalked into the kitchen, meowed, then sat at Matt's feet, staring up at him.

"Angora?" He held out his hand for Poofy to sniff. "Male?" She nodded. "He's beautiful." The cat stretched to reach his fingers. A second later, the hair on the back of Poofy's spine stood up, and he backed away with his tail in the air. Matt laughed, revealing an even set of white teeth. "He smells Sheba."

"Poofy's never seen a d-dog." She bent down to scoop the cat up. Still leaning over, her gaze met Matt's, only he wasn't looking at her face. His eyes were focused lower. Following his gaze, she caught sight of her tank top gaping open. Even though she was wearing a bra, from her vantage point *and* his, the wisp of fabric barely covered her breasts.

Tugging Poofy closer, she used the cat like an Angora pillow, covering her nakedness. She wanted to crawl into a hole and stay there until Groundhog Day.

Suddenly adjusting his position in the chair, the corners of Matt's lips lifted infinitesimally, which only accentuated the sexy five-o'clock shadow she'd noticed earlier on his chiseled jaw.

"So," she said, scratching Poofy's ear vigorously to hide her embarrassment, "what did you want to t-talk about?"

"Two things. Mainly, about you."

"Me?" She stilled her fingers on Poofy's scruff. "Why?"

Canting his dark head, he stared at her, and it took every ounce of restraint not to squirm beneath the intensity of his chocolate-caramel-coffee-brown eyes. Light from the small chandelier over the table glinted off his hair, which darker than she'd realized. It was nearly black.

Like midnight.

"I came here to make sure you're okay."

"I'm fine." She thrust out her chin and touched her neck. "See? No Band-Aid. Our c-conversation is over, so now you can leave."

He arched a brow. "That isn't what I meant, and you know it."

"Then you'll have to be more specific." *Don't you dare say anything about that kiss.*

"I don't suppose you can tell me what you're working on."

She gave him a *duh* look. "Not unless you've got TS/SCI, and you've been read into the program." As a CIA cop, he had to know that unless he had top secret clearance, plus the Sensitive Compartmented Information ticket on top of that, she could never discuss her work with him.

"That's what I figured." He nodded. "Has anyone been following you lately?"

"No." At least, not that she knew of.

"Any crank calls?"

"No." She rarely gave her cell number out as it was.

"Have you noticed any strangers in your neighborhood?"

"No, no, and *n-no.*" It was impossible not to suppress the irritation in her tone.

Leaning forward, his eyes darkened further. "Why are you so pissed off at me?"

"You're kidding, right?" Sensing her agitation, Poofy jumped off her lap. "Do I really need to explain it all over again?" She pointed to herself. "Security clearance? Revoked? Kicked out of Langley? Does *any* of that ring a bell with you?"

He leaned closer until his face was a scant two inches from hers. "Yeah, and you already chewed my ass out for that. But what you haven't done yet is take any responsibility for your own actions."

"*My* actions?" Trista nearly choked on the renewed flash of anger.

"Lady, you failed to file an incident report, which the agency considers to be a breach of protocol. Protocol that exists to protect you *and* this country."

Trista slammed her hand on the table, making her glass jump. "If you want to talk about breaches of protocol, revoking my clearance was a breach of protocol. They shouldn't have done it. There was no connection to the attack and my job."

Matt shook his head. "You don't know that."

"And neither does anyone else. That's my point." She threw up her hands. "Don't you think revoking my clearance was a bit extreme under the circumstances?"

"That's not my area of expertise and not my call to make. I don't work in the world of cyberspace or the black net. If you think they overreacted, then you should talk to your supervisor."

She gritted her teeth. "Don't you think I tried that?"

"And?"

"Aaand," she said, dragging out the word for effect, "both my supervisors refused to listen. I'm on the beach until this is resolved, whenever *that* is. Probably when I'm old and gray."

When Matt chuckled, she glared at him. "What's so funny?"

"You are." He chuckled again. "You're cute when you get all riled up."

"You bast—"

"Relax." He held up his hand. "Let's examine the facts. Did you get fired?"

"Of course not. I didn't do anything wrong." Now it was his turn to give her a *duh* look. "Well, okay. Except for not filing that report."

"Did they suspend you?"

"No." She reached for her glass of Scotch, grimacing at

the realization it was empty.

"So it's a paid vacation."

"You don't get it." She breathed a heavy sigh and pressed the empty glass to her forehead. "This job is my life. Without it, I have nothing."

When he clasped her wrist, tugging her hand from her forehead, the warmth of his touch zinged straight to somewhere deep inside her core.

"You said that to me once before, and I don't believe it. Don't you have a boyfriend?"

"N-no." She groaned. *It* was back. For a few minutes there, she'd been doing great.

Releasing her wrist, he leaned back in his chair, his forehead creasing. "I came here tonight for another reason. I want to apologize again for kissing you. I shouldn't have done it, and I'm sorry."

Seriously? Could he have bruised her ego and pooped on her day any more than he had already? This was the second time he'd apologized for giving her what was unequivocally the most intensely passionate kiss she'd ever experienced. Apparently, though, she'd been the only one enjoying it.

"Say something," he prodded.

Like what? Like, I'm disappointed?

"Don't worry about it." She grabbed the bottle of Dalwhinnie, uncorking it with a resounding pop, then pouring two fingers. "I g-get it."

"Get what?" He growled.

She paused with the glass a half inch from her lips. "Guys like you don't kiss women like me."

His expression blanked. "Meaning what?"

"Meaning—" *Hot, gorgeous men like you don't kiss plain women like me, let alone one who can't even speak a complete sentence without stammering like a babbling idiot.* "N-nothing. It means nothing. So, if that was the second thing you came here to say, you can leave now. For that matter, why did you really come here? You could have just called or t-texted."

He pursed his full lips and began strumming his fingers on the table, as if he was deep in thought. "I needed to see for myself how you were. To ask you in person."

"Why?" A tiny sliver of hope made her think he might actually care. *Get real, Trista.*

"I was worried about you. Is that so hard to believe?"

"I'm n-not your responsibility."

"Yes, you are." Leaning forward, he rested his hand on her forearm and again his touch affected her like no other man's. Her body felt like a computer that had just gotten a high-speed upgrade and was now totally aware of everything.

It was impossible not to glance down at his strong, tanned hand. Or to note how his long, scarred fingers contrasted with the paleness of her skin. Not for the first time, she wondered what had made those scars.

"*Every* employee in the CIA is my responsibility," he continued.

"Do you personally visit everyone you feel"—she hooked the fingers of her free hand into quotation marks— "responsible for?"

"No, I just—" A look of what she could only describe as bewilderment came over his features. "Hell, I don't know why I came here." When he removed his hand from hers and sat back, her heart sank with disappointment. She must have been off her rocker to think he truly cared about *her*.

Men like him don't go out with women like me.

With that essential tenet properly repositioned in her common sense, she took a deep breath and rose. "Thank you for coming, Sgt. Connors. Rest assured, you have done due diligence and fulfilled your obligation to verify I am indeed still living and breathing. I'll see you out."

Turning, she went to the front door and opened it, but when she looked back, he hadn't budged from his position at the table. Rather, he'd crossed his arms and was staring at her, doing that scowling thing again.

With their gazes locked for what seemed like an eternity but was probably only seconds, confusion clouded her thoughts. *What in the world is going on here? Why won't he leave?*

Finally, he pushed up from the table and came to stand by her at the open doorway. His perpetual scowl softened. "I'm worried about you."

"You shouldn't be. You saved me, and I'll always be grateful. But as Detective Sorensen said, it was a random attack."

The deep sound Matt made in the back of his throat led her to believe he disagreed with Detective Sorensen's assessment.

"I went back to the woods behind the Moose," he said. "Sheba found a piece of bloody cloth. The police lab is running it through CODIS. If they get a hit, I'll let you know."

"Thank you," she said, trying not to breathe too deeply lest she inhale his appealing scent.

"Call me anytime, day or night."

"I w-won't."

He opened his mouth as if to say something, then snapped it shut. After bestowing her with one last scowl, he turned and headed down her front steps.

When the door clicked shut behind her, she retrieved her glass from the kitchen table and took a healthy slug. Matt hadn't bothered to tell her what CODIS was. He knew she was an analyst and understood she'd be familiar with virtually every database in existence.

Since 1990, the Combined DNA Index System contained profiles from samples taken of anyone arrested. If the police lab got a hit in CODIS, it would mean her attacker had a criminal history. It would also mean they would then know the identity of the man who'd tried to hurt her.

A cold, terrifying shiver ran through her. With a shaky hand, she placed the glass on the table and ran to her front door, slamming home the dead bolt. Her pulse quickened as she raced to check the back door and all the windows in the remainder of the house. When she was satisfied her house was secure, she breathed a sigh of relief.

Meow.

Poofy sat in the middle of the hallway floor, his long, fluffy white tail swishing back and forth. Sorely needing feline comfort, she scooped the cat up and sat with him on her living room sofa. Poofy's soft, rumbly purring against her chest soothed her itchy nerves.

Why did Matt really *come to my house?*

He could have just called or texted, although she had to admit that she hadn't minded him showing up unannounced. There was something about the man that got to her, and it wasn't just his incredible good looks or all those manly muscles. There was an intensity about him, something dark and brooding just below the surface. Stupidly, she wanted to know what it was. Her interest in him was perplexing, but it was there. Plain as day.

Poofy stretched up a paw to her chin, and she took it in her hand, stroking her fingers along his fur. Much softer than a dog's paw, she imagined. Although she wouldn't know, since she'd basically never touched a dog in her entire life. Not by choice, anyway.

An old, frightening memory clawed its way to her thoughts, and she squeezed her eyes shut, struggling unsuccessfully to push it back into the box containing old images she'd rather forget.

She'd been six years old, in a park in St. Petersburg

with her mother, who'd gotten distracted reading one of her computer magazines and didn't see the dog charging through the playground. Trista had been sitting on the ground, blissfully playing, when the dog attacked, snatching her doll away from her. Even though the animal hadn't bitten her, the experience of being so helpless and frightened had forever left her petrified of dogs.

Being a K-9 officer, Matt could probably never understand that.

Resentful and exasperated didn't begin to describe how she felt about him. He'd single-handedly ruined her life by undermining the most important thing in her world: her job. She should have known he would have to file his own report whether she did or not. He was a cop, and they *always* filed reports. But her issue with him ran deeper. He piqued her on a basic, feminine level she hadn't seen coming. He was altogether too…too…male.

When she was around him, she couldn't think straight. Hell, she couldn't talk straight, either. Except when they were arguing about something. During those conversations, her brain had backed up her tongue with glib expertise, and she hadn't stammered once. *Why was that?*

And he *would* have to have a dog as a partner. The dog was an extension of him. Even Poofy smelled her on Matt when he'd tried to pet him. A shudder ran through her. Just thinking about Matt's dog made her edgy.

Sheba. Pretty name for a vicious dog. Or, at least, she assumed the dog was vicious. Then again, Sheba had bitten her attacker, then given chase and ripped off a piece of his clothing. Remote as it might be, that bloody cloth could become useful evidence if her attacker was in CODIS.

Dog aside, if Matt hadn't ruined her life, she might like the guy. She'd certainly enjoyed his kiss.

Groaning, she let her head fall back against the cushion.

"I *more* than liked it," she whispered, running her hand over Poofy's back. In response, the cat began purring, nuzzling her belly, his eyes big and blue as he demanded even more attention.

Instead, Trista closed her eyes, touching two fingers to her lips and rubbing them back and forth, imagining Matt's mouth on hers. Warm, curly tingles wound their way to her nipples, hardening them to the point where they jutted sharply against the thin fabric of her tank.

Poofy meowed, interrupting the direction of her X-rated thoughts. *Get real.* Fantasizing about kissing Matt again was about as realistic as her ever loving dogs. She needed to find something productive to do with all this time to kill.

Easing Poofy from her lap, she gently deposited him on the floor. "Sorry, I've got work to do, Poof." The cat glared up at her, unblinking, as if he couldn't believe she'd actually had the gall to dethrone him. Then in true discontented feline fashion, Poofy turned his tail on her and stalked regally into the hallway.

"Cats." She giggled, shaking her head as she got up and sat at her desk. Immediately, the purple-and-black icon on her laptop's toolbar caught her eye. Dark Curtain. Though she'd developed the program herself, it had been while employed by the CIA, making the program CIA property. If anyone knew she'd installed it on her personal laptop, *that* would be the breach of CIA protocol, *not* being the victim of a random attack outside a bar.

For all intents and purposes, she'd been suspended from her job, whereas what she was pondering could get her fired. It was a risk, but her job really was everything to her. If she couldn't work officially, she'd do it *un*officially. "Should I do it, Poofy?" The cat eyed her from the hallway then stalked back into the living room and stretched, arching its back with its tail high in the air. With the grace and agility of a gazelle, he hopped onto the far end of the sofa and curled into a fluffy white ball. "I know I shouldn't, but who will know besides you and me?" *No one.* And it would be worth it to maintain her sanity while she was stuck at home.

Taking a deep, cleansing breath, she double-clicked the icon and, when the program opened, typed in the name she'd heard in Karakurt's chat room: *Iqaluit.*

Chapter Eight

The digital clock on his personal F-150's dashboard told Matt it was well after midnight, and he was already late to meet his friends at the Moose. They'd driven in earlier in the day while he'd been working, and the small parking area south of his house was now jammed with other K-9-equipped Explorers.

As he drove past the lot and onto the main road, he yawned. All these double shifts were killing him, and he'd never quite caught up on sleep since pulling an all-nighter the evening Trista was attacked. That had been four days ago. Now it was Friday, and as much as he could use a quiet, uneventful night at home, followed by an equally quiet weekend working on his place, he was looking forward to hanging with the guys.

It had been over a year since he'd seen any of them, but when they hooked up, it was as if they'd never been apart. Going through basic training with them had forged an iron-tight bond. They were like his brothers. Each of them would be there to back him up without question, and he'd do the same for them in a heartbeat.

As he drove past Trista's exit, he found himself asking the same question over and over. Why *had* he gone to her house? She'd been right, of course. Calling her would have accomplished the mission of finding out how she was doing and to ask her questions. But then he wouldn't have been able to see her in person, and fuck, that was why he'd done it.

You wanted *to see her, you dumbass. You want to get to know her better.*

Part of Trista Gold was exactly as he'd surmised. She was an intelligent, analytical genius. Sure, he'd suspected there was something else hiding beneath that drab gray, but what he'd discovered had blown him away. Whether she realized it or not, she was an intriguing combination of sexiness *and* brains. He couldn't deny it. He liked her...to the point where when her friend Kevin had invited her to stay with him, a seriously annoying prick of jealousy rankled his ass. In fact, it bugged the shit out of him, and the thought had him gripping the wheel tighter.

When he'd arrived at Langley, he'd researched most of the employees. Without clearance, the only thing he'd managed to discover about Trista's current assignment was that it had something to do with the Russians. On the personal side, agency gossip didn't reveal Trista and Kevin were an item. Acknowledging that he'd even checked them out pissed him off even more. He had no business being jealous of who she stayed the night with. And yet...curiosity had him wondering whether she slept in plain cotton jammies or something sexy, like silk or satin.

He grinned. Based on what she'd been wearing when she answered the door a few nights ago, he'd guess cotton. But holy hell, she wore plain cotton like no other woman could. One look at those skimpy shorts and snug tank top, and he'd nearly swallowed his tongue.

The shorts barely covered the shapely globes of her ass

and a tiny waist, and the tight tank clung to a pair of full breasts, stretching the material to the point where he could totally envision how perfectly they would fit in his hands. When she'd leaned over to pick up her cat, he'd gotten a tantalizing view of creamy, mounding flesh. Enough of a view that his pulse had pounded faster, and he'd had to shift positions to hide the stiffening erection pushing against the zipper of his uniform pants.

Thinking of Trista had him reassessing relationships he'd had with women. They were always temporary, and he knew that going in. Occasionally, one of the women he hooked up with got hurt, mistakenly believing there was more to what they shared than just sex. But usually, they understood he wasn't looking for commitment, let alone permanency.

Exiting the highway, he turned onto the road that would take him to the Moose. Jerry would have liked the place... had he lived. Jerry's birthday and the anniversary of his death were on the same day. November 2. Groaning, Matt ran a hand through his hair.

In a few weeks, one member of Matt's family or another would come knocking on his door, inviting him to attend the fundraiser banquet that not only honored Jerry but raised money for a different charity each year. Jerry's folks had been holding the banquet every year on the same day since Jerry died. Not once had Matt attended. He couldn't. *Ever.* He could never face Jerry's parents again, and nothing would change that.

Up ahead, the Moose came into view, and as he pulled into the lot and parked, he automatically scanned the area where Trista had been dragged into the woods. Shoving the gearshift into park with more force than necessary, he realized the extent of his anger toward her unknown assailant. The asshole was still out there, and if Matt ever got his hands on the guy, he'd pummel the shit out of him all over again.

Trista might have more brains than most, but she was so slight she was helpless against anyone who tried to harm her. The world was such a dangerous place these days. In his opinion, every woman should take some form of self-defense training.

Less than a second after pushing open the door to the Moose, he spotted his friends at the end of the packed bar. Since they all towered over pretty much everyone else, it was hard to miss them. And, naturally, they were the rowdiest crew there, shouting and slapping one another on the back.

Friends aside, the Moose was definitely hopping. Loud music pumped from large overhead speakers, reverberating in his ears. Laughter and voices came at him from the many tables crammed with patrons.

"Matt!" Nick Houston, a sergeant with the Massachusetts State Police, met him before he even made it to the bar, then bear-hugged him, lifting him clear off his feet. The sincerity in Nick's steel-gray gaze confirmed that his best friend really had missed him.

"Connors, you son of a bitch." Jaime Pataglio, a tall olive-skinned Italian from the Port Authority of New York and New Jersey clapped Matt on the back.

Dayne Andrews from the FBI's Newark, New Jersey office shook Matt's hand, his emerald-green eyes as piercing as ever.

Next, Eric Miller, a blond, blue-eyed giant of an ATF agent, fist-bumped him, followed by a firm handshake from Markus York, a Secret Service uniformed officer with eyes as dark as the night sky and a fresh, angry scar over his left eye. Markus had recently transferred to D.C. and was bunking with Matt while he waited to close on a new house. Last but hardly least, considering he was over six-three, was Kade Sampson, a Homeland Security patrol officer from New York.

"Good to see you, buddy." Nick wrapped his arm around

Matt's shoulder, urging him to the bar.

"You, too," he replied, and meant it. It *was* good to see all his friends again. Knowing they were out there, only a phone call away, had kept him grounded during some of the crappiest of days, but it wasn't the same as hanging out with them and shooting the shit in person.

"Sheila, anything my friend wants," Nick said to the bartender.

The pretty twentysomething blonde Matt once had a brief fling with winked at him. "The usual, Matt?"

"You sure we can't convince you to have one beer with us?" Kade asked.

"Nah, I'm good." He nodded to the bartender. And he *was* good. Alcohol would always be a thing of his past and not a good thing, by any means.

After Sheila handed him a large mug of club soda with lime, everyone held up their drinks for a toast.

"To the dogs," Jaime said. "And the women."

"Hear, hear," they all repeated, clinking bottles together so loudly Matt was sure some of them would shatter.

"Hey, Matt. Long time no see." A curvy brunette with deep-red lipstick and carrying a tray of empties grabbed his arm, standing on her tiptoes to give him a quick kiss on the cheek. "Heard you saved some girl out in the parking lot. And by the way"—she glanced behind her—"I saw Charlene lurking around here somewhere. She was asking if you came in anymore."

"Thanks for the warning."

His friends snickered.

"Good to see you, too, Lynette."

"She's cute." Markus leaned around Matt to follow Lynette's swinging hips as she rounded the bar. "You dating her, too?"

He gave Markus a look of disapproval. "We dated a few

times, but no sparks. Just be nice to her or I'll have to kick your ass."

"Yeah, yeah, yeah." Markus flipped him off, then headed for the bar where Lynette was busy dropping off her empties.

"So," Nick said, "how *is* the woman in your life?"

Trista?

Shit, where did that come from?

Probably from being in her house twice during the past week and from getting royally chewed out by her. Or more likely, because he'd had more conversation with her lately than he'd had with any other woman since he and Charlene had broken up. *Yeah, that must be why.*

"You mean Sheba?" Though he knew full well Nick was referring to a *human* significant other.

"Yeah, Sheba." Nick laughed then took a sip of beer. "I take it you're not getting any at the moment?"

Rather than answer Nick's question, Matt took a swallow of his soda, which only made Nick laugh harder and Kade grin. His friends understood him well enough to know he didn't kiss and tell.

"You guys all settled in?" Knowing he'd be working a double shift when the guys arrived, he'd left keys to his house and the kennels, along with the alarm code, in a coded lockbox.

"We're good," Kade answered for the rest of them.

"Hell, we're better than good," Nick added. "With all the renovation you've done on the house, the place is sweet. And the brand-new kennels are kick-ass. Saxon was so excited it was twenty minutes before I could calm him down."

The image of Nick's black German shepherd, Saxon, scampering around the pristine kennels had Matt grinning. He was pleased that his friends appreciated his late nights and long weekends spent laboring on the house and the kennel addition.

Dayne, the eldest of their motley crew at thirty-eight, clinked his bottle to Matt's mug. "Jerry's Place is taking shape. You done good."

"Thanks, Dayne." Mixed feelings of pride and sadness flooded him. After nearly two years, the nonprofit he'd envisioned to help both troubled youth and rescue dogs was finally ready, although he still needed a major influx of outside cash to fulfill his promise. Not that he was broke. His wealthy grandfather had seen to that in his will. Still, if he wasn't careful with his own money, he'd soon be eating kibble every night with Sheba.

"How much land you got, anyway?" Jaime asked.

"About twelve acres." Which made him somewhat of a land baron in northern Virginia.

Eric whistled. "Damn, that's some high-priced real estate for these parts. You could sell the place and make a small fortune."

"I'd never sell." Not only was the place his grandfather's legacy to him, he was determined to make a go of Jerry's Place someday. Without his parents' handouts. No matter how many times they'd offered assistance, he'd refused. This was something he *had* to do on his own.

"That's an impressive security system you've got," Dayne added. "Cameras outside, monitors in your office, and some pretty high-tech computers. Why no locking gates on the driveway?"

Matt set his mug on the bar. "I want to keep track of things, especially when I'm not home, but I don't want the place to seem like a prison yard. It has to have an inviting atmosphere, or it won't work. The kids will feel like they're incarcerated."

"Sheila here," Jaime said, winking at the bartender as she wiped down the bar, "told us you had some trouble a few nights ago."

"Understatement." As succinctly as possible, he described the attack on Trista and how the son of a bitch got away.

"Any leads?" Nick asked.

"Long shot." He picked up his mug and took a long drink. "Sheba ripped off a piece of the bastard's clothing. The locals are running it through CODIS, but I haven't heard anything yet."

"And the girl?" Kade held up his finger to Sheila, signaling for another round "How's she doing?"

Frowning, Matt looked down at his mug, not realizing until just then that he'd emptied it. "Trista is...pissed at me." He laughed bitterly. "Her security clearance was revoked pending resolution of the matter, and she's mad as hell at me for filing an incident report with the agency."

"We've all pissed women off." Jaime smirked. "Exactly how pissed is she?"

"She ripped me a new one." Unable to stop himself, Matt grinned. Then he thought about the hot kiss that had followed the ass-ripping, and he sobered instantly. He still couldn't get that damned kiss off his mind.

"No shit." Nick barked out a laugh. "You save her life, and she chews you out? What the hell's up with that?"

"For Trista," Matt said, "her job *is* her life. Losing her clearance about killed her."

"Why?" Nick persisted. "Is she a dog? Too hairy in all the wrong places? No offense to Sheba, of course. On Sheba, hair looks good." The other men snickered. "Well?" Nick nudged him with an elbow. "What's she like?"

"Yeah, man." Jaime waggled his eyebrows. "Was she, ya know...grateful?"

Out of all of them, Jaime was by far the playboy of the group, and Matt found himself unexpectedly clenching his jaw at his friend's implication that Trista had given him gratitude sex. Forcing himself to relax, he faced another truth.

He might not be as vocal about his exploits as Jaime was, but they probably had about the same number of notches on their belts. The only difference was that Matt exercised far more discretion. Sleeping around wasn't something he planned nor was he proud of it. With him, it just…happened. Because he never stuck around long enough to give anyone a real chance.

"Trista is…different." He swirled the cubes of ice around in his empty mug.

"Buddy?" Eric scrunched his blond brows together. "You're scaring me. You've got this weird-ass, goo-goo-eyed look on your face."

Ignoring Eric, Matt struggled with how to describe Trista. "She's definitely not like any other woman I've gone out with."

The normally reticent Dayne chuckled. "So you *have* gone out with her. Told ya. Pay up." He held out his hand to Nick, who promptly slapped a twenty into his palm.

"No, dammit." Matt smacked his empty mug onto the bar. "I haven't gone out with her, and I haven't had sex with her." Not that he hadn't thought about it after that kiss, followed by ogling her sexy body in those skimpy clothes.

"Okay, man." Jaime held up his hands.

"Well, lookee here." Nick reached behind him for the next round of beers and another mug of club soda that Sheila had served up. "As if life wasn't exciting enough around our nation's capital these days."

Matt accepted the mug from Nick, eager to change the line of conversation. "Where's everyone assigned?" Each of his friends was in town working protection details at various high-profile events leading up to the presidential election in November.

"I got the White House," Eric said just before gulping his beer. "Probably a boring detail."

Matt nodded, thinking Eric was right. Having been in office for nearly eight years, the president and his administration were outgoing, and as such, had cut back on publicity events, save those to support his party's next candidate.

Nick waved his finger between himself and Jaime. "We're both at the Capitol. Anyone got Ashburn? Should be a happy occasion for him, come November. I think he's got it in the bag."

The other men nodded, and Matt had to agree. U.S. Senator Michael Ashburn from Nebraska was by far the favorite candidate, already tipping the polls at 60 percent. Ashburn was the first candidate in decades who seemed honest and well-intentioned. Ohio Governor Thomas Hughes, on the other hand, had baggage, including extramarital affairs and questionable fundraising tactics.

"We've got Hughes's detail." Dayne nodded to Kade. "That should be a hoot. That guy's so far down in the polls he'll probably hit every news show on TV to boost his ratings. We all start first thing Monday morning. What about you?"

Matt shook his head. "My office hasn't come out with pre-election assignments yet. They should be posted in the next day or two." He was looking forward to a change of scenery. Langley was nice, but every once in a while, he missed the action of being on the street, throwing himself out there into the mix.

No sooner had he taken another sip of his soda than an arm slipped around his waist, and he flinched. Before she uttered a single word, he knew who it was. The perfume preceded the woman, and it nauseated him.

"Hiya, baby." Charlene slithered her arm across his back as she came to stand close, doing her best to cuddle against him as if they were a couple. Hell, they'd *never* been a couple, as far as he was concerned, and they never would be.

Somehow managing to extricate himself from her clutches,

Matt cleared his throat, then nodded to each of his friends. "Jaime, Nick, Kade, Dayne, Eric, Markus, this is Charlene."

"Hello, boys."

As she held out her hand to each of his friends, giggling and batting her eyelashes the entire time, he wondered what he'd ever seen in her and instantly began comparing her to Trista.

Charlene was a model-perfect redhead, with perfect clothes, perfect jewelry and makeup, and expertly coiffed hair. Trista, on the other hand, was about six inches shorter, no jewelry, no makeup, but with a knockout body she hid behind seriously frumpy clothes.

Charlene was good in bed, but he'd quickly discovered that was the only place he enjoyed her company. It wasn't that the woman was dumb. But she just didn't make any attempt at a real-life, honest-to-God, back-and-forth conversation about anything that mattered in the world. He hadn't even *had* sex with Trista, and probably never would, but he enjoyed her company ten times more than he did Charlene's.

One of Charlene's hands slid from his back to his butt while she leaned in tighter to massage his chest. Christ, he felt like he was being mauled by an octopus. Her damn hands were everywhere.

Nick pressed his lips together, clearly trying not to burst out laughing. Kade and Dayne merely smirked at him while Jaime did his best to garner Charlene's attention and get her away from Matt. Unsuccessfully, that was. She was stuck to Matt like a giant burr no amount of shaking would kick loose.

"Uh, Charlene," he finally said, about to do his best to politely make it clear he wasn't interested, when the cell phone on his belt vibrated. *There* is *a God.*

He slipped the phone from its cradle. *Jake Sorensen.*

"Excuse me." He looked down into Charlene's blue eyes, then at her dark-red lips twisting into a disappointed pout.

"I have to take this." Figuring on heading outside to take the call, Matt turned to the door, only to have Charlene's perfectly manicured fingers curve around his bicep.

"You don't really have to go, do you, Mattie?" More pouting.

Fuck, but he hated being called Mattie.

"Ma'am?" Jaime to the rescue. "I would be honored to buy you a very large, very expensive cocktail. Something with a lot of rum and an umbrella perhaps?" Without waiting for a response, Jaime miraculously tugged Charlene off Matt and put his arm around her shoulders, guiding her to the bar with smooth finesse.

After shooting Jaime a grateful look, Matt answered the call. "Hold on." Unable to hear with the loud music and chatter, he deftly deposited his mug of soda on a passing waitress's tray and pushed open the front door. "What's up, Jake?" The pounding from inside still beat in his ears, so he walked into the parking lot toward his truck.

"That bloody piece of clothing you gave me? We got a hit in CODIS."

"And?" Matt snapped his head up. What Jake said next had him bolting to his truck, shouting, "Meet me at Trista's house."

With his heart pounding, he yanked open the door to his F-150, jumped in, and cranked over the engine. Every cop instinct he had told him this was bad. *Really bad.*

Luckily, no one had parked in front of him, so he slammed his foot on the accelerator. Tires squealing, he tore out of the lot onto the road and punched it.

He cued up Trista's cell number, but it went directly to voicemail. After leaving a message, he tried her number again with the same result.

He'd always suspected something about Trista's attack hadn't been random. Now his gut told him it was true.

Chapter Nine

"Oh, sh—pooh."

Trista rubbed her eyes, then stared at the computer screen. Since being relegated to the "rubber computer squad," she'd been on the verge of inventing new curse words. "Shpooh," a combination of "shit" and "pooh," was her latest effort. Sadly, her mother still wouldn't approve.

In the days since she'd been put on administrative leave, she'd managed to find Karakurt only once, in a sneaky chat room that was tough even for her to find. But as soon as she'd gotten in, he'd ended the chat. In between her Dark Curtain forays onto the black net, she'd taken a breather here and there to research the place referenced in Karakurt's chat from Monday: Iqaluit.

Picking up one of the hundreds of sheets she'd printed, she began reading again. Though she'd never heard of Iqaluit, she'd quickly discovered it had been in the news quite a lot lately, with numerous domestic and international news sources referencing it.

Iqaluit was the capital city of Nunavut, a snow-capped

Canadian territory situated opposite Greenland, and one of the northernmost populated areas in North America. From its strategic position on Baffin Island in Frobisher Bay, Iqaluit was poised to bear witness to major changes affecting the Northwest Passage, a shipping route connecting the Arctic regions and the Atlantic that was normally blocked by ice. She was surprised to learn that in the next two decades, the Northwest Passage was expected to open up year-round due to global warming.

Trista flipped to another article, noting that Iqaluit also had something few other locations in those parts had: an airport. One of the unidentified participants in Karakurt's chat had said he was leaving for Iqaluit in an hour. *Why?*

Poofy burrowed his head against her leg, demanding his usual position of honor on her lap, which was currently filled with internet printouts. Reading on, she learned that for such a small town by global standards, and inhabited by less than eight thousand people, plus caribou and Arctic foxes, Iqaluit had grabbed more than its share of headlines over the past few years.

Canadian officials had met there on numerous occasions to discuss building a military base somewhere in the Northwest Passage in order to closely monitor Russian incursion into the Arctic.

Leaning back in her chair, she noted that Poofy had abandoned all hope of sitting on her lap and was now sitting three inches from the front door, staring at it intently like a dog waiting to be walked. Except that Poofy was an indoor cat. Absently, she thought the behavior odd, then selected another article.

Even though Canada was the second-largest territorial country in the world, its military power had weakened significantly over time as the country chose to invest in other aspects of its economy rather than national defense.

Both Canada and Russia controlled thousands of miles of Arctic shoreline, but with all the recent Russian aggression around the world, Canadian officials worried Russia would take advantage of a weak Canadian military and assert its dominance to seize the Arctic's vast energy resources.

Not being an exploratory scientist, Trista had no idea that as much as 25 percent of the world's remaining oil, gas, and other natural resources were located on the Lomonosov undersea ridge in the Arctic. But with her knowledge of the current Russian regime's political agenda, she did know that the Russian economy was based primarily on energy exportation. The Russians were constantly searching for untapped sources of energy, exploiting them with insufficient, and, at times, zero, regard to protecting the environment.

Reading on, she pursed her lips. A major power struggle was brewing in the Arctic. Other countries were also trying to lay claim to the Arctic's untapped resources, but unlike those countries, Russia wasn't a NATO member, and as such, did as it pleased without answering to anyone.

According to the last article she read, the Russians didn't want any interference from Canada, but Russia was by far the biggest threat to—

A muffled *thump* from the back door made her jerk her head toward the kitchen, tensing. Then she let out a breath with a *whoosh*. It was probably just another tree limb.

The old oak tree in her backyard had been dropping branches lately. Having it pruned had been on her to-do list for quite some time, but she'd gotten so wrapped up with things at work, staying late many nights, that she still hadn't gotten around to it.

She went to the door and flipped on the outside light. Her tiny backyard and the equally small back porch were illuminated by a single light, but she didn't see anything. Not even a branch, although one could have fallen onto the edge of the decking and slipped to the ground where she couldn't see it.

Padding back to her desk, she resumed her research. After reading a few more articles about these meetings in Iqaluit, it became screamingly obvious that unless the Canadians beefed up their military in the Arctic, a military confrontation with the Russians was looming. As such, the Canadian government had approached both presidential candidates for a major influx of American cash to fund new naval and military bases in the Arctic, and both Governor Hughes and Senator Ashburn had heartily agreed that if elected, they would lend financial assistance. Anything to prevent Russian dominance in such a vitally strategic part of the world.

The cell phone on the desk vibrated with yet another incoming message from her parents. Groaning, she looked at the image on the screen. It was the tenth photo in the last ten minutes, this one of them posing in front of the Sydney Opera House.

Five years ago, her mother and father—both retired computer experts—had sold their home and been traveling the world ever since. Based upon this latest selfie, she'd guess they were on the last leg of their Australian tour, about to head for one of the many isolated Indonesian islands. She appreciated them staying in touch, but if they pinged her with any more photos, she'd scream.

Another photo came through, and she slammed the phone onto the desk. "Enough already!" This was the reason she never slept with her cell phone by her bed at night anymore. Getting woken up by her parents' three a.m. text messages got old real fast.

Before powering off her laptop, she considered one more search. Ever since hearing the name Thomas George in the chat room, she considered looking him up and reaching out to him, but that was an operative's job, and she wasn't an operative. Still, the idea was tempting.

She yawned and clamped a hand over her mouth. Tomorrow would be another fun-filled day doing next to nothing, and a perfect time to do more research.

After shutting down the laptop, she locked it in a small filing cabinet bolted to the floor beneath the stairs. When she turned, Poofy was still rooted to the same spot by the front door.

"C'mon, Poof." She scooped the cat up, cuddling him to her as she flipped off the other lights and went into the bedroom, closing the door behind her. The room was stuffy, so she cranked on the large window AC unit, sighing as the first blast of cool air hit her face.

By the time she'd finished with her nighttime rituals and changed into a white cotton camisole, Poofy had curled up on his usual spot at the foot of the bed. Pulling the covers back, she glanced at her short, unpolished nails. Having nails of any length had always been a nuisance, since she usually spent ten to fifteen hours a day tapping on a keyboard. With that time seriously curtailed, maybe she'd get a mani-pedi. Pink, or vixen-red.

Wearing colors had never been her thing, but since she'd be out of work for an indeterminate period of time, perhaps she'd do something fun for herself, something outside her usual, boring box. She tried imagining her vixen-red fingernails against the toned, tanned muscles of Matt's chest and arms.

Rolling her eyes, she fell into bed, repeating her mantra: *men like him don't go out with women like me.* On top of which, she doubted she'd ever be able to forgive him for his role in her being kicked out of Langley. *So stop thinking about him.*

As soon as she closed her eyes, sleep began to take hold,

along with unwanted images of Matt's powerful body, sweaty and naked as he stepped into the shower.

Meow. Meow. Meow.

"Poofy?" Trista woke to find the cat sitting on her chest, pawing at her frantically.

A high-pitched tone screamed from one of the smoke detectors in the house. Two seconds later, the detector just inside her bedroom door went off, screeching so loudly she flinched. Then she smelled it.

Smoke.

Bolting from the bed, she flicked on the overhead light, immediately noticing the faint haze pervading the room. There weren't any flames, but smoke curled in from beneath the door.

No! She lunged for the doorknob, jerking her hand back. The metal knob was hot.

There's fire on the other side of that door.

Her heart began pounding, her breathing coming quicker. Grabbing a shirt draped over a chair, she wrapped her hand in the cloth and twisted the doorknob. A wave of heat slammed into her, and she staggered back. The smoke and smell of gasoline were overwhelming, making her cough. Through the hallway and the haze of smoke, she could make out the flicker of orange and yellow, along with crackling, hissing sounds.

Fire. My house really is on fire.

She covered her mouth with her hand, feeling her way along the wall for the fire extinguisher. As her hand bumped into it, she got a better look at the living room, and a small scream escaped her.

Flames licked up the billowing curtains as they quickly

blackened and disintegrated. The sofa and wingback chair were on fire. Dead ahead, the front door of the house was fully engulfed in flames.

A perfect, straight line of fire ran from one window along the floor to her desk, which had also begun to burn but not so much that she couldn't see that her cell phone was gone. She'd left it there last night like she always did. As if her house being on fire wasn't enough, her missing cell phone set off alarm bells in her head.

Someone did this. Someone set my house on fire. With me in it.

No extinguisher in the world would be enough to put out this inferno. With her heart pounding like a jackhammer, she spun and bolted back to her bedroom, coughing as she pulled the door shut behind her.

Poofy. I have to get Poofy.

But her cat was nowhere in sight. For a second, her throat closed up, a sure sign of an impending asthma attack, but she managed to take a slow, deep breath, tamping it down. "Poofy," she cried, searching every corner of the room, still not finding him. Dropping to the floor, she whipped up the bed skirt to find him hunched against the far wall. "C'mon, Poof," she crooned, but the cat didn't budge.

Coughing worse now, she crawled under the bed, finding the air clearer and cooler. As she neared the cat, he meowed pitifully. Reaching out, she hooked her hand around Poofy's body, tugging him toward her as she backed out from under the bed. She cradled him tightly to her chest, then covered him with the same shirt she'd used to open the door.

She ran to the room's only window, intending to shove the AC unit out onto the grass, but stopped short. When she'd bought the unit earlier in the summer, the installers had securely screwed the flanges into the wooden windowsill. Nothing short of a sledgehammer would dislodge it now.

At the bedroom door, she took one last breath and held it before flinging it open. As it had before, a blast of heat hit her in the face, hotter this time. She burrowed her nose and mouth against Poofy's cloth-covered body, barely able to see through the thickening smoke. She had to get to the kitchen.

The hall runner beneath her feet was warm, and the air was hot against her bare arms and legs. Visibility worsened, and she slammed her shoulder against the wall. Stumbling, she fell to her knees, again realizing the air was easier to breathe near the floor.

With Poofy still tucked against her chest, she crawled awkwardly into the living room. Her skin grew hot and tears streamed from her stinging eyes until she almost couldn't keep them open. With most of the living room furniture and walls engulfed, the crackling, snapping, and hissing was deafening.

Keep going. Keep going.

She scrambled forward on the floor. Using the front door as an escape route was out, but the back door in the kitchen was still accessible.

After what seemed like an hour but was probably only seconds, she felt the hard tile of the kitchen floor beneath her hand and knees. The air was clearer here, enough to see another perfectly straight line of fire leading from the window curtain, down the wall, and along the floor to the table, although the fire hadn't caught on yet with the same intensity as in the living room.

Pushing to her feet, she grabbed the doorknob, twisting and tugging. It didn't open.

Beside her, the kitchen table and two of the chairs burst into flames. Tucking Poofy tighter against her, she verified the door was indeed unlocked then pulled repeatedly. It didn't budge. *This was not happening. I need another plan.*

Basement.

Even the floor tiles beneath her feet were growing warm as she ran to the basement door and turned the knob. When it opened, she flipped on the light switch and headed down the stairs, slamming the door shut behind her.

The air was better down here, and she sucked in breath after breath, still coughing but not as fiercely. Setting Poofy on top of the washing machine, she grabbed a wooden stool and placed it directly beneath the small, hinged window. She stepped on the stool and twisted the latch, but when she pushed on the window, it didn't open, either.

What the hell?

She looked around for something to break the window, only to see fire shooting between the door and the doorframe. A burst of flames made it through, hitting the stair rail. The old, brittle wood quickly caught on fire, sending a line of flame down the railing.

I will not die in this house.

She reached for the crowbar hanging on the wall.

Chapter Ten

"Dammit." Matt gunned the pickup off the highway, taking the circular exit ramp way too fast, but he didn't give a shit. What Jake had related over the phone had his guts twisting with fear.

The blood on the cloth Sheba had retrieved matched that of Viktor Solonik, a Russian mobster suspected of being a hit man. Solonik had previously been arrested on weapons charges that hadn't netted much jail time, but every arrest required a DNA swab. Hence the hit in CODIS. This had to be connected to whatever Trista was doing for the CIA. He knew that with every fiber of his being, and he damn well intended to find out what it was if he had to wring it out of her, or her supervisors.

As he turned onto her street, an eerie glow lit the sky. When he saw why, his heart nearly stopped. Trista's house was on fire, and from the looks of it, it was already fully engulfed.

Jake's black Charger was parked a few houses from Trista's, its blue strobes flashing. Matt gunned his truck the remaining distance, then slammed on the brakes in front of the Charger. When he jumped out, he heard Jake calling in the fire, reciting Trista's address.

"Where is she?" Matt shouted.

Jake threw the radio microphone into the open car window. "Don't know. Just got here. Fire trucks are on the way."

Matt ran toward the house. Flames shot from every window, and part of the roof was caving in. The fire roared, snapping and crackling. Timbers creaked under the onslaught, making an eerie, wailing sound.

With his heart in his throat, he ran all around the house, scanning the yard, searching for Trista. But she wasn't there. She wasn't *anywhere. She's still inside.*

Every door and window were on fire, flames shooting out into the night. There was no way in, and no way out.

A grisly image of her small, petite body on fire came to him...the pain she would have felt. Matt fell to his knees. He'd never been much for prayer, but right at that moment, he prayed the smoke had taken her before the fire did.

His stomach roiled, and he wanted to puke. A hand rested on his shoulder. Jake.

"There's nothing you could have done, Matt."

Shaking his head, he breathed heavily. He couldn't believe she was dead. He barely knew her, but already he felt her loss from his life.

Sirens screeched in the distance. Minutes later, he heard them pull up to the house, their hydraulic brakes hissing as they came to a stop. A burning piece of something landed a few feet away, followed by a burst of glowing embers.

"C'mon, Matt." Jake grabbed his arm. "We gotta get away from the house."

Still staring at the fully engulfed structure, he let Jake haul him to his feet. A door slammed, and he jerked his head around. The family next door was evacuating. Good thing.

A crash had him whipping his head back to Trista's house. *Glass breaking. Where?*

He couldn't see anything, but it sounded like it had come from the burning house. Could be the heat doing the damage, but maybe it was something else.

Both he and Jake froze. A few seconds later, the sound of metal on metal came to his ears. He ran around to the back of the house and heard the same metal sounds and more glass breaking.

"There!" He pointed and ran to the window well.

A crowbar, held by pale, bare arms cleared glass from the broken basement window.

Trista.

Matt jumped into the window well just as Trista pulled herself to safety. She fell against his chest and he picked her up, getting a glimpse of the flames flickering inside the basement.

"Poofy!" she shouted, dropping the crowbar and slapping at his hands. "Let me go."

"Stop fighting me!" Matt shouted. The basement was bright with flames. Smoke poured out the open window, making them both cough. He had to get her out of here, away from the house.

"Let me go!" she repeated. "I have to go back inside."

But she was no match for him, and he easily handed her up to Jake. Kicking her legs, she caught him in the jaw, and he fell back, whacking his head hard against the siding. For a moment, he saw stars and his vision blurred. He reached out his hand, leaning on the side of the house until the moment passed.

"Poofy!" she screamed, still struggling to free herself from Jake's arms. "I have to go back and get Poofy!"

Shit. The damned cat.

"Get her out of here!" he yelled to Jake. "Whoever did this could be out there waiting to take a shot at her."

A fit of coughing seized her, allowing Jake to grip her tighter as he ran from the house.

"Fuck." Taking a deep breath, Matt pivoted in the tight confines of the window well and began lowering himself into the basement, legs first.

Bits of glass cut into his palms, but he kept going until his feet hit something. A stool. He stepped onto it, then onto the concrete floor. The intense heat hit him first, then the smoke. He dropped to his knees, knowing the air would be better down there. *Not much.*

"Poofy! Poofy!"

He looked around the smoky room for the cat, not really expecting the animal to come to him like a dog. Hell, even a dog would probably ignore his calls under these circumstances, instinct driving it to go to ground for a hiding place.

This was beyond crazy. It was insane. But seeing Trista screaming, panicked over her cat dying tugged at his heart to the point where he'd do just about anything for her. If it had been Sheba trapped inside a burning building, he would have fought anyone who tried to prevent him from saving her as well.

A chemical smell came to him—gasoline—and he tugged his shirt from his jeans and pulled it over his head, using it as a filter to breathe through.

If I were a cat in a burning building, where would I go?

If the situation wasn't so dire, he would have laughed. Then it hit him. Years ago, he'd taken care of a friend's cat for a weekend, and every time he walked into the house, the cat took off and hid behind the dryer.

Matt grabbed the edge of the dryer and pulled it away from the wall. Hunkered down in a tight, soot-covered ball was the cat.

Meooooow.

"Hey, Poofy." He kept his voice low and easy, trying not to frighten the feline. If the animal took off, and he had to search for it again, he doubted he'd have time to get his ass out of there before the basement turned into an inferno.

Slowly at first, he eased his arm toward the cat. The animal braced itself against the wall and, from the looks of it, was about to haul ass. Dropping his shirt to the floor, Matt shot his arm out, grabbing the cat in mid-lunge, then hauling it to his chest.

He tensed, expecting sharp claws to dig into his skin, but all he felt were soft paws and a wriggling body. Mercifully, the cat must have had its claws trimmed recently.

Coughing worse now, he made his way back to the window and stepped onto the stool. Aiming carefully, he hurled the cat through the open window, over the edge of the well and onto the grass. Then he hauled himself through, grimacing as more shards of glass dug into his palms.

Hands grabbed at him, hauling him out. *Firemen.*

"You okay?" one of them asked, urging him away from the house.

Water sprayed from two hoses, hissing as it hit the burning timbers.

"I'm fine," he said, although his voice was rough from coughing. He turned to search the yard for Poofy. "You guys see a cat?"

"Yeah. Over there." The fireman pointed to a clump of bushes.

Matt made his way slowly to the bushes, again being cautious of scaring the animal and having to chase it all over the neighborhood. He caught sight of Poofy and managed to grab him before he could take off.

At the street, Jake stood by the open doors of an

ambulance. Matt made his way toward him, cradling Poofy tightly to his chest. Inside the ambulance, Trista lay on a gurney, an oxygen mask over her nose and mouth. But when she caught sight of Poofy in his arms, she sat upright and tore the mask from her face.

Matt stepped into the ambulance and handed the cat over to her.

With a look of relief, she held out her arms. "Poofy." Then she cuddled the cat against her breasts and smiled.

That smile did something to his heart.

"Hey," one of the medics blustered. "You can't have a cat in here." He stood and was about to take the cat from Trista, when Matt shot out a hand and grabbed the guy's arm.

Shaking his head, he gave the medic a stern look. "Let it go."

Reluctantly, the medic dropped his hands and resumed tending to Trista by placing the mask back on her face.

Tears ran down the sides of her soot-stained cheeks, but Matt couldn't decipher whether it was from the smoke, or because her cat was alive. He turned to leave, stopping at the sound of her voice.

"Matt," she said from beneath the mask. "Thank you."

For several seconds, their gazes locked. Even covered in soot with an oxygen mask over her face, she was lovely. He gave a quick nod, then turned to find the medic extending another mask in his direction. Ignoring the offer, he stepped outside. He hadn't inhaled nearly as much smoke as Trista, and conferring with Jake was more important.

Matt didn't understand the unexpectedly protective thoughts he found himself continually having where Trista Gold was concerned. All he knew was at that moment, he felt a hundred feet tall.

"This was no accident," he said to Jake.

Jake nodded. "I agree. A Russian hit man going after

her, then her house goes up in flames. Any idea what she's working on for the CIA?"

"Not specifically, but I *will* find out." Even if he had to beat it out of someone.

"Can you follow us to the hospital?" Matt glimpsed a patrol car pulling to a stop across the street. "Just in case."

"Already planning on it." Jake nodded to the two uniformed officers stepping out of the vehicle. "I need to ask her some questions."

"Join the club," he muttered. Something big, bad, and ugly was going on here, and he was dead certain the agency knew more than it was letting on.

He closed the ambulance doors, not wanting to leave them open in case Viktor Solonik or someone else was hiding somewhere, waiting to take a pot shot. When the ambulance began rolling down the street, Jake got into his Charger, and Matt hustled to his truck to follow them to the hospital. Along the way, he called his boss.

"Buck," he said when his boss's groggy voice growled in his ear. "We've got a problem. Someone just tried to murder Trista Gold. Again."

Chapter Eleven

"We're just about done here," the nurse said as she cleansed away the last of the blood from Trista's arms and legs.

Glass shards from the basement window had gouged into the tender undersides of her arms and the tops of her thighs. Luckily, the wounds were superficial, stinging only slightly, and none of them needed stitches. That, and her asthma hadn't kicked in again, despite the stress.

Still clad only in her cotton camisole, she shivered at the continuous blast of cold air coming from the overhead vent, but it was the only thing keeping her awake. It was three fifteen in the morning, and with the adrenaline rush quickly ebbing, she could barely keep her eyes open.

Through the gap in the ER curtain, she glimpsed Matt, Detective Sorensen, and Matt's boss, Buxton McIntyre, with their heads together. Discussing *her*, no doubt.

The nurse emptied the silver tray containing a pile of bloody gauze into a red biohazard container on the floor, then grabbed a tube of something from a drawer. "How are you feeling?"

She nodded. "Good." Relatively, that was. *Considering someone tried to burn me alive.* Her throat felt dry as a desert, but at least she no longer felt the need to breathe through the oxygen mask.

The nurse began dabbing ointment on the tops of her thighs. "As soon as your chest X-rays come back, the doctor will be in to speak with you and listen to your breathing one last time."

"I'm not staying here. I want to go ho—" She *had* no home. Not anymore. Everything she owned was probably burned to ashes in the fire. Her clothes, her books, photos, mementos. Her phone had been stolen, and her laptop had probably melted inside the cabinet where she'd stashed it. She didn't even have any food for Poofy, or a litter box.

"Oh, honey." The nurse laid her hand on Trista's shoulder. "Do you want to call your family?"

"No. My only family is, literally, on the other side of the world." And they were probably incommunicado on an island in the middle of the Indian Ocean. Tears welled in her eyes, making them itchy, and she blinked them back. Along with cat food, kitty litter, and clothes, she'd also have to get new glasses, contact lenses, or both. The lenses she still wore were irritating her eyes, but if she took them out, her world would go blurry.

"How about friends? Is there someone nearby you can stay with?"

"Maybe." She could take Bonnie or Kevin up on their offers to stay with them, but she wouldn't dream of taking advantage of their generosity for more than a few days. "I'll come up with something." She forced a smile, genuinely appreciative of the nurse's concern.

"Are you up for visitors?" She canted her head to the three men hovering outside the curtain. "That detective wants to ask you some questions, and your boyfriend seems pretty worried about you."

"My *what*?" She stared at the nurse as if she'd grown two heads.

"Your boyfriend." She glanced to where Matt and the other men stood, then squeezed a generous blob of white ointment from the tube. "The big handsome guy who hasn't stopped pacing since you were brought in. He's been interrogating the nurses every five minutes for an update on your condition. If he wasn't so darned good looking, we would have tossed him into the waiting room."

She looked through the curtains at Matt, who was deep in conversation, a dark, brooding look on his handsome face. Despite her mantra, she couldn't help wondering what it would be like to be his girlfriend. Would he be attentive and loving? Or aloof and hard, like so many law enforcement officers tended to be?

Taking a shallow breath so as not to induce another fit of coughing, she sighed. "He's not my boyfriend."

Without looking up from dabbing ointment onto Trista's cuts, the nurse uttered a high-pitched laugh. "Coulda fooled me, honey. He sure acts sweet on you. But if he's not yours, can I have him?" She winked. "While the doctor was examining you, I cleaned and bandaged the cuts on his hands and chest, and OMG. If I had a man with that body and that face looking at me every morning at breakfast, I'd never leave my house."

Matt sweet on me? Ridiculous. Surely the nurse had mistaken Matt's professional interest in her well-being for something else. Processing that absurd notion was about as realistic as the internet going away, and—

"Wait." She grabbed the nurse's arm. "He was hurt?" She hadn't known that, but he was standing right outside the curtain, and he seemed okay.

"Don't worry." She patted Trista's arm. "He has a bump

on the head and some cuts on his hands and torso. The gashes on his hands are deeper than yours, so I wrapped them in gauze to heal for a couple days. But they're not as bad as they look. I understand he saved your cat."

"He did." That must have been when he'd been cut, going back through the window to save Poofy. The more she thought about it, she doubted she could have managed to re-enter the house and get both her *and* Poofy back out on her own.

The anger she'd been harboring against Matt began slipping away. If her beloved cat had died, she would have been heartbroken. Because of Matt, Poofy was safe and sound.

Why was he at my house in the first place?

"There." The nurse capped the tube, handing it to her. "Apply this twice a day to all the cuts to ward off infection."

"Thank you." She watched the nurse leave and speak briefly to the men waiting outside.

She picked up a Styrofoam cup of water to ease the dryness in her throat. Through the open curtain, she caught Matt looking at her, and she froze with the straw between her lips. The scowl on his face was unmistakable. He was angry. On the other hand, he scowled quite a bit. But on him, a scowl looked *good*.

He turned as three more people joined the group—her supervisors, Wayne Gurgas and Genevieve Grujot, and Buxton McIntyre, Langley's chief of security. "Oh, boy," she muttered, as the entire group amassed inside her small, curtained ER room. Matt stood to one side of the gurney, Detective Sorensen to the other. Langley's chief of security and her two supervisors stood at the foot of the bed.

Whirring came from the overhead vent as the AC took that moment to blast her with more freezing air. Instantly, her nipples began to pucker and harden. She crossed her arms over her breasts, knowing full well it was already too late to hide her body's responses. She would have reached for the blanket at the foot of the bed, but that would only give everyone present a better opportunity to look down the top of her camisole.

As if reading her thoughts, Matt reached over and grabbed the blanket, draping it around her shoulders. Seeing the white gauze wrapped around both his hands, her heart squeezed at what he'd done to save Poofy. After pulling the ends of the blanket across her chest, she glanced up at him. *Who would have known the big bad cop had a sweet, thoughtful side?* "Th-thank you."

Nodding slightly, he still didn't look happy. He wasn't exactly scowling anymore, but his jaw was tightly clenched and the intense gleam in his eyes was one she hadn't seen before.

After Wayne, Genevieve, and Chief McIntyre expressed their concern and condolences over the loss of her house, Detective Sorensen began questioning her.

"Ms. Gold." He flipped open a pad. "I'd like to ask you some questions if you're up to it." When she nodded, he continued. "Did you see the fire start?"

"No." She shook her head. "When I went to bed around midnight, everything was fine. I don't really know what time it was when I smelled smoke. Poofy—my cat—woke me up and then all the alarms went off."

Detective Sorensen scribbled on his pad. "Cats and other animals can often sense even the smallest amount of smoke long before humans do. What happened next?"

"I opened my bedroom door and realized the house really was on fire. I was going to get the fire extinguisher, but it was too late to be of any use. The front door, all the curtains, and most of the furniture were already ablaze."

Pausing, she reached for the cup of water and positioned

the straw in front of her mouth, but her hands were shaking.

Matt covered her hands with his, guiding the cup to her mouth, patiently waiting while she sipped and swallowed. She cast him a grateful look before continuing.

"I went back to the bedroom, grabbed Poofy then crawled into the kitchen because it was easier to breathe on the floor. I was trying to get out the back door, but it wouldn't open."

"Did you unlock it?" Detective Sorensen asked.

"Of course, but it still wouldn't open." Her hands began shaking again, so she set the cup on her lap for fear of spilling it. "So I went into the basement. There's one window down there, and I'd just opened it yesterday. I do that regularly to prevent the basement from becoming too damp and musty."

"I take it the window didn't open," Detective Sorensen said, more than asked.

"It didn't, so I broke it with a crowbar."

"Did you see or hear anyone else in the house?"

"No." She thought back to Poofy's odd behavior. "But before we went to bed, Poofy sat directly in front of the main door, looking up at it. It was strange, since he's not an outdoor cat. I thought I heard something outside but thought it was just another dead tree limb falling from the old oak tree out back.

"Aside from smoke, did you smell anything unusual?" Matt asked.

She'd been about to say no, when she remembered that wasn't true. She *had* smelled something. "Gasoline, only maybe not quite gasoline."

"Could have been some other form of petroleum distillate," Matt added. "Kerosene or turpentine. I smelled it, too."

Detective Sorensen nodded as he jotted in his pad. "Did you see any lines of demarcation in the fire?"

"Yes." How could she have forgotten? "There were

distinctly straight lines of fire running from the curtains down to the floor and the furniture, both in the living room and the kitchen."

Matt crossed his arms, looking none too happy. "Those were probably made when he poured the accelerant all around."

Detective Sorensen looked up from writing. "Anything else you remember?"

She nodded. "When I went to bed, I left my cell phone on the desk in the living room. After the fire started, it was gone."

"Are you sure you didn't leave it somewhere else?" Matt asked.

"Positive." Her fingers dug into the Styrofoam cup. "That's where I always leave it at night so my parents don't wake me up with their three a.m. text messages. Someone was inside my house and took it."

Detective Sorensen looked first to Matt, then to her. "So it would seem."

Wayne cleared his throat. "What about your laptop? Did they take that, too?"

"No. I assume it burned up or melted in the fire."

He paused to stare at her for a moment. "Were you using it for anything work-related?"

Trista gulped, squeezing the cup tighter. "I, uh, was doing some internet searches on it."

"Searches on what?" Genevieve narrowed her eyes.

She hesitated, knowing that if she fessed up, she'd be neck-deep in trouble. *Someone's trying to murder me. I'm already in trouble.* "Iqaluit," she reluctantly answered.

Genevieve pressed her lips together then exchanged looks with Wayne. "And?"

And now I'm about to dive headfirst into deep, deep shpooh. "I had a copy of Dark Curtain on my laptop."

Wayne exhaled forcefully, telling her she'd pay dearly for that indiscretion.

"What's Dark Curtain, and what's Iqaluit?" Chief McIntyre looked at Trista, then to Wayne and Genevieve. "And don't invoke any of that top secret need-to-know shit, because at this point, it's safe to say we need to know. From what Sgt. Connors related to me about the attack on Ms. Gold earlier this week, the hit in CODIS on her attacker, and—"

"Wait!" She grabbed Matt's arm, forcing him to look at her. "You got a hit in CODIS?" That meant her attacker already had a criminal record. "Why didn't you tell me?"

"I only found out tonight." The muscles beneath her hand flexed, and she released his arm. "When Jake told me the guy's criminal history, we went to your house to check up on you."

"Well, who is he?" She looked from Matt to the detective.

"His name is Viktor Solonik," Detective Sorensen supplied. "He's a low-level thug with ties to the Russian mob. He's been suspected of a few hits, but nothing was ever proven. Do you know him?"

She gripped the bed rail tightly. For a moment, all she could do was give the detective a blank look while she processed what he'd said. *A Russian hit man is trying to kill me.* She shook her head to clear it, then wracked her brain for even the slightest recollection, but there was none.

"I've never heard of him. Why didn't he just shoot me? If he could break into my house and douse it with gasoline without me hearing a thing, why not put a bullet in my head while I'm sleeping? Wouldn't that have been a lot easier?" This time when she shivered, it had nothing to do with the air conditioning. The idea of being shot while she slept was terrifying.

"Overtly murdering a high-level CIA intelligence analyst would raise a helluva lot of red flags," Matt said. "Both a police *and* an internal investigation would be initiated. The first attempt on your life was almost labeled a random attack, which was probably what Solonik intended. In all likelihood, had he succeeded, he would have gone back and stolen your wallet from your car to make it look like a simple robbery. Even the fire could have been considered accidental, although using an accelerant that way was sloppy."

"Getting back to my point"—Chief McIntyre glared at Wayne—"someone tried to murder her. Twice. That makes it my and Sgt. Connors's business. So we *definitely* need to know what the hell's really going on here."

Wayne and Genevieve exchanged another look, this one longer in duration. Wayne poked his head around each side of the curtained room, then turned back and lowered his voice.

"Gentlemen, what you're about to hear is ten steps beyond TS, but in the interest of Trista's safety, we agree. You *do* need to know. The two of you," he said, tipping his head first to Matt then Chief McIntyre, "will both officially be read into the program." He gave the detective a pointed look. "You, however, were never here. Discussing a single word of what I'm about to say outside the scope of this investigation constitutes a breach of national security. And"—he indicated the detective's notepad—"no notes."

"Get on with it." Matt's tone was hard as he glared at Wayne, the muscles in his cheeks flexing. He looked...deadly. That was the word that came to Trista's mind.

Wayne shifted, looking uncomfortable under Matt's unyielding scrutiny.

"Ms. Gold is exceptionally good at what she does. To a fault." Wayne's gaze met hers, and she couldn't be certain what he'd said was a compliment. "Using a program that she alone developed for the agency, she tracked a target in the black net, then overheard something in a secret chat room that put her life at risk. After the attack Monday night, we reread the printout of the chat but weren't certain there was a connection to her assignment. Due to the content of that conversation and even the remote possibility that the two events were linked, we revoked her security clearance and banned her from Langley for her own safety."

Hearing the true reason for her clearance revocation made her feel slightly better, although all she wanted to do now was to go after Karakurt that much more.

"We now believe," Wayne continued, "that someone is trying to kill Trista for her intrusion into that black net chat room."

"If this program is so covert," Matt interjected, "how did they identify her, and how did they do it so quickly?"

"That's something we're not clear on," Genevieve said. "But we're working on that to prevent it from happening again."

"Kevin?" Trista asked, knowing her friend was the agency's go-to guy for troubleshooting all things online. Then she gasped. "I know what happened. There was a brief blip in power. It disrupted my program for a few seconds, but it could have been enough to enable a trace. Kevin's computer experienced a power glitch at the same time."

"We know." Genevieve nodded. "And we're implementing additional safeguards. Our backup power sources now have two additional reinforcements. Unfortunately, it looks as if that brief power shutdown was enough for them to trace your location and ID you."

"Who are *they*?" Matt asked. "And how could they have ID'd a specific person inside Langley?"

Again, Wayne and Genevieve exchanged meaningful looks that Trista easily recognized. Her supervisors were engaging in a silent debate about how much information to reveal.

"To answer your first question, the Russians," Wayne

said. "As for the second, we don't know yet."

Matt moved closer to the bed. "Who exactly were you listening to?"

"I don't think that's—" Wayne argued, but Matt's harsh tone cut him off.

"I don't give a shit what you think. The time for spy games is over." When he looked down at her, his voice softened. "Tell me exactly who was in this chat room and what they said. Don't leave anything out."

Despite Matt's commanding, no-nonsense tone, ultimately she worked for Wayne. And he was the one who called the shots regarding the dissemination of classified intel, although she appreciated Matt's to-hell-with-protocol attitude when it came to her safety. His fierce protectiveness made her feel cared for. Or maybe that was merely wishful thinking on her part.

"I'm afraid that's not possible." Wayne shot her a look of warning. "Ms. Gold is a CIA analyst and, as such, is privy to some of the most classified intelligence on the planet. To be fully read into this would take months of background checks and security clearances. We've already provided you with more information than you're entitled to know."

"You've given us jack shit." Matt advanced on Wayne, who took a step back, nearly tripping over a chair. "We know Solonik tried to kill her, but we still don't know who gave him the order. If you don't tell us who's really after her, it's clear as rain they'll keep trying until they get the job done."

"No, he won't." All eyes turned to Chief McIntyre, who, until now, had remained silent. "Because *you* are now officially assigned to protect Ms. Gold until further notice."

"What?" Matt barked.

"No," Trista said at the same time. So great was her own shock that her hold on the Styrofoam cup loosened, and it fell to the floor.

"It's already been worked out," Chief McIntyre continued. "As of this moment, your tours at Langley are being covered by other officers. Your only assignment is to get Ms. Gold someplace safe and keep her that way until the Intelligence directorate gives us the all clear."

"No, I won't do it." She shook her head so vigorously the blanket fell off her shoulders. "You have no idea how long that will be."

"Actually," Genevieve piped in, "we feel certain this will all be cleared up within the next thirty days."

"How do you know that?" Matt crossed his arms. The scowl on his face was the deepest she'd ever seen. Obviously, he didn't care for the idea of being saddled with her even for a month.

Neither Wayne nor Genevieve responded to Matt's question, but they did exchange another irritating, clandestine look that spoke volumes. They knew precisely what was going on but weren't about to say so.

"*My* life is at stake." She glared at her supervisors, still in disbelief. "Don't you think *I* need to know what's going on? I realize my clearance was revoked, but someone's trying to kill me, for Pete's sake."

Wayne shook his head. "Your only assignment, until you hear from either myself or Genevieve, is to keep your head down and do whatever Sgt. Connors tells you to do to stay safe."

"But—"

"That's an order." He pointed a finger at her. "The Intelligence directorate has operatives in the field who will follow up on the chat room, so you are not to do a damn thing. The only thing you should be logging on to a computer for over the next thirty days, is to look up your horoscope."

"Fine." She crossed her arms, feeling like a small child punished by her father. "I'll stay with my friend Bonnie for a few days, then maybe at Kevin's place after that. He's got a bigger apartment than Bonnie does."

Matt gave a snort. "You'll stay where *I* tell you, and it sure as hell won't be at Kevin's place."

"Why not?" She gave him her best angry glare, only to find he looked even angrier. His dark brows had drawn together and the skin over his nose etched into a deep V.

"Because Kevin can't protect you like I can," he snapped. "Besides, you wouldn't want to put your friends in danger, would you?"

Well, shoot. What did *he* have to be angry about? But he was right. She'd never forgive herself if anything happened to her friends because of her. Looking down at her hands, she gave a reluctant sigh. "Okay."

Beside her, Matt, too, exhaled a breath, as if he hadn't expected her to capitulate so easily.

Detective Sorensen pocketed his notebook and pen. "Fire marshals will investigate the remains of your house for evidence. We'll check for prints on the doors and inside the house, but assuming this was Solonik again, chances are he wore gloves and any prints would have been obliterated by the fire. We'll also check for boot prints around the house, although with all the firemen and the two of us tromping around, it's doubtful that will yield anything conclusive." He nodded to Matt. "As soon as I get the report, I'll send it over."

"Thanks, Jake." The two men shook hands.

Detective Sorensen paused. "Need me to tail you out of here?"

"Nah, I got this," Matt said, then Detective Sorensen turned and left, the ER curtains flapping in his wake.

A tall, young doctor wearing wire-rimmed glasses and scrubs entered the room and pulled a stethoscope from around his neck. "Folks, we need a few minutes here, then I think Ms. Gold can go home."

At the word "home," Trista winced, again reminded that she no longer had one. Her only remaining possessions were her cat and her car. Given how close to the house she'd parked her car, even that was questionable.

"Stay safe, Trista." Genevieve leaned over and squeezed her arm.

"Take care of her, Sergeant," Wayne said to Matt.

"Count on it."

Matt's tone held a discernible note of conviction, leaving Trista completely confused. Only moments ago, he'd seemed completely opposed to being her bodyguard.

Ah, yes. Must be that ingrained sense of cop duty. Given an assignment, he'd fulfill his duties and obligations. It had nothing to do with her personally, and she experienced a stab of disappointment. *Get real, Trista. A guy like that must have a hot girlfriend waiting for him at home.*

Both supervisors left the room, leaving her alone with Matt. Dark-brown eyes scrutinized her, making her feel like the proverbial bug under a microscope. It was unnerving. Plus, wearing nothing but her nightclothes made her self-conscious, and she tugged the blanket tighter around her, but it slipped off her shoulder. Matt tugged it back up, his knuckles grazing her bare shoulders.

"I'll get you something to wear over that...shirt." He frowned, clearly having no idea how to label her plain garment.

She wanted to die of embarrassment. He was probably used to sexy, exotic women wearing silk and satin, not boring cotton. "It's a camisole," she practically groaned.

"Yeah. Camisole. Whatever. I'll be back." He disappeared through the curtains.

"I'll be back," she muttered. *Is that his Terminator line?*

The doctor pressed the stethoscope against her chest, and she flinched as the cool metal touched her skin.

"Breathe normally," he said, moving the instrument around to different locations on her chest, then to her back.

She breathed several times until he said, "Excellent. Other than some smoke inhalation, your X-rays are clear and your breathing is good. No carbon monoxide poisoning, and your abrasions are minor. We just need you to fill out a few forms, and you'll be all set."

He picked up her chart to jot something down, then opened a cabinet drawer and pulled out a pair of slippers and surgical pants that he set beside her on the bed. "I understand you lost everything in a fire. These will at least give you something to wear tonight."

Fear and a sense of isolation crashed down on her. She wanted to cry, or scream, or throw something. Instead, she wrapped her arms around her legs and rested her chin on her knees. Her home was burned. Probably her car, too. She'd been banned from her job, and her parents were on the other side of the world.

"Get some rest," the doctor said. "Drink plenty of fluids, and if you have any trouble breathing during the night, don't hesitate to come back to the hospital."

"Thank you," she said before he left the room.

The AC kicked on again, and she tucked her legs closer against her body and began rocking back and forth. Someone was trying to kill her. Viktor Solonik. A Russian thug who wanted her dead for reasons unknown. To her, anyway. Wayne and Genevieve knew, and the more she thought about it, the faster she rocked.

Sitting around doing nothing to save her own ass wasn't working for her. They might have banned her from Langley, but that didn't mean she couldn't do a little discreet investigating on her own. Under the radar.

The question was how to do it without a computer, *and* while under the watchful, sexy eye of Sgt. Matt Connors.

. . .

Forty years ago, she'd been young, naive, and married to a horrible man who'd beaten her to within an inch of her life. Somehow, she and her son had survived and escaped a virtual hell. She had no regrets about what she'd done, except for what little Billy had been forced to endure.

Despite the tears trickling down her aging face, she smiled. Against all odds, her son had grown up to be a good man, honest and kind. Now, he had everything she could have wished for him. A beautiful wife, three adorable children, and an incredible future.

Who could have guessed that he would rise from the swamp of horrors in which he was born and become what he was today? *I'm so, so proud of him.*

She reached for a tissue and dabbed at her eyes. Sadly, their past had finally caught up to them. She didn't fear for herself, but for her son. She didn't know how, but after four decades of hiding, they'd been discovered.

The *Russians* had stumbled onto the truth. And it could ruin everything.

Chapter Twelve

Matt sat in the truck next to Trista and started the engine. When he gripped the wheel, his hands stung in protest from several shallow cuts dotting his skin, but he didn't give a shit. Trista was alive, and that was all that mattered.

She still wore that sexy cotton camisole that was slowly but surely driving him insane, a pair of scrub pants she'd rolled up to just below her knees, and one of his CIA windbreakers. On her lap was the not-so-fluffy-now Angora.

Until five minutes ago, he hadn't known where he'd be taking Trista, squirreling her away someplace safe. Now that he'd made the decision, he didn't relish breaking the bad news. But her eyes were closed, and the steady rise and fall of her chest beneath his windbreaker told him she was out like a light. It was just as well. When she realized where she'd be spending the next thirty days or so, she'd have a conniption. So would Poofy. *Understatement.* But by his reckoning, it was the safest option.

As he pulled out of the ER parking lot, he continually checked his rearview mirror for a tail. He hadn't even wanted

Jake or the uniforms following him. The agency would eventually figure out where he was stashing Trista, but since they insisted on keeping him in the dark, *let 'em work for it.*

Stifling a yawn, he headed onto the road, thankful for the darkness enshrouding them.

He couldn't decipher the twisted mix of emotions messing with his head. When Buck had given him his assignment— protecting Trista twenty-four seven—he'd nearly blown a gasket. The last thing he wanted was to be a bodyguard. But the more he learned about her predicament, the more he realized just how vulnerable she was. He wanted to be the one to keep her safe. Not because she looked hot as hell in that camisole, and definitely not because he'd caught every man in the room—including his friend, Jake—staring at her breasts. *Fuck, no.*

Something about her stirred the most basic, primal instincts within him. Even though she'd exhibited more guts than most women he knew, and her IQ probably topped the charts, she was so small and seemed so alone. Yeah, that's why he wanted to keep her safe. After the situation was resolved, they'd go their separate ways and things would return to normal.

I'll go back to living my solitary life.

Turning onto the highway, he yawned again. He was beat. It was nearly four a.m., and the sun hadn't quite begun to peek out over the horizon. Everyone else would probably be bunked out for the night. *Good thing.* All he wanted was to get Trista and Poofy settled, then fall into bed himself.

Thirty minutes later, after making several countersurveillance turns, he rolled into his driveway, past his friends' vehicles, and parked near the front door. Trista was still asleep, with her head lolled against the window and one arm tucked around her soot-stained, formerly white cat. He shut the engine off and the cat stared at him, as if he was suspicious already. Matt had no idea how he'd get through the next month. How *any* of them would survive.

Quietly, he stepped out of the truck and nudged the door shut. The air was cooler than it had been earlier in the week, a sign that fall would soon arrive. He went around to get Trista, but with her head leaning against the window, he didn't dare open the door or risk her falling onto the pavement. Gently, he tapped twice on the window. She didn't move. He tapped again, with more force this time, and her body jerked upright.

He opened the door and waited a few seconds for her to wake fully. "Home sweet home."

She looked up at his house, her eyes groggy. "Where are we?"

"Like I said, home."

Her green eyes widened. "This is *your* house?"

"Yup." The cab of the truck was high off the ground, so he held out his hand to assist her. "I've got eight bedrooms. Plenty of space for you and Poofy."

Looking over his shoulder, she asked, "Who do all the other trucks belong to?"

"Friends. K-9 officers working pre-election events in the D.C. area over the next couple months." Matt watched her gaze travel down the row of Explorers.

"There are *six* of them? Six men *plus* their dogs? And *yours*?"

He understood her wariness. Rooming with seven men would be intimidating to any woman. "They—and their dogs—are all highly trained officers. You have nothing to worry about. I trust them with my life, and yours. They'll be here for at least the next two months, backing me up. If anything happens, they'll be there in a heartbeat."

Her face paled. "The dogs," she whispered. "Where will the d-dogs be?"

As expected, her innate fear of all things canine was at the crux of the matter, not him or his friends. "See that building?" He tipped his head toward the main house's addition. "It's a kennel. Enough for a dozen dogs. Occasionally, we let them into the house, but I promise…as long as you and Poofy are here, no dog will be allowed inside."

Furrowing her brows, she looked cute as ever, but worried. He'd seen that look before on people who'd been terrorized by dogs, and he'd noticed it on *her* face during her encounters with Sheba. Something had definitely happened to make her believe canines were the devil. Maybe, since they'd be stuck here for at least the next thirty days, he'd work on getting her over that fear.

"You p-promise?" She glared at him, clearly trying to give him her most intimidating look. On her, it was cute.

"Cross my heart." He grinned, doing just that.

"Okay." She took a deep breath, then with Poofy still clutched to her chest, she placed her free hand in his.

When their fingers touched, he heard her quick intake of breath, felt the softness of her fingers, along with an awareness he hadn't expected. There was something sizzling between them, and she felt it, too. It was there in her eyes, just as he knew it was in his. She was a beautiful woman, one he might one day be interested in pursuing. *If my head wasn't so fucked up.* For now, he'd settle for protecting her, and he gladly accepted that responsibility.

He unlocked the door to his house and stood aside for her to enter. The alarm pad beeped, and as soon as he'd closed the door behind them, he entered the four-digit code and reset the alarm for what was left of the night.

As he led the way up the wide staircase to the room that would be Trista and Poofy's, he flipped on various lights. With the brand-new runner he'd installed on the stairs, their footsteps were quiet, which was a good thing, since everyone else was still asleep. Sure enough, before they even reached the top of the stairs, the sound of deep snoring came to his ears.

At the top landing, the faint, lingering smell of freshly painted walls pervaded the air, and he thanked whatever had driven him to bust his ass the past few weekends to complete all the interior painting before his friends arrived.

He led the way to the only vacant bedroom in the house. Unfortunately, it was directly opposite the master bedroom. *His* bedroom. If his friends hadn't been bunking with him for the next two months, he would have put her in the bedroom on the third floor. For safety's sake. Higher level rooms were inherently safer from break-ins. *Yeah, that's why.* Again, not because he'd kissed her and she'd kissed him back with enough passion to knock his fucking socks off.

Reaching inside the open door, he flipped on the light switch, illuminating the cream-colored walls and the newly refinished four-poster bed with its rich red brocade duvet cover. When he glanced back, Trista was busy taking in the whole room. A faint look of surprise lit her features.

"Like it?"

With her eyes wide, she gently lowered Poofy to the floor, whereupon the cat began inspecting and sniffing the antique rug. "It's beautiful. I had no idea."

The appreciative look on her face tweaked his sense of pride. He'd been renovating the old Colonial for two years, and he was finally finished. The place did look damn good.

"I'll give you the grand tour after we get some shut-eye. There are fresh towels and toiletries in the bathroom. I'll get you something to sleep in, and a litter box and water for Poofy." Rather than give in to his urge to take her in his arms and hold her tightly, he left to go gather up the items he'd promised.

When he returned to Trista's room, the door was almost closed, but not quite, reminding him it was still in need of repair. Through the opening, he glimpsed her sitting on the bed with her back to him, still wearing the overly long scrub pants, but she'd tossed his jacket on a chair. Poofy stalked back and forth across the duvet with his tail held high in that regal, self-important way all cats had. A sooty towel had been draped over a chair, and the cat's fur was nearly all white again.

She pulled her hair to one side of her neck and began speaking to Poofy in a gentle, soothing tone. He couldn't hear what she said, but it seemed to ease the animal's anxiety because it lay down, tucking its feet beneath it, gazing up at her as if he were soaking in every word she said.

Matt didn't know much about cats, having preferred dogs at a very early age. He supposed cats could just as easily be attuned to their owners as dogs. Maybe it was their inherent aloofness that made him think cats didn't give a shit about anything except themselves. Contrarily, dogs were all about pleasing their masters. Yup, he'd take a dog any day over a cat.

He tapped twice softly on the door, doing his best not to startle her. God knew she'd been through enough for one night—hell, for one *week*—and the last thing he wanted to do was to scare her. When she turned at the sound of his voice, his attention was first drawn to how smooth and graceful her bared neck and shoulders were. Then he noticed the dull, sleep-deprived look in her eyes and felt guilty for ogling her. He was used to going without much sleep—he'd been that way since the Marines—but she'd probably need to sleep half the day away.

"The door doesn't latch shut entirely unless you give it an extra tug," he said pushing it open enough for him to set a low plastic tub on the floor. "No kitty litter, so I lined it with newspaper. I'll go into town later and get whatever you need, so make a list when you wake up." He nodded to the old oak desk. "There's pen and paper in there."

She rose from the bed and came to where he stood. The cotton camisole was smudged with soot, but not enough to hide the curves of her waist or the fullness of her breasts. "I don't have any m-money, or checks, or ATM cards, or..." Her voice trailed off, and he knew precisely what she was thinking. *I don't have anything.* "But I'll go to a bank, then go shopping for myself."

"Negative." Matt shook his head, also knowing she wouldn't like what he said next. "I don't want you setting foot off this property."

The dullness in her expression instantly evaporated, her green eyes lighting with fire. "I'm *not* a prisoner here." She parked her fists on her hips, pulling that damned, soot-covered camisole tighter across her breasts.

"Of course not." He forced his gaze back to hers. "Whoever's trying to kill you may not know about my involvement, and probably won't figure on you being stashed at my house. But until I can get more information about what's going on, it's not safe for you anywhere."

"But—"

"No buts." He cut her off, pressing his lips together to keep from shouting. If it wasn't for the fact that his friends were likely in deep REM sleep at the moment, he would have. He leaned in until his face was a scant inch from hers, keeping his voice low and controlled. "Someone tried to slit your throat. When that didn't work, they tried to burn you alive. What part of the message are you *not* getting?"

That green fire he'd glimpsed moments ago dulled, and her shoulders slumped as the frightening reality of his words kicked in.

"Look," he said, handing her the T-shirt he'd draped over his arm, along with a shallow dish to use as Poofy's water bowl. "We're both dead on our feet, and..." *Bad choice of words.* "I don't know about you, but I'd really like to wash off the smell of smoke and get some sleep. I suggest you do the same. We can talk more later. Good night. Or rather, good morning."

Without waiting for a response, he turned and closed the door behind him, giving it an extra tug to verify the latch did indeed lock into place this time. Before crossing the hallway to his own bedroom, he stood outside Trista's door, pressing his fingers to his forehead. He hoped he'd made the right decision bringing her to his home. The practical logistics of the plan he'd just set in motion had more obstacles than Omaha Beach on D-Day. A cynophobic woman shacking up with seven K-9 officers and their dogs was a royally fucked-up scenario.

Once inside his room, he stripped out of his filthy clothes, dropping them on the bathroom floor, then tore off the bandages on his hands. He turned on the shower, waiting only a minute or so before stepping gratefully under the spray and turning his face into the hot stream of water. He uttered a groan of pleasure. But as the water hit all the shallow cuts and scrapes scattered all over his hands, chest, and abs, he sucked in a tight breath.

Great. He'd forgotten about those.

The headache that had been brewing behind his eyes had finally begun to hammer in full force. It had started when Trista kicked him in the jaw outside her house, and he'd hit the back of his head against the brick siding. Now blood pounded mercilessly throughout his skull.

When he finished showering, he stepped into a pair of clean knit boxers and went in search of aspirin. When he didn't find the bottle he was searching for, he figured one of the guys had snatched it in anticipation of a hangover. On the way to the kitchen, he caught sight of himself in the full-length mirror on the wall. *Shit.* His torso looked like he'd been hit with light shrapnel, and the left side of his jaw was turning three shades of purple.

When he opened his bedroom door, he paused, listening for any sounds inside Trista's room, but there were none. Hopefully, she could manage to get some rest.

Heading down the hallway, the same snoring came to his ears, louder this time, and definitely coming from Jaime's room at the top of the stairs. Knowing his friend's proclivity to snore like a freight train after a night of drinking, Matt had strategically placed Jaime as far away from the master bedroom as possible.

In the kitchen, he began searching the upper cabinets for the spare bottle of aspirin he knew was tucked away somewhere. He moved down the line, checking each cabinet, determined to find the little white pills that would be his salvation. Finally, he caught sight of them in the cabinet over the stove, hidden behind boxes of sugar and flour. Why the fuck he'd put them there, he didn't know. Reaching for the bottle, he froze.

Soft creaks sounded in the hallway, the kind made by someone stepping lightly, tentatively. Matt tensed, trying to decipher whether the source of the noise was friend or foe. The house alarm hadn't gone off, but given the violent events of the past few days, he readied to lunge for one of the dozen or so brand-new chef's knives sticking out from the butcher block inset in the kitchen island.

Trista rounded the corner. Her hair was damp, and his white T-shirt covered her from the neck down to her knees. The cotton shirt swamped her slight form, but he'd chosen it because it was well worn and would be comfortable to sleep in. But that also made the soft fabric cling lovingly to the mounds of her bare breasts. At least, he assumed they were bare, because the only clothes she had left in the world were that cotton camisole and probably panties. Although even the panties he couldn't be sure of.

At the sight of him, she gasped, her green eyes wide. She put her hand to her throat, then her breath came out with a *whoosh*. "You scared the pooh out of me."

"Pooh?" He barked out a laugh at her obvious reluctance to use the word "shit." In a house full of seven cops and seven dogs, she'd better get used to hearing it. Often.

"Yes, pooh." She straightened her shoulders and stuck out her chin, as if she was proud of the word.

"You don't swear, do you?" he asked, again wanting to laugh when her pink lips twisted into an indignant pout. His question reminded him of when she'd asked whether he drank alcohol.

"Of course I do. When the situation d-demands it." She padded hesitantly into the kitchen, her bare feet almost soundless on the tile. Her eyes dipped to his chest, down his body, all the way to his toes, and back again. Matt didn't know if she was checking him out or eyeballing all the scrapes on his body.

And speaking of cursing, hell, her shins were dotted with cuts the same way her arms were. He'd seen them at the hospital, on her pale, soft skin, and it had made his gut clench with anger at the nameless, faceless fucker who'd torched her house.

As she came nearer, his gaze was drawn to her feet. Christ, even they were cute. Unpainted, tiny feet with tiny toes. And shit, was that a...*no way*. Gracing the big toe of her right foot was a silver ring studded with pink, sparkly stones. "Nice toe ring. Who knew you were such an undercover rebel. You got a tattoo somewhere?"

That elicited a tiny smile. "No. But every now and then, I like to take a walk on the w-wild side."

He laughed, louder this time. "Honey, if you think that's walking on the wild side, we're gonna have to work on that."

Her smile faltered, and he realized why. He hadn't intended it, but his words were laced with sexual innuendo. *Fuck.* Why the hell had he said that? There might be something in the air between them, but he'd never be capable of giving in to it.

Clearing his throat, he turned and took two glasses from one of the cabinets. "Can I get you some water for your throat?"

"Yes, please." She stood beside him in front of the sink, and the smell of soap and shampoo wafted to his nose. "Do you have anything stronger? I'm exhausted, but I c-can't seem to fall asleep."

"Just beer." He filled both glasses from the tap, handing one of them to her. "I can pick up something for you when I go shopping."

Nodding, she took the glass. "I'll take that beer."

He padded to the refrigerator and snagged a bottle of River Horse ale, popping the cap off, then holding it to her.

She accepted the beer, but her gaze was on his chest. "Did the nurse put any ointment on those?"

"Some." He watched her eyes wander from his pecs to his abs, and his cock began to harden. Gritting his teeth, he angled his body away from her so she wouldn't notice the ever-growing bulge beneath his tight shorts, but she'd turned and left the kitchen without a word.

He blew out a breath. "Thank God," he muttered. Not having sex in a while would do that to a guy, and he'd noticed lately that his body was on a short leash.

Opening the refrigerator, he snooped around for something to eat. Luckily, his friends had shopped, and the shelves were jammed with everything from steak and chicken to eggs, cheese, and every vegetable in the produce section. He reached for a package of cheese when he heard the same creaking in the hallway and lifted his head. Trista re-entered the kitchen, and he glanced down to see that the cool air streaming from the fridge had brought his wayward cock to heel. When he closed the door, he noticed the tube in her hand.

"You really should put some antiseptic ointment on those cuts." She squeezed a dab of pale-yellow cream onto her finger.

You? The ointment was on *her* finger.

Taking several steps closer until she was standing directly in front of him, she reached out tentatively, pausing to lock gazes with him for a heartbeat before dabbing cream onto the longest of the cuts, the one on his right pec.

Her touch was gentle, soothing as she daintily massaged the cream into the laceration with the tip of her finger. When she finished with that cut, she moved on to the one immediately below it, near his right nipple. His nipples weren't normally an erogenous zone, but *holy shit.*

He willed her not to look down at the bulge growing again. Thankfully, she was concentrating on what she was doing. Her brows furrowed, and the creamy skin over her nose crinkled as she worked diligently to administer ointment to all the abrasions on his torso.

She really was a tiny thing, the top of her head barely reaching his pecs. Taking a step closer, her tantalizing scent filled his lungs, and he couldn't stop himself from breathing deeper.

"Your nursing skills are exemplary," he said, surprised at the husky tone of his voice.

Without looking up from her ministrations, she smiled. "It's a hidden talent."

It was on the tip of his tongue to ask what other hidden talents she possessed. He didn't, knowing it would come out screaming even more of sexual innuendo.

She'd made it to his lower abs, and when her fingers

began massaging a large cluster of tiny scrapes, he flinched, but not from pain.

"Baby." She snickered, glancing up. Her nostrils flared. Her eyes roved his face, then down his chest and back to his abs. She squeezed out another blob of cream and dabbed it onto a different spot. A *lower* one.

Her touch was getting *waaay* too close to ground zero. The skin above his waistband tingled, and he suppressed a shudder at the goose bumps parading up and down his back. Worse, his balls had grown tight, and he was hardening again like nobody's business. It felt…good.

The thought had the same impact as dousing *both* heads of his body with a bucket of ice water, and he was hit with the familiar, sweeping tidal wave of guilt that drowned him whenever he began to enjoy something in his life.

It was Matt's fault that his best friend would never know the gentle touch of a woman's fingers on his chest, inhale her delicate scent, or experience the aching pleasure of burying himself inside a woman's body.

So as much as he wanted to let Trista dab his entire body with ointment, he gently, but firmly, clasped her wrist and tugged it from his chest. Every bit of her warm skin he touched branded his fingers, singeing him with regret. Raising her brows, she gazed up at him in question. But he'd never tell her the answer. Ever. He was damaged goods and always would be.

"Go to bed, Trista." The minute the words were out of his mouth, he felt like a shithead. It was as if he'd just kicked a puppy. The flicker of hurt in her eyes was unmistakable but necessary in order to give him distance and to ram home the inevitable reality he was doomed to live with for the rest of his life. Solitude.

Turning away from her, he braced his hands on the porcelain farmhouse sink and waited until he heard her receding footsteps on the kitchen tile and the stairs creak as she went up to her bedroom.

He dragged a hand down his stubbled jaw, unwillingly facing facts he'd been trying to deny. Thoughts of Jerry had been intruding more and more lately, nearly every day, in fact.

Ever since he'd met Trista Gold.

Chapter Thirteen

Trista woke to dappled sunlight filtering in through the wooden slat blinds and stretched her arms over her head. The beautiful antique clock on the bedside table told her it was two o'clock. She'd slept a much-needed, solid eight hours and felt significantly better than she had when she'd fallen into bed.

What she'd done last night in Matt's kitchen was *so* not like her. It was as if her alternate personality had been released. Rubbing ointment all over his perfectly toned, incredibly muscled body... She'd been like a woman possessed. The memory had her groaning in embarrassment.

Maybe she should chock it up to the stress of the last week and everything that had happened. Perhaps she could blame her Nurse Nancy routine on gratitude.

No. That isn't it.

Sgt. Matt Connors was beautiful. With all that smooth, taut skin covering thick, hard muscle, she hadn't been able to keep from touching him. His arms were long and strong, as were his legs. From his pecs to his abs, his entire torso was covered with undulating ridges of incredibly well-defined muscle. Looking at him in the kitchen, with him wearing nothing but those tight boxer shorts, her mouth had literally watered. *That* had never happened to her before. Then again, aside from an occasional day at the beach, she'd never been around a man so scantily clad, and it did things to her body that she'd also never experienced.

Tingles had skittered across her skin, and beneath Matt's soft T-shirt, her nipples hardened to tight buds. Something deep inside her began craving something new. Something unfamiliar.

She'd been through hell over the past few days and hadn't given a thought to what it would mean to stray beyond her comfort zone. She'd nearly been killed twice in the past week, and for once in her life, she wanted to do something without second-guessing herself, without preparing an analytical plan to examine every action and reaction.

If she'd learned nothing else over the past few days, it was that life could be cut short, without any warning whatsoever. So she'd done what her feminine instincts demanded. And those instincts had screamed at her to rub that goddamn antiseptic ointment on Matt's body. *So there.*

Take that, Sgt. Connors. I can too curse. When the situation demands it.

Although it did occur to her that if she cursed to herself when no one was around to hear it, did it really count?

Even with the beer, sleep had come painfully slowly, and she'd lain awake for another thirty minutes, tossing and turning, unable to get comfortable. It had been impossible not to remember how he'd trembled at her touch, and as she'd administered the ointment progressively lower on his torso, the temperature of his skin had seemed to rise twenty degrees. But he hadn't stopped her. Not at first, anyway. Then something changed as quickly as a shifting wind, and he'd pretty much kicked her out of the kitchen.

The bed was warm, the air streaming in through the open window cool. Reluctant to get up, she tugged on the duvet to snuggle deeper into the plush bedding, but it wouldn't budge. Turning onto her other side, she came face to face with a pair of amber-gold eyes. For a fraction of a second, she couldn't move. Couldn't breathe. Then she opened her mouth, tilted her head back, and screamed like she'd never screamed before.

The dog leaped to its feet on the bed. Trista scrambled backward off the mattress, falling hard on her ass on the floor, which still wasn't far enough away.

Sheba stood on the bed, her tail wagging, her jaws open, and her entire body wriggling. If Trista didn't know better, she'd swear the dog was either laughing at her or was inordinately pleased with herself.

Trista's heart slammed against her ribs as she crab-walked backward on her elbows to the farthest corner of the room.

Sheba pranced in a circle on the bed, panting, smiling in that evil way dogs did.

Poofy!

Had Matt's dog eaten Poofy in the middle of the night while she slept?

Dear God, no.

Panicked, she searched the room until she spotted Poofy hunched into a ball on the desk, backed up as far as he could possibly get against the wall with the hair on his back standing straight up. Fear-filled blue eyes stared back at her, telling her this was all her fault. She should never have agreed to this arrangement, and now it was too late.

Sheba lay down on the bed and crawled to the side of the mattress closest to her, hanging her muzzle off the edge, facing her. Trista shut her eyes, her chest heaving as she gulped in air. The distant memory of another dog... She'd been helpless, only six years old. *Mommy! Mommy! Where are you?* Then her mother was there, picking her up and holding her tightly. More screaming. *Hers.* Only this time it was real, not a memory.

The dog's eyes glowed hotly from a brown-and-black face. There was no doubt in her mind that the devil dog on her bed was about to tear her and her beloved Angora to shreds.

Sheba rose to her feet, woofing, and Trista opened her mouth to scream again.

"What the hell?" Matt stood in the open doorway, his bare, broad chest heaving, and his hair was mussed, as if he'd just woken up. He had a gun in his hand. "Sheba! *Jdi ven!*"

Letting out another *woof*—one that sounded as if the dog were disappointed—Sheba spun, leaped off the bed, and trotted from the room.

"Tris." Matt set the gun on the desk and kneeled on the floor beside her, and the next thing Trista knew, she was in his arms, her head pressed against the solid wall of his chest. "Shh." He stroked her hair, and she realized he was now sitting on the bed with her in his lap. "I'm sorry about that. I didn't know she was in the house. One of the guys must have let her in while I was asleep."

"Sh-she was going to kill me and Poofy," she managed to say between shaky breaths.

Beneath her cheek, Matt's low chuckle reverberated in her ear. "That, I can guarantee you, would never happen."

"Bullshit."

To her annoyance, he chuckled again. "You *do* curse."

A stampede of footsteps pounded in the hallway, followed by a chorus of shouts.

"What's wrong?"

"What the fuck?"

"You guys okay?"

"Duh, what do you think?"

"Shit. Sorry, Matt." Another man's chuckle. "Didn't know you had company."

Lifting her head enough to look over Matt's shoulder, Trista's eyes widened at the sight of six enormous men—six *armed* men—filling the open doorway.

"We're fine." Matt twisted his body slightly, turning to the other men. "Could one of you put Sheba back in the kennel?"

"Sure thing, Matt," one of the men said.

"Everything really okay here?" another asked.

"Yeah. Just a little cynophobia," Matt answered.

"A little?" someone said in a sarcastic tone.

Dying from embarrassment, Trista tucked her head back down against Matt's chest and closed her eyes. His thick pectoral was warm and hard beneath her cheek, and that warmth zinged straight to her toes, then back up to the top of her head.

"Give us a few, would ya, guys?" Matt continued stroking the top of her head in a gentle, soothing gesture. "We'll be down shortly. We all need to have a meeting."

"Ten-four."

"Copy that."

"Later."

The door clicked shut, and they were alone. Except for Poofy, who remained frozen on top of the desk, although his hair no longer stuck straight up from his spine at a ninety-degree angle.

She expected Matt to release her, but he didn't. His arms remained securely around her, his hand alternately stroking her hair and her nape in delicious circles. And she was sitting on his lap. *His lap.* Aside from her father's, she'd never sat on a man's lap before, certainly not one whose legs were as big and strong as tree trunks.

As if only now realizing that her arms were still linked tightly around his back, she eased her hold, but not completely. Being cocooned in his embrace felt too damned good, as did the rippling muscle beneath her fingers.

He eased away, looking down at her. "You know we're going to have to work on that."

As she spoke, her lips grazed his chest. "On what?"

"Your fear of dogs."

Leaning back, she met his amused gaze with a horrified one of her own. *"No."*

"Yes." He nodded emphatically. His lips lifted at the corners, but there was a discernible hint of sincerity in his eyes. "You don't know what you're missing."

Involuntarily, her hands clenched into fists. "Oh, yes I do."

"The old adage is true. Dogs really are man's—and woman's—best friend, but it's so much more than that. Sheba is not only my friend and partner, but she's family. She loves me, and I love her. She'd take a bullet for me, and I'd do the same for her in a heartbeat." He laughed. "I swear she knows me better than any other female in my life."

The idea of Matt with another woman suddenly annoyed her, and not for the first time, she wondered whether he had a girlfriend. If he did, he hadn't mentioned it, and he didn't seem worried that she was now staying in his house for an unknown period of time.

"What happened to make you so scared of dogs?" he asked, his voice gentling, encouraging her to talk.

Not caring to relive that horrid nightmare, she hadn't told many people in her life what had happened. Before she understood why, the words came gushing out. "When I was a girl, my mother took me to a park."

When Trista finished describing that awful day, Matt asked, "Were you hurt?" His tone was laced with concern.

"N-no. Not really. It didn't bite me, but it slobbered all over me, and I couldn't breathe. I never saw Miss Annie again."

"Miss Annie?" He grinned, displaying even white teeth.

"Miss Annie was my doll." She punched him in the arm, noting his bicep really was as rock solid as it looked. "So don't you dare laugh."

His expression sobered. "Not laughing. Getting attacked by a dog under any circumstances is no laughing matter. Even though it didn't bite you, I can understand why it traumatized you." He gently gripped her chin. "Did Sheba attack you?" She shook her head. "Did she slobber on you?" Again, she shook her head. "Did she go after Poofy?"

"No, but—"

"I'm not discounting your fear. Based on your experience as a young child, there's a basis for it. What I'm asking is, what was Sheba doing that got you screaming like a banshee?"

Frowning, she had to force her thoughts back to the very moment when she knew Sheba was in her room. "She was on the bed…" Her voice trailed off, as she realized the truth. "Lying down next to me."

"Hate to be the one to burst your cynophobic bubble, but she was sleeping. I don't *ever* let her up on the bed, but at times, she acts like a teenager, pushing the envelope and seeing what she can get away with." The corners of his mouth lifted.

"She stays in the house with you?" Now that was an issue. A *big* one.

He shook his head. "Mainly, no. If I let her inside every night, she'd sneak onto a sofa or a bed the second my back was turned. Like she did on *your* bed. I don't want her to get lazy and lose the drive to work. That's a mistake a lot of K-9 officers go through with their first dog, then they have to spend more time getting their partner to re-engage."

Interesting. "Who knew the d-dog psyche was so complex?"

Again, he gave her a smile, and she realized she liked it. His smile made her tummy all fluttery. "My point is, not all dogs will hurt you. Most, in fact, never will. *Sheba* never will, nor will any of the other K-9s in my kennel. They're trained to protect the good guys."

Suddenly, the air between them got thick and hot, steamy even, although there wasn't much space between them at the moment. That's when she noticed the purplish bruise visible beneath his chiseled, stubbled jaw.

She touched her fingers to his face. "How did you get this?"

He snorted. "You kicked me."

"What?" Her jaw dropped. "I did *not* kick you." His grin turned into a full-fledged smile. "When?"

"Did so." He tipped his head to where Poofy had now mellowed on the desk and sat watching them. "You were so hell-bent on getting back inside to rescue that fur ball you kicked me, so hard my head hit the house. Got me good."

"Sorry." She gave him a regretful grimace. "Does it hurt?"

"Not much."

"Great. N-nothing like kicking the g-guy who risked his life to save my cat. Or me. For the second time in less than a week." Her arms were still loosely around his neck, and she knew she should move them, but she didn't want to. It felt too good being here like this. Wrapped up in his arms. Warm and safe. "Thank you."

Their gazes locked. Neither of them said a word. He swallowed, his eyes dipping to her mouth, and for a minuscule moment, she thought he was about to kiss her.

His chest rose and fell as he took a deep breath. "You're welcome. Just doing my duty."

His duty?

Right. Not that it was a shock, but it hurt to hear him say the words, a stark reminder of her unflappable mantra: *men like him don't go out with women like me.*

Desperate to hide her disappointment, she looked away, cringing inwardly.

"Trista, I—" Matt clenched his jaw, giving her a look that told her she hadn't hidden her emotions well at all. "I didn't mean it like that."

Taking a deep breath, she forced herself to accept the inevitable. "It's okay." She patted his chest. "I g-get it. I really do. I'm an assignment to you, probably one you didn't even want. Barely ten hours under your roof, and I've already created utter chaos."

As if sensing her change in mood, he stood and released the arm he'd had beneath her thighs so she could lower her legs to the floor. As she slid down his body, the T-shirt rode up her thighs, and for one agonizingly long moment, they were skin on skin, her legs brushing against his, her belly contacting the hard bulge between his legs. She widened her eyes, floored by the intimate knowledge that *she'd* done that to him. Perhaps it *was* more than just duty he felt toward her.

She froze, daring to think the unthinkable. *Was it even possible? Could a man like him actually be interested in a woman like me?*

Hesitant hope blossomed in her heart.

His hand remained at the small of her back a moment longer before he let his arm drop. "I'll meet you downstairs, introduce you to the guys. Then we'll have to talk about procedure while you're here." He went to the door, turning at the last second with his hand on the knob. "Tug it shut harder next time until you hear the latch click. That's probably how Sheba got in."

He closed the door behind him, and she heard a distinct

click. Well, he *had* warned her. In her haste last night to put distance between them, she probably hadn't pulled it closed hard enough.

Minutes later, she'd brushed her teeth, finger-combed her hair, and put on those ridiculously baggy scrub pants, rerolling them to her knees so she didn't trip over them. Before heading downstairs, she checked on Poofy one more time, but he was curled into a tight ball at the foot of the bed, so she left him alone.

At the bottom of the stairs, men's voices floated to her ears. When she rounded the corner to the kitchen, seven sets of eyes focused solely on her, including Matt's. Crossing her arms, she really, *really* wished she had a bra on underneath her shirt, and that she had something nicer to wear.

All of a sudden, she wanted to look nicer. For her own dignity, or so she kept telling herself, but not so deep down she understood she wanted to look nicer for Matt. Just in case…

Most of the men were sitting on stools at the kitchen island, wearing either jeans or cargo pants and T-shirts in varying colors. Matt poured two cups of coffee, but her eyes were glued to his tight, jean-clad ass and the way the snug black T-shirt tightened across his back, emphasizing the size and definition of all that hard muscle she'd had her arms wrapped around.

"Good morning," she said, feeling the men's intense scrutiny as any woman would in a room full of this much testosterone.

Glancing around, she realized the kitchen was larger than she remembered from last night, with white walls and cabinets and gleaming black granite counters. Antique schoolhouse pendant lights hung over the kitchen island, making something in the granite sparkle like diamonds. Everything looked new, but someone had obviously paid a great deal of attention in returning the house to its former grandeur. Funny how she hadn't noticed any of that earlier. Then again, she'd been just a tad distracted.

The kitchen might be huge, but with all these giant men in it, she felt like a microchip in a room full of desktop computers. "Sorry if I disturbed you with my, uh, screaming."

"No worries." One of them, a handsome, olive-skinned giant of a man with brown hair and smiling brown eyes, slid off a stool. "Keeps us on our toes so we don't go soft. Have a seat." He indicated the stool he'd just vacated. "Heard you had a rough week."

She snorted. "You could say that." While she sat, each of them either smiled or chuckled, and it was obvious Matt had already filled them in. Eyeing a plate of bagels, her mouth watered, and her stomach growled. She hadn't eaten since the day before. "Sheba scared the snot out of me."

"Snot?" The gorgeous, sandy-haired man with deep-set gray eyes grinned at her from across the counter, transforming his seemingly humorless face. Then he surprised her more by laughing in the smoothest, richest baritone she'd ever heard.

"She doesn't curse, and she doesn't talk trash. Much." Matt plunked a mug in front of her, reaching to the center of the island for the sugar and creamer, positioning them in front of her. As he did, she caught his freshly showered scent and couldn't stop from inhaling deeply.

"Trista, this is Nick Houston with the Massachusetts State Police." Still standing next to her, Matt pointed to the gray-eyed Greek god, then introduced the rest of the Greek god contingent.

"Dayne Andrews, FBI." Matt indicated the equally large man to her left with eyes so intensely green they reminded her of raw emeralds she'd once seen in a museum exhibit.

Dayne nodded but didn't smile, striking her as someone who said little, preferring to observe from the sidelines.

"Pleased to meet you."

"Eric Miller, ATF," Matt continued, and a Viking-size man with spiky blond hair and clear blue eyes held out a hand that engulfed hers twice over as he shook it. Trista could easily imagine him wearing a metal skullcap with horns sticking out of the top.

Matt moved on to the next man. "Kade Sampson, Homeland Security."

"Ma'am." A dark-haired man with hazel eyes smiled broadly, revealing two of the cutest dimples she'd ever seen grace such a chiseled face.

Next, Matt pointed to a man with reddish-brown hair and the most unusual obsidian eyes. "Markus York, Secret Service."

"Nice to meet you, ma'am." Markus winked at her, calling attention to the deep scar over his left eye, which was still red and puckered, as if it was a recent injury.

"And this"—Matt clapped his hand on the shoulder of the man who'd relinquished his stool to her—"is Jaime Pataglio, aka Romeo, for obvious reasons."

The comment had the men breaking into laughter. Even though she'd known them for a grand total of sixty seconds, their camaraderie was patently clear.

"I owe you an apology." Eric, the blond, blue-eyed ATF agent caught her gaze, his expression apologetic. "Sheba getting in was my fault. With the kennel being right next to the kitchen, she heard us and wouldn't stop whining to get in and see Matt. We had no idea Matt had brought a…guest."

As if on cue, a series of whines came from the other side of one of the kitchen doors.

"That's my girl." Matt gave a half smile.

"Just like a woman," Jaime said. "It's like they've got a sixth sense, always knowing you're talking about them behind their backs."

"Hey, Romeo." Kade nodded in her direction. "Be respectful of the lady present."

"My apologies." Jaime bowed to her so humbly she giggled.

"No apologies necessary," she assured him. "I guess I'll have to get used to all the manly banter, but I have to warn you, I have a pet peeve about the toilet seat being left up."

The men laughed, and she laughed with them. After everything she'd been through, it felt good to find humor in something. Then she caught Matt watching her through narrowed eyes. *He* wasn't laughing. *What was up with that?*

She held her arms out. "What?"

"Nothing." Although it didn't look like nothing to her. He looked pissed, and his friends had picked up on it, too. Half of them raised their eyebrows, while the other half looked like they were struggling not to snicker.

"We need to discuss procedure," Matt announced, sporting the scowl she was becoming accustomed to. He slapped a small pad and pen on the counter in front of her. "While we talk, make a list of what you want me to pick up in town, and call ahead for a new set of glasses or contact lenses. I'll pick that up, too."

"Okay." She reached for the everything bagel that had been calling her name for the past few minutes, then tore off a small piece and popped it into her mouth. Chewing, she asked, "C-can't I just go with you? How will you know wh-what size clothes to get?"

His gaze did a leisurely sweep of her body, starting at her neck, then progressing slowly to her bare feet then back up, lingering on her breasts. The heat in his dark eyes set her skin on fire, and she nearly choked on the bagel in her mouth.

"Get a room," Dayne said, rolling his beautiful green eyes.

"Think we should give them some privacy?" Kade whispered, grinning so broadly his dimples looked even deeper.

"Nah." Jaime snickered. "This, I wanna see."

She felt her skin flush at the implication that her and Matt's relationship was—or would ever be—intimate.

Matt's lips compressed into a tight line. "I'll take an educated guess. Write while I talk."

"Yes, sir." She gave him a mock salute, then set to work making her list, relieved to have something else to do besides face him.

"I've explained to everyone what went down this week and the presumption that this has something to do with the Russians. If I have to leave the property, one of them will always be with you." He paused to look around the table at each of his friends, who nodded. "Starting Monday, each of them is assigned to one of the many pre-election protective details around the Capitol. As for you, the only thing you have to do is to keep your head down. Don't tell anyone where you are. Don't call your friends, and don't check your email. If one of us tells you to hit the ground, you hit it and don't get up until you're given the all-clear. Got it?"

"G-got it." She bit off another piece of bagel, wishing like hell she didn't stammer so much around Matt. It either didn't bother his friends or they were too polite to say anything.

"I'll stop by the police station to get their report on the fire, then call my office to see if there's anything new we should be aware of. After that, I'll shop for your things. I'll be gone a few hours."

"No problem. We got this, Matt." Jaime put his arm around her shoulders, and Matt's gaze instantly went hard. "She's in good hands. And we'll take Sheba out with Hugo. You know how she loves my big guy."

Matt clenched his square jaw, staring at Jaime until the other man let his arm drop from her shoulders. "Good deal, then." Matt grabbed a split bagel, slathered it with cream cheese, then pointed to her list. "Done with that?"

Nodding, she tore it from the pad and handed it to him.

"Keep an eye on her, guys." Then he was gone, slamming the door shut behind him. A moment later, a truck's engine started, followed by the receding sound of Matt driving off.

"Well, damn, little pixie." Kade again grinned at her. "What'd you do to get ole Matt so worked up?"

As she reached for the tub of cream cheese, she raised her brows. "Worked up?"

Markus, who'd been silently watching them all up until then, snorted. "When Jaime put his arm around you, I thought Matt would deck him."

"Why would he do that?" She slathered her bagel halves with a generous amount of cream cheese.

"Lady," Nick said, uttering a low laugh in that smooth baritone of his. "That's something the two of you need to figure out." He went to the refrigerator, grabbed a six-pack, then pulled out a River Horse and handed it to her. "Gotta have beer with poker."

"Me? Play poker? I don't know how." Having grown up with almost no friends, except for her fellow computer geeks, there hadn't been much playtime in her life.

"Not a problem." Eric was already shuffling a deck of cards, and the other men were pulling bills from their wallets. "We'll teach you."

Trista took a bite of her bagel and swallowed. "Guys, I don't have any cash. Except for my cat, everything I own burned in the fire."

"I'll spot you."

Dayne handed her twenty bucks, and before she knew it, they were dealing her in and she was quickly learning how to play poker for the first time in her life. And she was also unexpectedly enjoying herself, feeling at ease with the men around her. They didn't make her hot and edgy, the way Matt did. More importantly, when she spoke with them, she didn't stammer a single word.

Chapter Fourteen

Nearly three hours after he'd left, Matt pulled into his driveway. He'd spent an extra twenty minutes taking a circuitous route home, repeatedly checking for a tail. Luckily, there'd been none.

He could still use a few more hours of shut-eye to make him human again. Trista's screams had shocked him out of some seriously needed REM sleep.

He'd jumped from the bed, grabbing his gun, prepared to throw himself between her and the threat. Hell, he remembered vividly how hard his heart was pumping as he'd yanked open his door to see Sheba standing on Trista's bed, her sleek, brown-and-black body wriggling with glee. Understanding immediately why Trista had screamed, he'd nearly passed out with relief. And then she was in his arms.

Her body was warm and curvy, her skin soft as velvet, her full breasts pushing against his chest as she'd clung to him with her arms wrapped around his neck. Only now did he fully appreciate the stupidity of holding her like that far longer than he should have. His brain kept telling him to let her go, but he couldn't because he liked holding her too fucking much.

Shutting off the engine, he remained in the truck, sitting with his forearm draped over the wheel, struggling with his new reality. Being around her was totally screwing with his brain.

Before he'd left the house, the urge to wrench his friend's arm from Trista's shoulders hit him with such force he'd been taken aback. The only recourse he'd had was to bolt out of there and simmer the fuck down.

His stomach growled, and when he glanced at his watch, he understood why. It was nearly seven p.m. The guys had better have some of those strip steaks on the grill.

Grabbing the bottle from the liquor store, two large department store bags chock-full of female stuff, cat food, and kitty litter, he barely managed to tuck the police report he'd picked up from Jake under his arm. It turned out Solonik really was sloppy. With all the evidence he'd left behind, there was no way in hell that fire could have been deemed anything but arson.

He kicked the door to his truck shut, and when he was still a good ten feet from the kitchen door, a burst of laughter came from inside. Female *and* male laughter, and lots of it.

A spurt of jealousy blew through him. *Why doesn't she laugh like that around me?*

Because you haven't given her a reason to, moron.

And just like that, he realized he *wanted* her to share that part of herself with him. The part that was happy he was there with her and wanted him to know it. *Was she?* Damned if he knew. Frowning, he managed to open the door and was met by a series of greetings.

"Mattie!" Jaime shouted.

"'Bout time you got your ass back here." Nick tilted a beer bottle to his lips and took a long swig. "This pixie is about to wipe us off the table."

Matt set everything he was carrying on the floor and stared. Trista and his friends were seated around the table, playing blackjack. Each had a beer in front of them, although from the looks of hers, she hadn't really touched it. His friends each had a couple dollars left in front of them, but Trista's pile of cash had to be nearly a hundred bucks.

"I'm out," Dayne said, flicking his cards across the table at Nick, who'd dealt the last round.

"Shit." Markus smacked his cards on the table in defeat, his obsidian eyes casting a dumbfounded look in Trista's direction.

"How does she *do* that?" With his big, beefy hands, Eric shoved his cards away.

"Hot damn," Trista exclaimed with glee, grinning as she leaned forward and, using her hands as shovels, gathered the cash in with the rest of her winnings. "Now I can buy myself something pretty."

The men laughed again at Trista's remark, another reminder that while he'd been gone running errands, they'd all been bonding and having a blast in his absence.

"You coulda warned us, Matt." Kade got up for another bottle of beer. "She's a ringer."

"I think she's counting cards," Nick said.

Trista gasped. "I was *not* counting cards. At least, I don't think so. Come to think of it, I don't really know what card counting is. It's illegal, isn't it?" Wide-eyed, she looked to each man at the table, then to Matt.

"Then how'd you do it?" Matt asked, filling a glass with ice water.

"Well," she said, arranging her cash into neat stacks. "After they taught me the basics, I approached the game analytically. It seemed logical to start keeping track of the cards being played in order to estimate the chances of hitting it big later. I'm good at memorizing things. I almost have a photographic memory."

"And?" Matt prodded, then took a long gulp of water. Curiosity was eating at him. He really did want to hear how she'd managed to beat six of the best card sharks he'd ever played with.

"And," she continued, scrunching her face as if she was only now realizing the tactics she'd employed to whip their butts. "I keep a running tally in my head of all the high and low cards. That way I can bet more with less risk, thereby minimizing my losses when I've been dealt an unfavorable hand."

Matt nearly snorted the water he'd been drinking. "That's *exactly* what card counting is."

"Oh, no." Her frown deepened, and her face fell. "I'm so sorry. I've heard of card counting, of course, but since I don't gamble, I guess I never really knew what it entailed. You should take this back." She looked to each of his friends and began handing them cash from her winnings pile. "I swear I didn't know what I was doing."

Not one man accepted the money she held out to them.

"Keep it." Nick crossed his arms, his thick biceps and forearms rippling with muscle. "You earned it fair and square, and you need it right now more than any of us."

"Thank you," she replied in a reluctant tone.

"Here." Matt plunked the bottle he'd gotten her into the center of the table.

She gave him a megawatt smile that did something weird to his heart. "Dalwhinnie," she cried.

"Pixie girl," Nick said, "I never woulda figured you for a Scotch drinker."

"There's a lot you don't know about me." Making quick work of peeling the plastic wrapper off the top of the bottle, she uncorked the Scotch and held it under her nose, closing her eyes and inhaling deeply. "Mmm," she moaned. "I love that smell. Honey. Vanilla. Spices."

"I think the lady's in love, Romeo," Kade said to Jaime. "And not with you."

"Pooh on you." Jaime gave Kade a look of mock annoyance.

Pooh on you? Shit. Now Trista has my friends talking non-trash, too? I'm in an alternate reality.

"At least I have money to pay for all this now." She glanced at the bags on the floor.

"I won't take a dime from you." Matt set down his glass, then picked up one of the bags and held it out to her. "Clothes, shoes, toiletries, disposable contact lenses. There's kitty litter and cat food over there." He indicated the other bag he'd set on the floor in the corner of the kitchen.

Slowly, she rose from the table and took the bag. "If you w-won't take my money, how c-can I repay you?"

Kade and Dayne snorted. From the corner of his eye, Matt caught Nick raising his brows. One sharp look from him and they all shut up. "Make yourselves useful by lighting that grill out back and getting some steaks going."

As a unit, they rose, pulled steaks, corn, potatoes, and squash from the refrigerator, and disappeared outside. Almost immediately, a cacophony of barking sounded from the kennels. Turning back to Trista, Matt saw gratitude in her eyes, although he fully intended to extract a price. It just wouldn't be what his friends' lascivious minds had been conjuring up.

To answer her question, he said, "I'll think of something. For now, get dressed, then meet me in my office." He canted his head to the kitchen door. "Down the hall to the left."

He watched her leave, then listened as she climbed the stairs. When he heard her door click shut, he went to his office and sat at his grandfather's enormous, inlaid leather-covered desk and powered up one of the many high-end computers and monitors.

When he'd set up the security system for his home and the new kennel, he installed top-of-the-line computers, alarms, monitors, and other hardware, although he'd been reluctant to wire the entire perimeter. If the funding he needed to get Jerry's Place up and running ever came through, the last thing he wanted was for the property to be a place of surveillance, one with Big Brother watching from every corner.

His plan was for a laid-back, camplike atmosphere, one that included a dog training curriculum and regular counseling sessions for kids with alcohol problems. The kids would be referred to Jerry's Place by juvenile court judges, probation officers, or even school guidance counselors. In addition to the counseling they'd receive, kids would work with and care for dogs Matt would rescue from local shelters.

Jerry's Place was intended to be a place of healing, learning, and peace. For kids *and* dogs in need. But reality was like a kick to his gut.

I'm the one who needs Jerry's Place most of all.

Deep down, he hoped it would be his salvation. His penance.

For killing his best friend.

Flicking on his monitoring station, he cued up the camera facing the road from his driveway, gratified not to see a single vehicle. Living where he did was another benefit for Jerry's Place. With most residents in the area coming from old, wealthy stock, each family still owned major hunks of land and hadn't sold off to developers. As a result, his neighborhood was peaceful, and any vehicles driving along the main road that didn't belong to one of his neighbors would stand out like a Belgian Malinois wearing a pink tutu. The image had him thinking of Tinkerbell, fairies, and pixies.

Speaking of pixies, it bugged the shit out of him that Nick

had called Trista a pixie. Christ, they'd *nicknamed* her. Three hours was all it had taken for her to tame the pants off six of the baddest, most kick-ass cops he'd ever worked with. Not that he wasn't glad she was settling in. He just wished she was more like that around *him*.

And why the fuck was he the only one she stammered around?

When she talked with his friends, Jake, and the paramedics, she hadn't done it once. Was she afraid of him? *Shit*. He didn't want that.

Shaking it off, he got online and began a search on all things Russian in the D.C. area. Twenty minutes later, he looked up to see Trista standing in the open doorway, holding a crystal glass of what he assumed was Dalwhinnie. Then he took in the rest of her, and swallowed. Hard.

She'd brushed her hair, which now curled around her face in thick waves of golden brown that reminded him of summer wheat in his neighbor's fields. Her face was devoid of makeup, but that didn't stop him from staring at her creamy skin, the becoming tint of red on her cheekbones, or lips that needed no help in appearing pink, rosy, and—*hell*—totally kissable.

Christ, he wanted her, but he couldn't have her. Ever. Not only was she under his protection, but he just couldn't go there.

The emerald-green short-sleeved V-neck shirt she wore was one of several he'd selected in different colors because he was clueless as to what colors she preferred. And he sure as hell didn't want to see her prancing around his house wearing any more of that mousy gray he hated. The shirt not only made her bright-green eyes even greener, it accentuated the lush curves of her breasts.

Had he gotten the shirt a size too small? He'd bought mediums, but maybe he'd been shopping in the teen department. Either way, he didn't give a fuck, because he loved what it did to her breasts.

Lastly, the boot-cut jeans he'd gotten her were slightly snug, and he loved that, too. The denim hugged her thighs, displaying just how shapely her legs were. She might be petite, but everything about her was perfectly proportioned. He was betting those jeans also hugged a cute ass, too. Seeing just how good she looked made him wonder if she'd discovered the green silk garment in the bottom of the bag or the matching undies. Yeah, that had been fun, shopping in the lingerie department for women's undergarments. He hoped she liked what he'd selected. Particularly the silver charm bracelet that, he noted with satisfaction, she wore around her left wrist.

Aside from the toe ring, he knew she didn't wear jewelry so the bracelet had been a risk, one that hadn't been completely altruistic.

A month ago, he'd ordered a tracker to hook on Sheba's collar, one he could link to a satellite in the event his dog was lost or stolen. Instead, he'd hooked it on the charm bracelet, figuring since it was also silver in color, it would blend in with the dangly heart, star, dragonfly, and other cutesy charms.

While he'd been ogling her assets, she'd walked up to his desk, trailing her fingers lovingly over his equipment, wearing an adorable look of wonder on her face, as if she'd just discovered the holy grail. Starting with his open laptop, she inspected his other two computers, the printers, scanners, and bank of monitors, touching every piece of hardware as if she were fondling a lover.

"Oh my." She smiled. "They're...beautiful. Why do you have all this?"

He laughed. So that's what it took to get her to smile at him? A bunch of inanimate hardware? Only a top-notch CIA analyst accustomed to operating the highest-end computers in the world would have such a complete appreciation of his operating system.

"Partly because my grandfather developed a fondness for technology late in life, and partly because of the plans I have for this place."

"Plans?" She leaned on the edge of his desk, swirling the ice cubes in her glass, making the charms on her bracelet jingle.

"Another time." Explaining would only make him start thinking about Jerry again, and there were more important things they had to discuss. He logged off the internet and pulled up a blank Word document. "Have a seat." He stood and indicated she should sit at his desk. After she did, he pushed in the rolling chair, noting her feet dangled a good three inches off the floor. "In as much detail as possible, type out what was said in that chat room, and who said it."

Swiveling the chair, she looked up at him. "You know I can't do that. It's beyond classified. It's ten levels above top secret."

"I don't give a shit." He grabbed the police report Jake had given him earlier and smacked it on the desk with enough force that she flinched. "Someone injected epoxy into your door locks and dead bolts, then glued all your windows shut so they wouldn't open. That same someone doused the inside of your house with kerosene. If by some miracle you escaped, I guarantee you he was out there waiting to finish the job he botched the other night. If Jake and I hadn't been there, he would have. That oughta shitcan any doubts you may have about the danger you're in. You were supposed to die in that fire. Do you know what happens to the human body when it burns?"

Without waiting for a response, he leaned in. "If you're lucky, you'll die of smoke inhalation before the flames get to you. If not, first your hair will burn off. Then the outer layers of your skin will start to fry and peel away. The pain will be excruciating, at least until your nerve endings are fried and you can't feel a damned thing."

He'd kept the inflection in his voice flat, devoid of emotion, but when he began envisioning what he'd just described happening to Trista, he lost it, and he couldn't stop his tone from hardening more. "Then your skin will shrink and split open. You might burn for as long as seven hours, but don't worry…" Leaning even closer, he planted his hands on the chair's armrests, caging her in, growling through gritted teeth. "You'll be dead long before then."

With his face so close to hers, barely a few inches away, he had an up close and personal view of the tears gathering in her eyes just before they tumbled down her cheeks. When her lips trembled, he felt like the biggest shithead on the planet, but he had a point to make.

Shit. He straightened, dragging a hand down his face, taking a deep breath to calm himself. "I called Langley while I was out, and those dickheads you work for still won't tell me anything. But they sure wanted to know where I'd stashed you. It pissed the fuckers off when I wouldn't tell them."

Matt laughed bitterly. "Eventually, they'll figure out I no longer live at the address listed in my personnel file. That won't stump them forever. Soon, they'll do a property search and find this place. For now, though, I'm keeping them in the dark." He rested a hand on her shoulder. "If I don't know everything there is to know about what's going on, I can't protect you. The time for secrecy is over. Understand?"

She sucked in a deep breath, her entire body trembling. The urge to take her in his arms and kiss away her fears blasted him from out of nowhere. Fighting that instinct, he straightened and stepped back. If he didn't put some space between them, he might very well lose the battle going on in his head and do something stupid. Like kiss her again.

"You okay?" he asked, gentling his tone.

Nodding, she swiped at the tears on her face and began typing. Matt stood over her shoulder, watching her fingers fly across the keyboard. Less than a minute passed, then she pushed the chair back so he could read what she'd typed.

Karakurt: *He is not who he says he is.*

White: *If this comes out, it will ruin everything. Who made the discovery?*

Banks: *A reporter. Thomas George.*

White: *Does anyone else know?*

Karakurt: *Aside from our own people, none.*

White: *He must be stopped before this information is released to the public.*

Banks: *Understood. Although, other matters are moving forward. I leave for Iqaluit in an hour.*

Karakurt: *I'll take care of it.*

White: *Good. Report in when—"*

"That's it?" He raised his brows.

She nodded. "Word for word. Photographic memory, remember?"

Then she looked up at him and gave him a smile, one of the few he'd gotten from her. *I'll take that.* "Can you identify who these people are?"

"Karakurt is the code name for Alexy Nikolaevich Lukashin. Officially, Lukashin is a cultural attaché to the Embassy of the Russian Federation in Washington, D.C. Unofficially, we—the CIA—know him to be the *rezidentura*, a legal resident spy."

"The others?" He pointed to the screen.

She shook her head. "I don't know. Everyone uses an alias, but I've been following Lukashin for so long, I know his code name. The other names I don't recognize."

"Lukashin referred to someone, although not by name." He reread what Trista had typed. "*He's not who he says he is*, and *if it comes out, it will ruin everything.* Do you know what he's talking about?"

"No idea." Again, she shook her head.

"Can you find Lukashin? Without letting it be known where you are?"

"Not without Dark Curtain."

"The hide-and-seek program you developed."

She uttered a feminine snort. "You *were* paying attention."

"It's my job. So let's try to figure this out with what we've got." He sat on the edge of the desk, angling the laptop so he could still see the screen. "Whoever White is, he seems to have authority over Lukashin, essentially ordering him to take care of the reporter, Thomas George."

"Banks, however," Trista interjected, "seems to answer to Lukashin."

"Agreed." He began massaging his chin, the side she *hadn't* kicked. "Iqaluit...don't know where it is, but I feel as if I've heard of it recently in the news. Is that an Inuit name?"

"That, I can answer." Her eyes sparkled as she opened a search engine and quickly pulled up a map of northern Canada and the surrounding Arctic Circle. "I was researching Iqaluit right before the fire. It's a tiny town by most standards, but the largest northern city in Canada. And," she added, zooming in, "it has an airport."

"Aside from the airport, there's not much up there." From what he could see on the map, the entire city was surrounded by absolutely nothing.

"Can I turn these on?" She pointed to the other two

monitors on his desk. "I want to show you the articles I found on Iqaluit."

When he nodded, she pushed the power buttons, and again, her fingers clicked on the keyboard with speed and expert precision. In seconds, a different article displayed on each of the three monitors. Resting a hand on the back of her chair, he leaned in and began reading. When she sat back, her thick, silky hair brushed against his fingers, making it tough as hell to concentrate.

Somehow he managed, and five minutes later, he'd read all three articles. "So there's a military power play at work here between the Russians and the Canadians. And the Canadians are scared the Russians will take over the shipping routes and control vast areas of untapped resources in the Arctic Circle. Iqaluit is where the Canadian government will meet to figure out how to thwart them."

"I'm impressed." Again, she smiled at him, and again, he liked it. *Too much.*

He slanted her a sarcastic look. "I did go to college."

"I never meant to imply you hadn't." She turned to face him full on, crossing her arms, plumping her breasts. "But not every college graduate can pick up on the subtle nuances of an international article with worldwide implications so quickly, let alone cut to the heart of the matter with such pinpoint accuracy." She scrunched her face, something he'd seen her do when she was pondering truly deep stuff. "What did you study in college?"

"Political science and law." With a few criminal justice classes on the side that he'd intentionally failed to mention to his father.

"Where did you get your degree?" she asked.

"Harvard."

"No shit." She clapped her hand over her mouth.

He snorted at her spontaneous curse word. She was

already getting the hang of it. "Try to contain your shock. Cops *can* read."

"I'm just surprised, that's all."

"Clearly." He scowled.

"How is it you wound up in law enforcement instead of practicing law?"

"Fate, I guess." And a life-altering event he wasn't prepared to share. "Sometimes life has a way of pointing us in the direction we were always meant to go, even if it wasn't where we thought we'd wind up."

Clear green eyes held his for several moments. "Sounds like there's a story there. Care to elaborate?"

"No." The word came from his mouth with more force than he intended. "We have more important matters to discuss than"—*my fucked up life*—"my past." Still, he'd enjoyed the spirited banter, finding she was easy to talk to and smart as a whip. Not that he was surprised. And she hadn't even noticed that she'd just had an entire conversation with him without stammering once. "This reporter, Thomas George. Did you get around to researching him yet?"

"No. I didn't get the chance before the fire, and after that, I assumed my boss would assign someone to contact him." She frowned, and a look of worry came to her eyes. "Do you think he really did?"

"He'd be stupid not to. Someone tried to kill *you* just for overhearing that chat, and the wording indicates George knows something critical enough that Lukashin's boss ordered him *stopped*." He hooked his fingers into quotation marks as he said the last word. "I'd say Thomas George was on their hit list before you ever made the top ten." Which presented one helluva dilemma.

As a sworn police officer, Matt was ethically and duty-bound to protect someone if he thought their life was in danger. But this was a CIA matter, and like Trista, he wasn't an operative. Sure, he had most of the training and skills, but that didn't classify him as a field agent. Regardless, he couldn't stand by and do nothing. What's more, he couldn't shake the feeling that Trista's boss was hiding something, and not just because Matt didn't have clearance.

He opened the desk's side drawer and pulled out a cell phone, handing it to her. "This is a burner phone. Unlisted and untraceable. Call your boss and ask him if he had someone call that reporter or notify the local PD that there might be a hit on him. Put the call on speakerphone but don't tell him I'm here. If he asks where you are, don't tell him."

Hesitating for only a moment, she stood and dialed, putting the call on speaker.

"Hello," a voice Matt recognized as Wayne Gurgas answered.

"Wayne, it's Trista."

A lengthy pause followed before Gurgas replied, "Why are you calling?"

Odd, Matt thought, surprised he hadn't asked Trista how she was doing, what with nearly being murdered in a fire less than twenty-four hours ago.

"I've been thinking," she answered, looking at Matt. "I'm worried about that reporter. Thomas George. Did you or someone else call him or notify the police that he might be in danger?"

"For Christ's sake, Trista. This is classified information you're discussing over an open line." There was another pause, then a door slammed shut in the background. "I told you to stay out of this."

"So you did warn him?" she asked.

"I've had someone trying to reach George for days. Don't worry, we'll take care of him." Another pause, this one lengthier. "Where are you staying?"

Matt shook his head, re-emphasizing his warning.

"Someplace safe." Her brows knit together, and it was obvious she was just as suspicious of Wayne's responses as he was.

Matt heard a *click* and grabbed the phone, ending the call.

"Oh my God." Her eyes went wide.

"Yeah." He powered off the phone. "He started to trace the call."

"Why would he do that?" She sank into the chair.

"I don't know." But he damned sure wanted to find out where she was.

While Matt had been out, he'd also called Buck. His boss had informed him that Gurgas had changed his mind, wanting to put Trista in a safe house of the CIA's choosing. Something had niggled at Buck, and his boss had refused. From Buck's description, Gurgas had gotten severely hot under the collar, trying to pull rank. Buck stood his ground and eventually Gurgas backed down. For the moment, anyway. Although Buck suspected he hadn't heard the last of Gurgas and ordered Matt to stay far away from Langley.

"I wonder if he really has someone checking up on George?" She began tapping her fingers on the desk, then looked up at him. "Even if I can find Thomas George, it would be an operative's job to contact him."

"Do you see any operatives around here?"

Grinning, she turned back to the computer and began clicking away. The speed with which she pulled up one database after another was nothing short of amazing. She really was a computer prodigy. A brainiac. Most computer geeks he'd met were just that. Geeks. She, on the other hand, was one *hot* geek.

In less than three minutes, she had a home address, phone number, and employer information. Thomas George was a freelance investigative reporter who wrote a lot of articles for the *Arlington Sentinel*. George lived in Charlotte, North Carolina, a six-hour drive from Langley.

Using the burner phone, he called George and left a message on the man's voicemail urgently requesting a callback. He debated calling the Charlotte police, but not having any contacts in that department meant he had no assurances they'd take him seriously. Besides, word might get back to Langley that a CIA K-9 officer was snooping around, way off his turf.

"Dinner's up," Nick's deep voice came from the kitchen.

"Go ahead," he said to Trista. "I'll be there in a minute."

She grabbed her empty glass and left his office. Staring at the monitors, he reprocessed everything he'd learned today and was just as disturbed by it the second go-around.

The same instincts that had kept him alive in the Middle East during his stint with the Marines, and later with the Alexandria PD, were screaming out a warning to him as surely as if it were painted on the side of a patrol car. Something was very wrong inside Langley.

And Trista still had a bull's-eye on her forehead.

Chapter Fifteen

For the tenth time that morning, Trista yawned. It was seven a.m., but despite going to bed at ten, she was still wiped out. All because of what she'd discovered in the bottom of the bag.

After slipping on the sexy emerald-green silk nightie Matt had bought for her, she'd run her hands down her body, luxuriating in the sensual slide of the slinky material over her skin. Then she'd imagined the feel of *his* hands doing the same, and from that moment on, sleep had been slow to come. In fact, she'd tossed and turned half the night.

What was he thinking, buying me that?

Although, she was glad he had. She'd never slept in anything so pretty. Even the charm bracelet had been a welcome surprise, and she'd fallen asleep wearing that, too. She didn't wear jewelry—her toe ring being the only exception—but for some reason, she *loved* the silver bracelet.

"C'mon, Poofy." The Angora mewed, circling her legs, rubbing his head against the back of her calf. With Matt's promise to keep the house canine-free, Poofy now had the run of the place, and that suited them both fine.

At the bottom of the stairs, she and Poofy paused at the sound of men's laughter coming from the kitchen. Last night had been fun. The poker part, anyway. The part where Matt had scared the shit—*er, pooh*—out of her with his description of human charred flesh, not so much. But working with him to reason out what was going on with the CIA and the Russians had been enlightening. Matt was intelligent and quick-witted, and she admired his dedication to his job. Hopefully, that reporter would get back to him today. She'd feel better if she didn't have to worry about the man's safety.

"Morning, pixie girl." Nick vacated his kitchen stool, motioning for her to sit.

Jaime poured coffee into a travel mug and handed it to her, along with the milk carton.

She accepted the mug and poured in a hefty amount of milk. "Where's everyone else?"

"In the kennel." Nick tipped his head. "Matt's outside."

Capping her coffee, she took a sip, realizing how nice it was to feel comfortable socializing with people. Such a simple thing had always been a major challenge for her. Bonnie and Kevin were the only constants in her social circle. Getting nicknamed "Brainiac" early on in life hadn't exactly garnered her many friends. No, she much preferred being called "pixie." Especially by a group of handsome, hunky men.

Why is that?

Her social abilities were definitely evolving since she'd begun staying with Matt and his friends. The stammering thing—even around Matt—seemed to be getting better as well. During their conversation yesterday in his office, she hadn't stammered once. Although, she had to admit, they'd focused on work matters, an area of her life in which she was totally confident. It was the personal stuff that got her all tongue-twisted.

As Jaime poured himself a cup, she noticed both men were drinking from earthenware mugs. "Why do I get a travel mug?" She lifted the silver cup with the black rubber grip.

"Matt's orders." Nick ushered her from the stool toward the back door, opening it. "You guys got a date. Outside."

Before stepping out, she looked from Nick to Jaime, sensing something was afoot as they both averted their gaze.

"Matt forbade me to go outside." She narrowed her eyes at them.

"Not in the front of the house facing the road. But you can go into the backyard if one of us is with you at all times." Nick gently shoved her out the door.

"Hey! Wait, I—" But the door had already shut behind her.

Taking a deep breath, she stepped onto the grass, inhaling the crisp morning air. The weather was finally beginning to cool off, but it was still comfortable. This was her first real look at Matt's property, and what she saw amazed her.

Some of the lushest, greenest grass she'd ever seen blanketed at least several acres stretching out before her. Surrounding the manicured field were thick stands of evergreens mingled with tall oak trees, the leaves on which were just beginning to turn shades of yellow. The center of the field was dotted with an assortment of ladders, ramps, hurdles, stacked drums, and cinder blocks. On one side of the field, separate from the house, was another building with a sloped, red roof. A door opened, and Matt walked out and began striding toward the equipment, beckoning her to join him.

As she walked to meet him, sunlight glinted off his dark hair, and she wondered if it was as soft as it looked. With his cop haircut, it was short, but she'd bet she could run her fingers through the strands.

Even in something as simple as khakis and a dark-blue polo, the man was all business, but it wasn't just the clothes.

It was in his bearing and his overall demeanor. The man positively exuded confidence in everything he did. She really, *really* wished she possessed even a fraction of his self-assuredness.

"Morning." He smiled at her, but there was a mischievous glint in his eyes that made her suspicious. "Sleep okay?"

"Great, thanks." *Like shit. There goes my language.* When had that started? Probably after someone tried to murder her, twice, so she was entitled to a few curse words here and there.

"Liar." His gaze drilled into her as he gave her that classic interrogative-cop look she'd seen on too many TV shows. "I can see the dark circles under your eyes. Is the bed uncomfortable?"

"N-no."

"Is the guys' snoring keeping you up?"

"Um, n-no." *Shit.* The stammering thing wasn't going away after all.

His eyes narrowed, intensifying his cop look until she worried she'd unintentionally blurt out the truth. "Then what?"

I was thinking about you running your hands across my silk-covered skin, then—

"I was w-worried about that reporter," she lied again. "Has he returned your call?"

"No." Matt shook his head. "But it's only seven in the morning."

"What is all this?" In a desperate attempt to derail his interrogation, she swung her arm to encompass all the equipment.

He followed the direction of her arm. "It's a training facility. Or, at least, I hope it will be one day."

"For K-9s?" She should have realized it immediately.

He nodded. "Partly, yes. Since September 11 and all the

recent terrorist attacks around the world, there's a shortage of trained K-9s. I've been gathering the necessary equipment here and building a classroom in there." He indicated the red-roofed structure. "It's not quite finished. I still need AV equipment and a few other things. But I could use some grant money to finish it up."

"You said *partly* K-9s. What else d-do you plan to do here?"

"I want to help kids. Teens with alcohol problems."

Wow. She should have seen that coming. The other night at her house, when she'd offered him a drink and he declined, he'd said he hadn't had one since he was sixteen. There had to be a story there. Whatever it was, she'd bet her last USB drive it was something bad. "Does the place have a name?"

"Jerry's Place." His eyes softened, and it was obvious there was more behind him opening up this training facility than he was letting on. "After getting a grant, my goal is to get listed as an approved community service facility, so that when a juvenile offender is sentenced to community service, he or she can come here and work with the dogs. To start with, I'll select a few rescue dogs from local shelters so the kids can work with animals that need them as much as the kids need the dogs."

Pausing, he looked off in the distance. He seemed to be somewhere far, far away, seeing something she couldn't. Something that wasn't really there, of course. "Who's Jerry?" she asked.

"My best friend. Or, he was. Jerry would have loved this place." Turning back to her, his gaze was sober, and if his face hadn't been composed of all those hard, chiseled planes and angles, she'd say he looked sad. He took a deep breath. "Jerry and I were both crazy about dogs, but our parents would never let either of us have one of our own. They said we weren't responsible enough, so…"

"What did you do?" she asked softly.

He chuckled and looked away again. "What any kids who wanted a dog would do—prove our parents wrong. We did everything to show our folks we *were* mature enough to take on that responsibility. We both got every dog-walking job we could find after school and took care of neighbors' and friends' dogs while they were on vacation. But we never did manage to get our own."

His face went sober again. "Jerry died a long time ago, and this is the best way I could think of to remember him. Helping kids *and* dogs in need. Taking care of a dog and training one can give a kid a sense of purpose and responsibility."

"How did Jerry die?" she whispered, inherently sensing whatever had happened had left a painful mark on Matt's soul. Their gazes met, and she hoped he'd tell her. Thus far, she knew him solely as a cop and her protector, but now, she found herself wanting to know the man inside.

His eyes went hard. "In a fire."

"Oh God." No wonder he'd gotten in her face about what fire does to the human body. "Were you there?" She had a sick feeling in the pit of her stomach that he *had* been. *The scars on his hands and forearms.* Only now, she realized they were burn scars.

"Nice try, lady. Getting you out here isn't about me." The corners of his mouth lifted, instantly transforming his somber expression back to mischievous. If she didn't already think he was the handsomest man she'd ever met, she did now. *Holy shit.* Right then, she was practically bowled over by him. "It's about you."

Before she could react, he turned to the red-roofed building and whistled. To her horror, a dog—Sheba—launched through the open door.

For a millisecond, she froze. The signals from her brain warning her to flee weren't transmitting to her limbs. The travel mug slipped from her fingers to the grass. She began to shake, and her heart hammered against her ribs. "What are y-you d-doing?" As if her words broke the spell, she turned to run, but he caught her arm, pulling her to him, her back to his chest. "N-no! Let me g-go!"

As the dog's athletic gait quickly ate up the distance between them, Trista tried backing up, but that only pressed her deeper against Matt's enormous body, giving her a small measure of safety.

"Relax," he said against her ear. "I keep telling you she won't hurt you. You need to trust me on that."

Sucking in deep breaths, Trista's chest rose and fell as Sheba came closer. In two seconds, the dog would be on them. "P-please," she whimpered, her entire body shaking with fear. "D-don't do this."

Sheba neared them, her jaws open, her tongue lolling out the side of her mouth. Trista squeezed her eyes shut, tensing, waiting for those sharp canines to puncture her flesh.

"Open your eyes," Matt ordered softly.

Still tensing, her body against Matt's, she realized his arms were around her. More to the point, she was still alive. The dog hadn't attacked.

Grimacing, she opened her eyes to slits and held her breath. Two feet in front of her, Sheba stood, wagging her tail. The dog's jaws were open, but it was due to panting, from the effort of running across the field at breakneck speed. Not because she was about to attack.

"*Sedni*," Matt said, and the dog sat.

Sheba's amber-gold eyes glittered in the morning light, and if Trista could rid her mind of the certainty that the animal wanted to pounce and eat her for breakfast, she could swear the dog was…smiling.

"See?" Matt's breath was warm against her neck. "Give her a chance. She only wants to get to know you. It's in a dog's nature."

Sheba stretched out her neck, bringing those jaws closer, but all she did was sniff the air in Trista's direction. Those amber eyes stared at her, and she couldn't look away. Suddenly, the dog opened its jaws, and Trista twisted in Matt's arms, trying to get away. Now they were chest to chest. Without thinking, she threw her arms around his waist, clutching him to her.

"Honey, turn around."

Squeezing her eyes shut again, she shook her head. "N-no."

"Yes." He eased away from her, tipped up her chin with his forefinger, then kissed her.

With her eyes closed, she hadn't seen his mouth come down on hers, but when his lips met hers, she snapped open her eyes and jerked back. When she looked up, his lids had lowered, and his darkened eyes were totally focused on her mouth. Her own gaze sought out his lips, and her belly flip-flopped, as if a swarm of butterflies were scrambling to take flight inside. He stared at her an instant longer before exhaling a tight breath through his nose.

"You only did that to distract me. D-didn't you?" Because there could be no other possible explanation as to why he would kiss her. *Or is there?* Stupidly, she hoped so. Logically, she knew there wasn't. *Mantra. Remember your mantra.*

Giving her his typical scowl, he forced her to turn in his arms and face the dog again. Sheba still sat obediently at their feet, but now the animal was wriggling in place, her tail wagging harder, her face still sporting that imaginary smile.

"You can do this. Dogs are a miracle, and once you let them into your life, you'll wonder how you ever lived without them."

"I don't need a d-dog." Again, she shook her head. "I have Poofy."

When Matt chuckled, his chest vibrated against her back.

"It's not the same. Poofy's a great cat, but no cat in the world can provide you with the kind of steadfast companionship, loyalty, and protection a dog can. Think of it as broadening your horizons. Right, Sheba?"

Lifting her snout, Sheba opened her jaws and responded with a low howling, intermingled with guttural grunts and yips from low in her throat. It was almost as if the dog was talking. Trista had to admit it sounded kind of cute, especially coming from this dog in particular. Because like Matt, this dog was a cop.

Again, he chuckled, and she liked how it pushed the muscles of his broad chest against her back, making her feel safe and secure. "Do you trust me?"

"No." Although she really did.

"Reach out your hand. Let her smell you."

Trista swallowed, then took a deep breath and slowly stretched out her hand. Her fingers shook, and when Sheba leaned forward, the dog's nostrils flared as she smelled Trista's hand.

"Good. Now pet the top of her head. Stroke her ears. She loves that."

With her fingers still trembling, although not so much now, she petted the dog's head. The fur was softer than she expected, and warm. Beneath her hand, Sheba blinked, looking up at her. Winking.

Sheba's body wriggled in a way that even Trista understood was sheer delight. The dog pushed her head more firmly against her hand.

"She wants you to stroke her ears," Matt said. "Do it."

Obeying, she eased her hand higher, delighted to discover the short, dark-brown fur covering the animal's ears to be even softer than that on her head. Keeping her snout closed, Sheba moaned, letting her know she liked having her ears massaged.

For several minutes, she quietly stroked and petted the dog, and before she knew it, she was using both hands, reveling not only in the feel of the beautiful coat beneath her fingertips but in the dog's obvious appreciation of her attention.

The more she touched Sheba, the more the dog wanted. As soon as she stopped petting her, Sheba nuzzled her hand with unexpected gentleness, yowling until Trista started the process all over again. And throughout it all, her tail never stopped wagging.

"You are beautiful," she whispered when Sheba stood and began pirouetting in front of her, practically dancing.

The dog's ears pricked up, and she gave Trista a light lick on the back of her hand. When Trista giggled, Sheba made a series of yipping sounds so similar to human laughter, it made Trista smile. The dog sat back on her haunches, lifting her paw and holding it in midair. Instinctively, Trista reached out and took the paw, as if shaking hands.

"*Lehni*," Matt ordered, and Sheba lay down on the grass.

"Is that Czech?" she asked, fairly certain it was.

"Yes." He nodded. "Sheba is a Belgian Malinois. The breed is originally from Belgium, but she was born in the Czech Republic. She received her initial training there. After the agency bought her, it was easier to keep talking Czech to her than to have her relearn another language."

"Fascinating." And it was. She knew next to nothing about dogs. "I had assumed she was a German shepherd."

"A lot of people think that." Matt knelt beside the dog and began stroking its back. In response, Sheba nuzzled his arm. "Malinois resemble German shepherds, but most are ten to twenty pounds lighter, and with much shorter hair. They were originally bred to be herding dogs, although their temperament and abilities make them perfect for police and military work."

"Why's that?" She was suddenly interested in learning

more about Sheba's breed.

"They're intelligent, athletic, intensely protective, and trainable. Not to mention," he added with a laugh as Sheba licked him enthusiastically on the chin, "highly energetic, and eager to please their handlers."

"How much does a Czech-comprehending Belgian Malinois cost?"

"It varies. Sheba cost about ten grand."

"Holy shit! Who knew?" She shook her head, amazed, not only at the price tag but that she'd ever be this comfortable around a dog. Glancing down at Matt, she smiled and he returned it with a rare one of his own. And just as it had when he'd dropped that peck of a kiss on her lips, her belly flip-flopped all over again.

He nodded to Sheba. "Look what you've done to my dog. Turned her into a worthless, wriggling blob of fur."

Turning back to the dog, Trista laughed. Sheba lay on her back, kicking all four paws into the air. Hesitantly, Trista kneeled a solid foot away from her and reached out to rub her soft belly. One of Sheba's hind legs began kicking furiously, and Trista twisted away to avoid getting poked in the eye by a flailing, furry paw and landed on her butt in the grass. Sheba lay on her belly, creeping closer and closer, then gently rested her head in Trista's lap.

Without lifting her head, Sheba looked up at her and blinked. Resting her hand on the dog's silky ears, Trista realized that in the midst of all the horrible things crashing down on her, a miracle had just taken place.

After spending a lifetime believing that all canines were the devil reincarnate, she now saw that she'd been wrong. She was well on her way to conquering her biggest childhood fear.

And she had Matt to thank for it.

Chapter Sixteen

Matt found Trista right where he expected. Seated at his desk, her fingers dancing across the keyboard. Again he noted she wore the charm bracelet, which jingled as she clicked away.

He leaned against the doorjamb, being careful not to make any noise. Watching her had become one of his favorite things to do. From where he stood, he couldn't see what she was searching for, but she kept pecking away at the keyboard, looking awfully cute engulfed in his big leather desk chair with her lips pursed. Incredibly *kissable* lips.

Distracting her had been his goal in kissing her, and it had worked.

Liar. You kissed her because you damn well fucking wanted to. Again.

He'd just gotten off the phone with Buck, who had no new information. After bumping it up the chain, Trista's bosses still refused to turn over any new intelligence on whatever was really going on. They knew damned well what was behind the attacks and that pissed him off big time. What could be so important that they'd risk Trista's life?

By kicking her out of Langley, they'd taken her out of the game. Perhaps that had been their goal. Either way, he didn't like being kept in the dark. If he was in the dark, he couldn't see it coming. Whatever *it* was, he'd be there for Trista.

Even if that meant taking a bullet for her.

The sight of Sheba stretched out on the floor next to Trista's chair made him feel good. He'd helped Trista overcome a fear that had been festering since she was a kid. Sheba flicked her ears, letting out a throaty, contented groan deep in her throat. Normally, his dog would be in the kennel this time of day, since he didn't want her going soft, but he'd made an exception so that Trista and Sheba could continue to bond. Even Poofy seemed to accept Sheba in his life. *Kinda.*

The Angora sat on top of the desk, hunched into a fluffy white ball. A look of wariness sharpened his blue eyes, but he appeared to be at least somewhat accepting of Sheba's presence in the room. It was as if Poofy and Sheba had formed a tentative truce.

That reporter still hadn't returned his call. Since he didn't trust Wayne Gurgas's word that the CIA was trying to reach Thomas George, he considered phoning the local PD to have them drive out and check on the guy in person.

Trista's fingers finally stilled as she intently read whatever article she'd pulled up. He took a few steps closer and froze. Every muscle in his body tightened as he read the familiar headline: LOCAL TEEN DIES IN FIRE.

Annoyance flared in his gut, and he balled his hands at the realization she'd cyberstalked him. The last thing he wanted was for her to learn about the absolute worst part of his life. Or discover that it was still an integral part of him, one that occasionally had him waking in the middle of the night drenched in sweat and shaking so violently his teeth chattered.

"Oh, Matt," she whispered, then covered her mouth with

her hand.

That did it. He could take her derision at what he'd done. Even her disgust. But he couldn't stand her pity.

"So now you know."

Whipping her head around, she gasped, her eyes glossy with unshed tears.

"Sheba, *kemne*." As he left the room, the dog scrambled to her feet, her nails clicking on the hardwood floor behind him.

"Matt," Trista called out. "Matt, wait!"

Ignoring her, he strode out the kitchen door into the backyard, grabbing a tennis ball from the grass. Whenever he thought of that horrific night twenty years ago, he felt trapped, and the only things that helped him get past it were fresh air and working with a dog.

Beside him, Sheba cavorted, excited at the prospect of playing fetch. Before the ball even left his hand, she bolted, running at breakneck speed. The ball landed about fifty yards in front of her. She gave chase, grabbed the ball in her jaws, then spun and bounded back in his direction. God, he loved watching her run. The animal was beauty and grace personified, and packed into the most amazing athletic body.

Dropping the ball at his feet, she wagged her tail, her entire body quivering with excitement as he picked it up and heaved it again. He'd known Trista was behind him, but he stiffened as she laid a hand on his back. It wasn't that her touch angered him. Hardly. It felt good, comforting, even, but he didn't deserve her touch, and he didn't deserve to be comforted.

Fuck. He *did* want her touch, wanted it badly and in every way possible. But not like this. He wanted to enjoy it without an ounce of guilt, and he doubted that could ever happen.

"Matt, I'm sorry." Her hand fell away. "I just wanted to know what happened. I didn't mean to make you angry."

In the distance, Sheba grabbed the ball and spun back toward them. "You have nothing to be sorry for. It's public information." Unable to bear the look of sympathy in her beautiful green eyes, he turned and strode toward the other building.

Sheba quickly caught up to him, but Trista was unable to keep pace. He flung open the door and Sheba bounded inside, dropping the ball on the floor and darting around the many desks and chairs, her tail in the air as she gave the place a thorough sniffing.

Hearing Trista's footfalls as she entered the classroom, he sat on the edge of a desk and crossed his arms, facing away from the door. The rage eating him up inside was directed at himself for fucking up his life. Knowing what she knew now, Trista would never look at him the same way. She would see him for the fuck-up that he was.

The asshole that had gotten his best friend killed.

She stood in front of him, silhouetted by the white instructional board on the wall behind her. Sheba padded to her side and sat, and for a split second, he wanted to laugh at how easily and naturally Trista dropped her hand to the dog's head, as if she'd been doing it all her life.

"I'm sorry." Her fingers absently stroked Sheba's ears, and the dog leaned into it. "I didn't mean to upset you."

"Forget it," he said. "You're an intelligence specialist. Looking shit up is what you do."

"You were just a boy." Her tone was so sympathetic it grated on his nerves. "So was Jerry."

"That doesn't excuse what I did." Unable to meet her gaze, he looked past her, focusing on the row of thick, padded bite suits hanging on the wall.

"It was an accident," she countered.

"It happened because we were drunk." Beneath his folded arms, he clenched his hands tighter. "We were two stupid kids, drunk off our asses and daring each other to do stupid things."

"Tell me." She took a step closer, and with him sitting and her standing, they were almost at eye level. "I'd like to know."

As he stared into her clear green eyes, the thick, hardened shell surrounding his past cracked wide open, and he wanted to tell her everything. *Why? Why her?* Never once had he told any of his girlfriends about what had happened. Not that she was his girlfriend. The answer to his question hit him with the force of a battering ram. He cared what she thought of him.

"Now I understand." She looked around the room. "Jerry's Place. What you're doing here is an incredible achievement. Not everyone could survive such a terrible accident and manage to create something so constructive and wonderful from it."

Gone was the sympathy in her tone, replaced by something equally annoying. Admiration. He was no one to be admired, that was for sure. She needed to hear it. *All* of it.

He took a deep breath, then held it a moment before letting it out. "It was Jerry's birthday, and we wanted to celebrate. We were sixteen but looked older. Old enough to have a set of pretty good fake IDs and buy a six-pack and a pint of Jack. We started out with the beer, then moved on to the hard stuff. That's when our brains went to shit."

Sensing his pain, Sheba inched forward to rest her head against his thigh.

"Jerry knew I wanted to be a cop," he continued, ashamed that he'd managed to fulfill his dream but his best friend hadn't. "He dared me to sneak into a police station and steal a uniform, so I did. Jerry told me he wanted to be a fireman, and I told him he couldn't put out a fire to save his own ass, let alone anyone else's. We relocated our drunk-fest to the nearest park, and the next thing I knew, he'd doused an old storage building with gasoline and lit it up."

Pausing, he ran a hand through his hair. Despite being totally plastered at the time, he could still recall the vivid images of what had happened next.

"Jerry was so plastered he didn't realize how much gas he'd doused himself with, and his clothes caught fire. His entire body burst into flames. I tried getting up, but I was so goddamn hammered myself I kept falling on my ass. When I finally got to him, I shoved him to the ground, trying to roll him and smother the flames, but it was too late. He died in the hospital, and it was my fault. *My fucking fault.* So don't admire me for erecting this place. I didn't do it because I'm a good person. I did it out of guilt."

But he still felt unworthy and probably always would.

Moving to stand between his parted legs, she cupped the side of his face. "It doesn't matter why you built Jerry's Place. What matters is that it's here, and soon it will be up and running, ready to help kids who need it. I don't need to tell you, you can't change the past. But you *can* change the future and make it better for others, which is exactly what you're doing." The hand against his face was cool and comforting. "Building this place was the easy part. Finding a way to live with the past is going to be a lot harder, but you have to try because it's eating you up inside. I'm guessing you don't think you deserve to be happy, but you do. Jerry wouldn't want you to suffer like this."

Matt gazed into her eyes, and for a moment, he could envision what it would be like to be happy again. As soon as he did, the image sparked and caught fire, burning to black ash. Closing his eyes, he exhaled through his mouth. The next thing he felt were Trista's arms around him, urging his head to rest in the crook of her neck.

One hand gently stroked the top of his head while her other massaged the tense muscles of his back. When she dropped a light kiss on his head, he wrapped his arms around her, spreading his legs wider so he could pull her slim body even closer. He breathed in the shampoo she'd used to wash her hair and the soap she'd undoubtedly rubbed over her smooth, soft skin. Her full breasts pushed against his chest, stirring an urgent need that zinged straight to his groin. But there was something deeper at work here. In the twenty years since Jerry's death, he'd never known a single moment of real peace, but he was finding it now. In her arms.

Taking a deep, shuddering breath, he sighed. And when she pulled back and gazed down at him with parted lips, he kissed her.

Slipping his tongue inside, he tasted her sweetness, savored it, craving more. Angling his head, he slanted his mouth, rubbing his lips gently across hers. Her fingers sifted through his hair, leaving a trail of tingles on his scalp that spread lower until he felt a discernible pressure against the zipper of his khakis.

Moaning lightly, she opened her mouth, urging him to deepen the kiss. Her tongue met his with an astounding expertise, swirling and tasting him as much as he'd tasted her.

He slid his hands lower, gripping her ass, hauling her against his now-full erection while he shifted his kisses to a sensitive spot just below her ear. When she arched her neck, the tops of her mounded breasts peaked out above the V-neck of her shirt.

It was a temptation he'd be a fool to resist.

Matt slipped his hand along her rib cage to caress one breast, then he slid his hand to her other breast, feeling her heart thudding wildly, matching the tempo of his own. In her eyes, he glimpsed pure, unabashed passion, and in that moment, he'd never wanted a woman more.

He bent his head, dropping kisses on the lush mounds, caressing both of her breasts before flicking at the hardened nipples with his thumbs. Vaguely, he heard another groan, this one canine as Sheba lay down on the hard concrete floor, clearly disappointed at no longer being the center of anyone's attention.

Just as he slipped one hand under her shirt, his cell phone rang. "Dammit." Now it was his turn to groan, as he reluctantly released Trista to tug the phone from his belt. It was Jake's name on the screen. "Hello," he heard himself growl.

"Hey, buddy," Jake said. "Sorry to bother you on a Sunday, but…"

Whatever Jake said next, Matt didn't hear, because Trista had her lips on his neck and was inching her way to his ear. When she got there, her tongue began doing amazing things, invading every groove with hot, wet heat and making the pressure between his legs grow to painful extremes.

Holy hell! Where did she learn to do that? He didn't really want to know because the idea of her doing it to anyone else had him gritting his teeth.

"Can you hear me?" Jake shouted in his ear.

"Uh, no." He reluctantly eased away from Trista, giving her a playful grin. "You must have blanked out for a second."

"I said, he's dead."

Matt stiffened. "*Who's* dead?"

"Viktor Solonik. The Russian who tried to kill Trista."

Chapter Seventeen

When Matt pulled his truck around to the back door, Nick helped her inside, handing up the overnight bag she'd quickly packed at Matt's direction. They were heading to Charlotte, North Carolina, a six-hour drive.

Early this morning, the man who'd tried to kill her—Viktor Solonik—had been found floating in the Potomac, his throat sliced. With the Russian thug dead, Matt had told her his theory that whoever was pulling the strings was tying up loose ends. Since Solonik had botched the job twice, the man had turned into a liability.

The reporter still hadn't returned Matt's calls, so they'd decided to take a road trip. Totally against CIA orders.

Sheba poked her head through the open window between the passenger compartment and the back of the truck. Lifting her hand to pet the dog's head, she realized the animal's presence was reassuring. Between Matt and Sheba, she felt very well-protected.

"I'll check in at six," Matt said to the other man.

"You sure you don't wanna leave her here with us?" Nick

gave Matt a cocky grin. "We love the pixie's company."

Matt scowled. "Not a chance in hell."

Nick threw his head back and laughed. "That's what I thought. But seriously..." His expression sobered. "Be careful."

"Will do."

"Thank you for taking care of Poofy while I'm gone," Trista said to Nick. "I left kibble and plenty of cans of wet food. He likes to be combed once a day, and—"

"Honey, I got this." Nick stretched a long muscled arm through the open passenger window and rested his hand on her shoulder. "I have the two-page instructions you left me. I'll take good care of him. It's only overnight. He'll be fine. I promise." Before removing his hand, he gave her a quick wink.

Glancing at Matt sitting beside her, she noticed his scowl had deepened. What was up with that?

"Later," Matt said as he cranked the gearshift and the truck began rolling along the grass back toward the driveway. "Stay down until we're on the main road."

She lay down on the bench seat with her head touching Matt's thigh. Something hard dug into her scalp, and she realized it was his gun hidden beneath his untucked shirt.

Directly above her, Sheba stretched her head down, the dog's black nostrils flaring as she sniffed the air above Trista's face.

Matt checked the rearview mirror more than once, and they weren't even on the highway yet. The look on his face was all cop. Funny, but she was getting used to it.

The muscles in his thigh bunched as he gunned the truck onto the road. From her position, she also had a mouth-watering view of his arms. As he turned the wheel, his biceps and the muscles in his forearms rippled and flexed, and she imagined running her fingers over all that firm, steely strength.

Even the scars didn't detract from his masculine beauty, although the way he'd gotten them certainly explained why he'd gone off on her about what fire could do to the human body.

Earlier, in the classroom when he'd kissed her, she'd only just begun to touch him. Even with all that coiled power, he'd been unexpectedly gentle. His lips had been soft, his fingers branding her skin, making her body quiver with anticipation of what it would be like to make love with this man.

"You can get up now."

When she did, he braked to a stop at a traffic light, then picked up his phone and hit redial. The reporter's voicemail picked up again, and Matt ended the call. When the light turned green, he gunned the truck toward the on-ramp.

"Maybe he's screening his calls," she suggested.

"Maybe." He glanced in his side-view mirror, then merged onto the highway.

"Let me try." She grabbed the phone and quickly hit redial before the phone locked up.

"Put it on speaker. If he answers, give me the phone."

After tapping the speaker symbol, the phone rang four times before Thomas George's recorded voicemail kicked in.

"This is Thomas George. I can't answer the phone right now. Please leave a message, and I'll get back to you."

A beep sounded, and for a moment Trista didn't say anything. Matt reached for the phone, but she swiveled in the seat so he couldn't reach it.

"Mr. George, my name is Trista Gold." Beside her, Matt shot her a dark scowl, his lips pressing into a hard line. To say he wasn't pleased that she'd identified herself was an understatement. *Too late now.* "I'm a CIA intelligence analyst at Langley, and there's something you should know. Someone tried to kill me because of something I discovered, and I think you might also be in danger. Please, when you get this message, call me back right away, and I'll explain more."

"Hello," a man's voice came from the phone.

Trista gripped the phone tighter. "Mr. George?"

"Yes," he answered. "What exactly do you want to explain?"

Matt gave her a quick nod.

"Part of my job entails monitoring online communications involving Russian operatives here in the U.S."

"What does that have to do with me?" George asked in a suspicious tone.

"I don't know," she answered truthfully. "You were mentioned in a black net chat room as having discovered something that could *ruin everything*." She emphasized the last words. "Does that mean anything to you?" Her question was met with silence. She waited several seconds longer, worried he'd hung up. "Mr. George, are you there?"

More silence, but shuffling sounds came through, telling her they were still connected.

"I'm worried for your safety," she continued. "These people are Russian operatives, and they said you had to be *taken care of*." Again, she emphasized the last words, hoping to get through to the man. "Are you working on a story that has something to do with the Russian government?"

"No," he answered immediately, followed by a lengthy pause. "But I *am* working on a story. Something big. Something *extraordinarily* big."

"What?" She glanced at Matt. His eyes were focused on the road, but she knew he was listening intently. "Mr. George, someone tried to kill me over this. Twice. We think you could be next."

An audible exhale came through the speaker, followed by more silence. "Not over the phone. I'll meet you in person, but come alone."

The truck's dashboard indicated it was eleven a.m., and

they had nearly six hours of driving ahead of them. "Five o'clock today? Your place?"

"No. There's a coffee shop on the corner of Central and Louise avenues. I'll meet you there."

"Be care—"

The phone beeped, indicating he'd hung up.

Unable to stop herself, she grinned and grabbed Matt's shoulder. His muscles were tense, the stark, savage beauty of his profile made more so by the clenching of his jaw.

When he glanced at her, his eyes blazed with anger. "Don't ever do that again."

"Do what?" She stared at him, wide-eyed and confused. "I just made contact with that reporter. Not even *you* managed that."

"That's not the point," he said, his jaw clenched. "You gave him your name after I expressly told you not to. We don't know what the hell is really going on here, and we don't know if this guy's phone is being monitored by the Russians, the CIA, or Bugs Bunny. You just identified yourself and announced to anyone listening exactly where you'll be at five o'clock."

His voice had risen to the point where he was yelling at her. Hearing the commotion, Sheba stuck her head through the window, and he reached out to stroke her ear.

Trista turned in the seat to face him, crossing her arms as her own temper rose. "Why are you so angry with me?"

"Because I—" He readjusted his hands on the wheel. When he spoke again, his voice was low and controlled. "I don't want anything to happen to you."

When he gave her a quick glance, the look in his eyes was tender and honest, diffusing her indignation. "Oh." Uncrossing her arms, she settled back against the seat.

What exactly did he mean by that?

He'd given her another passionate, toe-curling kiss, but

that didn't mean he truly cared about her. On a scale of one to ten, her experience with the opposite sex barely scored a two, but even she understood men had physical needs. Sexual needs they often satisfied without feeling an emotional bond with a woman. The statement he'd made about not wanting anything to happen to her could merely mean that it was his official duty to protect her. She was, after all, a CIA asset.

Having found that scratching Sheba's ears was soothing not only to the dog but to her as well, she reached out her hand, but her fingers never contacted the soft fur. Matt grabbed her hand, entwining their fingers and holding their linked hands on top of his thigh, something that had nothing to do with protecting her.

Immediately, her body heated and something deep in her womb contracted. She shivered. Matt's expression didn't change as he focused on the highway before them. Smiling, she reveled in the warmth of his fingers and the heat from his thigh. Uttering a contented sigh, she closed her eyes and fell asleep.

Chapter Eighteen

From beneath lowered lids, Matt adjusted the newspaper in his hands and slid his gaze from one side of the coffee shop to the other.

A few patrons lingered, drinking coffee, reading magazines, or chatting away across small, well-used wooden tables. Nothing was out of place, and there was no one around who tripped his bad-guy meter. Except for a couple of men ogling Trista. He still couldn't believe the flash of possessive irritation he'd experienced when Nick had leaned into the truck and touched Trista's shoulder.

While he knew none of his friends would ever hit on her, he knew they were attracted to her. *She* was the only one who didn't realize her hidden charms where men were concerned, something that was slowly driving him out of his mind with wanting her.

Sitting at a table on the opposite wall, she sipped a cup of coffee that had to be lukewarm by now, since they'd been there an hour.

Six o'clock. The reporter was a no-show.

He sent a quick text to Nick, updating him of the situation, then another to the burner phone he'd given Trista, telling her to meet him back at the truck. Remaining where he was, he waited until she read the text.

Before she had the chance to get up, he tossed the newspaper on the table and exited out the door. As he neared the truck, Sheba's brown-and-black muzzle stuck through the cracked window of the covered bed. Catching sight of him, the truck began rocking gently, showing the dog's eagerness to be let out and part of the action. Although tonight was a total bust thus far.

As he sat in the driver's seat, Sheba greeted him with a series of woofs and whines. They'd taken her for a short walk before going inside to meet the reporter, but she had to be hungry for the stash of kibble he'd brought along. A minute later, Trista joined them, and he nearly laughed at the irony.

Less than twenty-four hours earlier, she wouldn't have dared touch his dog, but as soon as she parked her butt on the passenger seat, she put her face right into Sheba's, allowing the dog to give her some serious licking.

"What now?" she asked.

"We call him." He picked up the burner phone from the console, then hit redial and put the call on speaker. The phone rang four times before going to voicemail. Without leaving a message, he ended the call. "Now we go to his house." He entered the reporter's address into his phone's navigation system, then pulled away from the curb.

Ten minutes later, he rolled past the address, a small white Colonial that had seen better days. The house was sorely in need of a paint job, and the foot-tall grass could use a hefty mowing.

"Hey, aren't you going to stop?" Trista gave him a questioning look.

"I'll park on the next block. I just wanted a look at the

place before we go in." And to check for vehicles parked out front. But there were none clearly associated with the address, and no garage in which a vehicle could be hidden.

He cut the engine, and Sheba let out a gruff *snort*, uncertain as to what was going down. "Patience, girl."

He leaned over to grab a leash from the glove compartment. "I want you to stay close behind me. Take this." He handed Trista the burner phone. "If everything goes to shit, call 911. Got it?"

She nodded, then swallowed. "Got it."

"Good." On impulse, he dropped a quick kiss on her lips and was rewarded with a smile that gave his insides an unexpected jolt. It felt good to make her smile, nearly as good as kissing her. And God help him, he wanted to kiss her all night long.

Outside the truck, he let down the tailgate, and as soon as he'd hooked the search harness and lead onto Sheba's collar, she leaped from the truck, excited as hell to be going to work. Working was like playtime for the dog. It was what she lived for. *That, and now for Trista's ear massages.* He'd have to keep a tight rein on that so his dog didn't go soft and get lazy.

"Let's go." Holding on to Sheba's leash with his left hand, he reached for Trista's hand with his right, coming to love the feel of her small fingers entwined with his.

Sensing where they were heading, Sheba led the way onto the sidewalk, then turned onto the walkway leading to the reporter's house.

At the front door he knocked, and when no one answered after a full ten more seconds he knocked again. Again, no answer. Releasing Trista's hand, he turned the knob. The door was unlocked, but he didn't push it open. Sheba tensed, her hind legs poised to catapult her inside the second he opened the door.

"Stay behind me," he reiterated, gratified when he felt

Trista's hand at the small of his back. He eased the door open, wincing as it creaked.

"Police K-9," he said in a raised voice as he crossed the threshold. "Mr. George?"

No one answered. The living room was empty. Of people, that was. Every surface was littered with books, magazines, and newspapers. Not unexpected for a man who made his living writing articles. A printer and a stack of white paper were visible on a small desk tucked under the stairwell. A loose cable from the printer dangled off the side of the desk. *No laptop,* he noted.

Sheba trotted briskly around the sofa and armchairs, ears erect. She sniffed the air and the floor, looking, listening, and smelling for signs of another human being in the house.

Matt cast a wary glance up the stairway, then over his shoulder at Trista to verify she was following him.

Sheba led them into the kitchen. A pizza box sat on an oak table, along with a dirty plate piled high with pizza crust. A can of coffee sat on the counter beside a coffeemaker. Matt touched his hand to the machine, which was cold. The door leading from the kitchen to a small, unkempt backyard was wide open. The yard was empty, save for weeds and overly tall, un-mowed grass.

"Where do you think he is?" Trista asked. "Do you think he left?"

Matt put his finger to his lips, indicating she should remain silent.

Sheba trotted from the kitchen back into the living room to continue searching for people. There was still no sound from anywhere in the house, but something wasn't right. Not only hadn't the reporter kept his appointment with them, but for a guy who was clearly suspicious, his house was wide open.

"Call him again," he whispered in Trista's ear. "Don't put it on speakerphone."

She pulled the phone from her back pocket and hit redial. A few seconds later, a phone rang somewhere upstairs.

A *thump* came from above them on the second floor. Sheba lowered her head and placed one paw on the bottom step. The only reason she didn't bound upstairs was that she was waiting for his command.

Hair on the back of Matt's neck prickled, and he yanked up the hem of his shirt, pulling his Glock from the holster. Beside him, Trista's eyes went wide.

"Get behind me," he whispered in her ear. "Stay close." He leaned down to the dog, again whispering. *"Revier."*

Sheba was so fired up for the search she practically pulled him up the stairs. Luckily, the carpet runner muffled his boots and her nails. At the top of the stairs, he pointed his gun in every direction, clearing the hallway. His heart thumped in a fast but controlled rhythm as his eyes darted in every direction.

The moment he unclipped Sheba's leash, the dog trotted into the first room. He and Trista followed closely behind, and Matt quickly determined the room was empty. They repeated the same procedure in the second bedroom, then Sheba picked up her pace, bolting toward the third open door at the end of the hallway. He knew the signs his dog was giving him.

Someone was in that room.

"Zustan," he whispered, and Sheba froze, her ears pricking into sharp points.

Matt pushed past Sheba and eased around the doorjamb. Before he'd even crossed the threshold, he smelled it.

Death.

He aimed his gun into the room. Sheba bounded in beside him, pausing briefly to sniff the man lying face down on the floor. No blood was visible, but he was dead just the same. Matt was sure of it.

Behind him, Trista gasped. Matt hazarded a glance at her. Her face had paled, and she held a hand tight to her mouth. Her shoulders began to heave, and he knew she was about to be sick.

She spun and darted out the door, her hand still over her mouth.

"Trista, no!" *Dammit.* He still wanted her to stick close.

In a powerful, athletic pirouette, Sheba spun and bolted into the bathroom, barking furiously. Her hind legs bunched, and she launched past the door. A strangled cry followed. From his position in the bedroom, Matt couldn't see what was happening yet, but he knew the audio cues.

Sheba had just bitten down on her quarry. Though she was trained not to inflict any major damage, a police dog's jaws clamped around a person's arm or leg was a terrifying thing.

"Call it off, call off your dog!" a panicked voice came from the bathroom.

Matt charge into the tiny master bathroom, aiming at the ground where Sheba did indeed have her jaws clamped around a man's upper arm. "Police!" he yelled, just as the man reached for the weapon holstered on his left side. "Don't move!" Matt shouted, and the man froze. "If you pull that gun, two things will happen. I'll shoot you, and my partner will rip you to shreds."

Now Matt's heart pounded. If the guy tried to shoot Sheba, he'd nail the fucker without hesitation.

The man's hand fell from the butt of the gun he was reaching for. When Sheba gave the arm clamped in her jaws another shake, he cried out again, louder this time.

"Stop fighting the dog," he ordered, and the man obeyed, his dark eyes wide with fear, his chest heaving. "Do exactly as I say, and do it slowly." The man nodded. "*Pust,*" he said to Sheba, and she released her grip and backed off, not letting the guy out of her sight. "Slowly, roll onto your stomach and interlock your hands behind your back."

The guy did as he commanded, and Matt quickly extracted the holstered gun, securing it behind his belt in the small of his own back, then patting the man down for additional weapons. Next, he backed away. "Roll over but stay on the floor and interlock your hands on top of your head again."

As he complied, Matt cast a quick glance behind him, worrying over where Trista had gone. A phone beeped, and he realized it came from beneath the dead body. Probably the cell phone he and Trista had just called, indicating an unanswered call had come in.

The guy in the bathroom wriggled backward to lean his head against the tiled wall. The movement had Sheba lunging to bite, uttering a deep, menacing growl in the back of her throat.

"Call your dog off!" The guy pressed farther back against the wall, his heels slipping on the floor as he tried pushing himself farther away in an effort to avoid Sheba's snapping jaws.

"Don't give me orders, asshole."

For a moment longer, Matt let him experience the terror of a K-9 in full-on attack mode. Not because he was a sadist but because he wanted to impress on the guy that both he *and* Sheba meant business. Not only did he still have his Glock trained on the guy's chest, but experience had shown him that even the most hardened criminals, ones who had no qualms about going hand to hand with a cop, backed down like a bunch of babies when confronted by a K-9.

"Okay, okay." The voice was pure American, not Russian, as Matt had expected.

Aside from the blooming shiner under his right eye, the guy was totally average in appearance. Average height, weight, and with brown hair and brown eyes. Even his clothes were un-noteworthy. Tan slacks, polo shirt, untucked short-sleeved overshirt to cover his gun. He dressed the same way a lot of plainclothes cops did.

"Make any quick moves, and I'll shoot you," Matt said with zero inflection in his voice.

"I'm CIA, dammit," the man growled, then thought better of it when Sheba upped his growl with a louder one of her own. "I said, call off the fucking dog. I'm on your side."

"That *fucking dog*," he snapped, "is *my* partner, and you'll treat her with the respect she deserves or I'd be more than happy to let her rip off your nuts with her bare teeth."

"My apologies, Sgt. Connors." A muscle in his face twitched as he warily eyed Sheba.

Matt narrowed his eyes. *He knows my name.* So maybe the guy was CIA after all. But he'd been hiding in a bathroom not ten feet away from the dead reporter. "Did you kill Thomas George?"

"No."

"Then what the fuck are you doing here?"

"I was ordered to check on him."

"Ordered by whom?"

He shook his head. "Can't say."

Not that Matt had expected the guy to give it up, but it had been worth a try. He assumed the order came from someone inside Trista's unit. Wayne Gurgas, most likely. "Using your right hand, pull out your creds and hold them out. Don't make any other moves." As an added warning, he subtly tipped his head to where Sheba stood bristling, her head lowered, eyeing the guy like she really did want to crunch down on his balls.

He reached awkwardly around to his rear pants pocket, extracting a black wallet that he held out to Matt.

Keeping his eyes *and* the muzzle of his Glock trained

dead center on the guy's chest, Matt picked up the creds and gave them a quick glance.

Mitchell Hentz. Central Intelligence Agency. An operative, no doubt. To all outward appearances, the creds appeared legitimate. He recognized the agency hologram, which was virtually impossible to replicate.

He threw the creds at Hentz's chest, then holstered his gun. "*Pozor.*" Sheba's body relaxed some as she shifted into guard mode. "When did you get here?"

"About fifteen minutes before you." Hentz reached down and pocketed his creds.

Matt was well aware that agency operatives were trained for all kinds of deception. Even so, he stared at Hentz, searching for signs of duplicity on his face and in his body language. But there were none. Besides, if Hentz had killed George, he wouldn't stick around.

Unless he was searching for something.

But the place hadn't been tossed. The reporter's laptop wasn't on his desk, but that didn't mean it wasn't in a drawer or a briefcase somewhere.

Where the hell is Trista?

Light footsteps sounded, and he readied his gun, uncertain of whom it was and hoping like hell it was Trista. He exhaled with relief when she burst back into the room. At the sight of George's body, she swallowed. "Is he really dead?"

"Looks that way." He nodded, returning his attention to Hentz.

The next thing he knew, Trista's arms went around Matt's midsection, and she pressed her body against his. "Thank goodness you're okay."

Still keeping an eye on Hentz, he wrapped an arm around her slim shoulders, surprised at the potent rush he experienced knowing she was worried about him. "We'll have to call the police," he said to Hentz, knowing the guy wouldn't like it and not giving a shit.

Hentz cleared his throat, an annoying smirk growing on his face. "Sorry to interrupt your little reunion, but if you're gonna call the cops, I need to be gone when they get here."

"Why's that?" Matt wanted to wipe the smirk off Hentz's face with his fist.

"Because I was never here, and if you're smart, the two of you were never here, either." He made a move to get up but jerked to stop when Sheba lowered her head and growled. He flinched, banging his head on the wall. "Sgt. Connors, I realize, as a uniformed officer, you're accustomed to responding to incidents with formalized police procedure, but try to understand the other side of the house. The world I work in is different. The world *she* works in is different." He indicated Trista. "It's gray because it has to be. I don't know exactly what you two stumbled into, but whatever it is, it's big and it's tied in with national security. Do you want to be responsible for fucking up our nation's safety?"

Matt carefully considered Hentz's words. He knew both CIA operatives and analysts worked behind the scenes and under the radar, but that didn't mean he could automatically let the man walk or that he'd lie to the local PD to cover for Hentz. But he did agree that he and Trista had stepped into something deep, dark, and dangerous. Add to that, something was sure as hell off with how Trista's supervisors were handling the entire situation.

He wasn't about to let this fucker go without asking a few more questions. "You said you didn't kill him and that you came to check on him." Matt nodded to George's body. "You also said you got here fifteen minutes before us. What have you been doing during that time?"

"Following orders," Hentz said. "Looking for his laptop and any other computer hardware and storage devices. Did either of you see any before you came up here?"

"No." Matt looked at Trista. She shook her head, but there was a subtle gleam in the way she was eyeing him, the same one he'd seen when she'd lied about filing her incident report. She'd found something and was keeping it to herself. *Atta girl.* "Do you know this guy? Says his name's Mitchell Hentz?"

"No." Again, she shook her head. "I've never seen him before, but I don't normally interact with operatives."

"How'd you get the shiner?" Matt asked, gesturing to the discoloration beneath the man's left eye.

"Got coldcocked the minute I stepped into the room." He touched a finger to his swelling eye. "When I came to, I was alone with a dead body."

That would explain the open kitchen door. When he and Trista arrived, they'd probably interrupted the other intruder, who'd escaped into the backyard.

Matt had been prepared to cuff the guy and arrest him as a material witness, but right now all he wanted was to separate Hentz from Trista and find out what she'd swiped. That, and there was logic in not calling the police right away.

The Russians could have connections anywhere, and the last thing he wanted was for Trista's name to come up in another police report, leaving a trail of bread crumbs for whoever was trying to kill her.

"Get out of here." He hooked a finger at the door.

Casting one last wary glance at Sheba, who sat panting with her tongue lolling out the side of her mouth, Hentz slowly got to his feet and held his hand out to Matt. Not to shake it, Matt understood. To retrieve his weapon. Reluctantly, he handed it over. "You're lucky I let you go without turning you over to the locals."

Pressing his lips into a firm line, Hentz made for the bedroom door with Matt following to verify he left the house.

On the way down the stairs, Hentz turned. "I'll have to tell them she was here." Then he was gone.

Matt returned to the bedroom and rested his fingers on George's carotid. He adjusted his fingers, still not feeling a pulse. The man was definitely deceased, but the cause of death eluded him.

Next, he hustled Trista down the stairs. "Did you touch anything down here?"

"N-no."

Again, he detected a faint note of deception, and it wasn't because she'd stammered her response. "You sure?" When she nodded, he hustled her out the front door, pausing to wipe the knob clean of his fingerprints with the hem of his shirt, then shutting the door behind them.

As they walked briskly to his truck, Hentz was nowhere in sight. After settling Sheba in the back, he opened the passenger door for Trista, then went around to his side and got in. Ten blocks away, he grabbed the burner phone from where Trista had dropped it in the console. He punched in 911, reported a disturbance—shouting—at Thomas George's address, then hung up without giving his name.

"Do you really believe Hentz didn't kill that reporter?" she asked.

He stared out the windshield for a moment, silently recounting everything Hentz had said and done. "I don't know for sure, but my gut says he's telling the truth." *Too bad they waited so long to check on the guy.* Then he pulled over onto the side of the road and held out his hand.

She raised her brows. "What?"

He let out an impatient breath. "I know you swiped something back there. Hand it over."

"How do you know that?" She crossed her arms, twisting on the seat to face him.

"I'm coming to know every expression on your beautiful

face. I know when you're lying, and you were definitely lying to Hentz."

Her jaw dropped, and she looked at him with something akin to shock. "You think I'm beautiful?"

"Very." He leaned in close, feathering his lips over hers. "You take my breath away." And he meant it. He took her mouth in a deep, wet kiss that lasted several long, sweet minutes. Then he reached behind her and tugged out a small external hard drive with a short USB cable that she'd tucked into the small of her back. "Where was it?"

She uttered an adorable little *huff* that made him want to start kissing her all over again, then to lay her out on the bench seat and strip off her clothes. Christ, he was hard as a rock.

"Taped to the underside of the big desk drawer."

"So you did touch something in the house." *Shit.*

"Worrywart." She rolled her eyes. "I didn't leave any fingerprints behind. Even when I went outside to puke, the door was still unlatched. All I had to do was shove it open with my forearm." Her eyes lit with excitement. "I hope you don't mind, but I grabbed your laptop and packed it in my bag. As soon as we get to the hotel, we can see what's on this little baby."

He should have known she wouldn't go anywhere without a computer. Truth was, he was happy she'd brought one. He was just as eager to discover what was on that hard drive as she was.

Matt looked in the side-view mirror, then pulled back onto the road. He had just broken so many rules of police procedure he'd lost count. But losing his job was the least of his worries. He could be charged with all kinds of shit. Tampering with a crime scene. Stealing evidence. Leaving the scene of a crime—a homicide, no less. The list went on and on.

What he *ought* to do was haul ass back to George's house to wait for the police and return the evidence, but the shit going down around Trista stank to high heaven, and it was getting deeper by the second. Keeping her off-radar was paramount. He didn't know where any of this was going, but the more time he spent with her, the more he understood one thing with unerring certainty.

For her, he'd do just about anything.

Chapter Nineteen

Trista tugged the thick robe around her silk nightie and got under the covers. The digital clock on the hotel's bedside table read nine p.m., and she was exhausted, yet sleep wouldn't come. Images of Thomas George's dead body kept flashing in her mind, making her tremble with anxiety. *Focus on something else.* Anything *else.*

An hour after leaving the reporter's house, they'd stopped at a deli for sandwiches, although she hadn't been able to eat much. Every time she'd taken a bite, her stomach roiled. Seeing a dead guy had totally taken away her appetite.

Before pulling in to a hotel, they'd found a dog park so Sheba could stretch her legs and do her stuff. Watching the K-9 interact with civilian dogs had been amusing and a welcome distraction from the ugliness of what she'd just seen. Sheba pranced, cavorted, and chased the other dogs as if she were a small child, leaving Trista wondering if the other dogs knew they were playing with a cop.

Despite the humorous thought, she doubted she'd ever forget that blank, dead stare in the reporter's eyes.

Giving up on sleep, Trista pulled Matt's laptop from the overnight bag he'd lent her, then lay back against the plush bed pillows, powered it up, and inserted the USB plug for the external hard drive she'd *borrowed*. As the icons began appearing on the screen, the shower in the bathroom came on, and she tried not to think about the pounding spray dribbling down Matt's bare shoulders and back, or his ripped abdomen. She swallowed, imagining where that trickling water would go as it headed south below his waist.

The TV droning on about the upcoming presidential election just over a month away was a welcome diversion from her wayward thoughts. A reporter detailed the many interviews and festivities both candidates would be attending, probably many of the events Matt's friends were detailed to for added security.

The bed started to shake as Sheba rested her head on the edge of the mattress, wagging her tail as she stared directly into Trista's eyes. She patted the dog's head, then clicked open the hard drive. Still the bed shook, and she looked down to see Sheba wagging her tail more forcefully, her entire body wriggling. She could no more ignore the dog's obvious plea than she could drive by a wholesale computer outlet store without stopping.

She patted the mattress once, and Sheba leaped effortlessly onto the bed with the grace and agility of a wolf crossed with a ballerina. After making three tight turns, the dog snuggled against her side with a satisfied *hmpf.*

At first, she'd been taken aback when Matt had gotten one room for both of them, insisting that it was the only way he could keep her safe. But as he'd grabbed their overnight bags and made a beeline for the shower, something warm and tingly settled deep inside her. With both Matt and Sheba on her side, she'd never felt more protected. Or cared for.

With one forearm resting on the dog's back, she began

clicking open file after file with the same irritating result. *Password-protected file. Enter password.*

For the next ten minutes, she struggled to find the password or a back door to get her into the files. At some point, she realized Sheba was snoring and the shower in the bathroom had been turned off. Granted, there were two queen-size beds in the room, but the idea of sleeping in the same room with Matt was…

Exciting.

But it shouldn't be.

Trista let her head fall back onto the bed pillows. *Okay, so he kissed me.* More than once, and not always a chaste, proper kiss. There'd been tongue. *Lots* of tongue, and she'd loved it. Loved what it did to her, how it made her body go warm and tingly in places that had *never* been warm and tingly. But that didn't mean *he* thought of her in that way. *Did it?*

He was there with her—in the same room—to protect her, not to make love to her. The thought of him holding her, stroking her naked body with those big hands, then entering her was both intoxicating and frightening.

The screen suddenly filled, and she bolted upright, upsetting Sheba, who jerked her head and took quick, snorting breaths.

"Sorry, girl. Easy there." She rested a hand on Sheba's belly until the dog calmed and lowered her head back to the mattress, seemingly satisfied there were no threats in the room.

I got in.

This file was a scanned copy of a newspaper article detailing a homicide in Ridgeway, West Virginia. William Sands, 25, was found dead in his house from a fatal stab wound. His wife, Erica Sands, and son, William Sands Jr., were missing. Mrs. Sands was wanted for questioning. The article was over forty years old.

"Interesting," she mumbled to herself, her heart beating a little faster as she used the same password to open up the next document, a police report, also forty years old. Some of the sections were redacted, completely obscured by thick black lines, but from what she could read, Sands had been found dead in his kitchen, lying in a pool of blood. The murder weapon, a large deer-gutting knife, had also been discovered. An all-points bulletin had been issued for Mrs. Sands and her son.

The next two files she cracked into were both West Virginia FOIA—Freedom of Information Act—requests, the second one specifically requesting the redacted portions of the Berkeley County Sheriff's Department report on the Sands murder.

For the next few minutes, she tried unsuccessfully to open another file, this one labeled *Article-Third Draft* and dated yesterday. But the password she'd used to open the other files wasn't working on this one.

Taking a break, she absently stroked Sheba's belly, smiling when the dog began kicking her hind legs in a jerky motion, tangling her paws in the bed's comforter.

"You are such a pretty girl."

Sheba opened her jaws. *Arrrr, arrrr, arrrr.*

"Yes, you are," she murmured, locking gazes with the dog's, giving her one more belly rub.

"What the *hell* are you doing?" Matt shouted.

"Nothing." Startled, she sat upright on the bed, as did Sheba. "What's wrong?"

"Sheba, *kemne!*" Matt pointed to the floor at his left side, and the dog bolted from the bed and sat obediently at his left side, leaning her head against his thigh, looking totally forlorn.

Trista guessed that by the heated tone in his voice, he was

berating Sheba for some doggie transgression, but she didn't really hear the words. How could she?

Though she'd seen him wearing nothing but jockey shorts before, her mouth went dry nonetheless. Sgt. Matt Connors stood before her wearing nothing more than low-slung jeans and a short towel draped around his neck.

He. Is. Beautiful.

Broad, thick shoulders tapered down to a slim, taut waist. Beads of water ran in rivulets through the grooves separating the six or eight or ten different packs of abdominal muscles. But it was the dark V of hair arrowing down from his abs to just above the button of his jeans that had her breath catching in her throat.

"Did you hear me?" He gripped both ends of the towel, his biceps flexing.

"Huh?" She shook her head to clear it of the X-rated thoughts racing through her mind. "What are you talking about?"

"My dog does *not* sleep on the bed."

Sheba looked up adoringly at Matt, who ignored her, his eyes blazing into Trista's. It was screamingly obvious all Sheba wanted was Matt's forgiveness, and it was breaking her heart when he didn't give it.

"Why not, Mr. Grumpy Pants?" Rising to her knees, she planted her fists on her hips. "She was keeping me company."

"She can just as easily keep you company if she's on the floor. *Lehni*," he said, and Sheba slunk to her belly, resting her muzzle between her front paws, still looking up at Matt with the saddest eyes she'd ever seen on a dog. Not that she'd ever been brave enough to look into a dog's eyes before Sheba. "I don't want her going soft. The last time I let her up on my bed, it threw her off her game for two weeks. Instead of working, all she wanted to do was lounge around and get tummy rubs all day."

"Don't be mad at her." She looked regretfully at Sheba. "It's my fault."

"Let me guess." He whipped the towel off his neck, exposing a set of gloriously pronounced pectorals. "She rested her head on the bed and looked up at you with those big eyes until you invited her. Trust me, I know all her tricks."

Sheba let out a breath that sounded more like a sad little whine.

Still, Matt scowled, looking all darkly handsome. "I can't believe you lifted my laptop. You're turning out to be quite the talented little thief. If this analyst thing doesn't work out for you, you might have a future as an operative."

"Hardly." She rolled her eyes, finally able to think straight. Although that tingling in her belly had her craving his lips on hers again. "Me without a laptop is like you without your gun, or Sheba. It would be like a part of you was missing. Wouldn't it?"

That got her a reluctant but agreeable grunt.

"Come see what I found." She opened several windows to show Matt the files she'd cracked into. "I've been trying to understand why George was so fascinated with a murder committed forty years ago in West Virginia. He even FOIA'd the police report, but parts of it were redacted."

When he sat on the edge of the mattress to get a better look at the screen, his arm and shoulder touched hers, and she regretted the thickness of the robe.

While Matt read the police report and the old news article, she inhaled the smell of soap, shampoo, and the musk of a half-naked man. A bead of water from his still-wet hair trickled down his neck, meandering in a fascinating line between his pectorals.

"I'll call the Berkeley County Sheriff's Department tomorrow. It's only a slight detour from our route home. I'll ask for the entire report. Maybe there's something interesting in the redacted portions."

"Will they really show you the whole report?" she asked. "If George had to FOIA it, won't we have to do the same?"

"I'll flash my badge and stroke the sheriff's ego. When feds and locals collide, that tact usually works best." His brows drew together in another scowl, but this one she'd come to decipher was his deep-in-thought scowl. "The question is, why would digging into a forty-year-old murder get the reporter killed?"

"We don't really know that's what happened," she said. "The chat room wording was that George knew something that would ruin everything if it came out."

"Can you open this one?" He pointed the cursor at the draft news article dated yesterday.

She frowned. "Not yet." Darn, she was better than that. By this point, she should have had it open, and a few others, too.

"You'll get it. I have complete faith in your clandestine file-cracking skills." He winked at her, and her belly fluttered.

Their attention was drawn to the TV, on which a color map of the Arctic Circle was displayed while an anchor for a political news show, Bob Foster, talked in the background. Small boxes on the upper part of the screen indicated Foster was posing his questions to both presidential candidates, Governor Thomas Hughes and Senator Michael Ashburn.

"Senator, Governor." Foster glanced at notes on his desk. "Both of you have previously vowed that, should you be elected president, you would dedicate U.S. funds to support Canada in rebuilding its military presence to counter any possible Russian incursion into the Arctic region." Both candidates nodded in unison. "But Senator Ashburn, last week you backed away from that promise. The Associated Press quoted you as saying, 'I plan to review the matter carefully and thoroughly before committing taxpayer dollars.' Senator, this is somewhat in opposition to your original commitment to support the Canadians in this effort. Why the change of heart?"

"Well, Bob, since I made that statement over a month ago, additional information has come to light that I was not previously aware of. I owe it to the American people to fully consider both sides of any international controversy that involves American troops and a significant amount of taxpayer money." Senator Ashburn smiled charmingly into the camera, playing on what Trista believed would probably win him a lot of female votes: his genuine smile.

"Recently," the senator continued, "the Russian Department of Geography and the Environment met with Canadian officials in Iqaluit and presented compelling evidence to suggest that the Arctic Ocean's resource-rich Lomonosov Ridge is part of the Asian continental shelf, which would give Russia primary control over most of the Arctic seafloor. Canada, however, still supports the theory that this ridge is an extension of the North American continental shelf, which would, instead, give Canada priority access to those resources. All I'm saying now is that before making a decision, I want to be as fully informed as possible."

"Thank you, Senator." Foster turned his attention to Governor Hughes. "Governor, does that change your position in the matter?"

"No, Bob. It doesn't." Governor Hughes shook his head. "I am just as committed to supporting our neighbors to the north as I was the first day I hit the campaign trail."

"Senator, Governor," Foster said, nodding to both candidates, "I know you both have extremely busy campaign schedules during the next month. I'd like to thank you for taking the time this evening to be on our show."

Matt killed the volume, and when he began tapping his fingers on his thigh, Trista suddenly noticed that he'd fully stretched out on her bed. That, and his dark brows were drawn together, his lips compressed into a thin line.

"You thinking what I'm thinking?" she asked. *Iqaluit.*

Turning onto his side to face her, he began absently stroking her bared thigh, sending fiery tendrils licking their way to her core. Beneath the thick robe, her nipples pebbled, and she shivered.

"What I'm thinking," he said, staring over her shoulder as if he didn't really see her, "is that for a tiny little town in one of the most remote and bitterly cold parts of the world, Iqaluit has become one hell of a burning hot topic. I find myself wondering why the Canadians, the Russians, *both* U.S. presidential candidates, *and* the *rezidentura* in a black net chat room can't seem to stop talking about it."

Trista nodded, urging him to continue, trying not to think about what his fingers were doing to her thigh.

"According to the chat," Matt continued, "George found out *someone* is 'not who he says he is,' and George had to be stopped before the public found out. Found out *what*, is the big question, along with who that other person in the chat room was that had to leave within the hour for Iqaluit. Then, a week after you overheard that conversation, George is murdered, and someone has tried to kill you twice."

As dire as their conversation was, Trista had difficulty keeping her head in the game. All she could think about was Matt's hand on her thigh. "We don't know what the reporter knew," she said, "but we do know he was on to a big story, which may or may not be connected to this forty-year-old murder he was researching."

"What we just heard about the Arctic could be totally unrelated," Matt said. "Still, we can't discount the possibility that this is all connected. But it's only a theory."

"Agreed." She appreciated how his sharp brain was totally tracking with her own thoughts. "Anything else?"

His fingers stilled on her thigh. His lips parted, his nostrils flaring right before he swallowed. "Yeah. We'd better get some sleep. We have an early wake-up call."

Without another word, he rose and killed the lights, then got into the other bed, still wearing his jeans. Disappointment flooded her. For a moment there, she thought—hoped—he'd kiss her again.

With a soft sigh, she closed the laptop and headed into the bathroom, stopping along the way to give Sheba a good-night pat on the head. Just before closing the door, she glanced over to see Matt lying on his side, facing the wall away from her bed. She quickly brushed her teeth, then splashed cold water on her face to cool her libido. After patting her face dry with a fluffy white towel, she opened the door and nearly screamed. She would have, but Matt wrapped his arms around her and covered her mouth with his.

His lips were soft, sliding gently back and forth across hers until she opened her mouth to him. He slipped his tongue inside, holding the back of her head. Warmth spread from where his fingers touched her scalp, all the way down her neck, to her breasts, and lower, until her insides clenched with anticipation. When he lifted his head, both their chests were heaving.

In the near darkness of the room, he gazed down at her, his dark eyes glowing from the flickering TV's light. "Trista." He cupped her face, skimming his thumb over her swollen lips. "You are truly beautiful, and sexy, and you're driving me up the fucking wall."

"N-no, I'm not." Although he certainly made her feel like she was.

To her chagrin, he chuckled. "You just spent the entire day with me and didn't stammer once. Why now?"

"I'm n-nervous." In reality, she was, but that wasn't why she'd begun stammering again. It was because she was coming to like him. *Really* like him, and that's what always happened whenever she liked a guy. With Matt, it was like that part of her went into hyperdrive.

She wanted him as she'd wanted no other man in her entire life.

"You've got nothing to be nervous about. Your body is a perfect, amazing little package waiting for me to unwrap it." He tugged on the belt holding her robe closed, then pushed it off her shoulders, letting it slide to the floor. His gaze lowered to her silk-covered breasts, his jaw clenching. "This nightie looks great on you. I knew it would."

Unable to wait a second longer for his touch, she gripped his wrists, placing his hands on her breasts. A muscle on the side of his face flexed as he held them in his incredibly large hands. Beneath the silky fabric, her nipples tightened, and he rubbed his flat palm over them, until they jutted sharply against the thin material.

Reaching around her, he slid his hand beneath her nightie to her buttocks, then picked her up, fastening his mouth over one nipple, catching it in his teeth. Instinctively, she wrapped her legs around his waist, arching backward, allowing him to bite at her other sensitized peak.

"I don't deserve you." His voice was husky with a definitive hint of self-reproach. "But I need to have you."

He carried her to the bed, lowering himself gently on top of her, taking some of his weight on his elbows. She tugged at his arms until he pressed fully on her, loving the feel of his bare chest against her.

"Honey, I'm going to crush you," he said with a note of worry in his voice.

In answer, she pulled his head down, and this time *she* took control of the kiss until they were both breathless, their chests heaving, his hands beneath her nightie, stroking her until she was writhing beneath him. She wanted more. She wanted him inside her, stroking her in her most private places.

She shoved her hands beneath the waistband of his jeans and under his tight jockey shorts, grabbing and kneading his taut buttocks, pressing him firmly against that part of her that craved him inside her.

He pulled her to a sitting position then peeled off her nightie, leaving her clad only in matching panties. In another moment, they were gone, too, pulled slowly down her legs as he stripped her bare. With heavy lids, his gaze roved her nakedness, his throat working. His hands came back to her breasts, stroking and massaging, until he lowered his head and sucked one nipple into his mouth.

A tight little moan escaped her lips as she held his head tighter to her breast. He shifted to her other nipple, plucking with his teeth, rolling it around with his tongue until she was moaning even louder.

His hand slid down her rib cage to between her thighs, urging her legs apart. As his finger penetrated her, she practically arched off the bed with a little scream that was swallowed up when he kissed her again. What he was doing to her…the incredible sensations…were like sparks exploding across every inch of her skin. She couldn't breathe, couldn't get close enough to him…

Slipping her hand between their bodies, she caressed his jean-clad erection, rubbing her hand up and down until he let out a harsh breath.

"Matt, please," she whispered against his neck.

He rose from the bed, and she watched, completely captivated as he stripped off his jeans and jockey shorts. His long, thick erection jutted proudly from between heavily muscled thighs, and for one panicky moment, she worried how he would fit inside her without splitting her in two. Taking a deep breath, she swallowed.

I want this. It's time. And he's the one.

She watched him grab a thin square packet from his overnight bag, rip it open, and deftly roll on a condom. He lowered on top of her, positioning his erection between her thighs, nudging gently at her opening.

Dragging her heels up and down the backs of his legs, her hands roved the broad expanse of his back, kneading and stroking the coiled muscles. She bit at his chest and was rewarded with a deep groan of pleasure.

"You are so damned sexy." He kissed her mouth. "You know just what to do to drive me absolutely crazy." His lips trailed down her chin to her neck as he palmed one of her full breasts. "Beautiful. I could spend all night feasting on these."

His words were like an injection of pure lust to her veins. Never before had she felt truly beautiful, but he made her believe it. Beneath his heated gaze and expert touch, her body responded in ways that both shocked and fascinated her.

Her skin was on fire. The craving deep inside her womb clenched with an unsatisfied need so powerful she thought she'd scream if he didn't take her right now.

She writhed against him, urging him to give her what she so desperately needed.

"You are so, so wet. I love it." He nudged his erection at her core, pushing gently, rocking into her until her tight walls began to relax.

Not enough.

Wrapping her legs tightly around his waist, she surged her hips upward while at the same time gripping his ass, pulling him fully inside her. She screamed in pain, although the moment was fleeting.

"What the *hell*?" He jerked his head up, his eyes burning brightly as his big body shook, and he quickly withdrew. "Trista!" Above her, his breath came in heavy gasps, warm against her face as he stared down at her. In his eyes were shock and regret.

"I'm sorry." Unable to meet his pained look a second longer, she covered her eyes. "I should have t-told you."

"Yeah, you should have." He tugged her hands from her eyes, but she squeezed them shut. "Look at me. *Look at me.*"

Reluctantly, she did, fearing what he would say.

I've ruined this. What was meant to be a special moment in my life, I've turned to shit. Shit, shit, shit.

"I'm no good at this." Hot tears pricked at her eyes, humiliation heating her cheeks. She shoved at his chest, but he didn't budge. "I was a thirty-three-year-old virgin, and I can see by the look on your face you're disgusted. Let me up."

"No, that's not it." He shook his head, his eyes filled with disbelief. "Honey, what I don't get is how? You are the sexiest woman I've ever been with. Your passion is so uninhibited it floors me. There is nothing about you that disgusts me. It's just the opposite. *Everything* about you turns me on like no one ever has. Do you hear me?"

She couldn't believe it, but there was such sincerity in his eyes. He turned onto his side, taking her with him. With gentle fingers, he wiped away her tears, then tipped her chin up with his forefinger. "Why haven't you ever made love before?"

Hesitating, she took a deep breath. He'd bared his soul, now it was time for her to reciprocate. "When I was five, my parents began to suspect my aptitude was off the charts. They took me to a facility that confirmed their suspicions. As a five-year-old, none of that meant anything to me until I started grade school."

"The other kids were intimidated by you." Matt's brows bunched as he scrutinized her intently.

"Understatement." Suddenly shy, she tugged the sheet up, intending to cover her breasts, but he stopped her.

"Too late for that now." He grinned. "I've already seen everything there is to see. Go on."

"It only worsened with time. In high school, it seemed like half the kids were mean, calling me a *brainiac*, a *geek*, or a *computer-head*. The other half wanted nothing to do with me. I never had any real friends until I was hired on with the agency."

"No boyfriends?"

"No, not really." She shook her head, dismally recalling the loneliness of her teenage years. "As soon as I met a boy I liked, I began to sta—" She clamped her mouth shut, pressing her lips together. Admitting to herself how much she liked Matt was one thing, but telling *him* was an entirely different matter. She wasn't ready for that.

"Stammer," he said, finishing her word for her. "So, you like me?" A boyish grin tipped the corners of his mouth as he began trailing a finger along her jawline.

She giggled. "Well, m-maybe a little."

"Just a little?" His grin widened.

When she punched his shoulder, his talented fingers instinctively found that ticklish spot on her waist, and she giggled louder, trying unsuccessfully to twist out of his grasp.

When he began caressing her breast, she leaned into his hand and held back a little moan. She loved how he touched her. How he kissed her and made her feel all tingly.

Matt pursed his lips and narrowed his eyes. "You didn't stammer once when you were talking to Jake Sorensen, or any of the guys back at the house. Does that mean you don't like them?"

"No, of course I like them." Point of fact, she thought they were terrific. "I just don't like them in that way."

"What way is that?" He pressed his lips to her neck.

As he began nibbling on her ear, she closed her eyes and shivered. "Like I want to tear off their clothes and jump their bones." Gasping, she snapped open her eyes. "Oh, shit. Did I really just say that?"

He laughed openly, something he rarely did and the sight of him enjoying a moment of unreserved happiness made her heart squeeze. She wanted him to experience more of that. Contrary to what he believed, he *did* deserve it.

"I love it when you go all truck driver on me. It turns me on." For a moment, they both laughed, then he stopped. "Why me?" he asked, sobering.

"Because I—" Because she didn't just *like* him. Even she knew the signs. *I'm falling in love with him.* But she couldn't say that. "Because I thought it was time, and I wanted you to be the one." *Not an outright lie. Just a shitload of omission.*

Matt brushed the backs of his knuckles down her cheek, then rolled her onto her back. "I'm honored you chose me to be your first." Then he kissed her deeply, settling between her thighs.

This time, when he entered her, there was no pain, only the smooth slide of him as he slipped inside her moist walls. Throughout it all, he kissed her, murmuring sexy words that once again had her writhing with pleasure, digging her nails into his back and shoulders, reveling in the flex and play of all those muscles as he rocked into her.

Pressure built in her womb, intensifying until she could no longer keep her eyes open. She gripped his ass, and with each stroke, pulled him in deeper. He picked up his pace, pumping faster, shoving them higher up on the mattress.

"Baby," he breathed against her ear. "Baby, let it go. Jesus, let it go."

Electric pulses shot from her belly outward, and she arched upward, crying out as the orgasm spiraled through her body. She clung to Matt as the aftershocks crashed over her, one after another until she was gasping for air.

With his arms wrapped around her back, he pushed deeper inside her and went rigid. He groaned, then spasmed against her.

They stayed that way, pressed together with him still inside her as their breathing slowed. Minutes later, he withdrew, then picked her up and carried her into the bathroom. He set her on her feet while he adjusted the shower spray, holding out his hand while she stepped in. Picking up a washcloth, he began gently washing away the thin smears of blood on her upper thighs, his muscles bunching and flexing as he washed her ever so gently. When he was finished, he proceeded to soap up and scrub her entire body clean.

Trista closed her eyes and held on to his waist for balance as she gave in to the sensation of his hands sliding over her slick skin and the heady emotions cradling her like a warm mist.

She was thirty-three, ancient for a virgin, and until now, it had been an embarrassment she'd kept to herself. But tonight...in the warmth of the shower and the safety of Matt's arms...she was glad she'd saved herself for someone special. And he *was* special. She knew that with every fiber of her being.

Just as she knew that with every moment she spent with him, she was falling more deeply, and more desperately, in love.

Chapter Twenty

Matt didn't know what woke him. The sound of Sheba's light snores on the floor beside the bed or Trista's warm, wispy breath against his neck.

She lay on her belly, snuggled against his side with her head on his shoulder and her arm draped across his chest. Strands of her thick, honey-blond hair tickled his chin, and he couldn't resist rubbing a few locks between his fingers.

Smiling to himself, he wanted to laugh. He was all but sandwiched by the two females in his life. Trista on the bed, Sheba beside them on the floor. After making love to Trista again, he'd fallen into such a deep, dreamless sleep, he hadn't heard Sheba get up to change locations.

Trista shifted, sliding her hand to his abdomen, making his cock begin to harden beneath the sheet. He wanted her again, but being that this was her first time, she'd be sore. He didn't want to hurt her.

Why she'd chosen him was something he couldn't wrap his brain around. He hadn't been kidding when he'd said he didn't deserve her, and he hadn't even known she was a virgin then. Finding out had not only shocked the hell out of him, it had humbled him. No other woman had ever made him feel special, but she had. Her virginity was a precious gift, one he would treasure for the rest of his life.

Making love to her had been mind-blowing. She'd surprised him with how sensual and instinctive she was. After showering, he'd let her explore his body with her hands, lips, teeth, and tongue, loving every moment. For a virgin, her inherent sense of just how to drive his body crazy with need was beyond amazing. Then it hit him. He was thirty-six years old, but he'd never really made love to a woman. *Until now.*

Over the years, he'd had lots of sex with lots of different women, some he'd even briefly referred to as his girlfriend, but with Trista, it was different. To her, he'd given more than just his body, although he didn't quite know what it was. All he knew was that last night, he'd wanted to go all out to make her feel good. Not that he hadn't made any of his previous sex partners feel good. From their responses, he definitely had, but with Trista, he'd gone way overboard, wanting to make her first time something she'd never forget. And afterward, he'd felt something more. Something he'd never truly felt with a woman.

Contentment and…happiness.

He was falling for her. This little pixie draped over his chest had begun to dig her way into his heart. He couldn't deny it, and he couldn't allow it. Nothing had changed.

I don't deserve to be happy.

Fuck, will I ever get past that?

For the first time in his adult life, he considered finding the answer to that question. *Not anytime soon.* Not with the annual banquet commemorating Jerry's death coming up in a couple months.

After his best friend's death, Jerry's parents had created a foundation that donated money to a different worthy charity every year. Ironically, he'd just gotten his nonprofit community service status and was now eligible to receive charitable donations for Jerry's Place. A moot point, since Jerry's parents would never consider giving his place a dime.

Mr. and Mrs. Wilshire never pushed for a criminal investigation, nor had they come after his family for any civil responsibility. But Matt hadn't had any contact with his friend's family in twenty years—since the day of Jerry's funeral. And given the family's state of shock, even that contact had been minimal.

He knew it was a lame excuse, but confronting the demons of his past would have to wait. Protecting Trista and finding out what the hell was going on were his priorities. No way in hell would he let anything happen to her.

Trista let out a sleepy sigh and stretched, her arm slipping lower to rest on his upper thigh. Before she could fully wake, he slipped from the bed, carefully stepping over Sheba.

"What time is it?" She rested on her forearms, her full breasts mounding on the mattress.

He resisted the urge to slide back into bed and hit the repeat button. "Time to get up."

When she pushed to her knees and held out her hand, the sheet fell away, revealing her perfect, naked body. "Come back to bed. Just for a little while."

The corners of her mouth lifted into a sleepy smile that did something to his heart, threatening his resolve. "I'd love to, honey." *That was the honest-to-God truth.* "But we've got another stop to make before we head home, and I've gotta take a shower." *Alone.*

Even if moments earlier he'd been contemplating carrying her in there with him again so he could personally see to it that her soft breasts, firm buttocks, and every other inch of her body was clean.

As he turned to head into the bathroom, he caught the

unmistakable confusion in her eyes, and it about killed him. He knew what she wanted, and part of him—the resistant side of him that needed something more than to meander through life alone—wanted it, too. *More than anything.*

Turning back to her, he slowly shook his head. "I'm sorry, honey. I just need..." Fuck, he probably shouldn't say it, but lying to her or leading her on would be worse. "Distance."

As soon as he spoke that one damned word, he instantly regretted it. The confused look in Trista's eyes had changed to one of blatant pain. Coward that he was, Matt padded into the bathroom and shut the door. Moments later, he was beneath the pounding spray of the shower, resting his palms flat against the tile wall.

I really am fucked up.

Worse, he hated himself that much more for hurting Trista.

By the time he'd gotten dressed, she was bundled up in a bathrobe, waiting for her turn in the shower. The hurt he'd seen earlier had morphed into anger. He could see it in the green flash of her eyes and the tightness of her lips. "Tris, wait." He made a move to grab her arm, but when she shrugged from his grasp, he let her go, feeling more and more shitty with each passing second.

The bathroom door shut—no, *slammed*—in his face. Sheba raised her head, looking alternately from him to the bathroom door, as if to say, *Are you two fighting?*

Exhaling, he sat on the bed. Sheba came over and rested her muzzle on his thigh, looking up at him with big, sympathetic eyes. Even his dog knew something was wrong.

Thirty minutes later, they were on the road to the sheriff's department in West Virginia. The space between them on the seat was wide, both figuratively and literally. Trista sat hunched against the door, staring straight ahead with her arms crossed. Mile after mile, her silent treatment had been killing him. He wanted to punch out a window.

Finally, when he couldn't take it a minute longer, he pulled into a highway rest stop and parked. "Trista." She wouldn't even look at him. He unbuckled his seat belt, leaned over to undo hers, and easily tugged her to his side.

"Hey!" She pushed at his chest, but he held her tight. "You don't get to touch me again."

He snorted. "The hell I don't." The idea of never touching her again...*not gonna happen.* Leaning over, he cupped her face and kissed her. Not a quick peck, but not the way he wanted to kiss her, either, since she refused to open her mouth.

"Let me go!" She pushed at his chest, and he complied. Reluctantly.

She glared up at him. "I gave you my virginity, and what do you do the morning after? Behave like a goddamn teenager and run away with your tail between your legs." She smacked her hand against her forehead. "I feel like a naive fool, which is exactly what I am. Well, I'm a fast learner, Sgt. Connors. You want distance? You got it."

Jesus, I asked for this.

With an angry *hmph*, she scooted back to her side of the truck and rebuckled her seat belt.

He dragged a hand through his hair. "I'm sorry. I've just got a lot on my mind, and I couldn't handle it."

"Handle *what*?" While she glared up at him, he was reminded again of just how petite she was. But right now, he felt like a pussycat facing down a lion. *More like a pussy.*

"You. I couldn't handle *you*." Somehow he'd missed it. His tentative, shy little pixie had morphed into a goddamn force to be reckoned with, and he admired that she hadn't hesitated to call him out on his shit. If she wasn't so pissed at him already, he would have smiled. "I never expected this to happen between us."

"But it did," she countered. "And now you're too much

of a chickenshit to deal with it. You're really a cold bastard."

True. Bull's-eye on both counts.

Other women had accused him of being cold, but he'd never cared before. With Trista, he cared. He had no fucking clue where, if anywhere, this was going between them. He only knew he cared what she thought of him.

"You can't have it both ways." She shook her head. "You don't get to make love to me, then walk away as if I don't mean anything, only to change your mind the next time the wind blows and you want to get laid again."

This time, she clapped a hand over her mouth, widening her eyes as if she couldn't believe she'd really just said that.

"You're right. I'm sorry. You have every right to be pissed." He gripped the steering wheel and stared out the windshield. He'd already told her about Jerry, but he hadn't told her everything. "There are still things you don't know about me."

"Then tell me." Her voice had gentled, giving him the courage to go on.

"I—" *Can't.* He couldn't tell her he was broken, that he could never be the man to make her happy, to make her dreams come true. Fuck, he wanted to. But how could he ever make someone else happy, when he was incapable of experiencing true joy himself? Anytime he did, the guilt was overwhelming. He'd even thought about eating his own gun.

"Don't shut me out," she said, her voice still gentle, yet now firm with conviction. "Apparently you can make love one minute, then shut out everyone around you. I don't operate like that. If you can't accept whatever it is I feel for you, or you don't want it, I'll ask for another officer to protect me."

Anger boiled inside him, and he turned on her. "Forget it. That's not gonna happen." She was his to protect, and he'd see this thing through to the end. That, and there was no way in hell he'd ever turn her over to someone else's care. *She's mine.*

The thought had him wondering exactly what he meant. *Was she his to protect? Or just plain* his.

"It *will* happen if I want it to. I can't make love with you one minute, then be cast aside the next." Her voice was choked with emotion, telling him how badly he'd hurt her. "If you want to walk away, then do it. Maybe I was stupid, thinking one night with a man meant something, but I can see by your complete lack of response, it doesn't. You've taught me a good lesson. Now that I've had sex, I want more. I'd rather have it with you, but if you don't want me, then I'll find someone else."

"Over my dead body!" He slammed the inside of the door with his fist, welcoming the pain shooting up his arm. Jealousy pounded his brain at the thought of another man touching her. He'd been her first, and the idea of not being her last filled him with an unexpected surge of rage for whoever that nameless, faceless son of a bitch would be.

"Then talk to me, dammit." Now it was her turn to punch something, although she wisely chose the considerably softer seat cushion. "What the hell is going on with you?"

Unable to look at her, he let his head fall back against the headrest. He paused a moment longer until his pulse slowed and he stopped feeling like he wanted to murder all of Trista's future lovers. He wasn't prepared to tell her everything. *Yet.* But he could be honest about what had been bothering him lately.

"There's a banquet in a couple months," he said quietly. "It's a fundraiser Jerry's parents hold every year, partly to honor their son's memory and partly to raise funds, which they later donate to a worthy charity in his name. They always send me an invitation, but I've never gone. I haven't seen his parents since the funeral. Hell, I've barely seen my own parents since I got back from the Middle East."

"Why don't you go this year?" she asked. "Maybe it's time. It might help you."

He raked his fingers through his hair. "I don't think I can. Aside from the funeral, I've never been able to face them." When he glanced at her, the sympathetic look in her eyes bothered him. "I'm not telling you this because I want your pity. I'm telling you because thinking about Jerry still tears me up inside. Whenever this time of year rolls around, it fucks with my head and I can't think straight."

"And this morning when you woke up, you thought of Jerry. You couldn't stand being in bed with me enjoying yourself, so you bolted."

Bingo. And that was about all he was prepared to divulge at the moment.

"We need to go." He cranked the gearshift and slammed his foot on the accelerator as he headed the truck back onto the highway.

"You need to get help, Matt. *Professional* help."

"Cops don't talk to shrinks." Although he'd thought about it a few times over the years.

"Why not?"

"It just isn't done." Archaic though it was, consulting a shrink was considered a stigma in the world of law enforcement. A weakness that could call into question his abilities to carry a firearm.

For a long moment, she didn't respond. When she did, her words were low and gentle. "You're killing yourself from the inside out."

He'd known that for years. He didn't need a psychiatrist to psychoanalyze that out of him. What was different now was the rising futility of it all. Of his whole life and what was left of it. If he didn't do something soon, he feared the worst would happen.

He'd be completely dead inside.

Chapter Twenty-One

Four hours later, they were seated in Sheriff Tulane Underwood's office at the Berkeley County Sheriff's Department in West Virginia. Trista was amazed at the speed with which everyone jumped to Matt's command once he flashed his CIA badge and requested to see the sheriff. Despite the emotional chasm that he'd erected between them, she liked how he'd introduced her as "my colleague."

"My secretary should have the file you're looking for in a few minutes," Sheriff Underwood smiled, revealing a number of crooked teeth.

Even though he was seated behind a ginormous wooden desk, in an oversize, squeaky antique leather chair that had seen better days, the man made an obvious effort to straighten to his full height. Still, he was nowhere near as tall or big as Matt, and that probably annoyed him, considering they were on his turf.

"Thank you, Sheriff." Matt gave the other man a deferential nod. "We surely do appreciate your assistance with this. We're hoping with your knowledge and extensive experience in this community, you'll be able to shed some light on this murder."

Trista stifled a laugh at how quickly Sheriff Underwood puffed up his chest, clearly drowning in Matt's flattery. Matt sure knew how to work the man.

"Always happy to help out the CIA any way I can." He leaned his forearms on the desk, clasping his hands.

"Always?" she asked. "Have there been others inquiring about matters within your jurisdiction?"

"Yes, ma'am." He nodded. "Quite a few. First, there was a reporter from the *Sentinel* who FOIA'd the file, then wanted the redacted parts, which we refused to provide. This case may be old, but since there's no statute of limitations on murder, it's still an open case, and we treat it as such. No critical evidence will be provided to the public, even under FOIA rules."

"You said a few." Matt narrowed his eyes. "Who else was asking about this case lately?"

"After the reporter, another one of your CIA colleagues— Hentz—was here demanding the original file and ordering me not to make any copies before I handed it over. Pompous little prick."

At the sheriff's reference to Mitchell Hentz, Trista and Matt exchanged glances.

Sheriff Underwood coughed. "'Scuse my language, ma'am, but he wasn't nearly as respectful as you two are."

Matt leaned forward. "I don't understand something. If this is still an unsolved murder case, how could you hand over your original file? As you said, the case may be old, but it's still an open case that could be opened at any time. Theoretically, anyway."

"Well, the agent had a forthwith subpoena with an addendum attached that strictly forbade making copies prior to surrendering the originals. Something about national security being at risk. How a forty-year-old murder could ever compromise national security, I can't fathom."

Now Matt was scowling outright, and she knew precisely why. Shortly after the end of World War II, the National Security Act of 1947 established the CIA to coordinate the nation's intelligence activities. But the act strictly stated that the CIA would have no law enforcement powers or internal security functions, so as not to conflict with the FBI's domestic enforcement authority. While Trista had never been an operative, even she knew what that meant.

The CIA had no subpoena powers. Whatever document Hentz had given Sheriff Underwood was total bullshit. Then again, Underwood didn't seem that gullible.

"This pompous little prick," Matt said. "Did he have company when he slapped that subpoena on you?"

"He sure did." Underwood nodded. "An FBI agent was with him. Special Agent Max Fenway."

"So the subpoena was issued by the Department of Justice and served by the FBI agent?" Matt asked.

"Precisely." Underwood nodded. "They seemed to be in cahoots."

Catching the sheriff's eye, Trista smiled. "Presumably, since your secretary is retrieving the file as we speak, you accidentally failed to comply with the addendum order not to make copies."

Underwood leaned back in his chair, crossing his arms behind his head and smiling smugly. "You are correct, ma'am. Dunno how that happened, but it did."

"Can't say I blame you," Matt agreed, a corner of his mouth lifting.

The sheriff frowned. "After those two federal guys, I had another guy asking about this case. A Russian."

Trista sat up straighter. "Who?"

"He never said."

"Did you give him any part of the file?" Matt asked.

"Hell no." Underwood grimaced. "Kicked him out on his Ruskie ass."

A plump woman wearing far too much pink lipstick entered the office and handed a manila folder to the sheriff. "Here ya go, sheriff."

"Thank you, Millie." Underwood winked at his secretary, then handed the folder to Matt. "There are two copies in there for you. Nothing redacted. This homicide occurred long before my time in office, but everyone around here remembers it, including me. A murder in these parts is big news."

"You're giving these to us?" Matt gave the sheriff a look of disbelief. "Without a subpoena?"

"Not exactly." Underwood grinned slyly. "Officially, I'd need that subpoena. But if I happened to leave these reports on my desk, it might take me days before I noticed one of them was gone."

Trista raised a brow. "And why would you be willing to do that?"

He paused, pursing his lips for a moment. "Something's going on here with this case, that much is obvious. If you or your colleagues can help me solve a murder—even a forty-year-old one—I'd be grateful. You see, I'm up for re-election in a few months."

Matt snorted. "And working closely with the feds to solve a cold case would boost your ratings."

"That it would." Underwood leaned back in his chair, smiling.

Matt handed Trista one of the copies. "Care to give us a briefing? Again, with your local expertise, that would be helpful."

She continued to admire the smooth way Matt worked the sheriff. Seemed like all Underwood wanted was mutual

respect from his fellow law enforcement officers, and both
Hentz and the FBI agent clearly hadn't picked up on that.
And, of course, he wanted to be re-elected.

"Will Sands was a mean son of a bitch. Bad temper.
Constantly in and out of jail for stupid stuff. I don't know
why that nice girl, Erica, married him in the first place. We
all figured it was because she got pregnant. Little Billy Jr. was
born seven months after the wedding."

Trista looked up from reading. "How old was the boy
when his father was murdered?"

"About eight. Nice kid. Smart, too. Got good grades,
respected his elders. Everyone had high hopes that Billy
would turn into something a whole lot better than his POS
papa."

Matt flipped to the second page of the report. "The
murder weapon was a deer-gutting knife. Any prints on the
knife?"

"Not many." Underwood nodded. "Someone had
cleaned the knife but didn't do a good job. We got a couple
clear prints. Only they came back not on file."

"You think the wife, Erica, killed her husband?" Trista
asked.

"She was always the number one suspect. There were
even bloody footprints in her size on the kitchen floor. But
after the murder, no one ever saw Erica or Billy Jr. again.
They disappeared into thin air. There was a BOLO out on
them for years. After a while, people began to forget there'd
been a bloody killing in their community. Besides, the guy
was bad news, so no one except for Will's brother—Avery—
really cared whether his killer was caught. The only reason
the investigation went on as long as it did was because Avery
and the old sheriff used to be friends."

Matt held up the enlarged color photo of the knife.
"These prints are pretty small."

Sheriff Underwood nodded. "That's another reason why the sheriff at the time figured Erica had killed Will herself."

Trista flipped to the page in the report Matt was referring to, and as her stomach lurched, she was grateful they hadn't stopped for lunch. The blade was long and ugly, with smudged, bloody fingerprints.

Matt massaged his chin as he continued staring at the photo. Then she realized he was staring at *her*. Her hands, more specifically. "Hold up your hand."

As soon as she did, he looked alternately from the photo, to her hand, then back to the photo. He pursed his lips, deep in thought.

"Something on your mind, Sgt. Connors?" Underwood rested his elbows on his desk, leaning forward.

"Have you ever considered anyone else as a suspect other than Erica Sands?" he asked, finally looking up.

"Not really," Underwood said. "The keys to Will's old truck were missing, and neither Erica nor Billy Jr. ever showed up in a hospital. Why do you ask?"

He held up the photo. "These prints are small. They *could* belong to a woman. Or, they could belong to a small child."

Trista widened her eyes. "You don't think the boy killed his own father, do you?"

"I doubt it," Underwood said. "According to witnesses, Billy adored his father. Will never touched the boy and was careful to take his anger out on Erica when Billy wasn't around. Besides, the coroner puts the time of death at ten a.m. Billy would have been in school at the time. That was confirmed by his teachers and several of his friends."

Matt made a sound in the back of his throat that told Trista he didn't necessarily agree with the sheriff's assumption about the identity of the killer. "Erica Sands would be about seventy by now, and the boy would be around forty-eight."

"That's right." The sheriff nodded. "What are you getting at?"

"I don't know," he answered, although she could tell something had piqued his curiosity.

As Matt and the sheriff continued discussing the case, Trista flipped through the remainder of the report, noting that Erica Sands was indeed a small woman, not much taller than five feet. Then she looked at the other photos, one in particular. That of Will Sands lying in a pool of blood, his eyes open, yet sightless. It reminded her all too much of Thomas George's body, minus the blood. But both men had been murdered.

Matt stood and held out his hand to Underwood. "Thank you for your time."

"Any chance you *can* tell me why all the sudden interest in a forty-year-old murder?" the sheriff asked as he shook Matt's hand.

"I wish I knew," Matt answered, dropping his copy of the report onto the desk. "But if we get any leads, we'll let you know."

"I'd sure appreciate that." Underwood stood and turned his back on them, a clear signal they should leave now and take the other copy with them.

Minutes later, they were back at the truck letting Sheba out to stretch her legs in the park next to the sheriff's department.

When Trista opened the door to get out of the truck, Matt stopped her. "Wait here. I don't want you exposed any more than necessary."

Reluctantly, she stayed in the truck while Matt jogged around the park with his dog. Sheba raced in front of him, her nose to the ground as she followed one scent after another before finally stopping to relieve herself.

Matt's stride was long and graceful. Athletic, like that

of a thoroughbred racehorse loping effortlessly around a track. As she continued watching, she was struck by the incongruities of this man. For someone so big and strong, he'd been infinitely gentle with her last night, both physically and emotionally. He'd been taken aback at discovering she'd been a virgin, but there'd been no judgment, not of her, anyway. He'd seemed more shocked that she'd chosen him to be her first.

A breeze rustled the tree behind her, blowing strands of hair in front of her face. Speaking of faces, Matt was so handsome and confident he could have any woman he wanted and yet he believed he didn't deserve her. *She* was the one who should be totally in awe of the fact that this beautiful man wanted *her*, not the other way around.

She wasn't a psych major, but even she understood the underlying issue. He was so guilt-ridden, he didn't think he deserved anything good in his life. For twenty years, he'd been torturing himself over Jerry's death, carrying around a pain so deeply ingrained it was slowly but surely killing him.

He'd already told her plainly he didn't want her sympathy, but her heart went out to him just the same. Not in pity, she realized. But she was equally certain he would never let her in until he could set aside the guilt and start living for himself.

As things stood right now, there wasn't a single part of his life that was devoted to his own happiness. His job was to protect others, and in his spare time, he'd been working on Jerry's Place to help others, not him. She understood his need to create the nonprofit. It accomplished several things he wanted so desperately. To do good for others in need, to memorialize his friend, and to assuage his guilt. Clearly, the last part wasn't working, and she doubted it ever could.

Sheba walked at Matt's side, constantly looking up at him for his next command. The animal was the only other woman in his life. The dog was devoted to him, and she could both see and sense their inherent bond. He would do anything for her, and she for him. That was love.

Her heart clenched, with both joy and sadness. What if he didn't let her in? What if he couldn't allow himself to ever love anyone?

As Matt and Sheba came toward her, only one thing was certain. She was head over heels in love with a man who might never be capable of loving her back.

• • •

Somewhere outside Washington, D.C.

The delicate China cup rattled on the saucer as she sipped her tea. Not even her habitual afternoon Earl Grey could settle the acid churning in her stomach or the fear that now kept her awake night after night.

Things were spiraling out of control, and she had to take matters into her own hands. Setting the cup onto the elegant, inlaid-wood coffee table, she shook her head in disbelief. Their entire world was about to crumble down around them because of some slip-up she must have made. Billy and his family would suffer the most and that was unthinkable. It was…*unacceptable.*

She glanced down at her perfectly manicured nails and clenched her hands in disgust. Her boy had come too far for the damned Russians to destroy everything he'd accomplished. This was his chance—his *dream*—and she'd be damned if anyone would stand in his way or undermine the very fabric of who and what he'd become.

There was only one thing to do. Billy might not agree with what she was about to set in motion, but it had to be done.

With trembling fingers, she picked up the phone and dialed.

Chapter Twenty-Two

Before Trista knew it, another week had passed.

After they'd gotten home, Matt had checked in with Buck, but there'd been nothing new to report. She assumed Hentz had informed Wayne and Genevieve that they'd been at Thomas George's house and that the reporter was dead. From online newspaper accounts, George's killer was still at large. There'd been no mention of any suspects nor were there any leads for the police to follow up on. She'd expected a serious reprimand from the agency about her and Matt sticking their noses where they didn't belong, and they'd both gotten it.

The message Buck had delivered to her from Wayne was that if she didn't stay put, she'd be thrown into protective custody whether she liked it or not. Matt had received a similar tongue-lashing from Buck, along with the reiteration to keep their heads low and he'd be in touch soon.

Soon can't come soon enough.

Since returning from West Virginia, they'd slept in separate beds every night and had minimal yet civil conversation. He seemed to be avoiding her, going out of his way to put physical distance between them but still remain close enough that he'd be there quickly should something happen. On more than one occasion over the past week, she'd caught him staring at her with an intensity that made her toes curl. There was heat in his gaze, and if she didn't know better, she'd even go so far as to call it desire.

Probably my own wishful thinking.

Even Matt's friends had detected the cold chill between them, especially Nick. His sharp gray eyes didn't miss a beat, and while he hadn't come right out and asked, she suspected he knew she and Matt had made love.

All the other men were out on one pre-election detail after another, and she missed them, especially Nick. Over the past week, they'd become friends. Probably, she guessed, because out of all them she sensed he was closest to Matt, and he'd gone out of his way to make her feel comfortable. Including giving her some instruction in self-defense.

Upon their return from West Virginia, she'd initially asked Matt to assist her. When he declined with no explanation as to why, Nick had stepped up. That was until Matt caught them grappling on the living room floor with Nick's muscular arms wrapped around her neck. From that moment on, Matt had taken over, but his instruction had been detached, as if he didn't want to be near her.

Sometimes she wished she could have fallen for Nick instead. Unlike Matt, Nick seemed to be capable of tolerating her company. Unfortunately, he didn't evoke the same physical or chemical attraction she had to Matt, even though with his sandy-blond hair and gorgeous gray eyes, he was striking enough to be on the cover of a magazine. And beneath that whole hard-ass cop thing Nick had going on, she was convinced he was really a sweetheart.

She stared at the computer screen, massaging her temples.

Breaking into the reporter's password-encrypted files was vastly more difficult than she'd anticipated, but she was close. Another few hours and she ought to have the password.

Poofy jumped onto the desk next to Matt's laptop and mewed, nuzzling her arm. Taking a break, she gathered the cat in her arms and held him close. The low rumble of his purr resonating against her chest was a welcome comfort.

The kitchen door shut, and Matt's boots clumped as he walked into the office. Poofy scrambled from her arms back onto the desk. When she looked up, she found Matt scrutinizing her intently again in that way she'd become accustomed to over the past week, and her heart beat a little faster with the fervent hope that he still wanted her as much as she wanted him.

"I put Sheba up in the kennel," he said as he wiped sweat from his brow. "I'm heading upstairs for a shower."

Disappointment swamped her, and she prayed the pathetic longing she experienced every time she saw him wasn't written all over her face.

His boots clumped up the stairs. From the dampness of his shirt and pants, he and Sheba must have gotten in another heavy training session. *To counter all the mushy stuff you're doing to my dog*, he'd said.

Now that she knew what he looked like totally naked, it was impossible not to imagine him standing beneath the pounding spray.

Poofy readjusted his position on the desk, tucking his tail beneath him and closing his eyes in that half-closed position cats were known for.

Focus. Focus on the files. Anything for distraction.

She began tapping on the keyboard, searching for other articles written by Thomas George, determined to find the connection between the reporter's big story that he may or may not have been killed for, the attacks on her, and whatever the Russian *rezidentura* had been referring to in the chat room. She had a feeling the answer lay in the reporter's encrypted files.

Maybe there's another way.

The burner phone Matt had given her lay on the desk beside the laptop. What she was about to do was exactly what Wayne had forbidden.

Thirty seconds of internet research later, she was on hold for Martin Denis, Thomas George's editor at the *Arlington Sentinel*.

"Martin Denis," a man answered.

Hairs on the back of Trista's neck tingled. She spoke Russian herself and had been exposed to many dialects throughout the course of her career. So she could recognize the faint accent of someone who'd been in the U.S. a very long time. Denis was also a shortened version of Denisovich, a common Russian surname.

Should I hang up? No, the phone is a burner and completely untraceable.

"Hello?" the voice said.

"Mr. Denis, my name is Elizabeth Winter. I'm a reporter for the *Charlotte Sun*. I'm calling about Thomas George, one of your reporters who was recently murdered."

"Ah, yes," Denis said. "A tragic loss for us here at the *Sentinel*."

"Since George was a Charlotte resident, I'm doing a small local-interest piece. I understand the police have no leads as to the motive behind his murder."

"No, they don't," he confirmed. "It's quite mysterious."

"Do you have any idea what story he was working on at the time?" She held her breath and, when he didn't respond, added, "He was an investigative reporter, so I couldn't help wondering if whatever he was working on might have a link to his death."

There was a lengthier pause on the other end. "Why would you come to that conclusion?"

Think fast. Keep him talking.

"I realize it is somewhat of a leap, but when the police don't have any of the usual motives, such as burglary gone bad or crime of passion, we have to think outside the box. Do you know what he was working on?"

"Even though Thomas is dead, I'm hoping someone else will pick up his story and complete it one day. In his memory, of course. In the meantime, it is the *Sentinel*'s policy not to comment on any unpublished articles."

"So you *do* know what story he was working on."

"What did you say your name was?" Denis asked, a discernible note of suspicion in his tone.

Trista hung up, letting out a frustrated breath. It had been worth a try.

Poofy raised his head, and a second later, the doorbell rang. Looking at the monitors on the adjacent wall, she saw a tall man and a slightly shorter woman standing on the front porch by the main door. She'd been given strict instructions not to unlock the door for anyone, but as she peered closer at the couple on the monitor, something about them looked familiar.

At the door, she pulled aside the sheer curtain covering the sidelight window. In a millisecond, she knew who these people were. The man was an older version of Matt, with the same solid build and confident bearing. His hair was a distinguished gray, but he was still an undeniably handsome man. There was no doubt he was Matt's father.

The woman standing beside him was about six inches shorter but still tall for a woman. She'd undoubtedly tower over Trista, just as Matt did. Her features were similar to Matt's and his father's but in a feminine way. The woman looked to be about Matt's age, so she guessed this was his sister. The next things she noticed were the stylish clothes, hair, and makeup. Trista could only dream of carrying off such a put-together look.

Even though Matt would be pissed at her for letting someone into the house, she entered the code to disengage the alarm, then unlocked the door. Both the man and woman stared at her, their eyes dipping first to her shirt, then down her legs to her bare feet.

The woman's mouth quirked into a grin that reminded her of Matt. "Nice shirt."

Oh boy.

Since the washing machine had been in constant use lately by all of Matt's friends, he'd given her one of his old Harvard T-shirts. The shirt was so long on her that she'd tied it off at the waist, revealing a couple inches of bare midriff.

The man cleared his throat. "I'm Matt's father, and this is his sister, Joyelle. May we come in?"

"Of course." Trista stepped aside for them to enter, then closed the door, feeling incredibly self-conscious at the obvious conclusion they'd leaped to. That she and Matt were sleeping together. Only they weren't. *Not anymore, anyway.*

"Matt's upstairs in the shower. Would you like to wait for him?" She looked at the other woman, who was grinning broadly now.

Heat rose to her face as Matt's father again took in her wardrobe. "No," he said. "That won't be necessary. We just came to make sure Matt received this invitation." He moved to set a cream-colored envelope on the hall table but stopped. On the table was an identical envelope. Unopened. "I see he already has one." His jaw clenched, and the scowl on his face again reminded her of the similarities between the two men. He tossed the envelope onto the table and turned and opened the door himself.

"It was nice to meet you," Joyelle said with a glimmer of

curiosity in her gaze. "Hopefully I'll see you again."

"Thank you." Trista smiled at Joyelle and would have said her goodbyes to Matt's father, but he was already halfway to the silver Jaguar parked in front of the house. She'd sensed some serious undercurrents in the man's reaction to seeing Matt already had an invitation and hadn't responded. She assumed that the invite was to Jerry's banquet and that Matt wasn't going.

After locking the door and re-engaging the security system, she went back to Matt's desk. The program she'd been running to decrypt the last of the reporter's files was still hard at work, with combinations of numbers and letters scrolling rapidly down the screen. She glanced out the window to the backyard, thinking about the visit from Matt's family.

Whether he realized it or not, Matt really needed to attend the banquet this year. Despite his father's anger, it was obvious the man loved his son and was disappointed he'd so blatantly ignored the invitation. She surmised Jerry's death had not only hurt Matt deeply but had also indirectly caused a rift in the family, one that would keep worsening if it wasn't repaired soon.

The laptop dinged, and she jerked her head back to the screen. "I have it. *I have the code!*"

With shaking fingers, she entered the reporter's password and opened up the first of the three remaining encrypted files, the one labeled "Erica Sands," documenting the flight of Mrs. Sands and her son, Billy Jr., to Nebraska shortly after the murder of Will Sands. The second file contained a search history of Nebraska birth records for—

"It can't be." Her fingers froze on the keyboard as she read the name again.

A second later, she opened the last encrypted file, the draft article. As she read the last story Thomas George had ever written, her heart began to race.

"Oh my God." She sat back in the chair, her mind whizzing at what she'd just learned.

She now knew who was trying to kill her. And why.

Bolting from the chair, she pounded up the stairs and flung open the door to Matt's bedroom.

Chapter Twenty-Three

Matt leaned against the shower tile, allowing the cold spray to pound against the back of his head and neck. He'd lost track of how many cold showers he'd taken over the past week. Being this close to Trista and not making love to her again was driving him insane.

Earlier, he'd nearly lost his resolve and taken her right there on his desk.

Blood surged to his groin, and he looked down. Just thinking about her made him rock hard.

The only things that had kept him grounded enough that he hadn't done something stupid were a grueling workout session in his basement gym every morning, followed by an equally intense session with Sheba. To eradicate Trista's effects on his dog, so she didn't go soft.

Bullshit.

Every morning when Trista came downstairs and parked her butt at his computer, he'd taken Sheba and practically fled from the house because he still needed space. His need for Trista was off the charts, but he couldn't go there again.

There was only pain there for her, and he refused to drag her down with him.

A hammering sound came to his ears over the spray of the shower. He flung open the shower door to see Trista standing in his bathroom, chest heaving, her eyes bright with excitement.

"Matt, I—" Her gaze dipped to his chest, then lower as she took in his nakedness. When she swallowed, he knew what she was seeing.

His rock-hard erection.

Neither of them moved. He gripped the shower door tightly and clenched his other hand to keep from reaching for her.

Don't do it.

Blood pounded in his ears. His heart thumped crazily, and he felt himself grow impossibly harder to the point of pain. When their gazes finally met, the searing need he glimpsed in her eyes echoed his own, and he lost all fucking control.

Reaching out, he pulled her into the shower, not giving a shit that she was fully clothed. He wrapped his arms around her, tugging her against his chest. Angling her head, he groaned, then crashed his mouth down on hers. When she parted her lips, he savored what he'd been denying himself and wondered if he could ever live without it again.

"Goddamn," he whispered, raining kiss after kiss on her sweet lips, her creamy neck, and the tops of her breasts. "You have no idea how much I've missed you. How much I *want* you." He wished he could say more, but that one word wouldn't come out: "love."

He might not be able to express how he felt verbally, but he could do it with his body. That was the easy way, the coward's way out, but it was all he had in him.

"Matt, I-I have something to tell you." Her head fell

back, giving him better access to that sweet spot beneath her earlobe. Her hands came around his back, then lowered to his buttocks as he pushed her against the tile wall.

He grabbed the hem of her shirt and made quick work of dragging it up and over her head. Next, he rid her of her jeans and panties until she was clad only in a lacy bra. Leaning down, he sucked her nipple into his mouth, but it wasn't enough.

"I want you naked." He yanked down her bra straps, freeing her beautiful breasts. Cupping them in his hands, he bent and suckled each one until they were hard and tight and puckered.

She clasped the back of his head, moaning. He reached around her back to tear off her bra, then skimmed his hands up the insides of her thighs, urging her to spread her legs for him. When she complied, he stroked the soft, wet folds of her core. Her body jerked at his touch.

Nuzzling his nose against the honey-blond curls covering her most sensitive parts, he looked up to see her watching him with glazed eyes. "I'm going to taste you." With the shower's spray on his back, he knelt in front of her and flicked his tongue against her wetness. A strangled cry escaped her lips, and he fastened his mouth on her, tonguing her until she was writhing against him.

Her fingers dug into his scalp, and he knew she was close. Inserting a finger inside her, he felt her tighten, then shudder as she came, clinging to his shoulders, crying out his name. Sinking his finger in deeper, he sucked on her folds, extending her orgasm. The feel of her body, so completely turned on by what he was doing, had him harder than he'd ever been in his life.

He turned up the water temperature so she wouldn't freeze, then ducked out and rolled on a condom. Back in the shower, he closed the door behind them and lifted her, positioning the tip of his cock at her entrance. When she locked her legs around his waist, he pushed inside and they both groaned.

He gritted his teeth, pressing his forehead against hers. If he didn't get his damned dick in check, this would be over in less time than it took for a bullet to leave the barrel.

Slowly, he began moving inside her, thrusting deeper with each successive stroke. His lips found hers, and as he thrust harder, faster, his heart pumped so furiously he thought it would burst.

"Baby," he whispered into her mouth. "I can't live without this. I can't live without *you*." Nor did he want to, he realized.

"Then don't." She kissed him back, her tongue doing amazing things inside his mouth.

Lifting her a fraction higher, he angled her hips, allowing him to push deeper inside her warm, tight walls. She tightened around him. Her breathing came faster, as did his. A beautiful, feminine moan escaped her sweet lips as she came, harder than before, her petite body bucking, her hips gyrating against his. A second later, his balls tightened, and he exploded with such force he cried out. With his face buried in the curve of her neck, he waited for his pulse to slow.

"Matt." Trista's voice was soft and breathy against his face. "I love you."

He stilled as if he'd been slapped, then lifted his head to stare into the depths of her crystalline green eyes. For one infinitesimal second, he was happy. *Truly* happy. Then he felt the bite of tile digging into the old scars on the backs of his hands.

Jerry's young, vibrant face came to him just before he'd lit up the old barn. In less time than it took for Matt's heart to beat again, the joy shooting through him seconds ago fizzled and he stiffened. Under the warm spray, reality burrowed beneath his skin, and his body chilled.

No matter how much he wanted to say those three little words back, he knew he never would. Never *could*.

"Let me go." Her voice was flat as she unclasped her legs from his waist and slid down the front of his chest. She brushed past him and out of the shower, stopping to wrap herself in one of his large bath towels.

As she headed out the door, he followed her into his bedroom, pushing the door closed before she could leave. What he saw in her eyes killed him. Pain. Anguish. Both of which he was responsible for. "I'm sorry." He shook his head. He really was sorry, for both of them. "You deserve better than someone who can't ever love you. Someone who doesn't have it *in* him to love."

"Bullshit." Her eyes flared, and her voice rose. "You have as much capacity to love as I do, but you refuse to let yourself. It's easier for you to wallow in this pitiful existence you've created for yourself than it is to fight past it. I told you before…you're dying inside, and if you don't get help soon, you *will* die. You'll be here on this earth, living and breathing, but you might as well *be* dead."

He dragged a hand through his wet hair, feeling despair like he'd never known before, knowing he was losing her. "It's too late. What happened to Jerry—what I *allowed* to happen to him—" He hung his head and stared at the floor. "I don't deserve *you*." It killed him to say the next words, but they had to be said. "When this is over and you're safe, you'll find someone else. Someone who *can* love." The thought of another man in her bed had him gnashing his teeth.

Taking a deep breath, she lifted her chin defiantly, although her voice trembled. "I already found that someone. You. But if you can't heal yourself, I *will* find someone else. I may never love anyone as deeply, but at least I'll try. *You've* already given up."

Unshed tears welled in her eyes, and it undid him not to

go to her, not to take her in his arms and say the words he desperately wanted to say: "I love you, too." All he could do was watch helplessly as she pushed past him and opened the door. When she turned back to him, he glimpsed the sorrow in her eyes. He'd been given a gift—a beautiful flower—and he'd crushed it.

"I almost forgot. Your father and sister stopped by to hand-deliver an invitation to Jerry's banquet. You really should go this year before you lose all touch with your family. I saw the look in your father's eyes. It took a lot for him to come here." She paused with her hand on the doorknob. "I'll call my boss and arrange to go into someone else's protective custody."

Matt gritted his teeth. He didn't want her to leave. Ever. But damned if he couldn't get his feet to move. *I am an asshole of the lowest order. A pathetic fuck*. The woman he wanted more than his next breath was on the verge of walking out of his life, and he couldn't get his fucking feet to move or his tongue to work. *Doesn't matter*. He could never be what she wanted him to be. What he wanted to be *for* her. Her friend, her lover...the only man to ever touch her.

With the towel clutched at her breast, she opened the door. "By the way," she said in a neutral tone, completely devoid of emotion. "I got into Thomas George's encrypted files. I left them open on your laptop. I know who's trying to kill me, and why." She turned and shut the door quietly behind her.

For two seconds, he stared at the door, unmoving, then shoved his legs into a pair of jeans and grabbed a shirt and boots from his closet. Moments later, he was sitting at his laptop, reading the decrypted files.

"Holy fuck." He reread the article, along with the supporting files, but the words didn't change. Trista was right. Now they knew why Thomas George was murdered and why someone would undoubtedly try to kill Trista again. This story was the biggest conspiracy in recent history.

Pushing from the desk, he began pacing the length of his office. The chat room Trista had overheard was the key to everything. *Iqaluit. He is not who he says he is.* "Now we know who 'he' is," he muttered. And *he* wants to kill Trista because of what she heard in the chat room. She could reveal his identity and his link to the Russians. The million-dollar question was whether the CIA was part of the conspiracy to cover up the truth.

The articles Trista had pulled up weeks ago detailed a fight for Russian supremacy in the Arctic region. Was this really all about Russia wanting to claim Arctic resources? *Shit.* This was so fucking beyond his pay grade, but he didn't know whom they could trust.

Despite his claim to the contrary, the CIA operative the agency sent to George's house—Mitchell Hentz—could very well have murdered the reporter. Then Hentz *and* an FBI agent had dropped in on the Berkeley County Sheriff's Department. Together. *Why?*

There was only one reason the CIA and the FBI would be working together. After what he'd just read, this was an international conspiracy involving Canada, the Russians, and U.S. government officials. But the CIA wasn't authorized to conduct investigations on domestic soil, therefore they needed an agency that could. Enter the great and powerful FBI.

Matt had known Trista's bosses were holding something tight to the vest, but this was beyond his wildest imagination. *You can't make this shit up.* His gut told him government officials were in it up to their eyeballs, and the fog of suspicion surrounding all of them was thicker than an Afghani sandstorm. He'd bet the U.S. government damn well knew the identity of the *he* in that chat room.

He stopped pacing. Only one thing was clear. Trusting any of them with Trista's life...*not gonna happen.*

The stairs creaked, and he guessed she was coming down. He wasn't looking forward to their next conversation. Awkward didn't begin to describe how things would be. There was no way in hell he'd ever let someone else protect her. Which meant she'd have to stay here with him.

The front door opened, and the security alarm began beeping. He jerked his head to the monitors. Trista was heading out the door, a plastic bag in one hand, Poofy in the other. "Shit." She was leaving. Where she was going without a car, he had no idea. Guess she wanted to get away from him badly enough that she'd walk or hitchhike, even. "Fuck. That." He clenched his fists and began to turn toward the door when another monitor beeped as three black SUVs raced up his driveway.

His blood ran cold as he turned and bolted for the front door. "Trista, wait!"

He raced to the open door and flew outside to see a man in a suit gripping her roughly by the arm. Poofy and the plastic bag she'd been holding were now abandoned on the grass.

She struggled in the man's grasp, twisting and pulling, but he held fast. "Let me go," she cried.

Matt leaped off the front steps, running at top speed, and tackled the shithead dragging Trista to one of the SUVs. They both hit the ground, with Matt on top. He pounded his fist into the guy's face, hearing bone crack. Blood spattered, and the guy cried out.

Hands pulled him off, and he spun, plowing his fist into the next suit, knocking him to the ground. His buddy got in a shot to Matt's jaw, sending him staggering but still standing. Breathing heavily, all he could think was that he'd kill anyone who tried to take Trista from him.

He charged at the suit who'd gotten in a lucky shot, barely

registering three other men standing nearby. Again, he hit the ground and pummeled the guy until he stopped moving. He bolted to his feet, preparing for another attack, when the other three suits tackled him, pinning him to the ground.

Using his elbows and knees, he incapacitated one of them, hearing more bone crunch amid screams of pain. He nailed the next guy in the jaw, taking satisfaction at seeing blood spurt from his nose. He rose to his feet, readying to take down the latest asshole now holding Trista, when his arms were grabbed from behind and the muzzles of three guns were thrust in his face.

"No!" she screamed.

"Anderson!" a man shouted as he got out of one of the SUVs. "Let her go or Sgt. Connors will beat the shit out of you."

To Matt's satisfaction, the guy released Trista, and she ran toward him. Ignoring the fact that his arms were pinned, she flung herself between him and the weapons trained at his chest. She wrapped her arms around his waist. "Trista, get back!" His heart lurched with fear that one of these bozos would fire off a round and drill her through the back.

"Don't hurt him." She hugged him even tighter. "Please, don't hurt him and I'll go with you."

"The hell you will." He struggled against the three sets of hands restraining him.

"Sgt. Connors," the man who'd gotten out of the SUV said. With the tinted windows, Matt hadn't noticed the seventh man sitting in one of the front passenger seats. The fucker must have been watching the whole thing from his air-conditioned SUV. "Allow me to introduce myself." He held up a black leather cred case. "Resident Agent in Charge Max Fenway, FBI."

"Since when is the FBI in the business of kidnapping women?" He glared at Fenway, wanting to wipe the arrogant smirk off his face.

"This isn't a kidnapping." Fenway approached closer. "You two have stumbled into something bigger than you could have imagined." He refocused on Trista, who still held him tightly around the waist. "And you, Ms. Gold, just couldn't stop digging. We have a wiretap on several of the *Arlington Sentinel*'s phones, including that of Martin Denis, whom you recently spoke to. Someone inside your own agency recognized your voice."

Matt frowned. He hadn't known she'd made that call.

"Sgt. Connors, I'd like to release you. But before I do, I need you to promise not to beat up any more of my men. I can't afford to have my team decimated."

Matt glared at the three other men he could see, all of whom had blood dripping down their faces. "What the fuck do you want?"

"What I want is more men like you on my team." He arched a brow at his battered men. "Clearly, the FBI could use a man of your skills. If you ever want to jump ship, I'm sure I could arrange it. But seriously, I'm under orders to bring you in for a meeting, and for the sake of my team's health, I'd sure appreciate it if you both came willingly. Let him go." Fenway tipped his head to the men restraining Matt.

"Why the hell would we do that?" He wrapped his arms around Trista's shoulders. "You haven't told us shit about what's going on here or who this *meeting* is with."

From the corner of his eye, he glimpsed Poofy bolting back inside the house. From the kennel, Sheba's constant barking told him the dog knew he was in distress and was probably clawing at her enclosure to get to him.

Fenway shook his head. "It's not my story to tell, but you'll have answers to all your questions soon enough. Suffice to say, these orders come down from the highest levels of both our agencies. I don't want to, but I'll tase you if I have to. You have my word that we'll return you here in time for dinner. It may not seem that way, but we really are on the same side. Consider this an official request from above."

Matt gave an angry snort. "Most requests don't come at gunpoint."

"I do apologize for the show of force. Now we really need to go." He nodded to the SUVs.

Damn, but he didn't like this. Apparently, though, they had no choice. He looked down into Trista's eyes, feeling her slight body trembling against his.

So much was left unsaid. So much was in his heart that could never be spoken. "Let's go, honey." He took her hand, and they followed Fenway to one of the SUVs.

Chapter Twenty-Four

Trista shivered at the chilly air blowing through the SUV. She and Matt sat in the back while Agent Fenway took a seat in the front. The driver was one of the agents Matt had punched in the face first. The SUV they were in was led and flanked by two other identical black vehicles.

Matt held her hand tightly in his, staring straight ahead through the windshield. His jaw was rigid, as if carved in granite. With her thigh pressed against his, she could feel the tension and rage vibrating in his big body. She pitied the next person who got on his bad side and worried he'd get shot trying to protect her.

She took a deep, shuddering breath, scared beyond belief at what was happening. These men were FBI, but they'd fought Matt and pointed guns at him. She didn't know whom to trust anymore. Her only rock in this whole mess was sitting right beside her. Physically, anyway, but emotionally, he might as well be on the other side of the world.

"You okay?" His voice was soft and gentle, a stark contrast to the fire burning in his beautiful chocolate-brown eyes.

"This is all my fault," she whispered. "If only I hadn't opened the door. You warned me not to go outside, but I didn't listen. I was just...upset."

"I know." He squeezed her hand. "That's *my* fault, not yours. Whatever happens, stay close. Don't let go of my hand. Okay?"

She nodded, her heart bursting with love for him now more than ever. He'd unhesitatingly risked his life for her more than once. But if they were alive at the end of the day, she would still walk away. Funny how she'd just discovered the biggest conspiracy and news story in decades, and all she could think about was how her life would never be the same without Matt in it.

Twenty minutes later, they drove through Langley's main gates. Oddly, though, they drove around to the rear of the building, where more black SUVs were parked and guarded by a small army of men in dark suits, all wearing ear wires.

Secret Service?

"Why is the Secret Service here?" Matt growled, voicing her thought.

As far as she knew, the Secret Service was primarily known for protecting high-level political dignitaries.

"Standard procedure." Fenway got out and opened the door beside her, holding out his hand. But Matt was already out of the SUV and shoving Fenway aside.

"I got this." As Matt held out his hand to her, his eyes never left Fenway, who put his hands in the air and backed off.

When she alighted from the SUV, he tucked her tightly to his side with his arm around her waist. Again the thought came to her that he would never be able to love her, but he'd die to protect her.

One of the Secret Service agents spoke into a microphone

at his jacket cuff. The large metal door opened, and they followed Fenway and two other FBI agents inside. An elevator whisked them to the top floor, which she knew housed the offices of the CIA's highest-ranking officials. Outside a set of cherry-wood doors, two more Secret Service agents stood guard. At their approach, one of them spoke into his cuff while the other opened one of the doors.

Fenway entered first, followed by Matt, who paused at the entrance. His shoulders were so broad, she could barely see around him. Once inside the enormous office, she saw more people standing to their left. Recognizing one of them, she gasped and backed away. Two hands on her shoulders prevented her retreat.

"You lying son of a bitch." Matt reared back and slammed his fist into Fenway's jaw. The agent fell to the floor, groaning.

Instantly, Matt was tackled by five men, two of whom pinned his arms behind his back. Even from his seemingly incapacitated position, he managed to throw two of them off and struggle to his knees, his chest heaving.

"Stop it!" someone yelled. "Let him go!"

The agents released Matt, who jumped to his feet and stepped back, shielding her with his body.

"Sgt. Connors," the man who apparently had ultimate authority in the room said. "Ms. Gold, please forgive me. Neither of you were ever supposed to be in jeopardy. You have my most sincere apologies."

"Apologies?" Matt clenched his hands, looking ready to launch like a ballistic missile. "She knows who you are. Who you *really* are, and you're trying to kill her for it. So excuse me, *senator*, if we don't accept your apologies."

Senator and U.S. presidential candidate Michael Ashburn sighed heavily and gestured to a large conference table. "Please. I beg you to have a seat. There is much to explain."

Someone off to the side cleared his throat, and she got

her first glimpse of all the other people in the large room. She hadn't noticed them before.

Stanley Windham, deputy director of the CIA, was flanked by her bosses, Wayne Gurgas and Genevieve Grujot, and another man she didn't recognize. She'd met Deputy Director Windham during several security intelligence briefings she'd given.

An older woman of about seventy came forward, standing directly in front of Matt. Her short gray hair was beautifully styled, and the cream-colored skirt and jacket she wore screamed political royalty. In response to the woman's nearness, Matt repositioned himself closer to Trista, still maintaining a protective stance.

Peering around him, Trista recognized the woman from the many photos taken posing with her son on the pre-election campaign trail. This was Senator Ashburn's mother, Barbara Ashburn. For a woman no bigger than she was, Mrs. Ashburn possessed a soft confidence that she couldn't help but admire.

"Sgt. Connors," Barbara Ashburn said. "It's obvious how much you care for this young lady, but please allow my son to explain."

Grabbing onto Matt's arm, Trista met the other woman's gaze. "You're Erica Sands, aren't you?"

She smiled, and the skin around her sharp blue eyes crinkled. "Yes, dear. Although, I haven't heard that name in a very long time." She held out her hand, waiting patiently for Trista to take it. "Please, come sit with us. You both have my word that no harm will come to you."

"Matt?" Trista looked up at him to see his brows bunched, his jaw clenched as his gaze swept the room.

"Hear them out, Sgt. Connors." Deputy Director Windham gave Matt a curt nod.

Without a word, Matt put his arm around Trista's shoulder

and guided her past Mrs. Ashburn to the conference table. He pulled out a chair for her, waiting for everyone else to sit. In all, they were ten at the table, including Fenway, whose jaw was quickly bruising from Matt's punch, and Mitchell Hentz, who'd apparently been lurking somewhere in the corner, staying safely out of the fracas. The only other man she didn't recognize introduced himself as Special Agent in Charge Bradley Gotesman, from the FBI's Washington, D.C., office. The other FBI agents and Secret Service agents guarding the presidential candidate stood discreetly by the closed doors.

Matt sat to Trista's left, Mrs. Ashburn to her right. Senator Ashburn sat directly across from them, allowing Matt to glare directly into the eyes of the man he believed tried to murder Trista and had Thomas George killed. Either the senator was an accomplished actor or the look on his face truly was one of sincere regret.

Beside her, Mrs. Ashburn took Trista's hand in hers. "I'd like to tell you a story of a very naive, stupid woman who married a very bad man. The only good thing to come from my marriage to Will Sands was my sweet boy." She paused to give Senator Ashburn a gentle smile, which he returned. "By the time Michael—or Billy, as you know him to be—turned eight, I'd long since figured out my husband was a domestic abuser. But he loved our son and restricted his abuse to the hours when Billy was at school. Any time he left marks on my face, I lied about how I got them."

"One day, I forgot my mitt," the senator interjected. "I wanted to play ball with my friends after school, so I snuck home to get it. Nobody at school even knew I'd left. We lived far off the main road and nowhere near any other neighbors. When I got home, my father was yelling so loudly at Mom he never knew I'd opened the kitchen door to see him punching her repeatedly in the face and the ribs. She was already badly injured, with multiple broken bones and internal injuries."

Mrs. Ashburn opened a manila envelope, then pulled out several photos and handed them to Trista and Matt. Trista gasped. The woman in the photos was barely recognizable. Both eyes were swollen shut. Her face was bruised and cut, with multiple stitches.

"This is you." She looked into Mrs. Ashburn's kindly eyes, and her heart went out to this courageous woman who'd suffered such incredible pain at the hands of her husband and still survived.

Mrs. Ashburn slid the photos back into the envelope. "I had these taken in case the law ever caught up to us. If they did, I wanted the police to see the damage Will's fists inflicted. But I couldn't take that chance, so I took Billy and ran. I didn't want any of this to touch him."

"You were in no shape to kill your husband," Matt said in a sympathetic tone. "The prints on the knife found at the crime scene were small, but they weren't yours. Were they?" The way he said it, Matt's last words were more a statement of fact than a question.

"They were mine." Senator Ashburn's face hardened. "I killed my father. Stabbed him with his own knife. I don't think I cut him very deeply, but I must have hit an artery. Before I knew it, the kitchen floor was covered in blood." The senator's eyes took on a faraway look, as if he was reliving that day all over again.

"The authorities assumed my mother killed him." The adoring look he gave his mother was filled with unshed tears. "I don't know how she managed it with all her injuries, but somehow she drove us out of there and across three states before stopping for medical attention. When we finally pulled into a hospital, she lied to the doctors, saying some men held us up at gunpoint, took everything we had, then beat my mother to within an inch of her life."

As Mrs. Ashburn met her son's gaze, a thin trickle of

tears ran down her cheeks. "I didn't know what the police would do to a little boy who murdered his father. They could have taken him away from me and thrown him in a cell somewhere. I didn't want that for him."

"Given your injuries, don't you think the police would have agreed it was a case of a young boy defending his mother's life?" Matt asked. "Even forty years ago, no prosecutor would charge an eight-year-old boy protecting his mother from an abuser."

"Perhaps." Mrs. Ashburn wiped at her tears. "But this was backwater West Virginia. My brother-in-law, Avery Sands, was friends with the sheriff at the time, and since sheriffs are elected officials, I couldn't risk him launching an investigation into Billy's actions just to pacify Avery. I considered confessing to his murder myself, but I had no other family, and Billy's care would have fallen to Avery, who was just as evil as Will."

Trista placed a gentle hand on the woman's shoulder, inherently understanding the unconditional love between a mother and child, and praying she'd one day get the chance to experience that love for herself. "You fled to protect your child."

Mrs. Ashburn sniffled, then smiled and covered Trista's hand with her own. "And I don't regret it for a second."

"What we do regret," Senator Ashburn interjected, "is the deadly sequence of events our actions kicked off forty years later and how many others suffered because of it. Especially you, Ms. Gold, and Thomas George."

"While it wasn't made public," Mitchell Hentz added, "trace amounts of digitalis were found in George's blood. But he didn't have a heart condition."

Matt leaned his forearms on the table, sending the senator a stone-cold look that would make most men cower. "Are you telling us you *didn't* have him killed to keep him from publishing his story and outing you as a murderer?"

"That's exactly what I'm telling you, sergeant. Thomas George's death will haunt me for the rest of my life."

"Then who killed him? Because whoever it was is still out there. And to them, Trista represents the same liability. You're still conveniently leaving out the driving force behind your so-called *sequence of events*."

"It was the *rezidentura*, wasn't it?" Trista asked, knowing with growing certainty that this whole thing was somehow connected to the chat she'd overheard.

"Concentrated digitalis," Hentz said, nodding, "is one of the many suspected favorite poisons of our neighborhood *rezidentura*, Alexy Lukashin."

"Why do the Russians care about who you really are or what you've done?" Not for the first time since they'd sat down, Matt narrowed his eyes on the senator. "They're blackmailing you."

For a moment, the senator didn't respond. Nor did anyone else. It was as if this entire meeting had been choreographed by him under strict orders that this was *his* story and his alone to tell. She suspected they were about to delve into deeply classified information of international significance.

Senator Ashburn glanced at his mother. "When we changed our names, we could never have imagined the path our lives would take. As a boy, becoming president of the United States never crossed my mind. The only things of importance in my life back then were that we got away from my father and playing baseball with my friends. We began a new life under new identities, never intending to mislead the American people about who I really was. The years sailed by and thanks to my mother's unfailing support, I became a U.S. senator."

Again, he looked at his mother. "We both knew me running for public office was a risk, but we felt enough time had passed that we were safe from being discovered. Things snowballed from there, and here I am. One of two remaining candidates for president."

"Your name isn't even your own." Matt shook his head. "Didn't you ever stop to think that the American people have a right to know who you really are?"

"At first, no." Senator Ashburn smiled ruefully. "Regardless of what my legal name is, I'm a patriot, through and through. An American who believes in what this country stands for. Freedom. Equality. The pursuit of happiness and the opportunity to be anything you want to be in life. In this day and age of political unrest, this country needs a leader who will take us back to basics and reunite the country, not tear it apart with petty differences and the pursuit of personal gain."

Senator Ashburn stood, pointing a finger at his chest. "I want the opportunity to be that person. I *can* be that person."

As he stared at Matt, his eyes took on a bright, determined look, and Trista understood precisely what it was about him that drew people in. Not only was he charismatic, but she believed that he truly wanted the best for the country.

"You said, 'at first,'" she reminded him. "Now?"

The excited light in his eyes dimmed, and he sat heavily. "Now, things have changed. As you rightly surmised," he said to Matt, "the Russians hope to blackmail me. We may never know how they did it, but the Russians discovered I've been living under a false identity most of my life. They traced backward and found out that I killed my father when I was a child. Lukashin approached me surreptitiously, threatening to *out* me publicly. Anyone this close to becoming president of the United States is not only inordinately powerful but surprisingly weak. A candidate will give up just about anything to achieve that goal, and the Russians were—and still are—counting on that. They made me a proposition. They would keep my past a secret, in exchange for certain favors in the future, starting with the withdrawal of all support to the Canadian military. *If* I'm elected."

"Iqaluit." Trista glanced at Matt, recalling the articles they'd read detailing the Arctic power struggle. "The Russians want to take control of the Arctic's natural resources, something they can't do if the Canadian military is there to stop them."

"Basically, yes." Senator Ashburn frowned. "Iqaluit has been the site of several meetings held lately between Canadian officials and myself to discuss details of exactly what support I would provide the Canadians. Unfortunately for Thomas George, he somehow stumbled onto my backstory. If it had been published before the election, it most assuredly would have destroyed my chances of becoming president."

Matt gave an incredulous laugh. "You still intend to run? Don't you think your ethics have been compromised?"

"No." He leaned forward and pounded his fist on the table. "I will *never* compromise my ethics. I love this country, and I want to lead it into the future. But I realize that's no longer possible." He sat back, supreme disappointment evident on his face. "By November, this will all be made public and withdrawing my candidacy will be a foregone conclusion. For the moment, however, it is imperative that my story remain hidden."

"Why?" Matt countered.

Special Agent in Charge Gotesman cleared his throat. "Recently, Senator Ashburn approached the FBI and told us about the Russians' attempt to blackmail him. We involved the CIA to obtain as much behind-the-scenes information as possible and to take advantage of their Russian intel."

"Talking to the FBI was my mother's idea," the senator said, looking directly at Trista. "And I agreed because the Russians have to be stopped. Things were quickly spinning out of control and too many people were getting hurt."

Deputy Director Windham looked directly at Trista. "As the senator said, you are extremely good at your job. So good, in fact, that you unexpectedly stumbled onto this conspiracy in that chat room. We did our best to keep you isolated from that point forward, but Lukashin was tenacious, as were you, putting your life in jeopardy that much more." He smiled. "You should have been an operative."

"Thank you." She smiled back, appreciative of the compliment. "But I think I'll stay right where I am, sitting in front of a computer."

Matt crossed his arms, wearing his all-too-familiar scowl. "The Russians will be counting on the senator to keep quiet, and now that the reporter is dead, they think Trista is the only one out there who could blow the whole thing for them. After the story breaks and the whole world hears about it, they'll have nothing to gain by killing her. But until then, her life is still in jeopardy."

She shook her head. "There's something I don't understand. I gave a printout of the chat room conversation to Wayne and Genevieve, who could have given it to countless others within the agency. Why are the Russians so fixated on me? Why aren't they trying to kill every other person with the CIA who probably knows by now?"

"Several reasons." Wayne joined the conversation. "First, they don't know who within the agency is privy to the chat, and they can't go around killing all of us. Second, and more importantly, you, Trista, and your top secret program are the source of the information. Without you to testify before Congress as to whom you were tracking in that chat room and how you obtained the information, the U.S. government would never be able to completely prove the Russians were behind this."

"Just how far up the Russian food chain does this conspiracy go?" Matt asked.

"We suspect," the senator said, "all the way."

"To the Russian president?" Trista couldn't contain the shock in her voice.

"Shit." Matt dragged a hand down his face. "So what's your plan?"

SAC Gotesman leaned forward. "That's need-to-know."

"For Christ's sake, Brad." Director Windham held his arms out from his sides. "They're already privy to the biggest international conspiracy in decades. They have a right to know what we're doing to end this, so they can get back to living their lives."

"Very well, but I don't like it." SAC Gotesman pursed his lips. "Senator Ashburn requested a private meeting with Lukashin, during which we'll record all conversation."

"You seriously think he'll admit to anything?" Matt asked. "Don't you think he'll check for a wire?"

With obvious reluctance, Fenway nodded. "It's possible, but it's all we've got. I'm betting he won't insult a U.S. senator by patting him down."

"Lukashin is a cagey bastard," Hentz said. "He's been around long enough not to get caught. He'll be uber-suspicious. This trap better be good. *Damn* good."

"The FBI and the CIA agree," Wayne said. "We should at least try. He's too big a fish not to."

"In fish size," Hentz added, "he's a whale. For years, we've suspected him of over twenty assassinations on U.S. soil, not to mention hundreds in Russia while he was with the KGB and the FSB. It's even been rumored that he was one of the last members of the KGB's Department 13, the Soviet Union's executive action operations unit that was known for surreptitious murders using various poisons that mimic death by natural circumstances."

"Like digitalis," Matt said, and Trista could tell his mood was darkening by the minute.

Hentz nodded. "Lukashin and the Russian president aren't exactly friends, but they were in the KGB together. Rumor has it, he reports directly to the president."

Matt shook his head. "Even if you get evidence he murdered Thomas George and tried to kill Trista, won't he still be immune to prosecution by virtue of his diplomatic status? The only way this country has ever prosecuted a diplomat for murder is when his own country of origin waives his diplomatic immunity. I'm guessing the Russian president will never agree to that, especially given all the dirt Lukashin must have on him."

"You're right about that," Fenway interrupted. "They'd want to keep him from being put in a position where he could provide intelligence on the Russian government. We've spoken to the U.S. Attorney's Office and believe he wouldn't have full immunity, only functional immunity. That means if he does something outside his official function as cultural attaché, then he's subject to prosecution. I'm no lawyer, but I'd say that being a spy and a murderer is outside his official function. The Russians will argue otherwise, but we need the *rezidentura*. Without him, we'll never prove any orders came down from the top."

"Don't get me wrong"—Matt turned to Fenway—"putting Lukashin behind bars is at the top of my list, but even if you could prove the Russian president is behind this, you can't charge into Russia and arrest him. So what's the ultimate goal here?"

"I think I can answer that question," Senator Ashburn said. "You're right. He's sitting in a glass tower that we can't get to. But we do have recourse. We can impose trade sanctions. *Heavy* sanctions, those impacting Russian trade to the point where they'll never try something like this again. We may be able to justify kicking out everyone in the Russian Embassy for a lengthy period of time as punishment. Last, we can put pressure on the Russian government to have their president step down."

Beneath the table, Trista fingered her charm bracelet, twirling it repeatedly around her wrist. *When will this really all be over?* She didn't think she could go into hiding for an indeterminate period of time. *Will I be looking over my shoulder for the rest of my life?*

"And after the story breaks?" She glanced from Mrs. Ashburn to the senator. "What will *you* do?" Her question was met with silence so thick and heavy it seemed as if everyone in the room had stopped breathing, waiting to hear his response.

The senator turned to look at his mother. "I intend to urge the *Sentinel* to publish Thomas George's story posthumously. It's the right thing to do. I'll let the American people judge as to whether or not I'm fit to be president."

"There's no statute of limitations on murder," Matt said. "Even though you were eight years old, you could still be subject to criminal prosecution in West Virginia."

Senator Ashburn didn't hesitate. "That's a chance I'm willing to take."

"Do your wife and children know?" Trista asked, unable to contemplate what a secret like this would do to a marriage.

"I'll tell them right before the story breaks."

"Senator, we should get you out of here." SAC Gotesman nodded to the Secret Service agents guarding the door.

A minute later, the only people remaining in the conference room besides herself were Matt and Agents Hentz and Fenway, who both waited by the door.

"We need to get you into protective custody, Trista." Hentz arched a brow at Matt. "*Official* protective custody."

"Where are you taking her?" Matt's forehead creased with concern.

"To a safe house," Fenway answered.

"That doesn't answer my question." Matt narrowed his eyes. "Again, where?"

Fenway shook his head. "Can't tell you that."

Matt sent Trista a look of disbelief. "You can't seriously go with these clowns. *They* can't keep you safe. *I* can."

"Matt, it's for the best." She glanced briefly at Fenway and Hentz, not wanting to air her and Matt's personal business in front of the other men. Blinking back tears, she lowered her voice. "You know I can't stay with you." *Not when you can't ever love me back. Not while my heart is breaking more and more every second I spend with you.*

She took a deep breath, then cleared her throat. "I guess this is goodbye." She held out her hand, which he took, tugging her closer. "Please," she pleaded. "Let me go."

"Tris, no." He shook his head, a look of incredulity on his handsome features. "Don't do this."

"I have to." She looked down at their linked hands, realizing this would most likely be the last time they would ever touch.

Somehow she mustered the strength to meet his gaze, refusing to see anything more in his worried expression than general concern for her well-being. *It will be like ripping off a Band-Aid. Painful at first. But it's better to get it over with quickly and put it behind you. Just say goodbye and walk away.* "Would you mind taking care of Poofy until I can get someone to pick him up?"

He nodded, still clasping her hand in his. "I'll take good care of him."

"Say goodbye to Sheba for me." She turned to leave, but he held fast to her hand, looking as if he was about to say something. Then he let her go. More tears pricked at the backs of her eyes and she blinked rapidly. *Be strong.*

With her heart aching, she turned and walked out the door without looking back.

Chapter Twenty-Five

Trista lay in her bed, snuggled up with Poofy while binge-watching episodes of *Saturday Night Live*. Watching late-night TV had become their custom in the two weeks since she'd been whisked away to an FBI safe house.

Poofy busily purred louder than an electric razor, nuzzling her hand, demanding even more attention than usual. Not that she could blame him. Even she was bored out of her mind. Stuck in a tiny house, God knew where, with nothing but a few books, magazines, and two stoic FBI agents in the outer room standing guard over her to make sure she stayed put and didn't misbehave. That meant no laptop.

The only things that had given her the remotest sense of joy were the notes Hentz had provided from Bonnie and Kevin, who were both worried about her, and the seven postcards from her parents that had been piling up in her mailbox. Apparently, they'd departed Hong Kong and were now island-hopping somewhere in the South Pacific.

She snorted at the idea that the postal carrier had continued delivering her mail even though her house was a burned-out shell. Not for long, thank goodness. Someone high up must have pulled some strings with her insurance company, because her claim was being processed in record time. The agents had delivered her the paperwork notifying her that she could start rebuilding in just a few short weeks. Hopefully by then, this would all be over, and she could start fresh. Maybe she'd even take a walk on the wild side and paint her house some funky color like magenta or chartreuse. The idea of a chartreuse house had her grinning for the first time in two weeks. It was all part of her newfound confidence in herself. Ironically, she had Matt to thank for that.

She held up her hand, looking at the charm bracelet that made a pretty, jangling sound whenever she moved. He'd broken her heart, and she doubted she would ever love as deeply again, but she didn't regret what had happened between them for a second. Not only had he been her first, but he'd given her many other wonderful things. Through his eyes, she'd learned that she could be beautiful and sexy, and that other men saw her that way as well. He'd helped her to view herself in a different light. A stronger, more confident light.

Rolling onto her back, she stared at the ceiling, counting cracks in the paint. She was beginning to regret her decision to let the FBI watch over her, but staying with Matt another moment longer would have been too painful. Although she really could use a swig of the Dalwhinnie she'd left behind at his house.

"Who am I kidding, Poofy?" In response, the Angora stood and began kneading his paws on her thigh. It was *him* she missed. More than anything.

Since the moment they'd gone their separate ways, her life seemed empty, devoid of something she hadn't known existed until she'd met him. Now that it was gone, she wanted it back. But the man had issues, deep-seated issues he needed to resolve before he could ever love a woman.

Cops don't talk to shrinks. She understood that it was his warrior mindset—that aspect of a person who spends a lifetime protecting others—that made it virtually impossible for him to admit that sometimes *he* was the one who needed help. It was also fear that prevented Matt from moving on. Fear that seeking help would make him appear weak, undermining his ingrained sense of strength. Not his physical strength. That would never be in question. It was his emotional strength he feared losing, and he'd been that way for twenty years. At this point in his life, he didn't know any other way.

"I tried, Poof." She sat and scooped the cat into her arms, snuggling him against her chest. Matt could have been everything to her, and she to him.

Was I wrong? Should I have stayed and tried to help him?

No. He didn't want her help. This was something he had to work out on his own. Still, it killed her not to be with him. To snuggle against his long, hard body as they'd done that one blissful night at the hotel. To feel his lips on hers, his tongue in her mouth, his hard length filling her.

When she groaned this time, it was out of sexual frustration. Now that she knew how wonderful lovemaking could be, she wanted more of it. But the idea of making love with anyone but Matt made her shudder with apprehension.

Lying back again on the bed, she sighed. "Maybe one day, Poofmeister. Maybe one d—"

Raised voices came from downstairs. A heavy *thud*, followed quickly by another, then… Silence.

Bolting upright, she froze, holding her breath. Doors opened and closed, but she heard no more voices. She set Poofy on the mattress and tiptoed to the door. *Something isn't right.* These weren't the normal sounds made by Donald and Angie, the two agents assigned to the overnight shift. Her heart began thumping crazily.

She pressed her ear to the door. Shuffling. Another door being opened. "Angie? Donald?" No answer.

Heavy footsteps pounded up the stairs, and she stepped back from the door. The knob rattled. Someone was trying to get in, and it wasn't Angie or Donald. They would have knocked. That was the prearranged protocol if they needed to speak with her.

They found me. Somehow the Russians found me.

She backed farther from the door, turning her head to search frantically for some kind of weapon. But she already knew there weren't any. The only weapons in the house were the guns Donald and Angie carried on their belts.

Her heart pounded so hard she thought it would beat right out of her chest. *My phone, where is my phone?* They'd given her another cell phone for emergencies and with strict orders not to contact anyone but Angie or Donald.

She yanked the covers off the bed, upsetting Poofy, who gave an indignant *mew* and jumped to the floor.

Again, the door rattled.

Getting to her knees, she searched under the bed. *No phone, dammit!*

I have to get out of here. But she was on the second floor. Could she really jump to the grass without breaking a leg? Probably not, but it was better than staying where she was and getting shot.

With trembling fingers, she shoved her feet into her shoes, then went to the window. Her hands were shaking so badly she struggled to twist open the lock.

Behind her, the wood splintered.

They were kicking in the door.

Turning back to the window, she flipped open the lock and gripped the handle, raising the lower pane. She glanced over her shoulder to see the door come flying off its top hinge, slamming against the wall.

Sweat dripped into her eyes as she grabbed Poofy from where he sat cowering in the corner. She stuck one leg out the window, preparing to slide down the angled roof, when an arm went around her waist, hauling her back inside.

For Poofy's safety, she dropped the cat to the floor, twisting and kicking backward, struggling to get free. "Let me go, you son of a bitch!"

The man laughed as he held her a foot above the floor, kicking and screaming. His hand clamped over her mouth, then a second man slammed the window shut, cutting her off from the outside world. *Shit, shit, shit!* If ever there was a time and a place for that word, it was now.

Bastards. She might be tiny, but if they thought they could kill her without a fight, they were sorely mistaken.

The hand over her mouth was large and smelled vaguely like borscht. She twisted her head back and forth to loosen his hold so she could bite down on his fingers.

"Don't move," the second thug said in heavily accented English, shoving the barrel of a gun against her forehead.

She sucked in a breath and froze. The barrel was long, with a thick cylinder on the end. *A silencer.* They could kill her, and no one would even hear the shot.

So why haven't they? Her heart lurched at the realization they'd probably already killed Angie and Donald.

"What are you waiting for?" With Thug One's hand still covering her mouth, the words came out muffled. She kicked backward and was rewarded with a mild Russian oath as her foot contacted his shin and his hand slipped from her face. "Just kill me and be done with it."

Even Thug Two's chuckle had a Russian accent to it. "Perhaps I will. Perhaps I won't. Behave and maybe the boss lets you live. Maybe not."

Is there really a chance they'd let her live after all this? She doubted it, but if it could buy her enough time for the FBI to find her, she'd play along.

The stairs creaked as they led her down into the living room. She cried out at the sight of Angie and Donald on the floor. Angie didn't move, but Donald groaned as he caught sight of her.

Thug One aimed his gun at Donald's head and pulled the trigger. The agent's body jerked, and Trista couldn't stop the scream that escaped her lips.

Oh my God! They're both dead.

She froze. The scene before her was totally surreal. Though she could see the agents' lifeless bodies right there in front of her, the shock was so great she almost couldn't believe it. *Two people died trying to protect me, and now they're gone.*

Unable to stop herself, she began sobbing. Thug Two pointed another gun at her, and she cringed, expected to hear the shot, feel the bullet penetrate her flesh. It never came.

A gun pressed into her back. "Keep quiet."

With one last look at the dead agents, she compliantly followed them outside, hearing the door *click* shut behind them.

Poofy.

Turning, she glanced up to the top window, worrying and praying that her cat would be all right.

The night was dark as ink, the autumn air cool as they shoved her into the back seat of a dark sedan and slammed the door shut. The car's interior lights hadn't come on, and she assumed they'd removed the bulbs.

The car started and pulled from the curb. She heard a tiny *click*, then threw up her hands as a bright light blinded her.

"Hello, Ms. Gold." Instinctively, she pushed herself to the far end of the seat until her back contacted the door. The interior of the car was so dark she hadn't realized anyone else was inside. "We've never met before. Not in person, anyway. Although I understand you've been *following* me for quite some time."

A frisson of terror crept up her spine. This was the man who now held her life in his hands.

Alexy Lukashin—the *rezidentura*.

Chapter Twenty-Six

Matt sat in the dark living room staring at the TV, much as he'd done every night for the past two weeks since he'd watched Trista being escorted out of his life.

Yawning, he glanced at the green dial of the watch on his wrist. It was well after midnight and still, he couldn't sleep. Unfortunately, his friends were all working the night shift that week, so he was totally alone. Except for Sheba.

He'd gone back to work, volunteering for every double shift on the roster, anything to keep his mind occupied. Trista—his little pixie—had dug deep under his skin, burrowing into his heart until she was all he could think about. But he couldn't burden her with being around someone who was so fucked up. He'd undoubtedly make her miserable, and she'd wind up leaving him anyway. *It's better this way.* Or so he kept telling himself.

Sheba lifted her head from his lap, her amber-gold eyes locking onto his, a supremely mournful expression on her face, one that mirrored the sadness deep in his soul. When he scratched her under the chin, she dipped her muzzle to lick his hand, as if telling him she knew exactly what he was going through.

"I know you miss her." Sheba let out a little whine and laid her head back on his lap. "I miss her, too." So much that he'd taken to letting Sheba up on the sofa during his late-night TV sessions, a mortal sin in the K-9 world and one that he'd railed at Trista for committing in the hotel. The one where he'd taken her virginity and made sweet love to her. That was a night he'd never forget.

Resting his hand on Sheba's belly, he sifted his fingers through her short coat, remembering with vivid clarity how he'd watched Trista overcome her fear of dogs. She and Sheba had even become friends.

He wanted to give her more. *Hell, I want to give her everything, but not the way I am now.* "Think I can do it, girl?" In response, Sheba raised her head and rested one paw on top of his hand, as if in a high five. He doubted she knew what he'd said, but he'd asked her a question and she inherently knew his moods well enough to understand whatever was bugging him and offer her moral support.

The hardest part would be making that first call to someone in the profession cops avoided at all costs. A shrink.

Dipping her head down and up repeatedly, Sheba looked as if she were nodding in encouragement.

"I can't promise you anything." He scratched her ears, knowing he was saying that more to himself. "Except that I'll give it my best sh—"

The cell phone he'd set on the coffee table rang, and he picked it up, not recognizing the number. "Connors."

"It's Max Fenway. Trista's gone. We think the Russians have her."

Matt jumped to his feet. In less time than it took for his heart to beat once, he was instantly awake, as if someone had zapped him with a Taser. "What kind of fucking morons did you have protecting her?" He began pacing the living room, Sheba keeping step with him, her body tense as she sensed something was horribly wrong. "And what do you mean, you *think* they have her?"

"I've got two dead agents, and she's not at the safe house. The door to her bedroom was kicked clean off the hinges. There's no sign of her."

His heart gave a heavy sigh of relief. If there was no sign of her... If she wasn't lying dead next to the two FBI agents, then she could still be alive.

Goddamn it. Damn it all to hell. "I never should have let you guys take her." *Fuck, I should have been the one protecting her, whether she liked it or not.* "How many people do you have out there looking for her?" Whatever that number was, it wouldn't be enough.

"Look, Connors, we've got it covered. I'm only notifying you because I sensed something between you two. I've got every FBI agent in the area out looking for her and every snitch on the agency's payroll keeping their eyes and ears open."

"I can find her faster." With Fenway still on the line, he charged into his office and pulled up the GPS program linked to the tracking device he'd hooked onto Trista's charm bracelet. "Fuck!" The system was down. He'd have to find her on the ground using a handheld device.

He bolted up the stairs. Behind him, Sheba followed closely at his heels. "What's the location of the safe house?"

"What's the difference?" Fenway shouted back. "She's not there."

Putting the call on speakerphone, he set it on his bureau, then shoved his legs into a pair of cargo pants. "The difference is that I can try to track her from her last known location."

"How?"

"She's wearing a locator. It's in the charm bracelet I gave

her."

"How do you know she's wearing it?"

"Since the day I gave it to her, she's never taken it off." Not even in the shower, but he kept that information to himself. He grabbed a CIA shirt from his closet and pulled it over his head. "I'm not about to rely on you and your incapable team of fuckup agents to find her. Now give me the goddamn address!"

Fenway rattled off the address, which Matt committed to memory. "Don't show up here half-cocked, or I'll have to call your—"

Matt hung up, not giving a shit who Fenway called. He shoved his belt through his holstered weapon and two fully loaded magazine pouches. As he punched in another call, Sheba danced at his feet, tracking his every move. It was a conditioned stimulus. When he geared up, his dog knew what was coming and was as ready for action as he was.

"Nick," he said when his friend answered. Then he gave the code phrase they'd all agreed on when they'd been in training together, the one signifying dire, life-threatening shit was going down and their unquestioned assistance was needed ASAP. "Lock 'n' load."

Chapter Twenty-Seven

An hour later, they were still driving through the darkness, uphill on a turning, twisting tree-lined road. So many thoughts—regrets, mostly—ran through Trista's head.

I'm going to die.

No one will find my body.

I wish I'd gotten married and had children. Now she'd never have the chance. At least her parents still had each other. When word got back to them that she was gone, they would carry on. The only one who truly needed her was her cat.

She bit back a cry. *Who will take care of Poofy?*

Matt. Even though dogs were his first love, she didn't doubt he'd either keep Poofy at his place or find him a good home. That was one regret she didn't have. The other was that she'd fallen in love with Matt and told him how she felt. Given her dire circumstances, that one thought gave her some measure of comfort.

Trista choked down another sob. She loved him too much to spend one more night under the same roof with him, but right now, she was sorely regretting that decision. He'd been right. Matt might not be capable of loving her, but he'd always kept her safe. Now it was up to her to save her own ass.

She missed what the sign on the edge of the road said, but as soon as they'd passed it, the car slowed and turned onto another road. The vehicle lurched as it traversed the rutted pavement. In the glow of the headlights, she glimpsed an enormous wrought iron gate. They stopped in front, and the doors' locks clicked open. Thug Two got out of the car.

This is it. Her only possible chance of escape. Glancing sideways at Lukashin, she saw his attention was focused forward on his man now struggling to open the gate. Her heart raced as she clasped the metal door handle, cranked it open, then jumped from the car and took off running toward the trees.

Shouts came from behind her. She'd never been much for working out, preferring to spend her time sitting in front of a computer screen, but she'd never run faster in her life.

Tree limbs smacked her in the face and arms, and she nearly stumbled over the uneven terrain. It was pitch black, with no moon to light her way. Her heart pounded, and her breath came in quick gasps.

As she ran, she held her arms in front of her face to bat away the constant assault from all the low-hanging foliage. She tripped and fell to her hands and knees. *Get up! Go, go, go!*

A second later, she was on her feet, pounding through the trees. She had no idea where she was going, and it didn't matter. Behind her was death. In front of her was her only possible avenue of escape.

She slammed into something solid—something that spun her, jerking her off her feet. She screamed, twisting in his arms, clawing at his face, but it was no good. One of the thugs had her solidly in a bear hug.

He threw her over his shoulder and began walking. She pounded on his back with her fists, but he ignored her. Blood rushed to her head, and she nearly passed out. Suddenly, she was exhausted and let her arms dangle uselessly. She wanted to cry but couldn't.

What good would it do?

A few minutes later, she was thrown onto the back seat of the car like a sack of potatoes. The door slammed shut behind her, and she cowered against the side, pulling her legs up to rest her head on her knees.

"I admire your tenacity, but it is a waste of time and energy." The car rolled through the open gates. "There is no escaping what's coming next."

"And what exactly is that?" Although the interior of the car was dark, she looked in the direction of his voice, noting that his accent was still there, though not as thick as that of his thugs, and his English was impeccable, no doubt from living in the U.S. for so long.

"You and I need to have a little chat." The sound of wrinkling plastic came to her ears. "Peppermint?"

She sensed he was holding something in front of her face, but she ignored it. The scent of mint filled the car's interior as they continued along the darkened road.

The car's headlights illuminated the unkempt grass and weeds. They continued on for at least another mile before the first building came into view, a large three-story stucco structure with at least thirty windows on the side facing the road.

They passed building after building, similar to the first one. After forty such structures, she lost count.

Finally, Thug One drove up to one of the buildings, continuing to the side, where he jumped the curb, then pulled around back and parked on the grass. The walls of the structure were completely covered with meandering vines. Wherever they were, she guessed the place had been abandoned for years.

This is not good. Even if I scream, no one will hear me. I am in deep shit. Funny how after a lifetime of not cursing, that word was now her go-to fave.

The engine turned off, and she was hauled outside and through a rusty door. Thug Two turned on a flashlight, illuminating a long corridor with tall, multipaned arched windows covered with dust, grime, and cobwebs. The floor was covered with dingy brown-and-black checkerboard tile and littered with debris and green paint chips from the peeling walls. A damp, musty smell permeated the building, probably from the occasional fuzzy gray patches of mold on the walls.

They passed door after door, each one dark brown and with a single square viewing window. On one of the walls, someone had hand-painted a mural of an American flag with the words *One Flag, One Country.*

As they propelled her farther down the hallway, she glanced up and around, searching for something—*anything*—that could help her out of this mess. An open door. A discarded knife. But there was nothing. Nothing but paint chips, an occasional ratty leather shoe, and a filthy stuffed animal.

"Where are we?" Not that it mattered. Wherever it was, they were in the middle of nowhere.

"This is an old psychiatric facility," Lukashin said. "One of the largest in the country. It was built in the 1920s. There are over six hundred acres and nearly a hundred buildings with nine thousand beds. It was built during a time when mental patients were considered outcasts, separated from society. Hence the remote location. Out of sight, out of mind."

As they walked, the glow from the flashlight partially illuminated some of the rooms they passed. In one of them, she glimpsed old mattresses piled high.

"The surrounding community experienced an exceedingly high murder rate, a statistic attributed to occasional escapees. Anyone recaptured was…rehabilitated." He chuckled, a creepy sound that sent fear up her spine. "This facility was at the forefront of shock therapy, lobotomy, and research into many varieties of antipsychotic drugs."

Speaking of psychotic…

At the end of the hallway, they guided her into a room and flipped on an overhead fluorescent light that flickered and buzzed. At one end of the large space were six chairs in a row that looked like they belonged in a dentist's office… except for the leather straps attached to the arms, legs, and padded headrests. Beside one of them stood a rusty metal tray on wheels. At the sight of what was on the tray, her blood ran cold.

Syringes. Lots of them.

Her eyes went wide. "No!" She turned to run, but strong arms grabbed her and she was no match for their strength. One of the thugs shoved her into the chair, quickly strapping down her arms and legs. Fisting her hands, she strained at the straps to no avail. She tried kicking, but her legs were bound just as tightly to the legs of the chair. Again, she fought the urge to scream, knowing only these Russian bastards and the few rats she'd glimpsed scurrying away at their arrival would hear her.

Jerking her wrists from side to side, she strained at her bonds. Blood trickled down her arm onto the filthy white tile floor, and it was then that she realized the charm bracelet Matt had given her was gone. Her body began to tremble. She'd held back the tears until now, but the loss of that one little piece of jewelry undid her. A steady stream of tears trickled from both her eyes.

Now that she could see Lukashin clearly, she compared

him to her memory of the photos she'd researched in the CIA data bank files, which were taken of a younger man. Lukashin was now sixty-five years old, with a thinning, receding hairline. That, and he had more lines at the corners of his mouth and eyes. But it was the black, soulless eyes that she would have recognized anywhere.

"For such a tiny woman, you have caused me a great deal of aggravation. Your technological and analytical talents are well known to us. Your skills far surpass those of our own people's in those particular fields. What you failed to note was that while you've been tracking *me,* we've been keeping an eye on *you*."

"Is that how you identified me?" It was a lingering question that still remained unanswered.

"Essentially, yes. You see, I'm a product of the Cold War, but I've made a point of keeping up with modern technology's impact on the world." Lukashin pursed his lips, giving her the impression he was pondering how much to tell her. "You've clearly invented a miraculous program enabling you to track my location on the black net. What you didn't know is that my programmers can tag anyone found trespassing in my chat room. Still, I'd love to hear about how you found me online in the first place."

"Is that why I'm here?" she cried in a trembling voice. "To divulge classified technological secrets to you? I assure you, that's not going to happen." She'd die before betraying her country. Heck, she *was* going to die anyway.

"What do you know about Senator Ashburn?"

"Nothing," she lied. "Except that he'll probably be our next president." They couldn't know for certain that she knew who the senator was and what he'd done. And they certainly wouldn't know she'd stolen Thomas George's external hard drive and cracked into his encrypted files.

"You listened in on my chat room conversation." He

pinned her with those cruel, dark eyes. "And you called the editor at the *Arlington Sentinel*, asking what story Thomas George was working on when he was killed. Why did you do that?"

Oh shit. She'd forgotten about that phone call. "I was curious."

"Did you find out?"

"No," she lied again, realizing he knew she was handing him a line of shit. She wouldn't be in this mess if he didn't suspect she knew Senator Ashburn's backstory. "You murdered him, didn't you? Over his story."

He made a sucking sound as he shifted another peppermint from one side of his mouth to the other. "I did."

She swallowed. Any possibility he'd consider letting her go just went out the window. The fact that he'd just confessed to murder was the final nail in her coffin.

I'll never get out of here alive.

He leaned in until his face was inches from hers. "Who did you tell about my chat room conversation?"

"No one."

"You work for the CIA. There is protocol. There must be a printout of what you overheard. Who has it?"

"I don't know." She did, and he knew it. Matt, Wayne, and Genevieve. But she'd never say their names. *Never.*

"You're lying."

"What's the difference?" She snapped. "You're going to kill me anyway. You've already tried and failed twice before."

"Yes, that's true. The difference now is that you have something I want."

"What?"

"Information."

"I'll never tell you anything."

He gave a soft chuckle, reminiscent of the way her grandfather used to laugh when he bounced her on his knee.

But his grandfatherly demeanor was nothing but a grand facade. This man was a cold-blooded killer.

"We shall see, we shall see." He plucked another peppermint from his pants pocket, unwrapped it, and popped it into his mouth. He nodded to one of the thugs, who handed him a syringe.

"No." She began shaking her head back and forth. "Please don't." She twisted and pulled futilely at the restraints.

A hand clamped over her forehead, jerking her back against the headrest. The leather strap she'd seen earlier was tugged across her forehead and buckled tight.

Lukashin pushed up the sleeve of her T-shirt, and she cringed as the needle moved closer. *I'm going to die.* The needle was sharp as it pierced her skin, and as he slowly depressed the plunger, her last thought was of Matt.

I love you.

Chapter Twenty-Eight

A few blocks from the address Fenway had given him, Matt glanced down at the handheld locator on the seat. Nothing yet. *Dammit.*

As soon as he rounded the corner, the number of vehicles with blue flashing strobes nearly blinded him. The sidewalk in front of the safe house was jammed with Crown Vics, Chargers, Impalas, and every other make and model in the U.S. government's fleet. A few curious neighbors stood on their front porches, watching the bevy of police activity.

The house was a two-story 1970s tract house that looked like every other house on the block. It should have been perfect for a safe house. Lotta good that had done Trista. He wondered how the fuck they'd found her. "Goddamn FBI," he muttered through clenched teeth as he double-parked next to a black Charger.

He hooked the locator onto his belt, then grabbed Sheba's leash and the last garment he'd seen Trista wearing: the green T-shirt he'd bought her the day he'd purchased the charm bracelet.

His friends hadn't arrived yet, but he didn't doubt for a second that they'd be there for him.

After he leashed Sheba, she bounded from the Explorer. Even his dog knew serious shit was about to go down. "Let's go, girl."

Fenway met him at the front door. Over the agent's shoulders, he glimpsed a half dozen crime scene agents wearing gloves, brushing for prints and photographing the interior.

"Connors," Fenway said.

It took every ounce of his restraint not to deck the fucker, but that would waste precious time. *Later*, he promised himself. *After* they got Trista back. "Find anything useful?"

"Negative." Fenway shook his head. "My guys are processing the scene. No one goes in until they're done."

"Fuck that." Without waiting for a response, he shoved the agent aside. As soon as he walked into the house, he smelled it. The coppery scent of blood and the awful stench of death. In the living room adjacent to the hallway lay the bodies of two dead FBI agents. He was saddened by their deaths and angry that they hadn't been skilled enough to stop Trista from being taken.

"Connors, dammit!" Fenway shouted, but Matt ignored him.

He grabbed Trista's T-shirt from where he'd tucked it into his belt and let Sheba sniff it. Immediately, the dog headed for the stairs. Keeping her on the leash, he followed. Sheba beelined for the second door on the left side of the hallway. He didn't have half the nasal receptors a dog had, but even he would have known this was the room Trista had occupied for the past two weeks. Her scent was everywhere. Flowers, vanilla and spice, and that shampoo at his house that she'd come to like. The FBI agents must have purchased some for her.

He ripped the receiver off his belt, desperately hoping to

get a blip, but there was none. It had been a long shot at best. Now he'd have to drive in all directions, praying like hell that he'd get a hit.

Sheba whined, dragging him to the far corner of the room behind the bed. Cowering on the floor, every white hair on his furry body on end, was Poofy.

"*Shit.*" The last thing he needed was a cat in a K-9 vehicle, but he couldn't leave the poor thing there to fend for itself. Besides, if Trista ever found out he'd abandoned her precious feline, his ass would be toast.

If. If she was even still alive. *Don't even think it.*

Sheba strained at the leash, trying to touch noses with the frightened cat, but Poofy wasn't having any of it and pressed himself farther into the corner.

"Easy, buddy." Pulling on his dog's leash to keep the two animals separated, Matt leaned down and scooped up the cat, tucking him under his arm.

Seconds later, he and Sheba were running down the walk to his Explorer. He deposited Poofy on the floor in front of the passenger seat, then quickly shut the door before the cat could escape.

"Matt!"

He turned to see six men in uniform coming toward him. Somehow, Nick, Jaime, Dayne, Eric, Kade, and Markus had gotten out of their nightly assignments to come to his aid. He didn't want to know how they'd managed it without getting their asses chewed.

"What can we do?" Nick gripped his shoulder.

"Name it," Kade added. "We've got the dogs, and we're ready to roll."

He quickly gave the details of what had gone down, who they were dealing with, and what his plan was to find Trista.

"Let's go kick some Russian ass." Dayne clenched his fist in the air.

"Damn straight." Eric fist-bumped Dayne's fist. "If those fuckers hurt our little pixie, we'll pound their faces into the ground."

A stab of fear cut through Matt's heart at the idea of Trista being hurt, in pain, or…worse. *Dead*. Taking a deep breath, he shoved his fears aside. "Let's roll. I'll update you over the radio."

As the other men headed back to their SUVs, he caught sight of Fenway practically running toward him.

"Connors!" The agent grabbed him by the arm. "Let me send some of my team with you."

"Your *team*?" He leaned down and got in the other man's face. Beside him, Sheba growled deep in her throat, sensing his barely controlled anger. "If your agents hadn't just made the ultimate sacrifice, I'd bring up the fact that I managed to kick one of your teams twice that size, and I did it single-handedly." He pointed to the front door. "Those dead agents…that's on you. Two clearly untrained agents were a cakewalk for a crew of Russian operatives who were probably all military-trained. So fuck you, Fenway. I'll find her, and I'll do it with *my* team."

Fenway began sputtering, and Matt knew why. The man's career was on the line. He'd let a key witness in the biggest case in decades get grabbed, and now he wanted to be part of the rescue team so he could at least save face.

Fuck. That. At this point, Matt wouldn't even trust the man to safeguard the cat.

Ignoring the man's protests, Matt punched the fob on his vest and the side door of the Explorer swung open, nearly whacking Fenway in the ass. Sheba gave the other man a parting growl, then leaped into the SUV.

When Matt pulled away from the curb, six other Explorers followed closely behind, red-and-blue strobes flashing. In the darkened interior, he glanced at the receiver, still getting nothing from the tracker.

Goddamn FBI. No offense to Dayne, who was FBI K-9. Dayne was a different breed than Fenway and his incompetent agents. If Dayne had been on the team guarding Trista, Matt had no doubt she would still be there.

Twenty minutes later, he hung a 180 and headed in the other direction. The handheld receiver alone without the satellite link wasn't nearly as capable. Not quite a needle in a haystack, but driving around until he got a hit would take time, particularly since he didn't know in which direction to head.

An hour later, there was still no blip on the screen. For the third time since they'd been driving around, he tried the satellite link, but it was still down. He pounded the steering wheel with his fist. "Damn." They were wasting precious time.

Reacting to his outburst, Sheba stuck her head through the cage opening and rested her snout on his shoulder. Matt glanced at the floor in front of the passenger seat to gauge Poofy's reaction, but the cat was nowhere in sight, having crawled somewhere underneath the seat.

Eric was right. If those Russian fuckers had hurt Trista, he'd do a helluva lot more than just pound their faces into the ground. He'd unleash a painful shit storm the likes of which they'd never seen. He'd make them wish they'd never been born. He'd—

His heart squeezed, and he sucked in an unsteady breath. *I will find her.* Then he'd do the right thing and let her go. *I have to. Because I'm in love with her. Totally, absolutely, fucking in love with her.*

A weak *beep* came from the receiver, and he jerked his attention back to the screen. The blinking blip flickered in and out, indicating it was at the very edge of the handheld's range, but it was there.

His heart raced as he slammed his foot on the accelerator and prayed.

Chapter Twenty-Nine

Trista's head lolled from one side to the other. Not that she was sleepy, exactly, more like dopey or drunk. Having difficulty focusing, she squinted, then forced her eyes open wider.

"There you are." Lukashin smiled.

"For a diabolical killer, you have a nice smile." She grinned, somehow realizing that was the last thing she ought to be doing under the circumstances, but she couldn't help it, and she just didn't care. "I'm guessing that's how nobody ever sees it coming."

"You may very well be right." He bestowed her with another charming smile. "What is your name?"

"Trista Gold."

"Who do you work for?"

"The CIA. But you already know that, silly." This time, she was the one to laugh, and somewhere in the back of her brain, she understood her reactions were inappropriate, given the situation. "Why am I saying such stupid things?"

"That's the sodium pentothal I injected into your arm.

In James Bond movies, it's called truth serum. In reality, it shuts down the higher thinking parts of the brain. It's more difficult to lie than it is to tell the truth, so people tend to be uninhibited, saying whatever pops into their brains."

"Oh, okay." She nodded absently. *That makes sense, although he's going to kill me, so why am I answering his questions? Because he's right. I just don't give a shit. Shit.* Her favorite new word. "Shit, shit, shit." Somehow that word seemed more appropriate, and yet she did care and vowed then and there not to tell him anything of importance. *Fight it.* Fight it! *You can do it.*

"Did you read the article Thomas George wrote about Senator Ashburn?" he asked.

"You betcha." She nodded emphatically. "Quite a shocker, huh?" *Oops.* Had she admitted to reading the article already? *I suck at this.*

"Indeed." He, too, nodded. "Where did you read the article?"

"M—" She clamped her mouth shut. She'd been about to say *Matt's house* but caught herself at the last second. "My computer." She smiled broadly, quite pleased with the quick recovery. *See, it isn't that hard fighting truth serum. I'm as good as James Bond. 007.* "On the external hard drive I stole from Thomas George's apartment." *Oops again. Didn't mean for that to slip out. Shit, sodium pentothal really works!*

"Ah." His brows rose. "Did you show the article to anyone?"

Matt. Technically, he was the only one she'd shown it to. *No! Do* not *say his name.*

"Who did you show it to?" Lukashin persisted.

"Nope, not gonna tell you." She shook her head, which had begun to feel as if it weighed a hundred pounds.

"Who?" He leaned in so close she got a heavy whiff of peppermint-laden breath.

Think before you answer. Take your time.

"Handsome man," she answered on a sigh. "*Very* handsome man. He's totally hot." She snickered. *Yeah, go with that answer.* It wasn't a lie, after all.

"What is the handsome man's name?"

She bit her lip to keep Matt's name from dribbling through her lips. *I got it!* "Hot Guy. His name is Hot Guy." She couldn't stop from grinning like an idiot. "No, make that *Totally* Hot Guy."

One of the thugs snorted, but to her delight, Lukashin straightened, his lips compressing into a thin line.

"What did you do with the hard drive?"

"I gave it to Max." *Shit.* She hadn't meant to say his name. *I'm slipping.*

The *rezidentura* grinned, reminding her of the devil. "You were under the protection of the FBI, so would that be Special Agent Max Fenway?"

"I guess the cat's out of the bag now, eh?" *Eh?* Where had that come from? She wasn't Canadian. And she suddenly felt inordinately tired.

"Unfortunately, my dear, it seems everyone knows about the article. The FBI. The CIA."

"Good. Can I go to sleep now?"

He looked at Thug One and Two. "Take her to the cemetery."

"The cemetery?" She frowned. "Why would I want to go to a cemetery? That's where dead people go."

"You are correct." He picked up another syringe from the metal tray, and the smile he gave her this time was anything *but* grandfatherly.

Chapter Thirty

The beep had been getting louder by the mile, the red blip progressively brighter as Matt tracked it on the digital map.

Behind him glowed the steady, comforting headlights of the other six SUVs. His friends would always have his back. He only prayed they'd be in time. Fear and worry snaked through him that they'd be too late.

They'd long ago gotten off I-66 and been driving steadily north along a narrow, twisting two-lane road skirting the edge of the Blue Ridge Mountains. There wasn't much around except wild game and a whole lotta Christmas trees—another thing that didn't bode well. Whatever those Russian fuckers had planned, it was clear Trista being released wasn't part of it.

Sheba whined, pawing at the partition separating her from the passenger compartment before sticking her head through the opening and snorting in his ear. Craning her neck toward the green T-shirt on the seat, she let out a mournful howl. Sheba knew Trista was in trouble.

The road got steeper as they headed farther and farther

north into the mountains, and with each passing mile, he gripped the steering wheel tighter. She'd been gone for more than two hours, and his mind raced with horrific scenes of the pain and suffering she might be enduring. *God, no. Not that.* He couldn't take it if she was in pain.

As he rounded the next bend, an elevation sign came into view, thirteen hundred feet. The next sign took him by surprise. Blue Ridge Psychiatric Center. He'd forgotten the place even existed. As far as he knew, it had been abandoned for decades.

But the buildings are still there. A silent, morbid reminder of the brutal and experimental electrical and psychoactive drug treatments administered to mentally ill patients back in the day. The place even had its own cemetery, filled with poor souls who hadn't been cured.

If it wasn't for the lousy road condition, he would have stomped on the pedal even harder. But the driving was treacherous enough as it was.

Light rain began to fall, forcing him to flip on the wipers. "Shit." Rain would kill any scent residue, making it harder for the dogs to track. This time he did pound his foot on the accelerator, sending the Explorer perilously close to the edge of the unfenced road.

At the next bend, the road straightened, and another sign announced the entrance to the psychiatric center. He slammed on the brake and cut hard left onto a broken, rutted laneway. Just as the facility's massive gates came into view, the receiver shrilled, indicating he was practically right on top of the tracking device.

Right on top of the charm bracelet.

Slamming the brake pedal again, he waited for the Explorer to come to a halt, then hit Sheba's door release. The dog flew from the SUV and bolted around the hood. Matt took off at a dead run, following with a flashlight to illuminate the darkened woods. There was no need to look over his shoulder to verify his friends were right behind him. They'd always have his back.

Sheba barked once, then went silent. Breathing hard, he pounded through the trees, barely feeling the tree limbs smacking his face. Up ahead, the flashlight caught Sheba's eyes, making them glitter like gold diamonds. She lay on the ground, panting, looking up at him. Crouching, he shone the light between her outstretched paws, immediately spotting what she'd hit on.

Trista's charm bracelet.

He picked it up, clenching his jaw. "No!" For a split second, he squeezed his eyes shut, then stood and swung the flashlight in a 360, already knowing she wouldn't be there. If Trista was anywhere in the immediate vicinity, Sheba would have hit on her first, instead of the bracelet.

The sounds of trees rustling and men running came to him.

"Matt, whatdya got?" Nick rested a hand on his shoulder.

He was quickly surrounded by Kade, Markus, and Jaime. He assumed Eric and Dayne had remained behind with the other dogs and vehicles.

"She was here, dammit." He held up the bracelet, then closed his fingers around it.

"The other dogs are in the trucks," Nick said as he caught his breath. "You want us to get them out here?"

"Not yet. Sheba knows her best." Matt let the dog sniff the charm bracelet again, then swung his arm in a wordless command. Sheba took off in the direction of the other vehicles.

Matt bolted after her, his friends not far behind. When they returned to the SUVs, Sheba paused in front of the massive iron gates, jaws open, nose alternately sniffing the air then the ground.

She circled round and round before sitting, indicating she'd lost the scent. Either that or Trista had gotten back into a vehicle.

"Something happened here." Nick swung his own flashlight in every direction. "They had to have driven here, then she somehow wound up in the woods."

"She tried to escape, and they caught her." Matt couldn't hide the panicked edge to his voice. "I'm guessing there was a struggle, and her bracelet fell off."

A hum sounded from the distance, growing steadily louder. Light rain began to fall on the trees and pavement. Matt looked up at the sky, which was pitch black. If it rained any harder, none of the dogs—not even Sheba, who was the best tracker he'd ever seen—would be able to pick up a scent.

"Back in the trucks," Matt shouted. "Follow me." He rounded the Explorer and indicated for Sheba to get in. He shut the door behind her and got back into the driver's seat.

They drove deeper inside the complex, not seeing a building for a solid half mile. At an intersection, he stopped, his headlights illuminating building after building along all three roads as far ahead as the eye could see.

"Fuck, they could be anywhere." And if they'd parked behind any of the buildings, he could have missed them and driven right by. He keyed the mic. "Split up. Check behind all the buildings."

"Copy that," each of his friends came back.

He gunned the engine and went straight. Nick followed, with the other vehicles peeling off, either left or right. This could take time. Time Trista didn't have. "Hang on, baby. Hang on."

At the tenth building, he jumped the curb, driving around back, still seeing nothing. With the rain coming down harder, he was forced to flick the wipers up another notch. Behind him, Sheba pawed at the partition, whining in frustration.

As he drove back to the main road, Nick's headlights flickered from behind an adjacent structure. Matt put the Explorer in park and keyed the mic. "I'm getting out with Sheba. There are too many buildings, and we're flying blind. Regroup at my location." He flashed his headlights several times.

"Ten-four." Nick pulled up beside him.

In the distance, Matt caught the headlights of the other SUVs speeding in his direction. He grabbed Trista's T-shirt and Sheba's twenty-foot lead, then got out and rounded the SUV. When he opened Sheba's door, she practically leaped into his arms, eager to get on track. He hooked the leash onto her collar, then stuck the T-shirt under her nose for her to reprocess Trista's scent. She nuzzled the green fabric, taking short, deep snorting inhales.

He stepped aside, and she lunged past him out the door, quickly taking up slack in the leash, her body straining to get on track. With the rain this heavy, it would be a miracle if she found something. "Get Saxon," he shouted to Nick. "Stay behind me." He didn't want Nick's dog or the other K-9s interfering with Sheba's track.

"Copy that."

Matt released the extra length of the leash, allowing Sheba to run ahead without getting loose. Even as good a shape as he was in, once she got loose on a hot track, he'd never be able to keep pace with her.

Lightning lit the sky, followed by a deep rumble of thunder. Rain pounded steadily heavier, sending a sharp jab of worry to his gut. Sheba lifted her head, then turned in another direction. A strong gust of wind shot down the road, powerful enough that Matt had to shield his eyes from the driving rain. Sheba stopped short, turning her head in several directions, struggling to reacquire Trista's scent.

He clenched his jaw. Wrapping the leash several times

around his hand, he reeled the dog in, bringing her back to the last spot she'd hit on. She put her nose to the ground, trotting in a serpentine pattern, then took off again.

Heavy rain had dampened his shirt, and water dripped down his face. Soon there'd be nothing for Sheba to follow. Another gust of wind tore the scent away, and she circled back, hitting again on something and charging ahead. Again he tightened up on the leash. If he let her proceed too quickly, she could overshoot the track and lose it. But she didn't.

Matt thanked God for his steadfast partner. If anyone could find Trista, it was Sheba.

Minutes later, she led them to a building covered in vines. Fifty yards back, his friends followed, two of them with their leashed K-9s. Too many dogs could be a clusterfuck.

Sheba led them around the corner of the building. A flash of lightning lit up a sedan parked on the grass next to a door.

Bingo.

His heart slammed as he unhooked the leash and drew his weapon, aiming at the darkened vehicle. Sheba bolted for the car, standing on her hind legs and pressing her snout to the driver's side window.

Nick and Saxon approached from another angle, while Eric and his K-9, Tiger, covered them. Markus, Dayne, Jaime, and Kade hung back, awaiting orders.

Sheba whined then dropped back to the ground and ran to the other side of the vehicle, repeating the same process on her hind legs. Based upon her reaction, Matt already knew the vehicle was empty, but out of caution, he clicked on his flashlight and swept the car's interior. Sure enough, it was empty.

With his free hand, he urged Sheba to the door where he holstered his weapon to hook the leash back on. He glanced over his shoulder to see his friends moving forward, readying to follow at a distance that wouldn't interfere with Sheba's track.

He turned the doorknob, praying it wasn't locked, then wincing as the door creaked. Pausing for barely a second, he aimed his flashlight through the opening and pushed it open the rest of the way with his foot.

With her nose to the floor, Sheba led him inside and down a long hallway. She continued past a mural of an American flag on the wall, past room after room. Other than the faint glow of his flashlight, which he'd set on low beam, the hall was pitch black. Luckily, the floor was so pitted and littered with debris and paint chips that the scrabbling of Sheba's claws and his boots were well-muffled.

Up ahead a faint glow came from the last doorway on the left, then he heard a low sob, followed by a scream.

Trista.

Reeling Sheba in, he unhooked her leash then drew his weapon and ran down the hallway after his dog.

Sheba bolted into the room. Matt couldn't see inside yet but heard a bloodcurdling growl followed by a man screaming.

At the open doorway, he dropped the flashlight and went in blind. Trista's scream shot tactics down the toilet. What he saw nearly stopped his heart. Trista was strapped to a chair, her head lolled forward.

He aimed his gun point-blank at the man holding a syringe just above her arm. A killing rage, the likes of which he'd never experienced, rolled through him, and it took every ounce of restraint not to pull the trigger. "Police! Drop it!"

Trista didn't move. *Jesus, am I too late?*

The syringe clattered as it fell onto the metal tray and the man—Lukashin, he guessed—threw his arms in the air, as did the other guy standing beside Trista.

Booted feet pounded into the room behind him. Sheba made a gruff snort, and the guy on the floor screamed again. "Get off! Get off!"

The man beside Trista looked at Sheba, then reached to his belt, pulling out a gun.

Matt swung the barrel of his duty weapon and double-tapped the guy in the chest. Gunshots reverberated in the room. The thug staggered backward, then fell sideways to the floor, his gun skittering a few feet away.

"*Zadrrz*," Nick shouted behind him, and Matt caught a blur from the corner of his eye as Nick's enormous black German shepherd bounded into the room. The man on the floor screamed again as Saxon clamped his powerful jaws around another limb.

Matt refocused on Lukashin, who stood calmly, his arms still raised in the air, a smug half smile on his face. He wanted to drill the bastard. Instead, he jammed the barrel of his gun in the asshole's face. "What did you give her?" Fury nearly drove him to the brink of doing something stupid. *Like blasting this fucker to hell.* But he needed to know what he'd injected her with.

Dayne and Jaime now also had their guns pointed at the *rezidentura* while Eric, Kade, and Markus helped Nick control the other two men, one of whom he was pretty sure was dead.

Matt glanced at the metal tray, noting the syringe the *rezidentura* had dropped appeared to be full. But there were other syringes on the tray. And one of them was empty.

Jabbing his gun harder on Lukashin's face, he gritted his teeth. "What did you give her, asshole?"

"Easy, Matt." Kade's deep baritone somehow penetrated the blood-red fog blinding him, and he eased the pressure off his trigger finger. "If you wanna live, I'd wipe that shit-eating grin off your face and answer the man's question before he drills you in the head."

The smile disappeared, replaced by a vicious sneer. "Sodium pentothal."

Matt slipped his finger from the trigger and glanced at Trista. When her head moved and she moaned, he blew out a breath. "If you're lying, you won't leave this room alive." No need for him to sic Sheba on the guy. He'd rip the man to pieces with his bare hands.

The sleazy smile returned in full force. "Do you know who I am?"

"I don't give a fuck *who* you are." Matt holstered and yanked a set of cuffs from his belt. Without a shred of gentleness, he jerked Lukashin's arm to the small of his back, clicking one cuff on the man's wrist, then repeating the process with his other arm.

"You should. I have diplomatic immunity. I'll be out of jail before nightfall."

"Don't count on it, asshole." Matt roughly handed the *rezidentura* over to Dayne and Jaime. "Pat this piece of garbage down. Careful of sharps. Son of a bitch likes needles." He nodded to the metal tray and began unbuckling the straps at Trista's wrists and ankles. Placing two fingers at her carotid, he checked her pulse, grateful for the slow, steady thumping beneath his fingers.

Gently, he picked her up in his arms, nestling her head against his shoulder. "I'm taking her down the mountain to a hospital. Kade, you're with me."

"You got it." Kade led the way out the door while Nick, Eric, and Markus remained behind to deal with the two thugs and the local authorities.

As they passed the *rezidentura*, Trista lifted her head. Before Matt could stop her, she lashed out with her fist, popping Lukashin in the eye. The man's head jerked back, and he uttered something Matt assumed was a Russian oath.

With Dayne and Jaime gripping Lukashin's elbows, the blow was hardly strong enough to knock him down, but it might just leave him with a little shiner.

"Thazzz fer burning down my house, you—you… azzhole." Her head fell back against her shoulder. "Sssorry, Matt," she mumbled. "Truth serummm gives me potty mouth."

"Well, look at that." Jaime snorted. "Little pixie learned a new curse word today. *Asshole.*"

Nick grinned. "She's definitely got the hang of that right hook I taught her."

Despite the seriousness of the situation, Matt's friends chuckled, and he resisted the urge to plow his own fist into the *rezidentura*'s face.

"Sheba, *k noze.*" As he made for the door, the dog heeled at his side, glancing occasionally up at Trista in his arms. She moaned, an adorable little smile lifting her lips, one that gave him reassurance that the asshole really had been telling the truth. Not that he'd ever experienced it, but sodium pentothal was old-school truth serum, the effects of which were similar to being drunk.

"Baby?" he whispered as Kade opened the passenger seat of Matt's Explorer. "It's Matt. Can you hear me?"

Her lids cracked enough for him to get a flash of green eyes. "Maaatt." She giggled sleepily. "Handsome man. Totally hot guy."

His heart somersaulted with relief. If she could joke around, she'd probably recover, but a checkup at the hospital was in her future, regardless of his medical opinion.

Kade had already loaded Sheba into the Explorer. "Right behind you, buddy."

After lowering Trista into the passenger seat, Matt gripped the other man's shoulder for a moment in silent thanks.

Luckily, the rain had eased and less than an hour later, he laid Trista down on a gurney and watched her get wheeled into the ER. He'd taken a step to follow, then stopped.

"You're not gonna go with her?" Kade eyed him with surprise.

He stood rooted, clenching and unclenching his hands. As things stood, he was unable to move forward and unable to go back. She'd changed him.

He wanted his little pixie so much, the thought of living his life without her now was unthinkable. He wanted to be all things to her, forever and always. *Friend. Lover. More, if she'd have him.* But it was too soon.

Taking a deep breath, he steeled himself for what he had to do next—confront his past.

"Promise me you'll stay with her," he said to Kade, who nodded. Then Matt turned and walked out of the ER.

Chapter Thirty-One

The early November air was crisp and cool as Trista jogged into Bonnie and Kevin's driveway. She and Poofy had been staying with her friends for the past month while her house was being rebuilt. Much to her surprise, while she'd been in protective custody at the safe house, her friends had finally hooked up and moved in together.

"'Bout time," she'd said, happy for both of them, although inwardly sad because now she felt like a third wheel. Lovers—especially *new* lovers—needed privacy, and her presence wasn't helping any. She'd lost count of how many times she'd rounded a corner and caught them in a major lip-lock.

After catching her breath, she leaned down to grab the Saturday morning paper and tossed it onto the porch before doing her stretches. Running every other morning and doing light weights or some sort of aerobic workout had become her routine, partly to get in shape and to give her friends some alone time.

"Who am I kidding?" She rested her hands on the side of her car for some calf stretches. True, her workout routine was all part of the new and improved Trista Gold, the vastly more confident version of her old self, but for a couple hours every day, it also had the added bonus of keeping her mind off what was missing in her life. *Matt.*

She alternated pressing one heel to the pavement then the next, deepening the stretch with each repetition. After awakening in a hospital, she'd looked for him, certain he'd been there, but all she'd found was Kade. When she was coherent, Kade gave her the rundown of what had taken place at the psychiatric center, including how Lukashin and one of his thugs had been arrested while the other had died from a fatal gunshot fired from Matt's weapon. Ironically, she had no memory of anything, starting right after being injected with sodium pentothal.

Kade also told her how Matt and Sheba had tracked her via the locator on her charm bracelet. She should have been mad at Matt for tagging her with a tracker without her knowledge, but it had saved her life.

Trista swallowed the lump in her throat. Part of her would always miss that piece of jewelry.

Markus and Eric had been the ones to drive her to Bonnie and Kevin's when she'd been released the next day. The rest of Matt's friends had sent flowers and humorous cards that put a brief smile on her face.

Days later, the lab analysis report had revealed the contents of the syringe Lukashin had been about to stick her with—concentrated digitalis. It had been no surprise after what Hentz had told them about Lukashin's proclivity for using poison as a murder weapon.

She shuddered at how close she'd come to dying. If Matt and Sheba hadn't burst in and saved her, the *rezidentura* would have murdered her and buried her in the old cemetery on the grounds of the psychiatric center.

Easing into a hamstring stretch, she tried not to think

about the vivid description Dayne had given her of the many unmarked graves in the psychiatric center's cemetery. Lukashin had been burying his victims there for years. An FBI work crew would be out there with a backhoe for months pulling out bodies, many of which were nothing more than bones that would have to be identified by dental records.

She shielded her eyes from the late-morning sun, wondering how the *rezidentura* and his thug's hearing had turned out yesterday in federal court. Lukashin could be facing murder charges for Thomas George and two FBI agents. Due to the myriad of debriefing meetings, Trista had been unable to attend the funerals for Donald and Angie, but she'd sent flowers and condolence cards to their families. They'd died trying to save her, and she would never forget their ultimate sacrifice.

Both Lukashin and his surviving henchman could also be facing other charges—attempted murder for what had gone down at the psychiatric center and likely others relating to the bodies in the unmarked graves. Wayne and Genevieve had assured her they would notify her of the outcome when the hearing concluded, but the phone had been oddly quiet last evening.

As predicted, the Russian government refused to waive the *rezidentura*'s immunity, but the attorney general refused to back down. Trista shook her head in amazement. Lukashin was now linked to multiple murders, yet the case would undoubtedly be tied up in diplomacy and the courts for years.

She inhaled deeply, loving mornings like this. No cares or worries other than working out and reloading all sorts of new programs onto her brand-new personal laptop.

Going back to work had been difficult. Every morning when she went through Langley's doors, her eyes automatically flew to the uniformed officer, both relieved and disappointed it wasn't Matt. She'd heard he and Sheba had been temporarily reassigned to a pre-election security detail, one of the ones his friends were in town working. *It's just as well.* After what had passed between them, seeing him every morning would have been torture.

She picked up the newspaper, then went inside. Bonnie and Kevin slept in late Saturday mornings, so she normally had this time to herself. Poofy jumped onto the seat beside her, purring, and she absently scratched his head. The front page contained yet another article about Senator Ashburn.

As promised, the senator had gone public with his story, and since the entire world now knew about his past—as well as the Russian attempt to blackmail him—the threat to Trista's life had been eliminated. Luckily for Senator Ashburn, the Berkeley County, West Virginia, DA's office had declined to prosecute for the forty-year-old death of the senator's abusive father, and both Senator Ashburn's party and his constituents had rallied around him, urging him to remain in the race. Come Tuesday, it would be up to the American people to decide whom they wanted the next president of the United States to be. *Amazing.*

Above her, something *banged*, and she covered her ears. Bonnie and Kevin's bedroom was directly above the kitchen. "They're at it again, Poofy." She caressed the cat's soft ears. "Those two have more sex than bunnies. We have *got* to get out of here." Listening to her friends' lovemaking was driving her crazy. More to the point, it reminded her of how wonderful it had been to experience that intimacy with Matt. *And how I never will again.*

Even now, the mere thought of their naked bodies tangling together as he'd driven inside her, making her world explode with erotic sensations she'd only experienced in his arms, made her start to sweat and tremble with desire. There was only one remedy. *Cold shower.*

Thirty minutes later, freshly showered and with her hair

still damp, she opened her bedroom door to find Bonnie in her bathrobe, fist raised, about to knock.

"Don't tell Kevin I said this, but there's a hot guy downstairs waiting for you." She bobbed her eyebrows. "I mean, *seriously* hot."

A flash of excitement had her heart thumping a little faster at the thought that Matt had come to see her. The momentary elation was fleeting. If it were Matt, Bonnie would have said so.

"Thanks." She headed down the stairs to find Nick waiting for her in the living room. When he rose from the sofa, Trista had to agree with Bonnie's assessment of the man. In her mind, Matt could never be replaced as the hottest guy on the planet, but with Nick's tall, muscular body and those incredible, penetrating gray eyes, he *was* seriously hot. And that beautifully smooth, rich voice… If her heart hadn't already been taken, she may very well have fallen in love with the man for his voice alone.

"Hey, little pixie." He wrapped his arms around her, engulfing her against his huge body. "How ya holding up?"

"Never better." *A partial lie.* Her life *was* better. Except that Matt wasn't in it. "Can I get you something to drink? Coffee, tea, or water?"

Nick shook his head. "I came to let you know we all miss you. Sheba even misses that cat of yours." His gaze swung to where Poofy sat regally on an armchair, looking as if he really did rule over the house.

"And I miss Sheba. How is she?" What she really wanted to ask was how Matt was doing, but he was gone from her life, and that was the way things had to be.

"Sheba's good." Nick's brows bunched in a frown. "What I really came here to talk about is Matt."

"Is he all right?" She grabbed his arm. Matt was out of her life, but that didn't mean she didn't care about his well-being. She'd probably never stop.

"Yes. And no." He clasped her hand before continuing. "Physically, he's fine. Mentally, he's doing better than ever, but he misses you. He's in love with you."

She pressed her lips together, fighting back the tears welling behind her eyes. "You're wrong. He's not capable of loving me. Of loving *anyone*."

"Look, pixie. Matt's never been in love before, but he is now. With you. Trust me. And I'm guessing you're in love with *him*."

She swallowed the painful lump in her throat. "I can't be with someone who's hell-bent on destroying himself." She tried to rise from the sofa, but he gently tugged her back down.

"Hear me out," he insisted. "If I'm wrong and you don't love him, I'll walk away now, and we'll call it good. No harm, no foul. Just say the words."

Unable to meet the intensity of Nick's gaze, she let her head drop, knowing with all her heart that she would always be in love with Matt. For her, there would only be one man.

"That's what I thought." He tipped her chin up with one long finger and grinned. "I'm about to betray a major confidence. Matt would kick my ass if he knew I was here, let alone what I'm about to say, but he's my best friend, and I love him like a brother." His visage turned serious. "Matt is...complicated. We've all got pasts, and they aren't pretty. But his is about as bad as it gets. He's been in pain most of his life. He told me you know about Jerry." She nodded. "Since it happened, life hasn't been easy for him, but he's finally getting help. *Professional* help. We've all been trying for years to talk him into it, but he wouldn't go. *You're* the reason he's finally going."

"Why didn't he tell me?" Hurt coursed through her that he hadn't let her know about something so huge in his life.

"Pride. He needed to do this on his own."

"I see." The lump in her throat got bigger. "I'm happy he's getting help, really I am. But I don't understand what this has to do with me."

"He wants to heal himself or die trying, and he's doing it for *you*. He told me how you called him out on it and left him that day. He wanted to go after you then but couldn't. Kade said it about killed him to leave you at the hospital, but he knew it was pointless." His tone softened. "He needed to be able to wake up in the morning and not be consumed by guilt over Jerry's death."

"Is he at that point now?" Hesitant joy raced through her, but by her estimation, he couldn't have been seeing a psychiatrist for that long. Opening herself up to him might be setting herself up for a big fall.

What if Nick's wrong? What if he doesn't really love me?

"I'm not wrong about this," he said, as if reading her mind. "He's really trying, and he's made great strides in a very short period of time. All he needed was the right motivation. Love." Nick's broad smile would make any woman's heart beat madly, yet she'd take Matt's scowl anytime. "But it beats the shit out of him. I see it every time he gets back from a session with the shrink. Now something big is coming down the pipe, and I'm afraid it might set back his progress." He paused. "The banquet."

"Jerry's banquet," she breathed, tugging one of her hands from his to cover her mouth. Torment didn't begin to describe the look on Matt's face when he'd mentioned the annual banquet honoring his friend.

"Yeah. That." Nick frowned. "He's going, but deep down, he's scared shitless. He says it's part of the healing process and he has to do it. You can help him get through it."

"How?" she asked, realizing at that moment that she'd do anything for Matt. Now it was her turn to feel guilty, and tears trickled down her cheeks. Not for the first time, she wondered if she should have stayed with him. But if she had, he might not have pushed himself to seek the help he needed. "I'll do anything."

"I was counting on that." He pulled out his cell phone, sent a quick text, then got up and opened the front door. A few seconds later, Matt's sister, Joyelle, and his father walked into the house.

Joyelle carried two shopping bags from Nordstrom while Matt's father hauled in a small suitcase and a garment bag slung over his shoulder. Both of them were smiling, and Trista gasped as Joyelle set the bags onto the floor and drew her into a tight embrace. "Thank you," Joyelle said. "You have no idea how excited we are that Matt's coming to the banquet this year."

Matt's father pressed his lips together and looked at her through watery eyes. "Thank you," he said on a shaky breath, clearly overcome by emotion as he joined the group hug. "Thank you for bringing me back my son."

"I don't understand." She pulled away, uncertain as to what was going on. "I haven't done anything yet."

"But you will, pixie girl." Nick laughed. "You will."

Chapter Thirty-Two

Matt left Dr. Lawrence's office and closed the door behind him. He took a deep breath, feeling both relieved that he'd survived another session yet looking forward to the next one. The first had been the most difficult, and he'd left feeling as if he'd been mashed into the pavement by a tank that had backed up and hit him again. But with each successive appointment, he'd been getting better, feeling more hopeful for the future than he'd been since Jerry died.

As he walked the short distance to his truck, he shoved his hand into his pocket, fingering the silver charm bracelet. It had given him strength to walk in the psychiatrist's door that first day, and he'd carried it with him ever since. Seeing a shrink was something he had to do for himself, but he always kept his eye on the prize. *Trista.*

Damn, but he missed her. He missed her smile, her soft charm and gentle touch. He missed her humor, her wit, and he'd loved watching her bloom into the beautiful woman he always knew she was. He'd loved helping *her* to see how beautiful she was. Hell, he missed every goddamn thing about her, and he couldn't wait to win her back. *Soon*, he kept telling himself. But he needed to be ready. He had to be further along dealing with the shit in his head or he'd only fuck things up again.

He opened the door to his truck and got in. There'd been a hundred times over the past month that he'd nearly broken down and called her. He knew she was staying with Bonnie and Kevin. His friends had all met with her for coffee and lunch a couple of times, and he'd been jealous as hell knowing they were making time with his woman.

My woman. At least, that's what he wanted her to be. *When the time is right.*

At first, he worried that another man would come along and steal her away before Matt was ready to see her again. Then he'd laughed at his stupidity. If another man tried to take her from him, he'd just have to beat the shit out of him.

He slid the bracelet from his pocket, holding it up and watching sunlight glint on the additional charm he'd added. Then he glanced at the digital dashboard clock. Six o'clock. Just enough time to get home and change for the banquet. Fuck, he didn't want to go. Just the thought of facing Jerry's family had him breaking out into a cold sweat. But he had to. It was part of his healing process. He'd known that even before Dr. Lawrence had urged him to attend.

As he pulled onto the road, his cell phone rang. *Max Fenway.* He frowned. Although he'd made a point of attending funeral services for both the agents who'd died to protect Trista, he'd never quite forgiven the FBI for allowing her to be kidnapped right from under their noses. He'd also heard that their deaths lay heavily on Fenway's shoulders and knew personally how difficult that would be for the man to live with. Because of that, he took the call.

"Fenway. What can I do for you?"

"I have interesting news about Lukashin's hearing

yesterday."

"Go on." He stopped at a red light just before turning onto the highway. Fenway had his full attention now.

"As you know, both our agencies were royally pissed that you arrested him before the senator got the chance to have his meeting. The opportunity to record a top spy admitting the Russian president was behind a scheme to blackmail a U.S. presidential candidate doesn't come around every day."

"Yeah, no shit." Matt snorted, gunning his truck toward the on-ramp as the light turned green. "I got a major ass-kicking over that." Not that he'd cared. Saving Trista's life that day had taken precedence over anything else in his world. The politicians would just have to deal with it.

"I should tell you, your name came up in court during Lukashin's initial appearance. The judge asked if you'd unnecessarily roughed up the *rezidentura*, because he had a noticeable shiner the day he was arrested. You shoulda seen the smile on this crotchety judge's face when I told him Trista popped him a good one in the eye."

Matt grinned. He'd heard from Nick that she didn't even remember doing it.

"As it turns out," Fenway continued, "things couldn't have gone any better. The AG plans to charge Lukashin and his surviving henchman with murder and attempted murder. Catching Lukashin with that syringe full of digitalis in his hands was the nail in the old bastard's coffin." Fenway chuckled. "Russia, as expected, still refuses to waive diplomatic immunity, but the AG, the president, *and* Senator Ashburn don't give a shit." Fenway laughed. "Last I heard, there was a champagne-popping party at the White House, and the heaviest trade sanctions ever imposed by the U.S. are about to slam down on Russia's head."

"What am I missing here?" Matt narrowed his eyes as he merged onto the highway. "How do the *rezidentura*'s actions translate into trade sanctions for an entire country?"

"Ah, my friend, here's the kicker. Lukashin's been in the business for a lotta years and he knows the system. He's got too much intel on the Russian president in his head, so much that he figures even if he did get released—which he won't—he probably wouldn't live a full day on Russian soil."

Matt uttered a disbelieving laugh. "You telling me he's talking?"

"About *everything*, including the plot to blackmail Ashburn. In exchange for not getting the death penalty, the old fart's singing like a fucking bird. Even though he's looking at life in prison for what he's done, our prisons are like hotels compared to a Russian gulag. He'd rather live out the rest of his life in an American jail than risk getting offed by his own people before he sees his first Russian sunset."

"Holy shit." Matt shook his head. Fenway hadn't been kidding. Things really had turned out better than any of them could have anticipated.

Matt and his friends had been a heartbeat away from being supremely reprimanded, if not shitcanned, by their respective agencies for going completely off the grid on an unapproved, high-risk rescue op that should have entailed a small army of feds, not seven officers and their K-9s. But given the overall outcome, which included saving the life of the CIA's top intelligence analyst, the higher-ups had wisely decided to give them a complete pass.

Even Sheriff Underwood had benefited from this whole mess. Matt had called Underwood to notify him that his cold case had been solved. From what Matt had read lately in the Berkeley County, West Virginia, polls, Underwood was well on his way to being re-elected.

"The holiest," Fenway agreed. "And by the way, I wasn't kidding when I said we could use a man of your skills. If you ever want to jump ship and join on with the FBI, say the word."

Matt laughed as he took the exit to home. "Not a chance. You guys are a bunch of pussies." Good thing Dayne hadn't heard that or his FBI friend would probably call him out. He hung up to the sound of Fenway's laughter.

The digital clock read six fifteen as he turned into his driveway. After shutting off the engine, he sat there several minutes unable to move, yet knowing he had to.

This will be the second most difficult day of my life. The first being the day he watched Jerry burn to death.

Taking a deep breath, he got out of the truck.

Matt pocketed the ticket stub the valet handed him. He stared at the Manor House's grand entry with its enormous columns and massive, hand-carved wooden doors. His hands were shaking, and his stomach was twisting so violently he thought he'd puke. *Fuck. Me. Now who's the pussy?*

He'd been fearless in combat, leading his unit into dangerous territory nearly every day. Later, as a cop, he'd arrested more violent criminals than he could count. But tonight...facing Jerry's family for the first time since the funeral...totally, unequivocally scared the living shit out of him.

"Sir, are you all right?" the valet asked.

"Yeah. Fine." *So fucking not.*

Walking up the stairs, he blew out several short, quick breaths, steeling himself for the emotional shit about to rain down on his head. Everyone who was anyone in his community would be there, not just his and Jerry's families. And they all knew his history.

For two decades, this charity event had been the talk of the town, attended en masse not only by people who knew the Wilshires, but by community leaders, local politicians, businessmen and women. Old money and new, plus philanthropists up the wazoo. Anyone who donated to the annual fund in Jerry's name would be there to cheer on the lucky recipient of nearly a hundred thousand dollars. Knowing the Wilshires would never consider giving him anything, he hadn't ever put his name in the hat. *Somehow, I'll get the money for Jerry's Place.*

As the doorman opened the door, Matt's throat constricted, and he ran a finger between the shirt collar of his tuxedo and his neck. But he knew the tux wasn't to blame for his throat closing.

Sights and sounds slammed into him. Other men in tuxedos, women in fancy full-length gowns. Glasses clinking, people chattering loudly to be heard over the orchestra playing on the raised dais. Using classic room-clearing cop technique, he "sliced the pie," scanning the room in wedge-shaped segments. Ignoring the curious looks thrown his way, he shoved a hand into his pocket, fingering the charm bracelet as he began making his way through the glitzy crowd.

Many people he hadn't seen in years greeted him along the way. Some stopped talking altogether, leaning in to whisper to one another. He didn't need to have ESP to know what they were gossiping about. *Him.* The dumb kid who got his best friend killed.

He swallowed the bile rising in his throat. *You can do this. You* can *do this.*

Amid the throng, he spotted his parents and his sister. Them he could handle. He'd been to Sunday dinner at his parents' house twice since seeing Dr. Lawrence, something he hadn't done in more than ten years. His mother had broken down and cried the first time he'd set foot in the door. The second time, she'd managed to make it to dessert before the waterworks had kicked in.

"Sweetheart," his mother said as he leaned down to kiss her cheek. "I was afraid you wouldn't come."

"Me, too." Next he accepted a tight hug from his sister. "You look great, Joy." And she did, wearing a body-hugging purple sheath that accentuated her tall, willowy figure. A fact, he realized, every other man in the room had already figured out. He'd already caught several of them ogling his baby sis. "I'm going to have to fight to keep the men off you all night, aren't I?"

"Very funny." She punched his arm, something she'd always done when they were kids and he'd pissed her off, which back then was pretty much all the time.

He turned to shake hands with his dad. They'd gotten off to a rocky start, but Doc Lawrence was also helping him to repair that relationship as well.

His dad surprised him by pulling him into a bear hug. "Good to see you, Son."

"You, too, Dad." He clapped his father on the back, grateful for his family's presence and support. *Maybe I can get through tonight after all.* Then he lifted his gaze and spotted Mr. and Mrs. Wilshire in deep conversation with a large group of people at the far end of the hall.

His stomach clenched. A bead of sweat ran down his back between his shoulder blades. Again, his throat constricted, and he could barely breathe. *What the fuck?* He had never had one before but knew the signs. He was on the verge of an all-out panic attack.

Clenching his hands to hide their shaking, he pulled away from his father. *I can't do this. I'm not ready.*

Like a coward, he turned to run but froze, barely feeling his father's hand grabbing his arm. He blinked, shaking his head to clear his vision. He had to be dreaming. Trista was walking toward him, looking like a beautiful woodland nymph, and he drank her in like a man who was lost in the desert and had just spotted an oasis.

The full-length green dress shimmered and swirled around her legs as she glided across the floor. The tight bodice held up by thin spaghetti straps drew his gaze to her beautiful breasts. Her honey-blond hair was piled high, with delicate tendrils framing her heart-shaped face. The only jewelry she wore were long, dangly gold earrings and a matching necklace that dipped low into her cleavage.

Stunning didn't cut it. She was…extraordinary. But it was more than that. Her unexpected presence lit up his world. Just when he thought he'd been about to choke and run, she was there, like a lifeline, saving him from drowning and dying right there in front of hundreds of people.

As the crowd parted for her to reach him, people began to whisper, but he couldn't make out a single word. Every fiber of his being, every cell in his body, was focused on the woman now linking her fingers with his.

"Hi," she said, looking up at him with smiling green eyes that looked even more verdant thanks to her dress. "You know, you could kiss me. That would be a good icebreaker."

Still in shock, he did as she asked and dropped a light kiss on her lips. Only then did he take in her perfectly applied makeup. Since he'd never seen her wear any before, he began to suspect his sister had something to do with it, and for Trista being here. And she smelled amazing, like flowers, and vanilla, and sugary spice. He also noticed that she was taller than he remembered and glanced at her feet.

"Like 'em?" She held out one foot, revealing a strappy gold sandal. "They took a little getting used to before I could walk in them without falling on my face, but I'm a full four inches taller. I *love* that."

And I love you, he nearly blurted, his heart about to burst with the power and intensity of the emotions he was feeling. But he was so blown away by the fact she was there that he was rendered speechless. Besides, with all these people crowding around him now—including his own family—he wanted to say it in private, when they were alone.

"You look incredible." He ran his hands up and down her bare arms, admiring the light muscle definition that hadn't been there before. "You been working out?"

"Every day."

"Looks good on you." He couldn't wait to see what other body parts she'd been working out.

More to his shock, his father leaned down to kiss Trista on the cheek, as did his sister and mother.

"You all had a hand in this, didn't you?" He narrowed his eyes, feigning annoyance, when what he really felt was gratitude for their foresight and thoughtfulness. They'd known he'd need help, that he would falter, and they were right.

"We might have helped out." His sister linked her arm through Trista's and the two women shared a conspiratorial wink. "A little."

"I hope you're not mad that I'm here." Trista suddenly looked worried.

"Mad?" He laughed in disbelief. "*Hell* no."

"Language," his mother admonished, and they all laughed.

Not caring that his entire family was watching, along with half the people in the banquet hall, he slipped his arm around Trista's waist and pulled her in for a none-too-chaste kiss. When he lifted his head, there was no mistaking the love he saw mirrored in her eyes.

He clasped her hand to his chest. "Come with me?" he asked, looking over her shoulder to where the Wilshires were watching him.

"Anywhere," she answered in a firm voice.

"Excuse us," he said to his family, then led her toward the

Wilshires. Along the way, his chest tightened, but his body no longer trembled, and his throat didn't close up on him. All because Trista was at his side.

Before they got to the Wilshires, she squeezed his hand and pulled his head down. "You got this."

He couldn't help smiling back at her, but when they reached Jerry's family, he sobered in a heartbeat. Jerry's parents had aged since he'd last seen them but not unusually so. In his black tux, Bob Wilshire looked distinguished as always. Jerry's mom, Anne, though frailer now, still reminded him of a debutante in her white evening gown. Liz and Alex, Jerry's brother and sister, looked pretty much the same, just older, and married now, with spouses at their sides.

Though he'd rehearsed this moment over and over in his head for the past week and a half, words fled him now. *What do you say to a family whose son died because of you?*

Mrs. Wilshire's eyes glistened, then she gracefully wrapped her arms around him, her body shaking as she cried against his chest. He held her gently, swallowing repeatedly, desperately holding back his own gushing waterworks.

Then it was Mr. Wilshire's turn to join the awkward reunion, as he dropped an arm across Matt's shoulders. "You should never have made yourself scarce around our household."

"Dear," Mrs. Wilshire said, pulling away, then reaching to cup his cheek, "we *needed* you with us. You were family, like a third son, and we missed you."

"What?" He gave Jerry's mother a bewildered look. The sincerity in her eyes stunned him. "*Missed* me? I thought you hated me."

Liz came forward, her cheeks wet with tears. "What Mom and Dad are trying to say is that we didn't blame you for what happened. Jerry craved action and adventure just as much as you did. Even at sixteen, he was his own man. There was no telling him he couldn't do something, because he'd do it anyway and wouldn't care if he was grounded for life."

Alex cleared his throat, obviously trying not to lose it. "My little brother wanted to be a fireman more than anything. We read the police report. We know what happened, and we know what led up to it. You were there, but it wasn't your fault."

Mrs. Wilshire pulled away from Matt. She grasped his wrists and held up his scarred hands. "You tried to save him."

"It *wasn't* your fault," Mr. Wilshire reiterated, squeezing his shoulder. "You have to accept that. We did then, and we still do now. You need to do the same."

I do. Finally, I do. His throat closed up again. Not due to a panic attack this time, but from emotion as he absorbed the Wilshires' compassionate forgiveness and faced down the ghost that had haunted him for two decades. Part of him now regretted not having been there for the Wilshires, sharing their grief, helping them through it while they did the same for him. But he understood now that back then, his guilt had been so overwhelming and self-destructive that he wouldn't have been capable of giving, let alone receiving, anything remotely resembling compassion. So he'd isolated himself from the Wilshires, from his own family, and fled, both physically *and* emotionally.

"I'm sorry. For so much, but most of all that I wasn't there for you. *Couldn't* be there for you." Without any embarrassment, he swiped at the single tear tracking down his face. Letting go of Jerry's ghost completely would probably never happen, but he was damned sure going to try to keep a lid on that specter so he could live his life and be happy again.

"We understood." Mrs. Wilshire extracted a lace handkerchief from a slim evening bag he hadn't noticed before and dabbed at her own eyes. "Please sit with us at dinner. We've reserved room for you and the rest of your family at our table." She peered around him at Trista, who he now realized had graciously stepped back to allow him this moment with Jerry's family. "Matthew, where are your manners? Aren't you going to introduce us to your lovely girlfriend?"

My girlfriend? Definitely, and hopefully more someday soon.

As he held out a hand to her, Trista gazed up at him with glistening eyes. She'd been there with him the entire time. His silent strength. Again, he wanted to tell her how crazy in love with her he was, but it still wasn't the right time. Instead, he reached for her hand, tugging her to his side. "Mr. and Mrs. Wilshire, Alex, Liz, this is Trista Gold. My girlfriend," he added, eminently liking the sound of it.

The beatific smile on Trista's face told him *she* liked the sound of it, too.

An hour later, when everyone had finished dinner and was awaiting the Wilshires' presentation of the annual charity check, Matt massaged Trista's thigh beneath the table, loving the way the silk of her dress glided over her shapely, toned leg. She linked their fingers together and gave him a look so full of promise his brain went wild with erotic thoughts of all the things he planned to do to her in his bed after the banquet.

He leaned in, brushing his lips over her ear. "When we get home, I'm going to strip you out of that dress, then kiss, and lick, and suck on every inch of your beautiful body." *Home.* His home *was* her home. She just didn't know it yet.

"I might just have to do the same to you." With a playful gleam in her eyes, she slowly, seductively ran the tip of her tongue over her upper lip, then the lower one.

Beneath the table, he went rock hard and pulled her hand over him so she'd know exactly what her little tongue teaser had done to him.

She began to grin when the room went silent, and he only now realized the Wilshire family had left the table and gathered on the dais. Mr. Wilshire stood behind the podium.

"Ladies and gentlemen, on behalf of my family, I want to welcome and thank you all for attending this year's annual charity banquet to honor our son, brother, and"—he looked directly at Matt—"best friend, Jerry Wilshire."

Matt dipped his head to Jerry's dad in silent thanks for the acknowledgment and swallowed the lump in his throat. When Trista leaned over and kissed him on the cheek, he drew in a grateful breath. His life was about to get a whole lot better.

"We normally take in about one hundred thousand dollars every year," Mr. Wilshire continued. "I am pleased to say that this year's donations far exceeded our anticipated goals. Without further ado, I would like to announce this year's worthy recipient." The crowd hushed as he opened the white envelope his wife handed him. "I am pleased to present this check for one hundred and fifty thousand dollars to Jerry's Place, owned and managed by Matthew Connors."

The crowd went wild, the applause and whistling so loud Matt couldn't think straight. His jaw dropped, barely able to process what he'd heard. The entire room was standing and cheering. In fact, *he* was the only one in the entire banquet hall still sitting.

"Matt!" Trista managed to pull him to his feet, then hugged him tightly. "Congratulations." It took her nudging him toward the dais for his feet to move.

The next thing he knew he was on stage, shaking Mr. Wilshire's hand while Jerry's dad handed him that whopper of a check along with a wood-and-brass plaque. Then he was hugged by every one of the Wilshire family, and the applause grew to deafening heights. Mr. Wilshire urged him behind the podium to say a few words.

Over three hundred guests sat in their chairs. The room was so silent he could swear he heard the blood pounding through his veins. He ran a finger under his collar, stalling for time as he surveyed the crowd. Receiving this check tonight hadn't even been a remote possibility for him. He hadn't applied. And he had no speech prepared. All he could do was speak from the heart.

He opened his mouth to say something but stopped as he choked up. *Fuck*. He looked over at the Wilshires standing to his left and to his right, at his own family still seated at the table. Last, he looked at Trista, absorbing her strength and love as if it was the antidote for everything gone wrong in his world. Everything that was now suddenly, unexpectedly *right*.

With her at his side, he could make it through anything.

"Jerry's Place has been a dream of mine for years. What started out as a selfish need to commemorate my best friend will, with this money"—he held up the check—"help young people in need of support, compassion, and healing. Building Jerry's Place did that for me, and I hope it will do that for others."

The crowd applauded, then went silent. The words he'd just spoken were true. He was finally on the road to healing, and he had Jerry's Place to thank for it. But there were others to thank as well.

"I'd like to thank the Wilshires for having faith in me and bestowing me with the honor and fiscal ability to bring Jerry's Place to life." More clapping. "Coming here tonight was the second most difficult thing I've had to do in my life. It's been a long journey to get here, and I couldn't have done it without my family, who have always been there for me, even if I was too stupid and thickheaded to know it." This time, the applause was mingled with good-natured laughter.

When the room went quiet this time, a sense of peace

enveloped him, and he looked directly at Trista, no longer able to hold back the words he'd intended to say to her privately. "Last, I'd like to thank the one person who pushed me to face my fears and start living again. Trista Gold, I love you and wouldn't be standing here if it wasn't for you."

As the room erupted, he left the stage and strode to the table. Trista held her hands over her mouth, her beautiful green eyes glistening. He pulled her to her feet and deep-kissed her right there in front of everyone. Vaguely, he heard the cheers and laughter, but his heart and soul—hell, every part of him—was focused on the incredible woman in his arms.

She pulled away, gazing up at him. "I love you, too."

The noise in the room was so loud he'd barely heard the words. His heart and soul were bursting with love, something he never believed could happen. But it had. Trista standing before him was living proof that he'd conquered his biggest fear.

This is the beginning of the rest of my life.

A life that had been waiting twenty years.

Epilogue

Sheba pirouetted around Trista's legs, barking and whining with such exuberance that Poofy scampered up the stairs and disappeared.

After leaving the banquet, they'd picked up Poofy at Bonnie and Kevin's, along with Trista's overnight bag. Matt had wanted her to pack all her things, but she'd politely declined, saying they needed to spend some time together before taking that big step. And she also harbored a secret fear. Although he said he loved her, Matt had just gone through an emotional roller coaster, and he needed time to process.

Aside from the animals, they had the house to themselves. Matt's friends were all working a midnight shift and wouldn't be back until morning.

"I missed you, too, Sheba." She knelt beside the dog and was rewarded with a wet muzzle in her face and a paw to shake. "Yes, I know. I do, I really, really do."

Matt let out an impatient sound, and she looked up to see him watching both her and the dog with an impatient expression. "Are you two done yet?"

"We missed each other." She gave Sheba's ears a good scratching until the dog leaned into her hand.

"What about me?" He scowled, making her realize just how much she'd missed him *and* his adorable scowls. "Sheba, *sedni!*"

Sheba leaped to her feet and sat obediently at Matt's side.

The abruptness of his tone shocked Trista, and she was taken aback by the even deeper scowl on his handsome face. If she didn't know better, she'd say he was anxious about something.

"What's wrong?" She stood and ran her hands up his chest then down his muscled arms, loving all the incredible things the tailored tuxedo did for his body. The man looked delicious but way too serious. "Whatever it is, I promise I'll make you forget all about it." To prove her point, she licked her lips as she'd done at the banquet, then slid her hand to the front of his pants. At her touch, he hardened, sending a jolt of awareness and red-hot need shooting from her belly to her core.

She tugged on his arm, intending to drag him upstairs to bed and peel off his tux to get at all those hard, smooth muscles, but he resisted. Trying to move a man his size was like trying to move a two-story supercomputer.

"I have something for you." He dug into his pants pocket, then handed her something, curling her fingers around it.

She instantly recognized what it was. "My charm bracelet!" As Matt nodded, she narrowed her eyes. "Is this so you can track me again wherever I go?"

"No." He smiled. "I took the tracker off, but I added a new charm to replace it."

She peered closely at the bracelet, nudging the charms around on the metal chain, searching for the new one. Her fingers stilled, and she gasped.

Hooked between the heart and dragonfly charms was a diamond ring. She hadn't noticed it at first because it was white gold and blended in with the other silver charms.

When Matt knelt next to Sheba and took her hand in his, her heart seemed to stop beating altogether.

"Trista Gold." He gazed up at her. "I love you with all my heart and always will. I want you. Now and forever, if you'll have me. Will you marry me?"

"Yes," she whispered without hesitation. He was the love of her life. She'd always known that, even when he'd been unable to return her love.

A look of pure joy mingled with relief seemed to wash over him. Then he took the bracelet from her trembling fingers and removed the engagement ring. The diamond sparkled in the overhead light as he took her left hand and slid it onto her finger. Instead of looking at the ring, she looked down at him, drowning in the love she saw in his sparkling eyes.

He stood and kissed her deeply for several minutes before swinging her into his arms and carrying her up the stairs.

Sheba's nails clicked as she trotted behind them into Matt's bedroom. Poofy lay in the center of the bed, already having decided to make Matt's bed his new throne. Startled, he leaped to the floor where, amazingly, both he and Sheba lay down and curled up only a few feet from each other.

Moments later, her dress and his tuxedo were scattered all over the floor. They lay naked in each other's arms in the center of the bed. Matt was about to kiss her again when Sheba made a rumbly sound. They both looked over at Poofy and Sheba, then back to each other and froze.

Matt snorted. "It's like making love in front of our children."

A sudden worry took hold, and she tensed. That was something they hadn't talked about yet. *Children*. She wanted them but didn't know if he felt the same.

"D-do you—"

"Want children?" he interrupted. "With you, I want it all."

He pressed his mouth to her lips, tangling his tongue with hers until she was writhing with the unquenched need to have him deep inside her.

Sliding her hands down his back, she reveled in the rippling play of thick muscle, loving the way his large body covered her petite frame, the feel of his weight atop hers, his strong arms around her.

His body pulsing inside her.

Large hands cupped her breasts as he suckled and licked her nipples into jutting peaks of pleasure. He nudged her legs apart, and she guided him inside her, urging him on until he was buried deep within her pulsing heat.

She clasped his head, locking gazes with his. Then she pulled him down for a deep kiss and made love to the first, and last, love of her life.

Author's Note

K-9s are a highly specialized component of law enforcement that few officers are blessed to be a part of and pose challenges most of us never encounter on the job. I've done my best to accurately reflect this unique aspect of law enforcement. Any mistakes contained within this novel are entirely my own.

Acknowledgments

So many people to thank… My brother, Matt, for his invaluable assistance with all things clandestine and the world of top secret code. My critique partners, Cheyenne McCray, Kayla Gray, and MK Mancos, for reading yet another one of my manuscripts. My editor, Brenda Chin—thank you for persevering through our first collaboration. And thank you to Karen Grove for suggesting I do a K-9 series in the first place. Great idea!

A special thanks to Cpt. Joseph King, Lt. Patrick Silva, and Sgt. Gary Hebert of the Massachusetts State Police K-9 Unit, and K-9 officers from the Chicopee, Springfield, Long Meadow, and Holyoke Police Departments. Your professionalism, courtesy, and expertise are priceless.

About the Author

Tee O'Fallon has been a federal agent for twenty-two years, giving her hands-on experience in the field of law enforcement that she combines with her love of romantic suspense. Tee's job affords her the unique opportunity to work with the heroic and sexy men in law enforcement on a daily basis. For Tee, research is the easy part! Besides reading and writing, Tee loves cooking, gardening, chocolate, lychee martinis, and her Belgian sheepdog.

Also by Tee O'Fallon…

Discover more Amara titles...

Reckless Honor
a *HORNET* novel by Tonya Burrows

Jean-Luc Cavalier has only ever cared about three things: sex, booze, and the dangerous missions he undertakes with HORNET—until the night he rescues virologist Dr. Claire Oliver. Someone wants her research and they're willing to kill anyone and everyone it, but that's the least of HORNET's concerns. An ultra-deadly virus with all the markings of a bioweapon is decimating the Niger Delta, and Nigeria is only the testing grounds...

Undercover with the Nanny
a novel by Cathy Skendrovich

DEA agent Sawyer Hayes never planned on being so drawn to a possible suspect. How is he supposed to do his job when his growing feelings for her are clouding his judgment? Romance is not on interior designer and nanny Kate Munroe's radar. But her hot new neighbor could change her mind, with his broad shoulders and Southern charm. Too bad his secrets could destroy her.

Wanted for Life
a *Love Under Fire* novel by Allison B. Hanson

Former DEA agent Colton Williamson misses the action of his past life since entering witness protection as a high school math teacher. He also misses Angel, who refused to join him in his new life. Now it's Angel who's in trouble, and Colton can't help but be there for her—before it's too late. But the killer may be closer to them than they think.

Hard Pursuit
a *Delta Force Brotherhood* novel by Sheryl Nantus

Trey Pierce has spent years helping the Brotherhood, using his computer skills to dig out secrets and help deliver justice. But there's one mission he's yet to finish—finding out who killed his best friend. A chance meeting with Ally Sheldon gives him a new lead, one that comes with some baggage. Never in his life has Trey been more attracted to a woman, but she's hiding something. And that something may just destroy them.

Made in the USA
Columbia, SC
07 May 2022

60111896R00221